HALF

"Simply put, Da... ing voices in ge...

—Saladin Ahmed, author of *Throne of the Crescent Moon*

"A damn good read . . . a hard-... Daniel José Older t... targets and hits ther...

—Simon R. G... ...side

"Smart and gripping, fu... ...sightful. It kicks in the door, waving the literary .44. Be warned: this man is not playing."

—Victor LaValle, author of *The Devil in Silver*

"Vividly imagined and rendered . . . this is a fantastic beginning to what will surely be a fantastic series."

—Jesmyn Ward, National Book Award–winning author of *Men We Reaped*

"Older has crafted a compelling new world. . . . *Half-Resurrection Blues* is not just a daring new mode of ghost-detective story; it's also a courageous effort to celebrate the diverse voices that surround us."

—Deji Bryce Olukotun, author of *Nigerians in Space*

"Noir for the Now: equal parts bracing, poignant, compassionate, and eerie. A swinging blues indeed."

—Nalo Hopkinson, Andre Norton Award–winning author of *Sister Mine*

continued . . .

Also by Daniel José Older from Roc Books

HALF-RESURRECTION BLUES

MIDNIGHT TAXI TANGO

A Bone Street Rumba Novel

DANIEL JOSÉ OLDER

A ROC BOOK

**Published by New American Library,
an imprint of Penguin Random House LLC
375 Hudson Street, New York, New York 10014**

This book is an original publication of New American Library.

First Printing, January 2016

Copyright © Daniel José Older, 2016
Modified portions of this book originally appeared on Tor.com as
short stories "Anyway: Angie," "Kia and Gio," and "Ginga,"
copyright © Daniel José Older, 2014, 2015
"Sus ojos se cerron" copyright © SADAIC, 1935
"Las cuarenta" copyright © SADAIC, 1937
"Las puñalada" copyright © SADAIC, 1951
"A la luz del candil" copyright © SADAIC, 1927
Map by Cortney Skinner
Frontispiece illustration by John Jennings
Penguin Random House supports copyright. Copyright fuels creativity, encourages
diverse voices, promotes free speech, and creates a vibrant culture. Thank you for
buying an authorized edition of this book and for complying with copyright laws
by not reproducing, scanning, or distributing any part of it in any form without
permission. You are supporting writers and allowing Penguin Random
House to continue to publish books for every reader.

Roc and the Roc colophon are registered trademarks of
Penguin Random House LLC.

For more information about Penguin Random House, visit penguin.com.

ISBN 978-0-425-27599-3

Printed in the United States of America
1   3   5   7   9   10   8   6   4   2

Penguin
Random
House

For Nastassian, my love

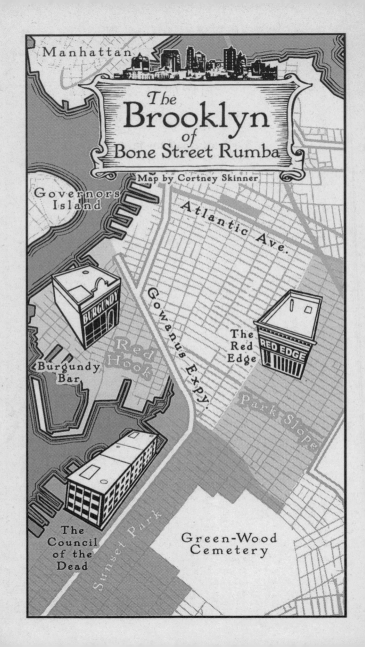

Manhattan

The
Brooklyn
of
Bone Street Rumba

Map by Cortney Skinner

Governors
Island

Atlantic Ave.

Gowanus Expy.

BURGUNDY

Red
Hook

The
Red
Edge

RED EDGE

Burgundy
Bar

Park Slope

The
Council
of the
Dead

Sunset Park

Green-Wood
Cemetery

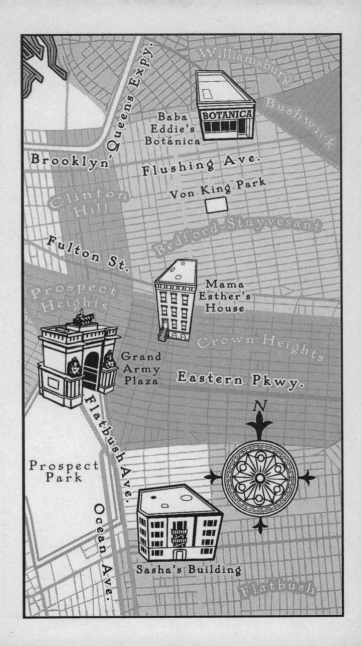

Convertir el ultraje de los años
en una música . . .

Convert the outrage of the years
into a music . . .

—Jorge Luis Borges, "Arte Poética"

CYCLE ONE

❧

RED SQUARE GINGA

Con el pucho de la vida apretado entre los labios,
la mirada turbia y fría, un poco lerdo el andar,
dobló la esquina del barrio y, curda ya de recuerdos,
como volcando un veneno esto se le oyó cantar:
Vieja calle de mi barrio donde he dado el primer paso,
vuelvo a vos, gastado el mazo en inútil barajar,
con una llaga en el pecho, con mi sueño hecho pedazos,
que se rompió en un abrazo que me diera la verdad.

With the cigarette stub of life pressed between his lips,
his gaze turbulent and cold, his stride a little off-kilter,
he turned a corner of the barrio, drunk on memories,
and like an eruption of venom, his song rang out:
Old streets of my neighborhood, where I took my first
        steps,
I return to you, my whole deck wasted with a single
        useless shuffle,
my chest on fire, dreams torn to pieces,
broken by an embrace that gave me only the truth.

"Las cuarenta"
tango, 1937
Francisco Gorrindo

CHAPTER ONE

Carlos

What song is that, man?"

I don't move. The rumble of this ambulance's diesel engine fills the air again; the park comes into focus around us, streetlamps fighting off the gloom. If I hold still, if Victor shuts the fuck up, if nothing happens for another few seconds, then maybe I can sink back in, grasp hold of that fragile thread of a melody, the line of her face fading into the darkness.

"Carlos?"

I rub my eyes and reach for the coffee cup on the dashboard. The thread is gone; Sasha is gone. Gone for good. "It's nothing, man. Just some song I heard." The coffee is lukewarm but strong as hell. Reality settles in fully around me. "Can't seem to shake it, is all. You get a job?"

Victor shakes his head. "Nah, man, go back to sleep." The ambulance radio crackles to life, a routine announcement that seat belts save lives, and then all we hear is the diesel *putt-putt-putt* and occasional snores from the passenger compartment, where Victor's partner, Del, is laid out.

"Look," I say, "if some shit don't go down by four, I'm out."

Victor nods. "I'm telling you, it's been every night, C. Without fail."

"Maybe accidents do take vacations after all."

"Carlos, I've been doing this job for twelve years and I ain't never seen a pattern like this. You know I don't even go in for all that woo-woo shit either. I don't get involved in your whatever spirit-hunting weirdo life. No offense."

"Thanks, man."

"And I ain't never come to you 'bout some shit in all the time I known you." He pulls out a cigarette and starts smoking it out the window.

Around us, Von King Park glowers with late-night shadows and a few scattered lights. The metal bars of a playground swing glint out of the gloom, a silhouetted pyramid against the cloudy sky. Darkened brownstones peer from behind the trees on either side.

Maybe there is something lurking out there. I get the faintest tinge of it—a rude kind of itch—but my cluttered-up memories make it hard to think clearly.

Anyway, if I say anything right now, Victor will interpret it as encouragement to speak more, so I light a Malagueña and glower along with the park.

Victor lets out a menthol-laced cloud and shakes his head. "Last night, a hipster on a bike got completely destroyed by a passing garbage truck. I mean, we were picking up pieces of him blocks away. The night before it was a prisoner that broke out the precinct over there, made it halfway across the street before the desk officer popped him, and *then* he got sideswiped by a motorcycle. The dude got dragged like four blocks, and when we got to him, his back was hamburger, Carlos. Hamburger."

I just grunt.

"Wednesday it was the suicide. That was on the far corner of the park over there. Jumped from the roof of that brownstone and lived, man. We had to decompress him though, full-on tension pneumo, tubed that ass and hauled him to Bellevue. Died in surgery."

"Damn." I have no idea what Victor's going on about, but all medical jargon aside, he's right. Three apparently unrelated gory deaths in a four-block radius is the kinda thing that puts me to work. He rattles off a few more while I smoke and ponder patterns and, inevitably, the past . . .

"Carlos?"

"Yeah, man?"

"You're humming again."

"Huh?"

"Like, while I'm talking." Victor narrows his eyes at me as I sit up and rub my face.

"Shit, man. Sorry."

"It's cool. I know you're not used to the nightlife. Anyway, they started calling the place Red Square on the strength of all this. And I'm just saying, seems like the kinda thing . . . you might know something about."

Vic's never known how to talk about me being half dead. It's not his fault—I've never come out and said it to him. But a gray pallor covers me like a layer of dust, and my skin is cold to the touch; my heart rate never surpasses a melancholy stroll. Plus I deal with ghosts. In fact, I'm employed by them: the New York Council of the Dead, a sprawling, incomprehensible bureaucracy, sends me to clean up any messy irregularity in the rigid, porous borderlines between life and death. I mean, since I'm a walking messy irregularity myself, I guess it makes sense the Council'd use me as their cleanup man, but truth is, it gets lonely.

Especially recently.

A whiny bachata song explodes out of Victor's belt. He curses, his belly shoved against the steering wheel as he squirms into what must be some kind of yoga pose to dig out his phone.

"Ay, shut the fuck up with that yadda-yadda horseshit," Del hollers from the back. Del is like eight feet tall with locks down to his ass. He's from Grenada, but he got hit by a school bus in the nineties and has been speaking with a thick Russian accent ever since. When he gets really worked up, his brain clicks fully over into Russian—some shit the neuroscientists of the world are still going nuts trying to figure out.

Mostly people try to be really nice to him.

"Sorry, man!" Victor yells, cradling the flip phone against his face. "Hello? . . . Uh, yeah, hang on." He hands me the phone. "It's for you, man. Some chick."

Sasha.

The thought wreaks havoc on my slow-ass heart for a half second, and then I mentally clobber it into submission. Of course it's not Sasha. There's eighty million reasons for it not to be Sasha, least of which being how the fuck would she have Victor's number and know I was with him? And why would she care? She walked out on me with no forwarding address, barely recovered from a nasty demon possession and pregnant with my child. And now all I have is a Sasha-shaped hole in my chest and a song I can't stop humming.

I mean, I did kill her brother. I was in no place to try to get her to stay. And still . . .

"Carlos?"

I have to stop disappearing from the world like this. I ignore Vic's raised eyebrow, take the phone, and say hello into it.

"Tell your buddy if he refers to me as 'some chick' ever again, he'll be driving his own ass to the ER so they can extract his nutsack from his mouth."

"Hi, Kia." Kia is sixteen and will probably rule the world one day. For now, though, she runs my friend Baba Eddie's botánica. Started on the register, selling *amor sin fin* and *espanta demonio* herbal mixtures, statues of saints, and beaded necklaces. Then she took over the books, which were a disaster, and, without bothering to ask Baba Eddie, she set up an online store and proceeded to build what appears to be a small spiritual-goods empire—one she rules with an iron fist—and all as an after-school job.

"You called?"

"Isn't it a school night? What are you doing up at four a.m.?"

"Returning your phone call."

"That was like eight hours ago!"

"Alright, man. I'll talk to you later then."

"Wait—you know anything about the park over on Marcy?"

"Know anything about it? I know a buncha motherfuckas been gettin' got there recently. Usedta be my stomping grounds for a while, then I moved on. Is that where you are right now, C? You might wanna not be there."

"I'm alright. Anything else?"

"My girl Karina babysits a whole boatload of little white kids at that park. You want me to ask her about it?"

"If you don't mind."

"I'ma see her at capoeira tomorrow. Maybe I'll swing through with her after."

The radio crackles, and Victor picks up the mic. "Five-seven X-ray, send it over."

"Be careful out there," Kia says.

Victor puts on his seat belt and cranes his head toward the back. "Del, we got a job."

"Morgala vikalyu, padla!"

"It's been like three weeks now," a little Humpty-Dumpty-looking middle-aged man in a bathrobe tells us. "I been coughing and hacking, but this is different."

Del towers over the guy, arms akimbo, perpetual frown deeper than usual. "You've been coughing for three weeks, yes?" He says it like he's about to launch into an eighty-thousand-page dissertation about peasants and vodka. "And now you decide for to call nine-one-one, why?"

"Well, tonight I coughed up something different. You want to see?"

"I really do not want to see this thing," Del says, but the little oval-shaped dude is already rummaging around a pile of used tissues and medicine vials on his coffee table.

Victor copies down the guy's basic information at the kitchen table. I'm sitting across from him trying not to gape. "Is this normal?" I whisper. "People call you for this shit?"

He peers over his dollar-store reading glasses at me for a hard second, then gets back to writing.

"Here it is!" the guy exclaims cheerfully. Then he erupts into a hacking fit. He passes a plastic Tupperware container to Del, who gingerly takes it in a gloved hand and peers in. He scowls and tips it toward us just enough for me to see a tennis-ball-sized clump of tangly brown hair.

"The fuck?" I say before I can stop myself.

The patient shrugs. "I know, right?"

Victor shrugs too, and then both radios in the room burst into excited, static-laced growls.

"Unit with a message, please repeat your assigned number and location. Unit with a message, please re—" Another desperate scramble of static and yelling cuts off the dispatcher. Victor and Del both furrow their brows and turn up their radios at the same time.

I hear the words "forthwith" and "imminent arrest" and then more static comes in. The dispatcher releases an angry tone over the airwaves and yells at the units to stop stepping over one another.

I stand up. "What is it?"

Victor shakes his head. "Sounds like they're calling for backup."

"Marcy and Greene! Marcy and Greene!" the radio screams. *"Forthwith! We have an imminent cardiac arrest. I need medics. I need backup. We about to roll."*

Victor and I lock eyes. "The park," I say.

He nods. "Go. We gotta wrap this up."

At full speed, I move with ease. You don't realize my left leg drags; this cane compensates just so: the full complex machinery of me lunging forward like a wave. It took practice, believe me. But I've had time. It's been more than four years since I died in some unspeakably violent way at the foot of the ornate archway at Grand Army Plaza and then woke up days later in a phantom safe house on Franklin Ave., body broken and every memory shredded. I find new life in each moment like this: the midnight brownstones breezing past me, the siren song of something foul dragging me forward. This is life, and really, anything is better than the sheer emptiness of so many lost memories.

"The streets is hungry," a little old lady mutters when I roll up, sweat-soaked and out of breath, at the southwest corner of Von King Park. She has a rusted old cart in front of her and a head scarf tied around her wrinkled brown face. "Streets be feedin' when they hungry."

A bloodstain the size of a trench coat shines up from the dark concrete at me. It catches the sickly orange glare of streetlamps and the pulsing blue emergency lights. They've already decorated the spot with police tape. The ambulance must've screeched off just before I got there; I hear its wail recede into the night. A few feet away from the bloodstain, a motor scooter lies in a heap, like someone just crinkled it up and tossed it there.

The cop nearest me has icy blue eyes and looks young and entirely unimpressed. I ask him what happened and he just shrugs and looks away. I turn to the old lady, still standing beside me and chewing her mouth up and down like she has the mushiest piece of steak in there she don't wanna let go of.

"One'a them Chinese delivery boys," she responds to my unasked question.

"What hit him?"

She nods up the block some, where a *Daily News* truck idles with its hazard lights on. A guy with a baseball cap and a goatee stands outside, talking on his cell phone, eyes barely holding back tears. An ugly human-sized dent marks the side of the truck.

I shake my head. "Damn."

"Streets is hungry," the old lady says again.

"You see anything right before? Anything weird?"

She turns her attention from the street; those ancient cataract-fogged eyes squint up at me. "Was just a small one, eh."

"A small . . . what?"

She flinches, eyes back on the street, far away. "Don't play stupid now."

"A small ghost."

"Ay."

"You see it clear?"

She shakes her head. "Just fleeting-like. Came and went, came and went." She chuckles softly. "He'll be back though, eh. He'll be back, yes."

CHAPTER TWO

～⁓⦿⁓～

Kia

I don't know why I can't stop thinking of Giovanni today. This is probably all Carlos's fault, with his damn incessant searching for an invisible past. Whatever it is, I can't shake it: it's like there's a tiny Gio hiding behind all the little potion vials and sacred pots on the shelves around me. I came in to the botánica early even though it's Saturday, because I couldn't go back to sleep and lying in bed with the sunshine creeping over me just wasn't cutting it. Yes, I have trig homework. No, I don't care. And Baba Eddie doesn't have any readings till two, which means he'll waddle in at 1:58, sipping his coffee.

But here I am.

The sunlight finds its way through the saint statues in the window display, lands on me and warms my skin. I feel old even though I'm not.

And then a breath of spring comes through the open door. It's tinged with frost but still carries that freshness, that new-soil, sunlit-fields goodness, and it should make me happy but it doesn't.

Giovanni.

This always happens, this second week of March, and I

always forget and turn myself in circles wondering why I can't find my way out of this hole, why every thought hurls me back to a dim, cramped place that doesn't know sunlight. But anniversaries will do that, creep up on you and settle in your bones.

Still, he's never been on me like *this*. Usually it's just the emptiness.

Giovanni.

It's been seven years, almost to the day.

I should probably give up and admit he's dead. Everyone else has. A boy like that, that bright a fire, seems like it'd be too much to ask to have him around for more than a decade or two. Instead I make up stories: Giovanni in Amsterdam, whoring around gleefully with poets and painters, smoking hash and making fun of American tourists. Giovanni in India, writing plays while riding elephants. Giovanni in Tunisia, fermenting a lusty new remix of the Arab Spring.

When I was nine, almost ten, and he was what? Sixteen? I was still plotting how to get him to marry me. I'd done all the math, checked and rechecked it: he would be twenty-three when I hit seventeen, the legal age to marry in New York. That seemed doable: seventeen and twenty-three. Shit, Uncle Freddie got married when he was fifteen and Aunt Bea was twenty-eight and they're still going strong. Then again, Uncle Freddie's been known to swallow his own teeth on purpose. Anyway, I scratched the equations out on my little *Powerpuff Girls* notepad and arrived triumphantly at the conclusion that it was doable, mathematically at least. The other concerns, that he obviously had no interest whatsoever in girls and that we're first cousins—that all seemed like secondary problems. Sex was gross anyway, right? Who wanted all that?

I'm gonna be seventeen next week and Giovanni is . . . nowhere.

A woman comes in, ignoring the CLOSED sign on the door. I can't tell if she's white or Puerto Rican or white and Puerto Rican. She's got loud purple lipstick on and she's almost perfectly round. Maybe she's been here before—Gina? Louisa? Then she opens her mouth and she's definitely Puerto Rican. "Hola, mi niña. Lissen, you have those collares for Babalu I asked about before? It was maybe two weeks ago, yes?"

Oh yeah, she was here before, but it wasn't no two weeks ago. Two months maybe. "We already sold 'em out, Iya." I use the respectful term for an elder santera even though I don't know if she's initiated or not. Whatever. One way or the other, she's older than me.

"Ay, mi madre, but I put in the order and everything." A singsongy whine enters her voice. I want nothing to do with it, so I end the conversation quick and she finds her way to the door. And then: Giovanni. Giovanni dressed in a hundred shades of violet, fro unruly. We were on our way home from school. That same chilly freshness teased the arrival of spring, and Giovanni was rolling his eyes because he got cast as the swan again in the ballet school's version of *Swan Lake*. "Gayest role ever," he said, sipping a cup of milk and sugar with a splash of coffee in it. "So stupid. Why can't we do a ballet based on *Ishigu*?"

I jumped up and down and did little pirouettes around him. "Ishigu! Ishigu!" That's the manga we both loved. Well, I loved it because he loved it and everything he loved was a holy relic to me. Plus, Ishigu was half boy-demon, half android and surrounded by the hottest anime chicks in Robot City. Gio could be Ishigu and I could be Maiya, who carried a staff with a talking ram's head on top that she used to disembowel all the tentacle-bots that came at them from the Red Death Chambers.

"I'm coming in late," Baba Eddie says when I pick up the landline. I hear him pull on his cigarette. "Something came up."

"I'm so sure." For no reason at all, I'm annoyed.

"Hold things down for me, okay? Why are you there so early anyway?"

"I dunno." I shrug as if he can see it over the phone, but really: it's Baba Eddie; he probably can.

"What's wrong, Kia?" That touch of charismatic condescension he always gets away with because he knows I love him like a father. Uncle. Fatherly uncle. Whatever. I let it slide. Again.

"Nothing."

"Good." He ignores my blatant lie. "See you at three . . . ish."

"You have a two-o'clock reading, and anyway, I have capoeira at three and I really hate being late."

"Who's the reading for?"

"Eliades."

"Oh fuck. He's always coming with some bullshit. Keep him entertained till I get there."

"I'm not entertaining."

"Just tell him I'll be a little late."

"But . . ."

The line goes dead.

Ishigu was a third-degree master of Shumanjo Levitating Robot fighting style, but Sunnyside Academy didn't have that as an after-school option, so Giovanni took kenpo instead. Gio also was a lead alto in glee club, treasurer of the debate team, assistant editor at the school newspaper, and president/ founding member of the Amiri Baraka Drama Club. Each met on a different day of the week, which I always took to be a special scheduling miracle devised solely to please my overachieving cousin—but it was really just a coincidence.

"Why you still wearing your tutu?" Gio narrowed his eyes at me.

"Because I'm a ballerina," I informed him.

"Ballet is so girly."

I matched his sneer with one of my own. "You do ballet and you're a boy."

"I'm not just a boy." Gio's hands extended to either side, palms out, like Ishigu does when he's getting ready to levitate. "I'm the baddest boy in town, bitches."

I was laughing, but then I stopped. "Don't call me a bitch." Both my fists found my hips, and I frowned, creasing my brow to show I wasn't kidding.

"I didn't mean you." The apology was sincere. "I meant it universally. All the bitches in the universe! Anyway, it's not a bad word if you say it right."

"It's not?" We started walking again all through the quiet suburbs of eastern Queens. When Gio was with me, I could ignore the creeping sensation that I don't belong, I don't belong; no matter where I am, I don't belong.

"Shh . . . We on a mission."

"Where we going?" I'd never been to this neighborhood before. Maybe driven past once or twice with my dad, but it was all white folks, and the feeling of *don't belong, don't belong* hung heavy in the air, like all the molecules wanted me to leave too. But I knew I was safe. Gio'd been studying kenpo since he was my age and he was a brown belt and not to be trifled with.

"It's a secret mission."

"But where we going?"

"If I tell you, it won't be a . . ." I made the face that I knew gets him, the one that I used to make right before I cried. He caved. "Fine. But don't tell *anybody*." He lowered his voice to such a shrill whisper on the word "anybody" that a little spittle escaped and he had to wipe his mouth. "We're going to see if Jeremy's okay."

I rolled my eyes. For three weeks, all I'd heard about was Jeremy Fern. Would Jeremy like this red leather jacket? Does he read *Ishigu* too? What kind of cigarettes would Jeremy smoke? If Jeremy were a crayon, what color would he be? (Yes, no, Virginia Slims, and plain ol' white, respectively, but who was listening?) The angle of Jeremy's chin: divine architecture; the perfection of his frown when he was thinking about a math problem; the timbre of his voice: angelic. Jeremy the Brave, bringing in articles about oil drilling in Antarctica for social studies. Jeremy the Agile, bounding effortlessly across the gym in tights for his *Swan Lake* solo. Jeremy the Cryptic, explaining his theory of how all six Star Wars movies were really one eight-million-hour rewrite of the Book of Job.

Or whatever.

If the boy had the slightest hint of self-awareness and looked out from the curtains of his thin blond hair once in a while, I'd actually feel like he was a threat to my impending marriage. But as it was, he displayed zero interest in anything more than a platonic friendship with Gio. Which baffled and relieved me at the same time.

So now we were off to see Jeremy the Clueless for some dumb "mission." Great.

Eliades shows up right on time, of course. I'm sipping some bodega tea, no milk, no sugar, staring off into nothing like some asshole in a nursing home, when the guy busts in with a loud jingle-jangle from the door chimes. He's always well dressed, but today his green striped tie lies half undone around his neck like a noose, and the top of his shirt is open, revealing pallid, moist flesh and a hint of chest hair. It's a chilly March day, but he's sweating like he ran all the way here from his Manhattan office.

"Hey, Eliades." I'm grateful for the company; all these memories crowding my head can't be healthy.

Eliades wipes a hand over his thinning hairline. "It's back." No *Hi, Kia*, no *How's school?* Just *It's back*. Okay. I hate small talk anyway. I don't even wanna know what's back.

"Baba Eddie's running a little late."

"But . . ."

"You can have a seat and wait for him."

Eliades may be self-absorbed, but he knows me well enough not to argue when I use my have-a-seat voice. He makes his way through the aisles, pouting softly, and settles in one of the big easy chairs we got at half price from the vintage spot on Myrtle.

A textbook lies open on the counter in front of me; I don't even remember taking it out. It's trig, some shit I already know how to do, and can't be bothered answering a bunch of mindless questions about. I know this is a terrible reason to be getting Cs, but the truth is, I'm bored out my mind almost every day in school. I mean, most of us are, and believe me when I tell you it's not us, it's them. Half the kids in there could be teaching advanced computer coding to a roomful of the aging millennials that are supposed to be educating us. It's all teach to the test, teach to the test, meanwhile, we got important, real-life shit to deal with that doesn't involve proving to a messy bureaucracy that their limp-dick machine functions properly.

Every time my report card comes back mediocre, my dad makes a speech about options being open and how I'm smarter than this and he's disappointed, and I get it, but that doesn't change the fact that doing mind-numbing work is mind-numbing, and my mind is numb right now. I'm over this shit. I've learned more running this botánica and trash-talking with my girl Karina than I ever did in a classroom.

Eliades lets out a massive snore.

I slam the textbook shut and roll my eyes.

"You wouldn't make much of a spy," Giovanni informed me as we sat in some bushes on a little hill behind Jeremy's house. It's just like all the other ones on this block: three stories, faded off-white shingles, all the decaying decadence of a middle-aged dad in a rumpled suit. "Too much chatter."

It hurt, but with some effort I kept the whine out of my voice. "Well, how am I sposta spy when I don't even know what we're doing here?"

Gio sighed and adjusted his position a little. "Because Jeremy said some strange men had been showing up around his house."

"How do you know he didn't mean you?"

"Kia!"

"Keep your voice down. You're gonna give us away."

"What I'm gonna do is take you right home and then come back all by myself."

The idea was so offensive to me I actually squealed a little when I said, "No!" This time when I made the pre-cry face, it wasn't a ruse.

Gio knew it too, and he softened. "Then shut the fuck up, Kia."

"Fine. But don't swear at me."

After a few moments, Giovanni sighed. "He said there were strange men that would whisper through his window late at night, all kinds of things about how he was destined for greatness and he was the chosen one. All kindsa shit. But it was like a whisper he could hear inside his head, not them speaking. They just made weird clicky sounds. They wanted him to come with them but would never say where, and when he'd ask, they'd just vanish into the night."

I didn't know what to say. My eyes were open so wide

they felt like they were gonna pop out. "And you gonna stop them?"

"I just want to make sure he's alright, is all."

Something is clogging up the air in the botánica. My eyes are watering, and I can't tell if it's because I'm getting all emo from thinking about Giovanni or if it's from whatever thickness has settled over the room. No, it's definitely not me. I peek through the aisles but Eliades is hidden behind a bookshelf. I can't inhale fully, my breath stops at the top of my chest and makes me cough.

"Eliades?" I say, and the silence that follows chills me.

It's back. His words echo through my head over and over again. *It's back.* I didn't even bother asking what—it's not my business and what could I do about it anyway? *It's back.* He'd elongated the "it" in that way people do when they're talking about something they don't want to speak out loud. He looked like just saying it was a punch in the gut.

It's back.

The room is so quiet now. I don't even hear the traffic outside or the shoppers around the corner on Graham or the bachata that usually streams out the music store across the street. "Eliades?" I sound like such a little girl: pathetic. The thickness hangs over everything, an ever-expanding balloon forcing all the air out of the place. I could call Baba Eddie, but I don't want to move from right here. Somehow I'm positive if I move, it's all over. So I don't. I wait.

It was getting dark; the foliage we were in was already swamped in shadows and the sky turned turquoise through the trees above us. Gio fumbled in his pockets and then produced a black cigarette. I gasped. He rolled his eyes, fumbled again, took out a lighter. The sugary scent of cloves filled the air; it was sweet and perfect, Giovanni's magic pixie powder.

"How you gonna be all mad that I'm loud," I hissed, "and then light a great big beacon of flame and send all that smoke out? You know he gonna see it."

"He's not even home yet. Look, the lights are out. Anyway, you can't really stake out a house and not smoke. It's, like, the rules."

"I guess. If by stakeout you mean *stalk*."

"Shhh!"

I was about to remind him he'd just said no one was home when a light went on. Jeremy appeared, pulling curtains out of the way and then lifting the window. He stuck his head out, smelled the spring breeze (the cloves too probably), and then disappeared back into his room. I elbowed Gio, for no real reason except to somehow indicate that I'd told him so, and he nudged me back but kept smoking.

"You're an asshole," I whispered. It felt good to swear, mature.

"Shh!"

Music swirled out of Jeremy's room. It was trancelike: a gush of strings and then a heavy beat. Jeremy sailed past his window, arms over his head, a perfectly executed grand jeté. He emerged, pirouetting, in the next window just as a pleading, luscious voice came in over the beat.

I tugged on Gio's sleeve. "What's this music?"

"It's Björk."

"What's a *Björk*?"

"Shh!" That was the moment I understood he would never marry me. The boy was entranced. I could see Jeremy dancing in his eyes, the glare from the bedroom lighting up his face, his mouth hanging slightly open. I might not've had the words for it at the time, but inside I knew: it was love. Not that bullshit TV love, not the corny love-song love either. *True love*. The kind that people got themselves killed for. The kind that made you do really, really stupid things.

"Gio?"

"Girl, if I have to tell you to shush one more . . ."

"What are we really doing here?"

The music churned on. Gio kept his gaze fixed on the window.

A stick of sage sits on the counter, its charred end resting in an ashtray beside Baba Eddie's cigarette butts. The lighter is . . . Where is the lighter? Usually in Baba Eddie's pocket, dammit.

The air still throbs with the heaviness of something about to happen, and I'm sure it's whatever spiritual crap Eliades dragged in with him. Which is some bullshit, but I guess it's what we're here for. Can't blame a sick person for coming to the hospital.

Baba usually squirrels away matchbooks in random nooks and crannies for when he misplaces his lighters. I turn my head slowly to the shelf behind the counter, scan past iron pots, little wooden axes, grinning stone heads, and there, tucked in between a bag of birdseed and a porcelain vase, sits a black matchbook from some Italian restaurant around the corner.

I don't really know why sage does what it does, but Baba Eddie swears by it, and listen: that shit works. I light it on the second try and wave it up and down the aisle like a cheerleader, leaving a floating river of fragrant smoke in my wake.

The place already feels more relaxed, but when I'm done I squirt some Florida Water around just to close the deal. Eliades manages to snore through the whole thing. I won't lie: those shits are comfortable as hell. Best nap ever.

It's twelve past two.

Fuck everything.

I call Baba Eddie, but he doesn't pick up. I've done no homework, no restock, no online sales. I just sat here, sulking, surrounded by Gio and memories and saint statues for two hours.

I throw my bag over my shoulder and shake my head. One way or the other, this'll have to sort itself out without me. I put some quiet Enya-type shit on the stereo, lock Eliades in, and head off to the rec center.

CHAPTER THREE

❦

Carlos

"It's new protocol time, gentlemen!" Bartholomew Arsten flashes a practiced smile, and Riley and I groan. We're in the misty abandoned warehouse in Sunset Park that the Council of the Dead calls home. As always, it's chilly and shrouded in darkness, just the way these creepy-ass dead folks like it. Also as always, the Council is on some fuckshit. Bart's office is on the second floor, a grim little windowless cubicle with peeling wallpaper. Below us, a few dozen soul-catchers flit around the wide-open factory floor, where they tend to assorted nefarious shit.

"Come, come now." Arsten rises. He looks like a sad pear with stubby arms and a comb-over. His dim translucence flickers in the haze, and he spreads his arms open, palms out, and shrugs. Even that seems rehearsed. "New protocols are the Council's way of staying up-to-date on the ever-changing landscape of the afterlife, ya know?"

Riley chuckles. "And here I thought new protocols were the Council's way of stumbling around like dickheads in the dark when one of our guys fucks up." That's why Riley's my best friend. My best dead friend. He's saved my life more times than I care to say, most importantly that first mysterious night at Grand Army Plaza. Sometimes I think he brought me into the Council fold just so he'd have a like-minded pain in the ass to cause trouble with.

Arsten looks like he swallowed a chili pepper. He recovers quickly though, ever the car dealer. "Ah, Riley. That's funny, really. In this particular case, yes, a soulcatcher did actually get herself in a little situation, it's true, but that's not the *only* reason we update the protocols. The protocols get revised and upda—"

"What happened?" I ask, more to cut through the bullshit than to actually find out. I am curious though.

"Oh, ha-ha!"

An uncomfortable silence lingers after Arsten's forced laugh.

Riley raises a ghostly eyebrow. "Bart?"

Arsten sits on his desk and shakes his head so hard his jowls flap. "You can't tell though, okay?"

We both nod and lean in.

"Soulcatcher Bell was on a routine collection run, right? Aw, man . . . Yeah, so anyway, there was, like, a bunch of unauthorized afterlifers envindigating at a particular location, over by—"

I raise my hand. "Hold up. Did you just say envindigating?"

"Yeah."

"That's not a word."

Arsten chuckles. "Sure it is. It means to hang around and make a nuisance of yourself."

"Like from the Latin 'envindigarus,' right?" Riley offers. I scowl at him.

"Right," Arsten says, smiling at Riley for maybe the first time ever.

"Alright, whatever, go on."

"Thank you, Carlos, I will. Yeah, they were over by Red Hook actually, by the hospital over there, and it was like a group of older spirits, in a nursing home, right, just hanging around."

Riley shakes his head. "Envindigating 'n' shit."

"Exactly! I mean, *in the open*. Like, with the living."

The Council can*not* fathom how or why any spirit would dare make itself known to the living. Call it one gigantic failure of the collective bureaucratic imagination—whatever it is, it's caused a lot of problems. Mingling with, appearing to, whispering words of wisdom within hearing range of the living, or any variation on the theme is strictly forbidden in no uncertain terms by the notorious COD. Except of course if you're in the upper echelon or you're one of the Ignoble Seven on the High Council.

But deal with the living? If an afterlifer's gonna stick around in the land of the living in full defiance of the Council's loosely enforced ban, they're also more than likely gonna eschew the Council rules on hanging with whoever they please.

"So the whole nursing home knew 'bout the ghosts?" Riley asks. "Staff and everyone?" You can tell he's intrigued by the idea. So am I.

"Just the B wing," Arsten says. "But still!"

"So you sent Sylvia and what?" I say. "She sliced 'em all into the Deeper Death without asking any questions or giving them a chance to cease and desist back to the regular old Underworld like good little obedient ghosts?" I wouldn't put it past Sylvia Bell. She's been known to be an overachiever when it comes to needlessly slicing ghosts.

Arsten rubs his face. "Quite the opposite, I'm afraid. She let them stay."

Riley sits up in his chair. "What?"

"Yeah. Just . . . left 'em alone. She had a whole team with her too, Soulcatcher Squad 9. Said they weren't causing anybody any harm. Can you believe that?"

"Unbefuckinglievable," I say, though not for the same reasons Arsten has.

"I know, right? I mean, sheesh!"

"So what's the new protocol?" Riley asks.

Bartholomew Arsten brightens. You can tell protocols

make the guy happy. He reaches behind him and retrieves some ghostly scrolls from the desk. "I'm so glad you asked, Agent Riley." He makes a big production of clearing his throat and adjusting the paperwork. Riley and I roll our eyes.

"Section seventeen, subheading six, column B: By order of the New York Council of the Dead, all new recruits, new being defined as having completed Soulcatcher Training Academy within the past twelve months, will hereafter be assigned to work with a senior soulcatcher, or Soulcatcher Prime, who will accompany them on all mission fieldwork as it pertains to and is related to the Council of the Dead activity, and at all times will that senior member of the force be by their (by which we mean the new recruit, as defined earlier in this paragraph) side and within their presence."

We're just staring at him when he looks up from the paper. In true protocol form, this one doesn't have shit to do with anything that actually happened.

"But . . ." Riley says.

"That doesn't," I try.

"Even . . ."

"Sylvia isn't even that new, Bart. What the hell does that have to . . . ?"

He waves a nonchalant hand at us. "Well, we figured what if she had been? Right? Would've been a whole lot worse, right? I mean . . . shoot. Think about it."

I just shake my head.

"Anyway, what are you guys working on?"

"Carlos. What we doing here, man?"

It's a chilly early afternoon in Von King Park. A few kids run around the playground, and some dog walkers stroll past with plastic baggies out, ready to collect the offerings. The sun's dead center in the sky, and even through the crisp air you can feel the first rumbling of spring announcing itself to the world: that fresh smell, the warm light. You'd never guess that the four corners around us have been scene to such vicious tragedy for the past week.

"We checkin' something," I say. Riley grunts. On my other side, Baba Eddie removes a cigarette from his pocket, places it between his lips, and pauses, eyes closed, for two breaths before lighting it and taking a luxurious drag. I look down at the wise little santero. "Every time, huh?"

Baba Eddie smiles. "Otherwise, what's the fucking point, am I right?"

"He's right," Riley says.

Baba Eddie deals with ancestors—it's what he does. At his house, a tall stick with ribbons and bells tied to it leans against one wall, and old black-and-white photos clutter around its base like sacred toadstools. He puts food down for 'em when he cooks and smokes cigars with 'em when he needs to suss out a situation. His clients flock to the botánica in droves to check in with their long-dead relatives or to get a cowrie-shell reading and see what the orishas have planned. He and Riley have known each other since before I came around.

"I do gotta be over at the store pretty soon though," Baba Eddie points out. "So if there's something, you know, important you wanted us to see, this would be the time."

"Word," Riley says. "I got shit to do too."

"The hell you do." I sit my ass down on a park bench. "This is my next assignment," I tell them.

"You gonna be a dog walker? Times's tough, huh, bro?"

"No, Riley. There's some shit going on in this park. I wanna know if either of you are picking up anything."

Riley raises an eyebrow. "What kinda shit?"

"Dead-people shit, man, what you think?"

"I know that. I mean . . . You know what, lemme have a look-see and find out myself."

The three of us sit there quietly for a few moments, Baba Eddie smoking and me and Riley just staring out into the park. A chilly breeze sweeps across the soccer field behind us and rustles some leaves overhead. A pug strolls past, followed by a yuppie dude typing away on his phone-a-majig. Pigeons come, bob their pigeon heads, and then flock away in a huff. Ain't much going on, really.

"I ain't got shit," Riley says.

Baba Eddie opens his eyes. "Me neither. You might wanna find a better assignment. This park's boring."

"But I will say this." Riley leans in, and so do Baba Eddie and I. "There something going on with you, homeboy."

I scrunch up my face. "Me?" I'm not in the mood for this shit.

"Yeah, bro. You seen yourself recently?"

I have no slick response to this, so I just give him dead eyes.

Baba Eddie nods. "You losin' weight, papi."

"What?"

"And I'll tell ya something else," Riley says. "You look like shit."

"What?"

"I mean, metaphorically *and* physically."

"The fuck you talking about, Riley?"

"You ain't well, C. That's what I'm talking about."

I actually laugh. What else can I do? "I feel fine, man."

"I'm happy for you, but you ain't. You been off for, like, a few weeks now, by my count. What you say, Baba E?"

I look at Baba Eddie. He squints one eye and then the other, calculating the duration of my fuckedupness, I guess. "Since the girl," he finally says, and I laugh.

"You guys, listen." A jogger passes without headphones on, and I pause until he's out of earshot. "Ain't shit wrong with me. I'm okay. Yes, that was fucked up, but I ain't still fucked up about it. Period. Punto. Fin."

"Listen," Riley says a little too gently, "we all been hurt, man. It's okay to feel pain. I mean shit, she was carrying your child. You ain't seen her in what, four months?"

"Six months and seven days."

Riley leaps up. "See? That was a test, and you failed. You counting the days, man. Just be upset and be okay with being upset."

"That is the best way," Baba Eddie muses. "The first time Russell and I broke up, I shut down for like three weeks. You couldn't find me for nothin'. I'm not gonna say I cried, but . . ."

"C'mon!" Riley reaches across me and jabs Baba Eddie with his ghostly arm. "You cried a little."

Baba Eddie looks thoughtful for a moment, retrieves another cigarette. "Niagara fucking Falls."

"Word up," Riley says. Baba Eddie lights his cigarette and sighs.

"So I need to cry is what you're saying?" I have a series of brutal accidents to unravel. I have my past to uncover. I don't have time for this shit. I can tell Riley's not gonna let me off easy though.

He shrugs. "All I'm sayin' is: whatever it is you need to do to get right, do that."

Baba Eddie nods and stands. "I'm late as fuck now, and Kia is going to kill my ass, but, Carlos, I sincerely hope you deal with your shit. Let me know if you ever want to talk or you know . . ."

"I don't want a reading, Baba, but thank you."

He doffs his baseball cap at both of us and strolls off toward Bushwick.

I look at Riley. "You happy?"

"Always, partner."

I sit back and, as we watch the day stroll past, let a simple melody slip from my lips.

CHAPTER FOUR

Kia

All the way down the bustling avenues of East Williamsburg, bright and audacious with hot new sales, Dominican cats throwing game, old ladies selling mango, and bachata on ten, Gio stays with me. If I turn around quick, maybe I'd catch him, that flash of a second before he vanishes again into the ether. I have some trippy drum 'n' bass shit in my ears, a new track from an underground DJ out of Jersey I downloaded last night, and it moves me along at a steady strut, past the cavernous prison facade of Woodhull Hospital and into Bed-Stuy, and Gio remains. It is a friendly haunting, this; got none of the wretched desperation that some folks come in to see Baba Eddie about. But then, Baba always says most ghosts aren't as bad as all that, not like in the movies where every ghoul is dedicated to emptying all your cabinets and then eating your brains. That, Baba has informed me, is a big bag of bullshit.

I pass a young white cop standing in front of a vacant lot. "Hey, Sideshow Bob!" he yells. *Ignore, ignore, ignore.* "Can I get your number?"

I stop in my tracks. Turn. "The fuck part of you calling me a cartoon character seems like it would be endearing?"

He raises both hands and eyebrows. "Whoa, easy! I was just—"

I turn around, keep walking. "I'm a child, you pervert. Suck my sideshow dick."

It doesn't make sense, I know, and probably dangerous as fuck—those weed-strewn lots would be easy to disappear into—but Gio's absence rages through me and all I know is that fire. The cop doesn't follow, probably just shrugs and tries his luck with the next teenage girl. And still, the memories press down, relentless.

I gasped when I realized we weren't alone in the wooded area behind Jeremy Fern's house. The men standing around us— they didn't walk there; we would've heard them. They just appeared out of the darkness. There were six of them. They had pale, almost greenish skin, broad shoulders, bugged-out eyes, and smirking, deeply lined faces. They hunched over slightly, all of them the same way. I almost screamed when I noticed them, but I kept it in. They just stood there—staring like Gio at Jeremy's entrancing performance. Ever so slowly, I wrapped my little hand around Gio's wrist. He was about to shush me, but I squeezed, squeezed so hard he shut up. It was just the tiniest of gasps he let out when he finally saw the men. I thought it was too loud, but they didn't look over, just kept those pushed-out eyes squinting straight ahead at Jeremy's house. The air filled with whispers—a dissonant hissing and clicking.

Then they started walking, all at the same time. They moved through the trees into the backyard. It was a slow, deliberate walk, each step careful and precise, long arms dangling by their sides. I couldn't stop staring at them, but something else in the corner of my eye was tweaking for my attention. Something was moving. I looked, but it was so dark, the trees were just shadows against the night. Still, there was movement. The trees, the trees were moving. They were alive somehow, shifting, writhing in the darkness. No.

I stepped closer to look at the nearest one to me. No. It was alive with insects. Shiny-backed cockroaches swarmed over the thing, the big kind, but they weren't the normal dark orange. They were pale, almost pink.

I opened my mouth to scream, and a hand wrapped around it. I was about to start fighting for my life when I smelled that shea butter/BO mix that I knew so well. Giovanni. He lifted me up and turned me around. "Don't say a fucking word," he hissed. "Don't even fucking cry."

I nodded, tears streaming down my face. Giovanni would make everything alright. He always did. Giovanni would get me out of here.

"Listen to me, Kia. Go home." My stomach plummeted. "Go now."

"N . . ." I started to say, but he shushed me with a look.

"Don't look back. Just go. I'll be home soon."

I shook my head.

"Kia." No debate, no whining. This was not a game. And I had no choices. "Go." He put me down, turned to where the six men made their slow path toward Jeremy's house.

The trees all around me crawled with pale roaches. I took a step backward, but Gio didn't even look to see if I'd gone. He launched down the hill, quiet as a ninja. I saw the light glint over his muscly arm, saw a splotch against it, another roach, just before he swiped it off. I cringed. My whole body wanted to vanish, burst out of the trees and get as far away as I could. But my heart wouldn't let me turn away from my cousin. I stood perfectly still, caught between the two impossible choices, and anyway: useless.

Gio came up behind the first man at a sliding crouch. He anchored one leg in the dirt and flew up into the air, flashing the other leg out in a stunning roundhouse kick. His foot found its mark; the man collapsed with an eerie silence. I think Gio was as stunned as I was—for a solid three seconds he just stood there gaping at the man sprawled on the ground. The others didn't seem to notice, or if they did they didn't care; the slow march toward the house continued.

I took a few steps down the hill. I couldn't watch, couldn't stop watching. Gio stepped over the one he'd taken out, but a hand came up from the ground and wrapped around his leg, dropping him to one knee. The man rose up fast, faster than he should've been able to after taking a hit like that. Two of the other men stopped and turned slowly toward the fray. Gio stabilized himself in a sturdy horse-riding stance, so he was ready when the blow came. It was clumsy and slow, like the man couldn't quite get his limbs to do what he wanted them to, but I could tell from the way Gio leaned to the side that there was an unnatural force to it. Gio side-stepped and let the weight of the guy's hit do the work, just like we'd been taught. As the man stumbled forward, Gio brought his elbow down on the back of his head.

The two other men moved in from either side. Gio's hoarse yell cut through the quiet suburban night: "Jeremy! Run!" Even the attackers seemed startled. Jeremy appeared at the window, and everyone looked up at him. Gio took advantage of the confusion, kicking in the kneecaps of one man and then spin smashing the other with another roundhouse. The first was done; I saw him crumple, again with that impossible silence, but the second guy recovered quickly and barreled into Gio.

The back door of the house swung open, and Jeremy gaped out. "What's going on? Giovanni?" It was like an electric shock went through the three men not busy with Gio. They lurched forward, crowding around Jeremy, blocking the door from closing.

"Get inside!" Gio yelled from the ground. Then the man smashed him hard across the face, and he fell limp.

I ran. I ran straight into the center of all that hell. Felt something tickle my arm and swiped it off over and over without bothering to even look at what it was. The man was crouching in the dirt with his back to me, and me, I thought of death. No strategy, no caution: just death. Because all my little body could do was surge forward even while my mind screamed at it to turn back, and the man was only a few steps from me now.

Gio's leg came out of nowhere, swept like a lightning bolt along the ground and took the guy's legs right out from under him. You could actually hear the swoosh of wind, the guy fell so fast. Before I could even yell, the man was on the ground and Gio was over him, and then Gio's foot was smashing down again and again on the man's face. I heard the squishing destruction of flesh, then a much sharper cracking sound, and then it was just a dull thud, over and over again, and Gio's sobbing breaths.

And then something started moving. I saw Gio tense, but it wasn't the man. It was something else. The broken skin of his face writhed to life, and a thousand pale cockroaches that had been his skin scattered away. More poured out of his sleeves, from under his collar, swarmed off his hands to reveal shreds of flesh clinging to raggedy bone. Gio and I both stepped back, but the roaches weren't interested in us; they scattered outward in a confused swarm and then flushed as one toward the house. Jeremy.

"No!" Gio yelled. I couldn't even catch my breath before he'd turned and stormed past the roach swarm through the back door.

"Gio!" I yelled. We were still alive. Why couldn't he understand what a miracle that was? A few minutes ago I thought everything was over and now we were alive: both of us! I hated my cousin almost as much as I loved him right then. The night was so quiet. I heard a few night birds chirping in the trees above me. Someone was watching TV in a house nearby, a reality show, from the sound of it. Had no one heard us screaming? For a terrible moment I wondered if any of it had even happened. Then I walked shakily toward the house, barely breathing, barely conscious.

Inside, there was a dim little alcove with winter jackets hung up and a cubby area full of weathered board games. Something glinted up from the short stairwell leading into the kitchen. Not roaches; it was perfectly still: blood. I moved faster, stepping around the wet spots and up into the kitchen: all dark, no one there. From somewhere in the house, Gio was yelling: "Jeremy? Jeremy?" I released a little dark sandbag of weight from my heart. Gio was safe for the moment. If he was looking for Jeremy, he wasn't fighting the freaky cockroach men. If he was looking for Jeremy, he was alive. The thought of ending this with Gio still intact made me want to sit down at the kitchen table and sob, but I kept going, through a winding hallway, past the living room, moderately fancy and very lived in, and up the stairs.

"I told you to . . ." Gio mumbled when he saw me. "I thought I told you to . . ." His eyes were so wide, the way a horse's look in movies when they get shot, like you didn't know they could get so wide, that such a noble, magnificent creature could actually be afraid. "He's gone." Gio fell against the wall and slid down into a crouch, sobbing. "They got him."

"Gio." My little nine-year-old voice sounded calm, authoritative, for the first time in my life. And there I was still in my tutu. I felt ridiculous. "We gotta go, Gio. We gotta go now."

He looked up. I'd broken through to him. He nodded, took the trembling hand I'd reached out to him, and stood.

The pulsing beat settles into a wide-open synth drone, echoing high hats and wandering sax riffs, and I'm standing outside the rec center, sniffling back tears.

The night of the roaches wasn't the last time I saw Giovanni, but it might as well have been. In the weeks after Jeremy disappeared, Gio withdrew deeper and deeper into himself until one day he was just gone. His parents had kicked him out years earlier, but my dad loved Gio like a long-lost son. We wallpapered the neighborhood with flyers, pestered the police about it every day, put search teams together to scour all the back corners and abandoned fields. Nothing. The boy was just gone. It barely got a blurb in the papers, of course—a little "missing" notice in the local crime section of the same issue that had a moving tribute to Jeremy on the front page.

I've made up so many stories. But the practical part of me knew he was just a hurt kid who had been through some fucked-up shit he couldn't make sense of, couldn't even tell anyone about. But then again, so was I.

And then he was gone and I was truly alone.

The ugly metal door squeaks open and Karina pokes her head out. "You comin' in, Kia? They got a new teacher, and he fine as fuck."

I laugh and tell her I'll be in in a sec and sniffle again, quickly so she doesn't notice, and then she's gone and I'm alone with the ugly empty sky and big-ass brick project houses and lingering winter and there's no more memories, no more Gio, just me and the world.

I should've told Karina to come out and then told her everything. I want to. But I also don't. Because right now, I'm busy saying good-bye. Giovanni has been with me all day, just like those ghosts that Carlos and Baba Eddie always talking about. Which means Gio's gone. Really gone. I pull off my headphones and open the metal door. Pause to take a deep breath and make sure my eyes aren't leaking. Dead and gone. I walk inside. Gone. Which means I have to stop pretending, stop making up stories, and finally, finally, for real this time, let go.

So I do.

CHAPTER FIVE

❧

Carlos

All the way at the far end of Court Street, long after the
chic provincial bakeries have given way to old-school
pizza parlors and barber shops, there is a pay phone.
There ain't many left in this city. It sits outside a train station
right where bourgie residential Brooklyn becomes industrial-
wasteland Brooklyn. The Brooklyn-Queens Expressway
looms over it, a hulking mass of corrugated steel and concrete; traffic lurches along in groans and honks.

The regular ol' fully dead folks use their telepathy shit to
get in touch with each other—it's like each one got a cell phone
implanted in their translucent-ass brains. Whatever asshole
makes the rules for botched resurrections and inbetweeners
decided that me being half dead meant I only got one-way
reception: the Council can blurt their damned protocol updates
and bossy, micromanaging messages directly into my brain,
but when I want to reach out, I gotta use the phone.

I plop in some quarters and wait as my own voice asks
me to please leave a message for Jimmy's Hat Shop (their
idea). "Yeah, listen," I say after the tone. "Send me Bell. I
know she's on disciplinary hiatus or whatever y'all call it,
but I'm working on something and I think I can bring her
back into the fold."

I pause and roll my eyes. They have this new thing where they want names for cases and brief descriptions, and I know without one they'll never send me Bell. I exhale, and my breath becomes a small cloud and rises toward the highway.

"Situation: Park Disaster. Status: Open. Summary: Dudes are getting fu . . . hurt. At Von King Park. In repeated succession. Reason enough to suspect nefarious spiritual . . . shit."

I shake my head.

"That is all."

I have the unusual thought that maybe that really is all and then I hang up. Maybe the rash of disasters is the uncaring hand of chance, playing with all of us. It doesn't matter really. I grab a coffee from the corner store and settle into my regular spot beside a massive concrete leg of the BQE. Pigeons flutter off, consult with each other in the shadows of the dingy overpass, swarm back. Some loud-ass tweens run across the street, screeching each other's names to the tune of some rap song that's been playing every point-seven seconds on the radio. Two old men in parkas stroll past, muttering to each other. A businesswoman stands in front of me, checks her phone, looks left, right, left again, and then wanders off.

None of them are Gregorio Franco.

I sip my coffee and scowl.

Sasha, her brother, Trevor, and I died the same rainy night at the foot of the archway at Grand Army Plaza. They woke up a few days later at a safe house along with Gregorio Franco, Marie St. Pierre, and a few others who would go on to become the Survivors. They compared notes when they came back around, but there was barely anything there; they were half-dead amnesiacs. Some fully alive but grim-faced and mostly silent man known only as Terra was there at first—Sasha told Baba Eddie about him as she recovered on my couch last year. Terra tended to their wounds, got a mournful faraway look in his eyes when they asked him questions, and then vanished shortly after and no one was able to track him down.

And me? I woke up at Mama Esther's. Only a shred of that night remains with me; it's all I have left of my life before dying. Three figures, hooded, with ski masks on, staring down at me as I die. One's wounded, breathing heavy, and as the night sky behind them bleeds over everything else, I'm relieved I did some damage before getting got myself, that I went down fighting. That's it.

A ghost named Pasternak was anchored to the archway and witnessed the whole thing, but all he gave me were vague, obnoxious riddles—*There were seven of you, and none survived. And then there were five.* The Council sent me after Trevor when he tried to help an ancient necromancer named Sarcofastas tear open a hole to the Underworld. I offed Trevor and then tracked down Sasha and, like an asshole, fell in love with her. She has a slender, sullen face with perfectly round cheeks and then she grins and tilts her head just so—there's mischief in that smile; it lets you in on a secret and then light catches the length of her neck, a caress, and it's a wrap. Besides all that, she understood. Without using all that clever finding-shit-out magic that we halfies have, she just knew. Sure, some of it was because she was like me, but there was an intuition at work deeper than all that.

When she figured out what I'd done, she impaled me on my own sword and aligned with Sarco, which caused the Council to send me after her (once I'd healed up, thanks to Baba Eddie and a Haitian surgeon named Dr. Tijou), and one sweltering afternoon last summer, I traced the woman I loved to this very spot, under this very highway, across the street from one of the few pay phones left in Brooklyn.

The man she was meeting with had a full beard and wore a long brown jacket and fedora; Gregorio Franco, Sasha told me later, as she recovered from the fight with Sarco.

Gregorio looked tired; deep lines etched his face and his off-gray paleness. They exchanged something, a small package, and then I stayed on Sasha's trail and Gregorio ambled off slowly toward the bay.

And then Sarco destroyed Pasternak, and Sasha and I killed Sarco with the help of a ravenous squad of tiny soul-devouring creatures, the ngks, and Sasha vanished again, this time for good, leaving behind the vague sense that she was as heartbroken as I was about the whole thing and an old cassette tape with the saddest song in the world. Which means Gregorio Franco is the only lead I got to figuring out what the hell happened that night and who I was before I died.

And where Sasha is.

It's not much.

Probably this was a random meeting spot. Probably they were smart enough to change up their rendezvous locations. Probably. But she abandoned her apartment on Ocean Avenue and went underground after shit hit the fan, and I have nothing else to go on. And it's a few hours before sunset still, a breezy March day, and I have a warm coffee in one hand and my cane-blade in the other, and despite what I told Riley and Baba Eddie, ever since Sasha left, all I feel is broken inside.

"Why you always hang out here?" Riley asks when he shows up next to me.

"Good afternoon to you too."

"I mean, you pigeon hunting? Do you have a sudden affinity for neo-postwar pregentrification, mediocre residential architecture and highways? Are you perhaps . . . high?"

I just shake my head.

"Or are you just depressed and this is one of those weird depressed-people things?"

"Riley, I'm not depressed, man. Get off it."

He eyes me and then lets it go. "What we doing?"

Before I can answer, a squat shining form slides up on my other side. "Soulcatcher Bell," I say. "Meet Agent Riley Washington."

Bell nods curtly. She's middle-aged, white, and entirely unremarkable. Up till her sudden change of heart, she'd been one of the Council's most effective and ruthless 'catchers.

"How you feeling, Sylvia?" Riley says. "They got you on admin work since the fallout?"

"Desk duty at Sunset Park HQ while they sort through the paperwork and decide what to do with me." She pauses, looks us both over. "Why am I here?"

"I was wondering that too," Riley says.

"Why'd you do it?" I ask.

Sylvia's glare is unwavering, her frown sharp. "Honestly," she says, and her shoulders relax like the word let out some long-pent up air. "It just didn't seem right to me, cutting those old ghosts down. I was always taught to respect my elders. Put my mom in a nursing home out in Hempstead when I was alive and I never felt right about it."

She glares at me again, gauging my reaction. I nod at her to go on.

"And there they were, all these geriatric spirits crawling into bed every night with their living loved ones and then mingling with them in the day, playing bridge, joking around, you know—what folks do. Being friends. They weren't hurting anyone. They were just being."

"And your squad?"

Bell inhales deeply and closes her eyes. The shadows have grown long around us, the orange haze of sunset seeping in past factories and support beams. Pigeons glide a smooth spiral over the rooftops toward the darkening sky. I can see that whatever it was that snapped in Sylvia Bell that night remains snapped. She's tired of making shit up,

tired of the bureaucracy and bullshit and resigned to whatever ridiculous fate the Council assigns her.

"Soulcatcher Squad 9 has been through a lot these past few
years since I took over as commander, Agent Delacruz."

"Carlos."

"Carlos. They are loyal to a fault, and when I ask something of them, they comply. They functioned that night
exactly within the parameters of Council protocol."

"By which you mean," Riley puts in, "they did what you
told them to, knowing full well it was a blatant infraction of
Council protocol."

Bell nods. "They're good soldiers."

Riley glares at her for a few seconds, and when she doesn't
flinch, he smiles. "I like you, Sylvia."

Sylvia Bell doesn't respond.

"You want to help us with a fucked-up situation in Von
King Park?"

"I'm on desk du—"

"Don't worry about that," I say. "We'll work it out with
the dickbags upstairs. I just wanted to make sure you were
in before I pulled you off the desk and back into the field.
For all I know you like the des—"

"I'm in," Bell says. I figured. Desk duty is like the Deeper
Death to soulcatchers like Bell. A tiny smile crosses her
face before she fades into the late-afternoon twilight.

"You plottin' something?" Riley asks as we meander through
the industrial Brooklyn backstreets.

"Right now—just gathering folks." It's a little after sunset, the sky a hazy navy blue. Streetlights blink to life
around us. Some unspoken purpose calls me forward, beck-
oning like a siren song from Von King Park.

"Then why you walkin' so fast, man? You only fast walk
when you plottin'."

"I like what Sylvia did."

"Me too. Council love being on that Council-type bull-shit. But she gotta be more strategic if she wanna stick around and keep fucking shit up."

"That's what I'm thinking."

We cross Atlantic Avenue, four bustling lanes of traffic, and cut north toward Bed-Stuy. "And so do we."

CHAPTER SIX

Reza

Tonight it's Shelly.

If I were capable of having feelings since Angie disappeared, I might have some for Shelly. Not because she's finer than the rest of them—she is fine though; don't get it twisted—but because at the beginning of the night, when she crawls into the back of my Crown Vic all prettied up and glittery, she always catches my eyes in the rearview and asks me how I'm doing. Not in the concerned way but not in the throw-off way either; she really wants to know.

Anyway, I don't think she's into women, especially not middle-aged skinny butch ones with salt-and-pepper hair and angry lines in their faces and memories of vanished lovers tattooed across their sleepless nights.

And anyway, I'm not sixteen anymore. In fact, I'm not even forty anymore, and I'm not here for the quick thrill of teaching straight girls that what they really want is this, and this, and this. Been there, done that. Far too many times.

And anyway: Angie.

So I nod. Yes, there's a glint in my eye. I can't help that; it's who I am. But I keep it to the trivial bullshit, and then we roll out into the midnight streets of Bushwick to whatever fancy scum made the call tonight.

It's one of those suburban blocks. Trees and pretty old houses that Germans and Russians abandoned in terror when we Puerto Ricans started moving in a few decades back. This one is all dark with a well-manicured lawn and draped windows, just like all the other ones. In other words, it gives me nothing. If it were a face, it'd be a blank stare. I don't like it.

"You want me to come in with you?" My voice is raspy, disarming at first, but it turns out to be sexy when I'm whispering late at night. I put a cigarette to my lips and then take it out again because I quit smoking last week and I really mean it this time.

Shelly rolls her eyes in the rearview. "You're such a worry-wart." She finishes putting her lipstick on, atrocious pink against her light brown skin, and flutters her lashes. She's Trini, I think, mostly Indian; she's getting a master's in social work and has a set of tits that can call you from across a room, but her swagger's a little pressed, if you ask me. She's better when she just stays genuine.

I'd tell her that, but she might either slap me or fall in love with me. Probably both. Instead I just mutter, "Okay," and look out the window.

When the ritual of mirror coquetry is done, Shelly clomp-clomps out my cab and up the porch steps. She rings the bell twice and then tries the door; it's open, and she walks on in.

I shake my head. This isn't how any of it's supposed to go, but what can you do? Johns will always be unpredictable and finicky with their creepy little preferences and pecu-liarities. And I'm just the muscle. My gnawing discomforts mean nothing, especially since they've been there since Angie went missing six months ago, so who cares if that plunging knell of despair is a little louder than usual? I blip the base that I'm here, and the scratchy reply is in Charo's voice. That's one thing I've always respected about Charo: he runs the whole operation, both the legit end and this side of things. He keeps his eyes on the bank; he checks in with his employees; he must handle an absurd amount of cash every day, and still he sits in on the radio board when someone can't come in. I've known him since he was little, know his parents and his sick fuck of an abuelo. I know them all, and believe me—Charo's the only one worth a damn. We've had our disputes, but he gets it done.

Charo wants to know if I'm okay. Stupid question and he knows it, but I guess it's in his gentlemanly code to ask.

"I'm fine," I say. "But I don't like this place."

"Maybe," Charo says, "because it's only a block or two away."

I'm about to ask away from what, but then rub my eyes and sigh. How could I not realize? The house that Charo and I turned inside out and upside down looking for Angie stands around the corner from here. It was the last place she was seen alive, and we took it apart a hundred different ways and didn't bother putting it back together and found not a single trace of the girl. Nothing.

"Reza," Charo says.

"Hm?"

"You want me to send you Miguel?"

Miguel's the biggest driver we got. No, that's not true: Carbrera is the biggest driver we got, pound for pound. But that's all lechón and batidos. Miguel is made of muscle. He's on the legit end, doesn't know jack about this side of things, in fact, so I guess all the other heavies are off on jobs. I used to think he was a wuss, all that muscle notwithstanding. He has an on-again off-again chick that he never shuts the fuck up about— Virginia? Vanessa? Vanessa—but outside of my team, there's really no one else I'd rather have my back in a fight. Except Charo himself, of course, because sometimes sheer wrath will take you farther than any workout video or Tae Bo bullshit.

"No. It's fine. I'm strapped and there's nothing wrong—just us being paranoid. No te preocupes, Charo."

I'm sure he shrugs at this point, probably lights a Conejo. Then he says, "Suit yourself, Rez."

I roll down the window and let the Brooklyn night in.

I usually clean the Vic to pass the time, but I ran her through thorough last night and once-overed her with a rag earlier, and now she's immaculate, even by my standards. My suit pants are pressed and spotless; the perfect line runs down the center of each leg and stops just above my steel-tipped alligator shoes. The matching gray vest I'm wearing hangs just right over the Glocks tucked securely under each arm. There's a dagger strapped to my ankle, and the bigger hardware in the trunk. May seem like a lot to you, but I still have some habits left over from the Bad Years and one of them is Never Be Outgunned. There's a gold crucifix around my neck and a locket that Angie gave me that sometimes brings me comfort and sometimes nightmares. I never take it off.

The radio's playing old salsa, the good Cuban shit that's so true and raw they can only play it late at night on one of those 88.whatever college stations. I take the cigarette out of my mouth again and replace it in its gold case, shaking my head. I'm not thinking about Angie.

I'm not thinking about Angie.

The doctor Charo made me go to said, "Try not to think about Angie so much." Might as well've told me to try not to have an arm. But I try. The song wants to take me elsewhere, but Angie's smile keeps wrenching me back. And then the emptiness her smile left behind. And then the frantic search. And then the feeling of gnawing desperation. And then giving up.

And then giving up.

Which I never really did, probably. Give up.

On Angie.

Even though Charo has told me to again and again.

Probably I dozed off, because a muffled scream wakes me from some kind of dazed stupor.

Fuck.

I'm out of the car, breaking toward the doorway, accosting the night air for any hint of another scream, anything.

It sounded like Angie.

Everything sounds like Angie when I first wake up.

On the porch, I stop. This is no way to move. I'm wide-open to attack. I'm barreling forward recklessly. This is not me. There may not have been a scream at all. My haunted head. There may have only been silence, like right now. I stand perfectly still on the front porch. Cars are passing on nearby streets. The Jackie Robinson isn't too far from here; it cuts through that big old cemetery on the border of Brooklyn and Queens.

No one is screaming.

No one is screaming, but something skitters over my foot in the darkness of the porch, and I jump back so fast it almost sends me toppling down the stairs. One of my guns is out by the time I regain my footing; it's pointed at where my foot was, but whatever it was is gone. It looked like a thing I hate more than death itself, a thing I would prefer not to even mention, thank you very much. And if it was that thing, there are more of them. There are *always* more of them. That's the rule about that thing. Many more. Seething, writhing masses of more. I reholster the Glock, walk back to my car, resist the urge to jump in and drive straight into the house, madman-on-a-rampage style, and come out firing. Instead I go into the trunk, bypass the secret compartment with the heavy guns, and dig through a duffel bag until I find a can of bug spray. It seems ridiculous, I guess, but like I said, I'll never be out-gunned. Not by no killers and certainly not by no six-legged hairy monstrosities. No, sir. I get a flashlight too, and then I walk onto the porch again and test the door.

It's open, and I slide ever so quietly inside.

Everything is in its right place in this standard American front hallway. There's an old staircase, coats on the coatrack, an open door leading off to the kitchen, a few closed doors on the way. It's dark, but some hazy streetlight comes in through a window. I can make out the old-fashioned swirly motifs along the wallpaper leading up the stairs. It's dusty in here, and the air is thick with mold. But nothing moves. No one screams. No creatures crawl across the walls. I don't lower the spray, and my gun hand twitches slightly, ready. The kitchen is the same; so is the living room. Everything's just so, and that's how I know something's off. It's all been carefully placed there, but no one lives here. The place is dead, a mask.

I'm standing in the kitchen looking out the window into the backyard when I see it. I can stand so still I almost disappear, and it makes every tiny movement crisp, shrill even. A tree is waving around outside, making a wild shadow show on the far wall. A digital clock on the microwave blinks 12:00; a car passes. And: something scurries across the floor and disappears under the fridge. I don't freak out. I don't. I let the freak-out wash over me and pass; it's only a jittery tremble now, and I'm about to take a step forward when another one of 'em shoots out of nowhere and makes its silent, frantic sojourn to the fridge. It pauses a couple times along the way; before it's gone, two more appear.

Even in the darkness I can tell there's something different about them. They're pale. Instead of that dark maroony swirl glinting with light, these are pinkish.

Anyway, maybe there's something rotting in there; they're making their way to a wretched feast. Maybe I swallow a little bit of vomit that found its way up into my esophagus and inch toward the fridge, my finger shuddering against the spray button.

There's nothing in the fridge but an unfortunate brown stain that's dark in the center and spreads into lighter, crusty circles. At any second, a thing will fly out from under there and up my pant leg, I'm positive. I step back from the fridge, carefully, and take it in. My brain knows there's something wrong, but my eyes can't decide what yet. It's one of those old antiquey ones, all bulky and aqua blue, and it stands next to the door coming in from the hallway. The front steps climb straight alongside the hallway, so the landing on the second floor should be right above my head and . . . there should be a basement. All these old houses have basements. There should be a door along the hallway wall that leads under the front steps. But there isn't. I stare harder at the fridge.

I know what I'm about to do and I already hate myself for conceiving of it. But there's no other way. I place my half-gloved hands on either side of the fridge and with two quick moves tip the thing onto one side and then lurch it forward at a diagonal away from the wall. About fifty shadows skitter out around my feet, and I catch my breath, dancing backward, point the can down, and push hard on the trigger button. They scramble away in a frenzy, and I'm left panting, sweating, and cursing as quietly as I can. I still myself, will my terror back into the iron box I keep it tucked away in. Breathe. There's something behind the fridge. Something besides ungodly insects, I mean.

Shelly, a voice whispers in my head. But all I hear is *Angie.*

It's a small door, wood-carved and old-fashioned, but just a brass hole where the knob's supposed to be.

Fuckers.

I want to hold my breath, but I know that'll only make things worse when something awful happens, and I'm positive something awful is about to happen. So I breathe, reluctantly, deeply, as I reach my finger into the hole. The door swings open with a creak, reveals more darkness. And I'm actually relieved I finally have real cause to unholster this Glock and point it into the emptiness as I step-by-step it down some old stairs.

The wall doesn't crawl to life when I swat it with my hand. It's solid and cool, not even the bumpy decay I was expecting in my less wild nightmares. I flick something and a fluorescent glow blinks on from the ceiling. It reveals a recently remodeled basement: shiny white walls and gray carpets, even that fresh-paint smell. A couple of boxes are stacked in one of the corners, and the floor is covered with children's toys. There are stuffed animals, plastic trains, and action figures. It makes me nauseous, so I try to keep my eyes away from the toys as I work the perimeter of the room, checking the wall for irregularities. There are none: everything is solid-sounding, support beams right where they should be, paint even. I shove the boxes over to the side, and there behind them is another small doorway. This one is just big enough to fit through if I duck, and it has a doorknob.

I realize I'm sweating. And my breathing's not quite right. None of which is usual for me. I won't go into details, but the Bad Years put me in the face of every imaginable form of death, my own and others', and I'm one of the only ones who made it out of that time alive. Charo's another, but even he had it relatively easy compared to what I got mixed up in. They say Death walks just a few feet to the left of every man. Fuck that. Me and Death are kissing cousins. But right here, right now? I don't know what the hell is wrong with me. Besides the obvious things. I guess I'm still not right. Maybe I'll never be. Or maybe it's the skittering death monsters, whose absence from the basement is somehow even more unnerving to me than their abundance in the kitchen. Or maybe it's those toys, which have no business being in a place like this.

Whatever this is.

Or maybe it's the muffled grunt that comes dancing out of the darkness in front of me. I almost yell, "Angie?" but then I remember Angie's gone. She's gone. Dead. It's Shelly I'm trying to find. Shelly. And maybe that was her. It could've been. There was a wetness to it, like whoever grunted was choking on her own saliva. Or blood. Enough. I shut down my imagination and duck into the darkness.

CHAPTER SEVEN

Kia

Karina's right: the new capoeira teacher is fine as hell. The dude's not even my type; I usually go for really overweight dudes with skin dark as mine. He sits on a foldout chair facing us in the big meeting room, his muscular arms crossed over his muscular chest. There's a shiny bruise on his left cheek, but otherwise, his face is perfectly symmetrical, like he might be an android. His left eyebrow is raised slightly, making him look just the right combination of arrogant and thoughtful. He's got big, perfect lips and a carefully trimmed goatee. Golden brown shoulders bulge out of that sleeveless shirt in a way that's almost profane, like just sitting there, being all burly and shoulderful in front of a group of teenagers seems somehow inappropriate.

And I'm here for it. We all are.

"Thank you all for coming today, kids!" Sally says. Sally's the white lady that runs things. She's barely taller than the new capoeira teacher and he's sitting down. She looks like a sack of mediocre potatoes next to his glowing golden perfection. Shit, we all do. "I'm really excited to introduce you to Rigoberto, our new capoeira instructor."

"What happened to Gilberto?" Devon asks.

"You scared him off with ya loud-ass farting last week," Karina tells him.

Devon flips her off. "Shut the fuck up."

"You guys," Sally says. "Let's not do this, okay? Gilberto unfortunately had an altercation in a bar the other night and won't be able to . . ."

"Somebody faded Gil?" Devon translates helpfully. "Shit."

Tarik jumps up. "Wait! Gil gets jacked up at a bar and the new homey got a shiner? Y'all ain't seeing what I'm seeing?"

A general murmur ensues. Sally looks *vexed*. "Guys, it's Rigoberto's first day here and—"

Mikey B. raises his hand. "Rigoberto a Dominican name, right?"

Rigoberto smiles. Teeth: perfect. At least four audible sighs happen. "Actually, I am from Brazil, like your last teacher."

"You speak Spanish, man?" someone yells.

"Well, I do, but in Brazil we . . ."

"Dumbass, he speaks Brazilian."

A bunch of us roll our eyes at the same time.

"Y'all so stupid," Karina says. "He speaks Portuguese. Now how 'bout we let the man talk and stop showing off how ignorant y'all are, 'kay?"

Laughter breaks out, and then people settle down and look at Rigoberto. Sally smiles a little too broadly. "I'll just let you talk to the kids now, Rigoberto. Thank you!" She pats his majestic shoulder and skitters out of the room.

Rigoberto stands up. Dude must be six three at least. He's perfectly proportioned; each piece fits into the other just right. His arms hang just right; his loose white pants fit just right—it's almost sickening. "Hello, guys and girls," he says with a doofy wave. "You can call me Rigo."

"Do we have bulge?" Karina whispers, peering over Devon's baseball cap.

We do. "We appear to have bulge," I report.

Karina nods. "Confirmed bulge."

"Rigo, you married, boo?" Kelly yells out. I want to punch her in the face. Everybody groans.

Rigo chuckles. It sounds a little forced. "Today we're going to talk about capoeira, yes? Not Rigo's personal life."

"Fat chance," Karina mutters.

"Let's begin by seeing what we know so far, okay? Because I don't know this other teacher, Gilberto, yes? But he may be, how do you say . . . incompetent? Capoeira is how my people survived European domination in Brazil. It is beautiful, but deadly."

"Just like him," Karina mutters.

"It is a martial art disguised as a dance, but it is also a dance disguised as a martial art. Why? Because we were not allowed to train to fight. We had to disguise our training as dancing, yes? We had to become clandestine warriors in a system that did not believe we are human, yes? Maybe this is something you can understand today, or maybe not. I don't know. But for this reason, it is very serious, the study of capoeira. We can have fun, but we also must remember it is survival, class, okay?"

Everyone just stares at him.

"That time, it was not rhetorical, the question."

As one, the whole class yells: "Yes!" It's the first time we've done anything in synch with one another.

"Holy fuck." Karina sighs. "He's beautiful and rebel deep."

"Now, why don't we have demonstration?" Rigo says. "Which one of you is Kia Summers?"

My heart lurches into overdrive. I suck at capoeira. And I hate standing in front of people. And. And. And. People are snickering and turning back to stare at me. Karina shoves my shoulder. Rigo searches our faces till his eyes lock with mine. He smiles that eerily perfect smile and says, "Ah, you are Kia, yes?"

I nod, praying he'll change his mind, knowing he won't. Why would he call me by name anyway? What kind of . . . ?

"Go!" Karina hisses in my ear. The moment has grown long, awkward. I stand, somewhat shakily, and make my way through the group to the front.

Rigo wears altogether too much cologne. It's something synthetic and overbearing, and it makes me dizzy. "You remember how to do a basic ginga?" he asks, smiling down at me.

I shrug. "I mean, kinda."

"The ginga is the basic step of capoeira, yes? Everyone has their own ginga. It is as personal as a signature. Just like everyone has their own rhythm."

"Devon doesn't!" Karina yells.

"When you understand the ginga, when you find your own"—Rigo swings one leg back and raises his forearm toward me, then switches sides, moving so smoothly it's like he's gliding a few inches above the wood-paneled floor—"it becomes like just walking down the street! You see? Natural. Come, we do it together." I try to mimic him, sliding my left leg back and then shifting my weight to the right. I feel like a broken mannequin.

"Clap, kids, yes? For the rhythm?" He lifts his hands over his head, and those thick triceps glare at me. I lose my entire sense of rhythm and have to start over. "Clap, clap!" Rigo yells, breaking into a syncopated beat in time with his hovering step.

The group claps, and I work my way back into a steady ginga.

"Yes, yes, very good!" Rigo yells over the clapping. "Now what happens when I go with one of these?" He spins; one foot anchors and the other flies up toward me. I know this part—I'm supposed to dodge-bend backward like in *The Matrix* and then spin into some impossible acrobatic shit and kick. I arch back and throw myself off-balance, hurl sideways, and catch Rigo's sneaker in the face.

Everyone in the room yells, "Oh!" as I stumble. I hear Rigo

mutter, "Porra!" as a whoosh of wind brushes past. Arms wrap around me. Thick arms. Rigo somehow evaporated and reappeared behind me. Again, audible swoons erupt, not all of them from the girls.

My hands cover my eye and Rigo's hands are on my wrists. "Let me see," Rigo says softly. "Let me see. I'm so sorry, Kia. Let me see what I did."

I shake my head. I probably look like one of those deepsea monstrosities right now. The hell I'ma let Brazilian Ken gape at me.

"We probably need to ice it. Can you see, Kia?"

I relent. The collective gasp is all I need to tell me what an instant freak show I've become. Rigo scrunches up his face. "Is not so bad, minha. Let's get some ice, okay?"

"I'll take her!" Karina yells.

Thank God.

In the rec center nurse's office, Karina informs me that I have a boyfriend.

"Don't be an idiot," I say. The ice pack pulses a numbing void against my forehead. From the wall, a cartoon condom explains, with the winningest of grins, that he's not reusable.

"I'm just saying," Karina says. "He called that ass out by name. He was like"—she drops her voice to an absurd baritone and affects something like a Polish accent—"'Kia Summers! Please for to come to ze front of ze el roomio.'"

"Karina."

"You in love, girl. That's okay. We all are. Homeboy is eight feet tall and fine as fuck. And he's packin'. I'm just mad it's you, not me, but I support you, Kia. I got ya back all the way. And when it come crashing down because he's too old for you, I'll step in and pick up the pieces on that distraught friend tip and get me some too."

"How that even make sense? You the same age as me."

"I'm more mature though. And I'm Jamaican, so . . ."

"What does that even . . . ? Just be quiet, woman. You're giving me a headache."

"That headache is called Love. A love ache."

All I can do is roll my eyes, but even that hurts. "You going to the park after class?"

Karina scoffs. "It's Saturday, ain't it? You know I got all those baby beckys to take care of."

A bunch of the new white folks in the neighborhood linked up on some social media site, and now they have regular Saturday-evening dinner parties where they plot, I'm sure, how to make the perfect vegan cupcake and take over the world. Karina got the gig watching their rug rats, and she usually just lets 'em loose in Von King.

"They ain't scared by all the shit been going on there?"

"Pshaw! It's added flavor and excitement to the urban adventure."

"I'ma come with," I say.

Karina sits up real straight and wipes off her stupid grin. "If Renny there, I got ya back."

I sigh. "It's not like all that, Karina. It's cool. I'm cool."

Renard Deshawn White, of all the old-man-ass names for a teenage boy, is this kid I used to talk to. He's big and black and beautiful, all those loving folds of flesh to get lost in, and he got a quiet easy way about him like I do when Karina's dumbass isn't around riling me up. We used to walk the length of the park after school just talking. I mean, he talked most of the time, and I just let him. He talked about his favorite video games and his moms and his little sister and how he wanted to be an engineer and okay, yeah, it seems pretty boring if you not in it, if you don't give a crap about Renny, but I devoured every word and then waited in the silences for him to look over at me and then wrap around me and I could disappear into him and and and.

And in February he started dating Maritza Lavoe. And

then they started walking the park, same path we took, same leisurely loving pace, and I sat hugging myself next to Karina while all those little white kids ran screaming around us and wondered if Maritza made him laugh more or if she listened better, if they'd made out yet, and if they kissed when they had sex. Dumb shit, I know, but that's where my off-kilter mind went and that's where it stayed. Me and Renny didn't even put our lips against each other, but I felt like I could go through things with him and come out on the other side a better person. I put the best King Impervious breakup rhymes in my ears and walked out of Von King Park one night. And I haven't been back since.

"You sure you cool?" Karina eyes my faraway look, and I snap out of it, flash a smile.

"Girl, fuck Renny and his video-game-playin' ass."

"That's what I'm talkin' 'bout."

We dap and then I say, "For real though, he still roll through there with Maritza?"

Karina shoves me, and I almost fall over the desk I'm sitting on. We're both laughing so hard we don't notice that Sally's standing in the doorway, arms akimbo, until she says, "Young ladies," and then all we can do is bust out laughing again.

CHAPTER EIGHT

Carlos

New York weather doesn't give a fuck about any of us. It wants us confused and off-balance, and if it has to become absurdly warm after the sun sets on a brittle afternoon in a brittle icy week, so be it. Folks are shedding jackets and sweaters, unraveling scarves, looking around dumbfounded and annoyed. Old people step out onto their stoops and stretch muscles cramped and tight from flinching against a long, hard winter. They smile as I pass, turn to each other and wonder who gonna get it tonight and how, what unaccountable tragedy will strike which corner of the park, and why . . . They shake their old heads, jowls dangling, eyes squinting in the streetlights, and wonder.

I stand in the center of Von King Park and let the whole universe of it spiral around me. Little kids swarm the brightly lit playground in the southeast corner. Dog walkers stroll along in small clumps. In the field behind me, a baseball game wraps up. I'll say this for the community: the recurring traumas have not deterred people's impulse to commune. Who can resist the first night of spring? The thaw has come early, and knowing New York's tempestuous temptress ways, tomorrow will see another frost.

"Mass random disasters be damned, huh," Riley says, appearing next to me.

"I was just thinking the same thing."

"The people gonna have their park."

"Ain't mad. It's a beautiful night." I'm sweating into this damn overcoat.

"Game plan?"

"Bell's at the southwest entrance." I nod toward the Marcy Ave. gate at the far end of the field. "Posted some'a her soulcatchers at the northeast end; the rest are scattered along the edges. You take the northwest."

"Where the little doggy park is? Man, fuck dogs."

"You have no soul."

"All I am is soul, brother."

"I'ma be over at southeast. Kia got a friend that watches some kids there. Gonna see if I can rustle up any information."

"Kia, as in Baba Eddie's little botánica badass?"

"Uh-huh."

"Alrighty. You worried? You look worried."

"That's my face, man."

Riley shakes his head and moves out to the edge of the park with long ghostly strides.

Am I worried? No. Not worried, but a growing unease rumbles through my core. I don't have a name for it, can't trace its roots. It's been there for the past couple days, I realize, unnamed and rising. I'm just getting myself together when I see Kia sitting next to her friend on the bench. One of Kia's eyes is swollen and blue. The unease erupts into a full-blown swath of rage.

"The fuck happened?" I say, quickening my pace as I cross the playground. "Who I gotta kill?"

Before Kia can answer, her friend is up in my face. "The fuck are you, homeboy?"

"I . . ."

"You gonna back up off my friend 'fore I—"

Kia's hand lands on her shoulder. "Karina, it's cool, girl. That's Carlos. He's my people."

Karina glares up at me for a solid three seconds before backing off. She has a shock of blue hair pulled back in a ponytail and glittery lipstick. Her eyes say she'll kill me if she has to and I believe them. I smile—not to seem condescending; I'm just relieved Kia has someone else around, someone her age, who will throw herself in the line of fire to protect her. I know I would.

"Karina, Carlos, Carlos, Karina."

I nod at the girl, and she appraises me with a squint.

"Ya hair *laid*, Carlos," Karina says.

"What?"

Kia puts her hand over her face and groans.

Karina is undeterred. "What you put in it though?"

"I mean, shampoo."

"Ugh! I hate men! Y'all so simple!"

"What happened to your eye?" I ask Kia.

"It's fine. It was an accident, is all."

Did the disaster ghost strike already? Seems there are no accidents these days . . . "Here?"

"Nah, man. At the rec center. Capoeira-related injury."

"What is this capoeira of which you keep speaking?"

"It's an Afro-Brazilian martial art. They came up with it during slavery, when they had to disguise their combat training as dance. Or their dancing as combat—can't remember which. I suck at it."

"She'll be aight," Karina puts in. "She was struck by an angel."

Kia swats her. "Shut it."

"A Brazilian angel."

Kia wraps both arms around her friend from behind and covers the girl's mouth. "Ignore her, C. What did you wanna ask about?"

They're so easy with each other and for a second I'm a hundred miles away. Physical contact with the living? I tend to avoid it.

"Carlos?" Kia says.

"You take care of all these kids, right?" I ask over Karina's muffled giggles.

She pulls away from Kia's hands and straightens herself. "Indeed I do."

"Every Saturday?"

"Unless the Ministry of Whiteness decides to give me a night off."

I squint at her. "The Min . . ."

"Never mind, C," Kia says. "She here every Saturday, yes."

"You saw the old guy get hit by that wheelbarrow from the construction site last weekend?"

Karina shakes her head and inserts a stick of gum in her mouth. "Uh-uh." She offers me a piece. I decline. Kia grabs one and starts chewing loudly. "I heard about it though. And the lady that ran into a city bus the next day. She lived though, I heard. But yeah. Whole lotta disaster up in these streets, man."

"You seen anything weird, like, around the park?"

"Besides white people jogging through Bed-Stuy after dark?" Kia says. They both fall out laughing for a minute and then collect themselves. "Nothing really. Same ol' usuals. Ol' Drasco and his cat parade. The cops making rounds. That's it."

"What about the kids?"

"You wanna ask 'em?" Karina stands and makes a pretend

megaphone with her hands. "WHAT WE GON' DO WHEN DI REVOLUTION COME?"

An eerie choir of high-pitched voices rises in the night around me. "Burn dem houses and kill dem sons."

I boggle at Karina. "What the hell is that?"

Little white kids pour off the slide and swing sets. They repeat the line in unison as they make their way toward us.

Karina shrugs. "Song my grandma usedta sing. It gets their attention."

"I don't think . . ."

"WHAT WE GONNA DO WHEN DI CITY BURN?" Karina yells.

The kids bustle in around us. "Light dem mothafuckas in dey turn," they chant.

"Karina . . . Do their parents know you have them—"

"Shit, I hope not. I'd probably get fired. I get nothing but tips and thank-yous, so I'm guessing nah. I swore them all to secrecy. Right, soldiers?"

"Ashé!" comes the yelled response.

"Ashé though?" Kia says. "You confusing these children, Karina."

"Hell, I'm a Jamaican in cold-ass New York City. I grew up confused—why shouldn't they? What'd you wanna ask 'em, Carlos?"

Pale expectant faces stare up at me. They all have big cheeks and wide eyes. "Anybody . . . notice anything . . . strange?" I ask them. I don't really know how to talk to kids. Not living ones anyway.

They just keep staring at me.

Karina furrows her brow and stamps one foot. "Ay, soldiers. Tell Mr. Carlos the truth."

A pudgy hand goes up.

Karina points at the kid. "Musafa."

"You gave them African names too?" I ask.

"Naw. Their parents did that. You know how some'a them white parents be."

All I can do is shake my head.

"Jimmy has fingerprints."

"Shut up!" another little boy yells. His blue eyes well with tears.

"It's true!" Musafa insists.

"Jimmy," Karina commands. "Come here, love." The little guy waddles through the pediatric throng, sniffling back a sob. "Yes, be strong, little mister. Don't cry now. Lemme see ya hands."

He holds up both palms, but there's nothing strange, no ink, no prints to speak of.

"Musafa, what you mean Jimmy has fingerprints?"

A girl in the front with strawberry blond pigtails and a bright pink jumpsuit stands up. "Not on his fingers."

"Where, Esme?"

She walks up to us and lifts Jimmy's superhero shirt. "On his body. Look."

I crouch down to squint at the shimmering blue markings on the boy's torso. Musafa was right: little handprints criss-cross his back and flanks. They're not from dirt though . . . These are ghost prints. "Shit," I say.

"Ooooh!" the crowd of kids hums.

"What we say about what Mommy and Daddy find out?" Karina says.

"Nothing," they answer as one.

"Alright, then." She looks down at me, and I can tell she'd just been playing cool for the kids' sake. "What . . . the hell . . . is that?" Karina whispers.

I stand up and turn because a strange motion flickers at the edges of my consciousness.

Something is happening. My hand goes to my cane-blade as I scan the perimeters of the park. Nothing.

"Carlos?" Karina says.

"Keep the kids close," I say. "Especially Jimmy."

"What is it?"

At the far diagonal from us, a car's brakes screech, and someone lets out a stream of curses.

"What's happening?" Jimmy moans.

I'm about to tell Kia to keep an eye on things when I realize she's nowhere in sight.

"Where's Kia?" I demand, fighting the edge out of my voice.

Karina spins around, panicked. "I don't know . . . There!"

Kia has her back to us as she fast-walks toward a fat kid and a girl with a massive weave by the northeast corner.

"Fuck." I hop the small fence around the playground and break into a run. An eruption of translucent fluttering bursts to life along the northern edge of Von King Park. I hear a revving engine, see a newspaper fly up into the air beneath a streetlamp and start to drift down like giant falling leaves.

"Kia!"

CHAPTER NINE

Kia

Renard Deshawn White.

Dark brown like me and round and those perfect arms, thick as my thighs with great dangling dollops of flesh. Folds I coulda sunk into on a lazy Sunday, some Sunday locked forever in my imagination, some faraway woulda, coulda type shit, as in coulda been all mine but instead, instead, instead . . .

Renard Deshawn White, sitting serene and stupid like a beached manatee on that park bench in Von King, Maritza perched on his lap, her long manicured fingers stroking his cornrows. Fuck this.

If they'd been making out, that woulda been predictable. Fine. Make out. That's ya girl. Alright. But this . . . this uninhibited performance of domestic bliss? Unacceptable. No little teenage love affair has any business looking this much like an ol' middle-aged couple, no way, no how. It's a ruse. Unacceptable, and unacceptable shit gets called as such. That's how I move. And regardless of how I move in general, this is how I'm moving now: flushed forward on long strides, fists tight at my sides, face tight so they know I truly will smite down a bitch lest they test me.

I'll not be tested.

No plan, no words formulated to blast out upon arrival, just fire and the simple truth that this shit, *this* shit, this *shit* will not stand. Nuh. Uh.

Maritza turns first. Renny's eyes are still closed, his head leaning back and his pleasant smile still splattered across his big, stupid, beautiful face. Her fingers stop caressing those cornrows; her mouth crinkles into a shrill frown.

"What happened, babe?" Renny murmurs, and it's then, in the second before he opens his eyes, that I remember my own eye, my newly damaged face, what a true disaster I must look like. My mouth drops open, panic rises in me, and instead of fire, nothing comes out: air. I wonder if I can vanish before he sees me, just be a story Maritza tells and surely she's kidding; Kia would never roll up on us like that, right? Right?

A commotion rises from the edge of the park, newspapers flutter down in the orange glow of a streetlight. I remember the disasters everyone keeps talking about, and then Renny looks at me, face scrunched with concern, and opens his mouth.

The voice that says my name isn't his though. If Renny did speak, it got run over by Carlos's hoarse shout from behind me. I've never heard Carlos sound scared. The next thing he yells is "Run!" But I don't run. I turn to look at him.

The motherfucker is crazy. Carlos Delacruz is barreling full speed toward me from across the park. I don't know where he thinks I'm going to run to. I don't even know what I'm running from. Then his eyes go wide at something in the air between us, something I can't see, and he pulls a long, shiny blade out of his cane. Behind me, Maritza lets out the girliest scream I've ever heard. I stumble back a few steps, and I'm about to run when an icy grip slides around my ankle, then up along my leg, and swings me around.

A thousand tiny icicles needle into my neck. Pain blurs the world around me, a dull roar and a cloudy haze. Then the haze lifts and I'm looking into two wide translucent eyes.

Dark rings circle them, and a shimmering face, its mouth stretched out into a scream, chipped, malformed teeth, buckets of gelatinous drool, an eternity of darkness down its throat. This is a child's face, haggard and broken but still so young. Those eyes burrow into mine; I realize the ice on my neck is from its two tiny hands crushing my windpipe.

The face takes up my whole vision—it's pressed up so close to mine I feel the frigid air around it, its stale breath— but a figure stirs in the hazy world beyond this thing. Carlos. He's poised to strike, that blade of his raised and ready. The thing turns and I see Carlos clearly—his brow furrowed and frown uncertain.

I'm trying to figure out why he doesn't just kill this demon-ass child mothafucka when the creature hurls into him, throwing Carlos on his ass. The sudden absence of pain is the first breath of air after drowning. I gasp, scramble a few steps, and then break into a run.

So many people have come out on this warm end-of-winter night, like their collective presence can somehow ward off whatever evil's been plaguing this park. Surely that *thing*, that horrible, broken-faced, icy demon child of frosty fucking death will find one of the many other folks here to attack once it's done eating Carlos's soul or whatever. Or maybe getting shoved will wake Carlos's aloof ass up and he'll take care of business finally.

Either way, I'm out.

I dip and dodge between concerned onlookers, ignoring the stares and the icy feeling that hasn't left me, cross Lafayette, skitter out of the way as a biker flies past and curses me out, and then cut around a corner and run hard. I don't know where I'm going. Everything inside screams, *Away, far, far away from that hell*. I pass the Junklot where the old guys used to play dominoes beneath that dazzling dragon mural

and the bodega I used to get candy at with Karina. Start to
slow as a stitch erupts in my gut, cross another street, and
then my hands are on my knees and I'm leaning over like I'm
gonna hurl. Then I do hurl, right there in the street, just watery
yellow crap—bile, I guess. And I look up, back toward the
park, and then I scream.

It's just a hazy flicker in the night, but there's no mistaking
it: the demon child is a block away, swimming toward me in
watery, uneven strides with its arms outstretched. I can't move.
A city bus passes, oblivious to the nightmare my life has suddenly become, and the whoosh of air wakes me up. One more
glance—the thing launching upward into the sky, mouth
stretching wide—and then I turn and run.

My breath is still short—I don't have much left—and
immediately the sharp ache reopens beneath my ribs. Carlos
is who knows where, and I have nothing to fight with, no
idea even how to come at a ghost, but I won't get got running.
I whirl around, fire raging in me again, ready to die.

It's closing on me from above, long fingernails stretching,
mouth twisted into a silent howl. My left legs shoots back,
and I pivot just so, twisting my body out of the way. The
ghostling rushes past with a chilly gust of air, spins back
around and charges. For this perfect second, I am smooth.
Born from unholy terror, this is my ginga. I don't know how
long I have before either this grace abandons me or I get
strangled again, so I anchor my right leg and spin kick the
little motherfucker right in the face.

The air is chilly and thick on my foot. The ghostling hurls
backward, and then something yanks it out of the sky.
Another shimmering shape, this one taller, wider. It thrusts
the demon child into the ground and unleashes a solid
thrashing on it. My breath comes in sudden fitful gulps; my
whole body shivers.

The taller shape looks up: a woman's face with a surly
frown, eyebrows creased down toward each other. "You okay?"

I don't answer; I just stare at her with my eyes filling up with tears. Another shape appears beside her, a man. He peers down at the subdued child demon squirming under the woman's shimmering foot.

"Nice catch," the man says. Then he looks at me. "She aight?"

The woman shrugs.

He looks back down at the demon, now writhing. "The fuck we gonna do now?"

CHAPTER TEN

~ ○○○ ○ ~

Reza

Each tiny shuffle of my feet echoes through the tunnel around me. Water streams down the middle, and an ancient, moldy smell pervades the thick air around me. And I realize something, something I've been wondering about since the moment Charo reminded me how close we were to the house we tore up all those months ago: they are connected, the two sites. Some underground tunnel links one to the other and who knows how many more. And I'm in the dank belly of that tunnel, trying not to get my feet wet or make too much noise and gliding along toward those occasional muffled grunts. Or sobs. Or moans. Each one is a little different. I'm not even sure they're all from the same person.

I step forward and almost yell because my foot doesn't find the floor; it just goes down into a thick, wet muck. I come down hard on the other knee, soaking that pant leg too, but stop myself from crashing all the way in and pull my feet back. When I catch my breath and make sure nothing's crawling on me, I probe around the edges of the hole with my steel-tipped toe point. It's not so large. I can easily hop across. The question is, how many more are there? And how deep do they go? I hadn't wanted to use my flashlight because there's really no better way to warn someone you're coming than shining a light down a dark tunnel, but at this point I'm not even sure if it matters. I didn't scream, but I've definitely caused some ruckus on the way.

Something else I've learned: I take power from my dapper. Perhaps I have some well-dressed angels watching over me, whoever they are, but when I have my slick on full charge, I am unstoppable in combat. It's just how things work for me. And now my pants are definitely ruined, I've probably got some awful fungus living in my sock, and who knows what else?

Up ahead, a dim light pours out of some larger room, delineating the edge of the tunnel. I'm so transfixed by it, I step forward again and slip into a world of shit, all the way to my waist in ick. I slosh forward. Things are rubbing against my legs and I don't have to reach down to know they're body parts. But I do. I do, and I pull out an arm. It's thickly muscled and green with decay and it's not the one I want, but now I know something; I reach again into the muck and retrieve another arm, discard it and then another and another. And then I stop, because the ring I gave Angie is staring back at me from the rotten, gray-green finger. It is connected to a hand, an arm. It's not Angie's—not the way I remember her. Peels of dead skin hang off the water-bloated forearm, and the whole thing is tinged with that sickly rot green. I don't want to see the face. I can't see the face. I have to see the face. I'm about to pull her all the way out when a scream bleats out up ahead. Then the walls around me come to life.

It's dark, so I can barely make it out, but everything is moving. It's not just the walls. The black water froths with tiny ripples, and little shiny pale backs dip and wrestle across the surface. I catch the scream in my own mouth, bury it back down. Holding tight to Angie's dead arm, I raise my eyes toward the edge of the tunnel. All the movement is directed toward the light. Shelly—it is her; there's no doubt—is screaming like her skin is being flayed off. In between screams she whimpers, sobs, and pleads. It's the worst sound I've ever heard.

I can't lose Angie again. Not even her rotten corpse. I can't. The burden of it is holding me up, but there's nothing else to be done. I leave her hand sticking out of the water at the edge of the tunnel.

The tunnel opens into a dim cavern. In the center, a cement platform rises out of the black water. Shelly's dangling a few inches over the platform, suspended by ropes that reach into the darkness. There's a pale man in a long black robe standing behind her, and beside him is a short, lopsided man with yellowish skin and a sweat-soaked button-down shirt. He looks familiar somehow; maybe I knew him during the Bad Years, although it's hard to imagine forgetting a face as collapsed on itself and anguished as that one. Then again, there are a lot of things I've erased from that time.

I have one Glock out and leveled steadily at the air around Shelly. She's still in her clothes, but they're hanging at weird angles, and she's trembling, gasping, screaming. She's between me and the two men. I can't make out what they're doing to her, but it looks like both have their pants on, so that's something. All I need is for one of them to move just far enough away for me to get a clear shot. The water around me is still frothing with its millions of swarming vagrants; they're paddling frantic billions of legs, propelling their shelled monstrosity selves toward the platform. They don't even seem to notice or care about me, and that's just fine, because it gives me the mental space to keep my aim steady.

Just when I think I'm going to have to change my position and risk blowing my hiding spot, the tall, robed one steps to the side. Before I fire, I make out his face—a middle-aged man, white, with light brown eyebrows and a tensely furrowed brow. His eyes squint with intense concentration, and his mouth opens and closes in what I can only imagine to be some demonic prayer. He's alongside Shelly now, reaching to her face with a long, ugly hand—too long, I think, just before I squeeze the trigger and blow a nice hole in it. My second shot rips through his chest. That should be the kill shot, but he doesn't fall, just turns toward me.

The little sweaty one roars, a terrible high-pitched sound that I wish I'd never heard, and then vaults across the water into the darkness of the far side of the room. He moves fluidly; he's somehow short and gangly at the same time, and his head is so big and boxy it looks like it should throw him off-balance. But this one's the least of my concerns right now, considering the guy who I just shot twice is still standing there staring at me and Shelly is screaming again and the army of insects has begun swarming up the platform toward her.

This is the part where I don't panic. It'd be easy to. It's what my body aches to do. But I don't. I unholster the second Glock, train one at the head and the other right at the heart. Before I can squeeze the triggers, though, the slippery fuck ducks down. At first I thought he was finally collapsing, but no. Instead he slides into the water and wades quickly toward me.

This is the part where I panic. A little. I don't know how many shots I squeeze off, only that I'm firing and firing and the air is exploding around me, the cruel bursts of gunfire echoing up the dark walls of the cavern, and I don't stop shooting until the clicks that mean I'm out of bullets.

For a second he just stands there. Angry holes pockmark his face, his hands, those long robes. Little curls of smoke plume out of each one, and I can only imagine what the blowout from the exit wounds must be like on the other side. Then I see the skin on his neck shudder; it's moving. It's alive. It's one of those evil fucking insects, making its skittish, evil way up his chin and across his startled face. Another one detaches itself from his flesh and then another, and I finally understand: they are his flesh. They pour across his face, burst from his sleeves. What's left is a trembling skull, tattered skin barely hanging on, two wide eyes. The robes he was wearing cave in on themselves and sink into the water as a thousand little shiny monsters swarm out of the murk where the man was just standing.

I'm frozen. Nothing in the world is alive except the billions of crawling fuckmonsters and the memory of Angie, and Angie's dead, she's definitely dead now, and that thought alone, her monstrous corpse, her empty eyes, that is what finally breaks me from this nightmare of stillness. Shelly is still dangling and whimpering. I move toward her at first without thinking, automatic pilot, through the scattering of life, careful not to get caught up in the thing's robes. Something moves in the darkness beyond the platform, and I snap to attention. My Glock is reloaded and pointed at the nothingness; little splotches dance across my sight line. I see nothing.

"Please," Shelly moans. "Please." I move closer to her, but I keep my eyes on the emptiness and my gun ready. And then I finally turn to her, because something keeps calling my attention, something just out the corner of my eye. It's a splotch on her leg. She's filthy and her light brown skin shines with sweat, but there's something else. I heave onto the platform, finally out of that filth, and she looks up at me. Black rivers of eyeliner and sweat swivel down her cheeks. Her lipstick is smudged straight across her face, and her dress hangs loosely from her shoulders. But most important of all, that dark smudge on her calf: it's red. Dark red. A bullet hole. Shelly's been shot, I realize as I fuss with the ropes around her wrists. I shot her.

We're at the tunnel's edge when I hesitate. You can judge me if you want, but if you haven't felt a girl like Angie move against you, look at you the way she looked at me, and then lost her forever, you just don't know. I hesitate because I can't have both, but I can't stomach the thought of leaving Angie's sad corpse behind. Not now. Not when I just found her.

Could this love be greater even than my will to live? I think if I hadn't shot Shelly I'd really be in a fix. I'd probably try to bring them both, and then we'd be caught for sure. Shelly lets out a series of gasps. I don't think the wound is too bad—looks like it went straight through without clipping any major arteries, but still: it's there. I look at the spot where the top of Angie's green-brown hand breaks the surface, and then I shoulder Shelly and we hobble through the tunnel and carefully, painfully up the stairs.

It's behind me. That gangly long-armed motherfucker. I can hear it scrabbling around, limping with that horrible grace through the tunnel toward us. Shelly screams, a horrible gurgly sound, and we break into a pathetic, ungainly run. We're out of the kitchen and into the front foyer when I hear the wooden door bust open and smack against the wall. It's panting and sniveling. I would turn back and take a shot, but we're already at the front of the house. Someone's standing there in the darkness of the porch, a short, stocky figure. I raise my gun, bracing myself against the wall.

"Reza?" Charo. My God, it's Charo.

"Charo!" I gasp, and drag Shelly with me out into the fresh night air. Charo raises a shotgun as we pass. He points it into the hallway. His face—I catch a glimpse of it before I hurtle down the stairs—it's calm, not tensed or sweaty or nothing; his eyes so peaceful, almost sleepy. I know that face. It means he's about to kill.

The last time I cried was in the fourth grade, and it was the first time I'd been shot. And the first time I ever shot anybody. That was it. Angie used to cry when she came hard enough, great heaving sobs as her pelvis rocked into my face

and my hands worked her nipples. It would move me—
believe me, it did—but never in a way you could see. She
knew how to decipher those small shudders along my cheek-
bones, the way I'd look away, the patterns of my breath. But
no one else. No one else could ever know.

Now, running full bodied and barely breathing out of
this house, I still don't cry. I almost do though. It's the closest
I've come in all these years, the tears sneaking around the
edges of my eyes, waiting. The truth is, I'm too afraid to
cry. Too in it. I hurl forward, and it's like Shelly is barely
there, might as well be floating above me for all I notice,
but we're both out and breathing and panting and she's
throwing up, bleeding still, and I'm not thinking about Angie's broken, abused body being back in there all alone with
the monsters. I'm not I'm not I'm not, but I am.

Miguel is standing there in front of his Crown Vic. He's
got one of those emergency gray rescue blankets opened up,
and I've never been so happy to see him in my life. I hand
Shelly off to him, and he makes a little Shelly burrito with
that blanket around her and lifts her easily into the cab. Then
he looks at me. I'm soaking wet and panting, put my hands
on my knees and lean forward to catch my breath, but otherwise I'm okay. I wave him off.

"The fuck happened?" Charo wants to know. No boom
came from the doorway; the thing must've held back. Surely
it's watching us, lurking.

"Angie" is all I can say. "Angie."

It's all I need to say. Charo nods his chin toward where
Shelly is writhing in the backseat. "¿Y esa?"

"Flesh wound," I say. "But I don't know what else happened before I got there. They were doing something when
I showed up."

"How many?"

"At least two. A . . . thing . . . man, I guess. Long arms.
Fast. And something else. Something cockroachy in a robe.

I got it though. But there's more. I know there's more. But, Charo . . ."

He looks at me. His expression's still that muted emptiness that means someone's about to die, but I know he's listening. "I have to get her. I have to go back in."

Miguel knows better than to say anything, but I see him start forward with horror. Charo just nods toward the door. "She's . . . ?"

"She's dead, yeah." First time I've said it. First time it's felt true. It only makes the need to bring that body back stronger. I won't take a full breath until it's done. "I can't leave her."

Charo studies me for a fraction of a second. "Miguel," he says, still staring at me. "Take Shelly to the base and call Dr. Tijou. Tell her what happened."

"What the fuck *did* happen?"

"Tell her what you know."

Miguel shakes his head, walks around to the driver's side. He gives me one last doubtful look, mutters, "Be careful," and then hops in and speeds off.

"Your trunk is full?" Charo says.

"Always."

The street is empty. It's late, a quiet night. We gear up quickly: more ammo clips, more bug spray, some shock grenades. We move fast up the porch and into the house. Our motions are aligned: a singular two-headed four-armed angel of death, a perfect killing machine after decades of staying alive side by side. The place is empty again—no movement, no shadows spring to life. That smell lingers though. It's a decaying type of stench. It's everywhere.

Down the stairs and through the freaky-clean playroom, into the tunnel. Nothing comes. No bugs, no gangly man. Nada.

"Here." The first word I've spoken in what seems like a long, long time; it's just a hoarse whisper. I wade back into

the dark waters, Glock leveled at the blackness around me.
The light at the far end is out, so I have to feel my way along.
Behind me, Charo makes barely a sound as he enters the
water, the slightest intake of breath and then a tiny splash
as the waves circle outward from him.

I have one hand stretched out ahead of me, just over the
surface of the water. I feel those body parts rub against my
legs as I move forward. I should be near the edge by now, but
there's no Angie. A little desperation creeps into my grasping,
a whisper of nervousness. She's not here. I make a little splash
noise as my hand pats the water. She's not here. I reach down,
holding my breath, swipe from side to side. Nothing.

Charo moves past me, gun first. The tunnel opening interests him. I'm considering the possibility that I imagined
Angie being there in a fit of desperation when my hand
brushes past something that feels like metal. The ring. *Angie.*
I wrap around the hand it's attached to and pull; a dark shape
breaks the surface.

"Charo," I whisper. He doesn't answer, so I look up and
he's frozen, staring past me down the tunnel where we came
from. There's something behind me. It's true in the tiny hairs
standing up on the back of my neck and the clenching in my
gut, true in my finger as it tenses over the trigger.

"Down." He says it so quietly. It's a whisper, just for me.
If I'd hesitated even a second, I'd be splattered across the
tunnel, another body for the collection. Charo's double barrel
comes up as I fall face-first into the water. I tuck forward and
glimpse behind me as I fall: silhouetted in the dim light of
the tunnel, there's another tall robed man, just like the one I
blew away. He's there for only a second before Charo
unleashes that deafening blast and the man disintegrates into
a raging swarm.

For a moment, the water closes over my head. I come up
sputtering, still clutching Angie's wrist. Charo's gone. Something's there, a bluster of movement in the darkness. It's

Charo, I realize, but he's covered, every inch of him, covered, in the pale swarm. He's not screaming, but only
because he knows what'll happen if he opens his mouth. I
belt the gun and retrieve the can of spray, put it directly on
my friend, and blast away. It only sort of works. A few flutter
away, a few move aside. Mostly they are unperturbed. We
have to get out of here.

Charo's brushing them off with quick, deft slashes of his
hands as we grope through the darkness out of the water. In
the tunnel, I help him find his face beneath the writhing,
squirming creatures. I can see he's doing everything he can
not to lose his shit. For a few seconds the only sounds are
our hands brushing feverishly against his skin, his clothes,
and then his panting, coughing back the urge to scream.
Finally he nods at me. There are still a few on him, but we
can't stand here anymore, not knowing what's coming from
where. I hoist Angie onto my shoulders. She's too heavy,
and water and black ichor pour from her flesh. Something
falls off, maybe a foot. I ignore it. I have to. We make it up
the narrow stairs, back into the brightly lit playroom, so
sterile and full of untold horrors. I know the short gangly
one is watching us. He's close. I can smell him, feel his eyes
all over us. Then we're bumping through the kitchen and
once again into the hallway and finally, finally, out into the
blessed night. There's a little den above the Medianoche Car
Service garage. It smells like air freshener with a hint of
mold; a large window looks over the fleet of black Crown
Vics to the big iron gate that keeps the world out. This is
where they brought Lizette after she was gang-raped. She
lay on this couch, staring at the ceiling, barely moving at
all, achingly calm, while Charo and I took to the streets for
revenge. The couch is draped with old blankets; one of the
armrests is falling apart. This is where Santo lay dying after

the Canarsie firefight, Dr. Tijou frowning over him, his arms
flailing out like they were trying to grasp at some lifeline
that wasn't there.

This is where Charo first told me Angie was gone. I don't
come here much ever since that day, but right now I feel
peaceful—that calm the world brings after a battle. That
calm of finally knowing after all these months.

I'm wearing sweatpants tied tightly around my waist
because they're about eight sizes too big. My graying hair is
slicked back against my skull and my skin is raw from so
much scrubbing. Charo's industrial-strength antibacterial
soaps have done their thing and I actually do feel moderately
clean, considering. Considering. I shudder, run a hand over
my face, and plop onto the couch.

Charo comes in wearing workout shorts and a Yankees
T-shirt. It's been decades since I've seen the man wearing
anything but his usual button-down shirts and slacks. He
stands there looking at me and then takes two Conejos out
of his pack, lights them both and hands me one.

It feels like an angel is giving me mouth-to-mouth, that
first sweet inhale. A blessing.

"Shelly?"

"Dr. Tijou says she's gonna be okay." Tijou had been one
of Haiti's top trauma surgeons until she treated the wrong
minister's estranged nephew and ended up in Brooklyn patch-
ing up the survivors of various gangland massacres. She's
worked on all of us at one time or another, saved all our lives.
Tijou's always smiling and muttering things to herself in Creole and she's smarter than anyone I've ever met. If she says
Shelly's gonna be okay, then Shelly's gonna be okay.

"There was something on her back though." Charo
scowls. "An opening."

I raise an eyebrow.

"Tijou says it seems like they were trying to implant
something in her. Eggs, she thinks."

"Eggs?"

"Like they were using the girls as some kind of incubators. That's what the doc says anyway. I don't know. They're still checking . . . Angie."

I nod.

"Oh, and she gave me these for you." He hands me a plastic baggie full of colorful pills.

"Morphine?"

"Retrovirals and antibiotics."

"Boo."

"Take them all. I got some too."

"Alright, alright." I pocket the baggie.

"I have something to say," Charo announces. I do too, actually, but I stay quiet. Charo looks uncertain, another first for him. We smoke in silence. When we finish the cigarettes, he retrieves two more.

"Want me to start?" I ask.

"No."

"Okay."

He takes a deep breath. "I'm done." It's what I was gonna say too, and in a way I'm not surprised. We've always walked parallel paths. "In fact, I'm mad that it took this"—a vague gesture toward the hell we've just been through—"to get me to this place. But no, I can't . . . We can't keep doing this. It's"—a deep tug on the Conejo, a mountainous release—"not right. It's wrong."

I nod. Tonight is full of surprises.

"It's been coming ever since Angie went missing," Charo says. "I've seen it in you too. We can't . . . We have to stop." He's staring out the window at the pipe-lined rafters over the garage.

"You want to disband the whole operation?"

"No."

"Oh?"

"A change of direction, is all." He shrugs, looks at me, and suddenly he's the old Charo again. A mischievous glint dances in his eyes. "This work has connected me to a lot of very powerful, very evil people. Even more evil than us, I mean. People with genocide and child rape on their résumés. These are men who can nod and wipe out an entire village in Guatemala."

He's not just talking about other gangsters either. I'd steered clear of the corporate connections Charo sent the girls to, mostly because I had the feeling I might lose my cool with them and cause problems for the company, but I've heard stories.

"So you want to start a cleanup operation," I say carefully.

Charo smiles. He likes that. "Yes. Cleanup. Exactly. A balancing of the scales, we could say." The smile grows wider, stretches to the far ends of his face; his eyes become squinty above those great big dimples. "Justice."

Charo can call it what he wants. I'm calling it revenge. "I'm in," I say. "But there's somewhere I want to start."

Charo nods. "I know."

Out the window, the iron gate shudders and rises with a groan. We stand there side by side and finish our cigarettes as morning pours into the garage.

CYCLE TWO

❧

BURN THE WHOLE SHIT DOWN

Fue mia la piadosa dulzura de sus manos,
que dieron a mis penas caricias de bondad,
y ahora que la evoco hundido en mi quebranto,
las lagrimas pensadas se niegan a brotar,
y no tengo el consuelo de poder llorar . . .

The sweet compassion of her hands: it was mine;
their caresses soothed my agony,
and now that I evoke her, drowned in all I've lost,
the tears I once imagined refuse to flow,
and I'm without even the consolation of being able to cry.

"Sus ojos se cerraron"
tango, 1935

Alfredo Le Pera

CHAPTER ELEVEN

Carlos

H ave you ever mourned?"

I looked up, met Sasha's deep stare. It was four a.m. and snowing—the worst night of my short, twisted life, the best night of my short, twisted life. My partner Dro's screams still echoed through me; I could still see him fade into the oblivion of the Deeper Death as a swarm of tiny demons overcame him. Riley was in a coma; I'd barely made it out alive. And here I was, looking into the eyes of this woman, wrapped in the embrace of her apartment. She sat with one knee tucked up against her chest and her bare shoulders glinting in the dim lamplight. Her brown skin was tinged ever so slightly with gray, and her lips pouted just so as she stared at me, eyebrows creased.

"Have I mourned who?"

We hardly knew anything about each other, but we knew the one thing that made us different from everyone else. When we met a few nights before at a yuppie bar in Park Slope, we'd silently agreed to refrain from reading each other's wandering spiritual information. We didn't ask—we just didn't go there at all. It was understood.

So when she frowned and said, "You, man," it caught me off guard.

Snow pirouetted wildly through the glow of streetlamps. The heater clattered an arrhythmic dirge and then sighed.

Sasha didn't rush me. The winter night felt infinite. Her stare didn't demand answers, and when I met it again I felt a deep sadness open up inside of me. It was perfect and alone—a single long note from a trumpet.

"No."

One corner of her mouth curved upward, just slightly. "Maybe you should."

I nodded. "Did you?"

"Trevor and I did a ceremony about a year after it happened."

Trevor—her brother and only friend. Trevor, who I murdered on orders from the Council. I closed my eyes and sucked it all back in. There would be a moment to explain all that, I told myself, and this wasn't it.

"He wasn't really trying to do all that, of course." Her scoff held no humor. "But I convinced him. He was so sad and sulky all the time—at first, I mean. We both were. He knew he needed something to change.

"I went to a vivero—one of those live poultry spots on Classon, you know? Got two pigeons. They put 'em in whatever ol' box they have lying around, this busted Nike box, right?" She's smiling now, and her eyes shine with oncoming tears. "Went to the bridge one warm night in October. The Manhattan Bridge. It was late, maybe two a.m., and we walked right to the middle of the bridge with this shoe-box birdcage and then we both said a little something, a prayer I guess, and then we let them go. They flapped up into the crossbeams and then out into the night."

"And that was it? Who did you pray to?"

She shrugged. "I dunno. The universe? God, I guess? I don't have a name for it. Don't need one really."

I nodded. I knew exactly what she meant.

"And then?"

"And then I went on with my life, or whatever this is."

"You felt better?"

Sasha put on her mean face: eyes slit, both brows raised, neck craned toward me. "No, Carlos, I felt like shit. Yes, I felt better. But it's not just about feeling better. It's about letting go. Sometimes you have to do something, you know, something real, to wake yourself up."

I hadn't known I was asleep, but then, maybe I had.

A bunch of dumb comebacks tried to surface and I discarded them all.

She was right.

In a few hours we'd be making passionate love while the morning broke. In another day, she'd figure out what I'd done and impale me with my own sword. A few months after that, we would save each other's lives amid the near destruction of the natural order of life and death and then say good-bye once and for all.

But in this moment, I watched her fuss with her hair and I thought about everything she'd just said and everything she was, what I was and how I got there. And I batted away all nagging demons of the future and past and smiled at her with my whole face.

"Carlos!"

That's Riley's voice.

"Wake the fuck up, bro."

But Riley's in a coma.

"Yo, C!"

Riley stands over me, arms crossed over his broad chest, one eyebrow raised. Lips pursed. This is Riley's unimpressed face. A crew of soulcatchers lingers behind him, their face guards lifted; I recognize a few of them from the park earlier: Squad 9.

A thick, surly ghost steps beside him. Sylvia Bell. The horrible night comes back in jolted shivers.

"He okay?" Sylvia asks.

Riley shakes his head. "I guess."

I'm in my apartment. The windows are open, letting in a cool early-morning breeze. Outside the sky lightens toward dawn. A tiny shimmering phantom bursts through the air, wrapping his hands around a slender brown neck. I jolt up. "Kia!"

Riley's barely there palm against my chest sends me sprawling back onto the couch. "Easy, C. She's alright. Sleeping it off in your bed. But we gotta talk." He looks at Sylvia. "Give us the room, Syl."

Syl?

She nods at her team and they disperse, mingling with the shadows and then vanishing completely. Riley looks back at me, shakes his head again. "Get up. Make coffee, whatever, but listen carefully to what I'm saying to you."

I stand, find my balance, shuffle into the kitchen. Nothing seems too damaged, just a general crappiness that resounds across my body. I fuss with the cafetera. Riley leans over the kitchen counter and gets up in my face.

"Are you listening?"

"Mothafucka, you ain't speaking. Speak and I'll listen. But get out my face."

For a second we just stare at each other. Then Riley says, "You fucked up."

I curl my upper lip into a snarl and squint at him. I don't know what he's talking about. Hell, maybe he's right, but it's what you do when someone throws down like that. It's protocol.

"Think I'm kidding?" Riley says.

"I think you should just tell me what you're talking 'bout rather than going comandante on my ass."

"Kia," Riley says. He doesn't waver in his glare. Doesn't flinch.

I run it back in my mind. The child ghost, the park around us, the newspapers fluttering in the streetlights. Kia, her eyes wide. She hadn't seen the dead before last night, I realize. All her dealings with spiritual folks at the botánica and she'd never actually seen a spirit herself. But in that moment, her eyes fixated right on the ghostling. And then the ghostling turned to me.

"You understand what I'm talkin' 'bout yet, C?" Riley has stepped back. I'm standing there still holding the half-full metal basin for the cafetera, and Riley just stares at me.

"I hesitated."

He nods. "Why?"

"I . . ."

"Stop," Riley says. "Think about it before you answer."

The face. It was just a child. I mean, you could tell from the back it was a child ghost, but then he turned and that young face was still pudgy with baby fat but contorted with rage, eyes sunk deep in his skull, mouth stretched wide, teeth long and sharp.

"Why'd you pause, C?"

But past the demon there was still something in there, a glimmer of what that kid had once been, some flicker of life. He'd turned to me, and in that millisecond I'd seen through the mask of rage and into its core. "Because I saw past the demon."

"Wrong."

"What?"

"You're missing something, man. Go deeper." The instinct to push back rises again, but Riley cuts me off before I can start. "You've sliced demon kids before. I seen you do it. No one likes to. It's never easy, but we do what we have to do, right? We always do what we have to do."

I nod. The worst was two years back: a toddler who had burned up in a tenement fire started plaguing the ER waiting room at Woodhull. Asphyxiated an old man and was about to possess one of the security guards when Riley and I caught up to him and put him away. The shit doesn't usually bother me, but I didn't sleep for a week after that night.

"And your friend was in danger last night, C. You had every reason and cause to move with unfettered ruthlessness. To be that unhesitating bad mothafucka that I personally know you to be in a time of crisis."

"But I paused."

"Why?"

"Riley." Sylvia Bell appears in the doorway. "He's up."

I hear the cafetera clatter into the sink. "He . . . the ghostling? He's *here*?"

Riley squints at me. "This conversation isn't over, Carlos."

"You brought him *here?*"

Sylvia vanishes into the hallway. Riley shoots me a final, penetrating glare and then heads after her. "We locked him in your bathroom. Come have a look."

The Council has an official policy against hiring child ghosts. It sounds good on paper, but the result is a bunch of young souls loitering around the living world. Most of them end up running dumb errands in exchange for toys or candy, and when the Council's dumbass telepathy shit breaks down, they head right to one of those deserted alleyways full of little floating ghosticles with a handful of mints.

So there you have it.

Every once in a while one goes malignant. I've never gotten anyone to explain how this happens. Pent-up bitterness, some unresolved shit from their life, the infinite angst of being dead and aimless among the living. Everyone's got theories. However it happens, it's a terror to behold. They tend to lash out in random bursts, exploding through a room like tiny translucent Tasmanian devils and leave it a disaster area in seconds. And then they'll vanish, sometimes for days, and pop up again a whole borough over, kill or maim a bunch of folks real quick again, with no apparent pattern or logic, and be gone. It's rare, thankfully, but when it happens, it means they gotta get got quick. That's the rule. See one, take it out.

And yes, it's fucked up, slicing a tiny shiny ghost, even when you know you're sparing the world from an endless series of massacres. Doesn't matter. We're hardwired to protect anything small and helpless-looking, even if you walk up on it strangling a little old lady.

Or your good friend.

I shudder, soft-stepping down the hall behind Riley's shimmering glow. I know he's right and I still don't know how to answer the question, which makes me want to kick his ass. A dull thud comes from behind the closed bathroom door, followed a few seconds later by a scratching noise. Riley smiles back at me, and I flip him off. The thud happens again, then more scratching.

"You put down one of those oogy-boogy ghost boundary things y'all love using?" I whisper.

Sylvia nods. "He's not going anywhere."

We stand in a semicircle facing my bathroom door. The thing thuds again, scratches. "Tell me again why y'all subdued this thing and brought it here for a sleepover instead of taking him out like we supposed to?" Sylvia opens her mouth, but I cut her off. "Because I seem to recall about five seconds ago having my ass handed to me for not dispatching him myself."

Riley shakes his head. "That was different. You hesitated and got jumped. We captured him. Tell him, Syl."

"He's not acting right," she says.

"No shit. He's been killing people in the park for a week."

"One." Sylvia raises a finger. "He's stayed within a set four-block radius. Two." And another. "The attacks have happened one at a time and usually with twenty-four hours between them. And three, he followed Kia."

Thud.

"What?"

Scratch-scratch-scratch.

"Yep," Riley says. "After your milquetoast-ass save-the-day fail, Kia ran and the ghostling went after her. Followed her halfway up Marcy, and then she dropkicked the thing. Then Syl snatched him out the sky and we bagged it."

"Shit. So he's . . ."

"Not just some random angry child spirit gone bad," Sylvia finishes.

I look back and forth between them. "The fuck is it, then?"

Riley shakes his head. "I hate to say this, but it seems like he's been weaponized."

Thud.

"Weaponized?"

Scratch-scratch-scratch.

"Like someone caught a child ghost, broke him, made him their own personal killing slave, basically, and then released him into the world."

"And who was he trying to—" I start to say, but I don't have to finish. Riley's staring at the bedroom door. And he already said the ghostling chased her. "No. Why would anyone—no."

Sylvia nods.

"She did used to hang out at that park every day," I whisper. "And then she stopped for a while, over some boy, I think. So you think"—*thud*—"the thing was operating on old intelligence, and when she wasn't where she was sposta be, he just started killing folks randomly, waiting for her to get back?"

Scratch-scratch.

"Man." Riley shakes his head. "Something like that. I know it's not a perfect theory, but what else we got to go on? I never seen a wild ghostling act like that. I never seen anything act like that."

"So you brought the demon-child assassin to my house and locked him into the bathroom across from the girl he's trying to kill?" My whisper is more like a strained cough.

"The fuck else was I sposta do with him, man? This the only way we gonna find out what the fuck is going on. And anyway, I'm not really interested in your opinion at this moment. Consider your decision-making skills in question. Feel me, Dr. Hesitation?"

"*My* decision-making . . . *My?*"

"Listen, boys," Sylvia says, inserting her formidable bulk between us. "You gotta relax. This isn't going to . . ."

The bedroom door opens, and we all whip around to see Kia staring wide-eyed from the darkness. "What . . . the . . . fuck?" she gasps.

I feel my heart crumble a little. She heard everything. She stares at Riley's floating translucent form, then Sylvia's. The ghost's touch gave her the Vision, alright. She blinks away tears, mouth a twisted frown.

"Kia," I say.

She slams the door.

CHAPTER TWELVE

Kia

I get my stuff together while Carlos knocks on the door and tries to sound reassuring.

Fuck that. I heard what they said. I saw what I saw.

Don't have much. My phone and house keys are on the bedside table with my glasses and a hair clip.

"Kia, answer me. We have to talk."

I brush down Carlos's burgundy sheets—what kind of creep has burgundy sheets?—pull out the wrinkles, and find my jacket and shoulder bag in a big leather chair next to a bookshelf. Creep.

I try to pull my mass of hair into something I can fit under a du rag. Give up. It's doing what it wants and so the fuck am I.

"Kia?"

The thing . . . the demon child—its face flashes, that huge mouth stretches open, rows of sharp teeth and those dead, sunken-in eyes bore into mine. It's just across the hall, thumping away in the bathroom. Trying to get to me.

Fuck everything.

"Kia, I'm coming in. I know you're upset. I just need to talk to you, okay? I'm coming in."

I open the door and try to push past him. I just want to make it outside before I burst into tears or get my soul eaten by that demon child, but Carlos steps his tall lanky-ass self right in front of me.

"Kia."

"Move." I shove, hard. He must've been caught off guard, because I'm sure I'd never be able to actually move Carlos if he didn't want me to. He stumbles back, a satisfying look of shock on his face. I'm halfway to the door when he grabs my arm, and I can tell by the grip there's no shaking it. I try anyway.

"Let the fuck go!"

He spins me toward him and then holds both my arms.

"Listen to me," Carlos snarls. "This is not some teen-angst situation, Kia. Your life is in danger."

"That's exactly why I'm trying to get the hell out of here, man." My voice is wet with an oncoming sob, but I'm not gonna cry in front of Carlos. That's not gonna happen. "Maybe I can find someone better equipped to save my ass out there."

Carlos blinks and straightens like I just clapped him across the face. I guess in a way I did. "I . . . I deserved that."

I stare at him. The urge to run seeps from me, and now I just want to hug Carlos and tell him it's gonna be alright. Confusing-ass emotions. Then the thing thumps against the bathroom door again. We both look at it.

"Let's go up to the roof," Carlos says. "We gotta talk."

I nod.

A muted daybreak opens across the warehouses and fancy new high-rises around us. The East River sparkles beneath the growing dawn, still alive with the last of Manhattan's shine.

We absorb it in silence for a few minutes, and then Carlos takes out one of those nasty-ass cigars he likes and offers me the pack with his eyebrows raised.

"No, thanks, man. I want to reach voting age without my larynx rotting out."

He shrugs and lights his.

"So." I put my hands in my pockets and keep my eyes on the gray sky above the rooftops. "Turns out you're not some crazy hallucinating guy."

Carlos barks a laugh. "And neither is Baba Eddie."

"Well, I knew that. And this Riley guy?"

"My partner."

"He's . . . dead."

"Very."

A seagull circles in front of us, caws its complaint, and then veers off toward the bay.

"I guess I always thought . . ." I pause, search for the words. What did I always think? Everything's a jumble right now. "I thought the whole ancestors thing Baba Eddie's always talking about is more like a metaphor, you know? Like, he puts down food for them and smokes cigars with 'em and shit, but I thought that was just like . . . you know, symbolic."

"Nope."

"And you're . . . Carlos, you're dead too?"

"Half."

I shake my head. "Alright, man. It's all just a lot."

"I know. And I know last night was scary. Really scary."

I rub my neck and try to cast off the unceasing memory of that face in mine.

Carlos pulls on his cigar, exhales a pillar of smoke into the sky. "And we're gonna figure out what the hell is going on, Kia. I know I was ragging on Riley about it, and I know it seems ridiculous, but he was right to bring the thing here."

My whole body tenses. I stay quiet, push back a sob.

"There's no other way to find out who sent it and why."

The sun emerges from a hazy muddle of clouds; it throws the scattered shadows of circling pigeons across our faces.

"What . . ." I pause. Collect myself. "What am I supposed to do now, Carlos?"

"I wish I could say everything's just gonna be alright," he says, "but that's not a promise I can make you, Kia. You gotta live your life, but you gotta be careful. You have the Vision now; you're gonna be seeing ghosts."

I shudder. "Like, everywhere? Man, I can't handle this shit. I didn't ask for this."

"Not everywhere, just . . . around. And I know it's a shock at first—believe me—but you have to stay sharp. Just stay away from them. If one starts coming at you, you gotta run. I mean, most of them are harmless, really, and I don't want you to walk around the rest of your life being afraid of the dead . . ."

"No, why would I ever do that?"

Carlos has already learned when not to take the bait with me. He stays the course. "Look, right now it's clear something's after you. And we got this one, but we can't be sure there ain't another one out there looking for you."

"Great."

He crouches and unstraps something from his boot. It's a dagger, sheathed in a metal holster wrapped in worn leather. He holds it out to me with both hands, all ceremonious-like.

"What's this?"

"It's a blade like mine. It kills ghosts."

"Carlos, man . . ."

"Kia, take it. I don't usually give things to people, especially not ghost-killing things. This is important."

I scowl at the dagger, my arms crossed over my chest. It is pretty cool though. "Where am I supposed to keep that thing, man? You do realize I'm black, right?"

"I . . ."

"Can't be walking 'round BK with a dagger hanging off

me just chilling like *ayy*. You gonna pay for my funeral when the cops blow my ass away?"

"Kia, I—"

"Y'all brown folks don't get got like us, C. You might get ya ass beat for being brown, especially gray-ass brown like you. But I'm black. Ain't no kinda ambiguous either. *Un*ambigously black. They shoot us for having a wallet or a sandwich, how I'ma roll around with a medieval-ass ghost-killing-ass dagger?"

Carlos finally stops trying to interrupt me, which is all I really wanted. He moves his mouth around his face a few times, eyebrows creased. It's fun to watch. He still holds the knife out like I'm a knight and he's a king.

"You right," Carlos says. "It is different for me. I hadn't thought about it like that."

"Course you hadn't." I snatch the dagger. "I'll take it though. I'll figure it out." I like this thing. It's heavier than I thought it would be. I draw it, and it makes that *shhiiiin-nnngggg* sound they do in movies and the blade catches the orange glow from the rising sun, damn near blinding me, and *yesssssssss*.

Carlos steps back. "Careful, now. Listen . . ."

I sheathe it up again because when it's out, I won't pay attention to a single thing he's saying: too shiny and cool. "Go 'head."

"You trying to really kill a ghost for good, you stab or slice at the head or torso. One or two good cuts and that's it; the deal is done. Most of the time. Sometimes a particularly strong one might last longer. If you cut the limbs you might incapacitate it, but it won't be gone."

"How a ghost die, though? They not dead already?"

"It's called the Deeper Death. Means they're really gone, like ether. Just gone."

"Cool."

"Not cool," Carlos says, his voice stern now. "Be careful with this thing. Sometimes when folks are new to seeing spirits, they just bug out and stab up any ol' ghost wandering by. Never rush to the kill." His eyes go misty for a second, then swing back into focus. "Find out what's going on. But stay ready. Shit gets hairy fast with the dead, even if *most* spirits aren't gonna try to hurt you."

"If they do," I say, drawing the blade, "they gonna taste Ethereal Juniper."

Carlos frowns. "Ethereal Juniper though? Try harder."

"You name yours?"

"No, Kia. I'm an adult, and I don't live in Middle Earth. But do you."

"You're no fun."

"Also: I'ma have Sylvia Bell keep an eye on you."

I shake my head and sheathe the blade again for emphasis. "Hell no."

Carlos turns to me. "Kia, listen . . ."

"No. I listened. Now you listen: you're not putting no middle-aged dead white lady on my ass."

"Well, Riley's gonna be busy with—"

"And you're not putting no Riley on my ass either. It's not happening. I reject it. Do you understand me, Carlos? I did not invite this situation and I do not welcome this situation into my life. Yesterday, besides almost dying, I made an utter jackass out of myself in front of the one boy I ever had a crush on. I am sixteen. I got a job, a black eye, trigonometry homework, and plenty of other shit to worry about besides having your dead-ass friends following me around. Feel me?"

Carlos squints and moves his mouth around, probably swallowing back some retort. He can see I'm not playing. "I do," he finally says. "I do and I'm sorry. Part of this is my fault. I shouldn't have hesitated. I fucked up and I'm sorry." He shuffles back and forth on his feet and looks out at the city. "Really sorry."

"It's alright," I say, squinting at him. "Maybe it's better anyway. Like you said—this way y'all can maybe figure out what's going on. If you'da just cut the little fucker, it'd be a done deal and we'd be stuck guessing."

He brightens a little. "It's true."

"But the next time it's between me and some demon child, stop thinking about how you're probably a brand-new father now and just do what you have to do."

Carlos's mouth drops open and the cigar tumbles out, lands in a puddle, and extinguishes with a fizz. I walk to the doorway at the edge of the roof. "See ya 'round, man."

"You . . . tag-teamed me," Carlos stutters.

I shrug and head down the stairs and out into the day.

I feel good, actually.

My body's relaxed, like I didn't get kicked in the face and choked out by a demon child yesterday. The breeze feels perfect against my skin as I step out into the Bushwick streets. I cross under the tracks as the wary bodega workers trundle up metal gates and retrieve the morning papers. I should feel like shit. I have eighty-seven reasons to. Instead, everything is crisp. I told off Carlos, and now I forgive him for almost getting me got. I really do. His sadness hangs all over him. He's coy and aloof, yes; I'd hug him and tell him it's gonna work out if I was that kind of douche and I thought it might help. I'm not though, and it wouldn't, and for all I know, nothing's gonna be alright. Especially with his jacked-up life.

My stride is long today, my fro magnificent. I tall-step in and out of long shadows, watch my own shadow dance along beside me; the great gravity-defying waves of my hair make my head a wild dark star against the pavement. King Impervious thunders another verse into my ears and the beat is sick—it carries me along on its own gale of blasting bass drones and the mischievous *clack-clack snicker* of the snare. *Ain't a mothafucka here make sense like me / My bitch a mermaid, a mothafuckin' manatee.* I stop in a bodega on

Bushwick to grab a buttered roll and a tea. I don't know what the fuck she's talking 'bout in that line, but she says it like she's fucking dying, like if she doesn't get those words out, they'll tear her in half from the inside. I always imagine her literally killing bitches while she lays down verses, because no matter what the song's about, King Impervious always killing a bitch.

I hang a left and then a right and then, "Ay, what happen, girl? Ya man get mean wichya?" I'm so riled up on this song, I almost deck the middle-aged bearded guy when he falls into step with me. "You want me to fuck him up for ya, girl? I do that for you." His ass so loud I can hear it *over* King Impervious, but he doesn't need to know that. "You know the domestic violence a serious problem in the community, girl. Lemme get that number."

I almost bust out laughing, but that would only encourage him.

A cat come close I kill him / let this bitch clean up the spill and / make a coat out of ya puppy like Cruella de Vil.

"Girl, I'm just tryna help," the guy calls from the corner. "You actin' like I ain't even exist, disrespectful-ass ho!"

I stop. Not because he called me a ho—I stop because everything is different now; I have the Vision or whatever the fuck Carlos calls it. I turn around, squint at homeboy.

"Hold up, now. I didn't mean no disrespect by that, girly." I start walking back toward him. "Calling you a ho, I mean." He waves his hands in front of his face. "I formally apologize, girl."

When I'm close enough to smell the morning's first vodka on his breath, I give him a good up and down. Everything looks normal. He's not all shimmery the way Riley and Sylvia are.

"Girl?"

I lift a hand and the dude cringes. I ignore him, put my finger up against the dusty worn leather of his overcoat.

"I'm sorry! I will never disrespect hos again! I swear."

I push. It's soft, like he has three sweaters on underneath. And then I must come against his shoulder blade. He's real.

I look up at him. "Good." And then I turn and head off toward Cypress Hills Cemetery.

CHAPTER THIRTEEN

Carlos

"Whatsamatta, bro?" Riley asks when I walk back into my apartment.

"Nothing. Got something in my eye up on the roof. I think a bug flew in there."

"You want me to take a look?"

"No, man. Last time I let you anywhere near my eye, you popped your own out and stuck it in mine."

"Suit yourself, C. Kia leave?"

I stand there rubbing my eye for a few seconds, very like an asshole.

"Carlos?"

"Yeah. She left."

"She alright?"

"She will be. Wouldn't let me put a bodyguard on her though. Gave her my dagger."

"Can't blame her. There's coffee if you want it."

Bless him. Ghosts can move physical stuff around, but even for a badass like Riley, all that intricateness and precision gets exhausting. I take his effort as a peace offering and walk over to the counter. "You alright, Riley. Sylvia still here?"

"She headed out to make her report."

"Fuck." I pour out two cups, throw some sugar in Riley's and stir it. "I should probably do that."

"I guess."

I pass Riley his and we enjoy the first sips in silence.

Thud.

Well, mostly silence.

"What's the move?" I say.

Scratch-scratch-scratch.

"I dunno, but we should probably get his ornery little ass outta there, cuz at some point your living half is gonna have to pee."

I shrug. "Ah, I peed when I was on the roof."

"Out ya eyes?"

"What?"

"Nothin'. Shall we have a look?"

I throw back the rest of the coffee. "Can't hardly wait."

The thump and scratch stops when we step up to the door.

"This is what I think," I say. "The ghostling had a mission: wait in the park and then get at Kia. He did that, causing hell and havoc all the while, and then she showed and he failed."

Riley nods. "True."

"What's the next move?"

"He tries again."

"Maybe, but maybe not. What's our protocol for when a mission goes south?"

Riley smirks. "Wouldn't know."

"You go back to the base, man."

We stare at the door for a few seconds.

"It's risky," Riley says.

"I know. The fuck else we gonna do though? Doubt he's gonna be open to chatting."

As if on cue, the ghostling thumps against the door again.

Riley draws his blade. I take a deep breath and turn the knob. The little shimmering creature collapses across the doorway, gasping.

"Well, damn," Riley says. "Now I kinda feel bad."

"*Psh*. You didn't have his hands on you."

The ghostling drags himself onto his knees, crumples forward again, and crawls a few agonizing steps.

Riley shakes his head. "If he does go home, it's gonna take a week or two to get there."

The ghostling snarls up at us and swipes a little hand at Riley's pant leg.

"Hey!" He steps back.

"You don't think he'll do something to throw us off the trail now that we've been talking like he doesn't exist right in front of him, do you?"

The ghostling scowls at Riley and finds his footing.

"Nah, this guy's been programmed. It's a horrible, horrible thing to do to a spirit. They break them and then give them a singular mission, and that's it. The most they'll get is a backup plan if it fails, like you're hoping, but these guys aren't functioning on any kinda high-strategy levels, trust."

The ghostling lurches forward faster now that he's up, angling toward the front door in a lopsided canter.

"You don't think he's gonna try to pull some slick and murderous move on us?" I ask.

Riley draws his blade. "I think his slick and murderous days are over, but I got my eye on him. Something about getting caught and locked in the bathroom seems to have taken the wind out of his creepy little sails."

"That and Kia's dropkick," I say. "Let's see where this goes."

We amble along beneath the tracks, an odd parade or just one weirdo staring at the ground a few feet in front of him, depending on who's looking, and then cut east along a quiet residential block, past an elementary school, across Bushwick Ave. toward Queens.

"You think he's going to the cemetery?" Riley asks.

The ghostling's been moving faster and faster as we go, and now I'm getting winded, keeping pace behind that still-raggedy shuffle.

"Might make sense, I guess," I huff.

But instead of turning right on Cypress, the ghostling lopes left, takes us along another quiet little street, and then halfway down, he pauses in front of a very ordinary-looking two-story house. Ordinary, I realize when we get closer, except for the tall, gangly phantom floating outside the front door.

"Garrick! Tartus!" the ghost announces.

"That a fact?" Riley says, shooting him the stink-eye.

The ghost doesn't respond, doesn't acknowledge us, just stares off, his lower lip hanging slightly open, shoulders slumped.

"I hate it when the dead do this shit," I grumble.

"Garrick! Tartus!"

We all stand there for a few seconds panting, and then the ghostling stumbles up the front steps.

"Whoa there, little guy," Riley says, yoinking him back. The ghostling sputters and hisses but doesn't have much fight in him.

"What you think, Carlos?"

"Garrick! Tartus!"

Besides the repetitive-ass ghoul, the place looks like every other house on the block. It's shingled, painted a dull gray-green. Wooden stairs lead up to the front door. The shades are down on all the windows, but that's not unusual.

I shrug. "Got nothing. Maybe somebody's home."

"Maybe Garrick Tartus's home," Riley says.

"Garrick! Tartus!"

I walk up the front steps. I'm reaching toward the brass doorbell when Riley says: "Carlos," and I hear a click behind my head.

"Turn slow," a woman's gravelly voice says. "Hands in plain sight."

She's standing perfectly still in a perfectly tailored gray suit. Her stance is just wide enough to brace for the recoil from the hand cannon she's aiming at my face. It's clear from the bulges between her vest and bloodred dress shirt that she'll never be outgunned. Even her goddamn footwear is perfect: elegant alligator-skin dress shoes, perfectly shined. For the first time in my weird little life, I am outdappered.

Also: Riley is standing beside her, his blade poised to slice through her skull. The ghostling squirms under his other arm.

"Have you heard the good word about Jesus Christ today, ma'am?" I say, flashing the cheesiest grin I can muster.

She smiles for a half second. "Try again." Not a cop—way too smooth and she would've ID'd herself by now.

"Vote yes on question six," I say, but it doesn't really matter. She had her chance to catch me off guard and passed on it. Riley relaxes his blade some.

"I'd like to know," the woman says, "why of all the doors on all the blocks in Bushwick, you walked up to this one right here." She says it evenly, with no trace of threat. Of course, she doesn't have to threaten when she's pointing that gat at my face. Still, I believe she really wants to know.

"It's a long story," I say.

She shrugs. "I'm in no hurry."

"And I'd like to ask the same thing of you."

There's a pause, and then the woman holsters her weapon so smoothly it's like it just evaporated in the midmorning sun. She's not just a professional; she's a fucking panther.

"Excellent," she says. "Coffee?"

There are still a few diners in Bushwick where the hipsters that come to gawk at locals leave with bruises. Tucked amid some abandoned factories and a tattoo parlor, the Rosebud is just such a place. The woman drives us there in a spotless black Crown Vic with MEDIANOCHE CAR SERVICE stenciled in a circular logo on the door. Riley hovers in the backseat, the ghostling tucked under his arm like a naughty child.

She says her name is Reza, reaching a hand over to me. I take it, watch her register the coolness of my skin. She doesn't flinch, just notes it with a solemn nod.

"Carlos. And I'll meet you inside; just give me one sec."

"Alright," Reza says, closing the doors and bleeping the alarm. "But don't run off. I'll find you and kill you." She turns around and walks into the diner.

"Welp," Riley says. "That happened."

"Yeah, she wasn't kidding either."

"Nope." The ghostling squirms in his arms. "I'ma take this guy back to the Council, see what they can do with him. You arright?"

I scoff. "Sure. She seems nice enough."

Riley snickers as he vanishes into the Brooklyn backstreets, the wee killer ghostling whining softly.

Four hours, eight cups of coffee, three unfiltered cigarettes, and two Malagueñas later, Reza studies me for a second, takes a drag, and then says: "I'll be honest with you, Carlos . . ."

"You mean you haven't been all this time?"

"Shut up. I don't usually talk this much. Especially not to strangers. And even less so to strangers that are men."

"Fair enough."

"I can count on one hand the number of men I've had

honest conversations with and not regretted it." She holds up one finger. "There, I counted. But you've been very honest with me this afternoon, and I appreciate that. I'm sure most people think you're fucking crazy or full of shit."

"You don't?"

"I didn't say that." She doesn't smile.

"But?"

"But if I did think so, I wouldn't have told you my side."

"To be honest," I say, "I don't usually tell people about this shit either. I don't really talk to that many people, come to think of it, unless they already know or I have to for . . . work."

"But?"

"I'm not totally sure, to be honest. You have a trustworthy face?"

Reza almost spits out her coffee. "These words have never been said."

I shrug and light a Malagueña. This has to be the last diner in New York that you can smoke in. The air is thick and murky with our combined pollution. The only other customer is a dusty old guy reading a paper in the far corner.

"So," I say, "there's a house, a tunnel, a rec room with toys, a fucked-up long-armed guy, a cockroach-for-skin guy . . ."

"Pink cockroaches," Reza says.

"Right. And then there's Shelly, Angie, and at least a few others, yeah?"

"At least." When I say *Angie,* Reza flinches ever so slightly. It's the first involuntary thing I've seen her do all afternoon.

"And on my end, there's this child ghost that led us back there, and that's it really; that's all I got. I'll say this though: someone who knew what they were doing fucked with that kid. Takes a high-level necromancy to make a single-minded killer like that."

Reza frowns and stubs out her cigarette. "Well, that's an

angle you're gonna have to handle, clearly. Meanwhile, this roach situation has gotta get ended. This what I'm thinking: someone has to own that house, right? We got a guy that—"

"Wait—we who?"

The waitress, a surly octogenarian wearing all the makeup ever, approaches to refill our coffees. "You alright, lovebirds?" she snarls. "Need anything else?"

Reza smiles. "We're good, Cathy, thanks." She turns back to me. "We: my people. We got a guy that can look that shit up. I'll see what he can find tonight when I go in."

"Can I ask you something?"

"You're not my type."

I narrow my eyes. "You were just waiting for that moment, weren't you?"

"Eh." She shrugs. "What you wanna know?"

"Why'd you tell me all that—everything you just told me? You seem like the type that information has to be pried out of."

Reza studies me for so long I get uncomfortable. She must've been wondering the same thing. Finally, she takes a sip of her coffee and says, "When you do what I do for as long as I've been doing it, you learn to figure people out quickly and break down everything you need to know about them to two things."

"What things?"

"Doesn't matter."

"Huh?" I furrow my brow, and she smiles.

"Two essential things. They're different things for everyone. But you don't have time to sit there analyzing eighty million little quirks and who loves their father. You have however many seconds to decide if they can kill you and if they will kill you, and then you either kill them first or you don't. And if you don't, you either die or you—"

"Have a four-hour cup of coffee at the diner."

"Basically."

"And?"

"You're a genuine person, Carlos."

I try not to be flattered, but I am, I am. "I'm actually a pretty good liar though, just FYI."

"No, you're not."

"My line of work has me—"

"You lie to people who want to be lied to. That doesn't count. You just collude with their denial. That's not lying. It's an ongoing charade we all participate in. Try lying to a liar."

"How can I get better?"

"Shut the fuck up," Reza says. I do, and she lets out a congested chuckle. "No, man. I mean let them do the talking. The less you say, the better. Find the part of the lie that's true and tell everything else to fuck off. But really, just shut up. They'll usually tell you what you want to know."

"That's what you do?"

"Nah. I know how to lie. That's for you. Believe me, Carlos—you're better off wielding that sword you keep in the cane than trying to get over."

"How'd you—"

"The second thing is, you're a killer."

I shut my mouth. A single word floods my mind, spoken in the harsh whisper of the man who created me: *murderer*. I had demanded to know who I was and it was all he said. Sarco was an ancient sorcerer and everything he got he had coming to him, but I could never let go of that single scrap of knowledge about who I'd been before I died. And then I'm holding Sasha's brother, Trevor, as he dies from the blade I just hurled into him. Trevor was the first person I ever found who was like me. The ghosts I dispatch to Hell, well, they're already dead. It's different. Trevor looks up at me, begs me to find his sister, and I'm so lost in the smile that glows from her photograph, I barely register the life that's slipping away in my hands, and then I do and he's gone.

"Carlos."

"Hm?"

"You went somewhere."

"I'm here." I find my coffee, sip it, and concentrate on the lukewarm bitterness. Reza and I lock eyes. "If you could tell I'm a killer, why did you—"

"Because I can also see you're good at what you do."

"Well . . ."

"And I need help."

CHAPTER FOURTEEN

Kia

Peace to the bitches who ain't have no faith in me
All up in ya faces now ya can't keep pace with me
I've played through all of *Red-Handed Royalty* at least six times. Got other albums on here, but none of them fit my mood. No Gio. No Gio and no Ma Sinclair and no Uncle Terence and no Great-Aunt Gene. None of 'em come through. Six rounds of *Red-Handed Royalty*—it ain't a short album either; King Impervious got a lot to say—and none of my dead made a showing. I'm at the family plot, my ass in the dirt, my back against the granite stone with Ma Sinclair's name carved in elegant all caps on it.

I give not one, two, three, or four fucks
Come watch me scatter 'cross the world like a horcrux
Every once in a while I close my eyes. I've drifted in and out of naps. I keep thinking, when I open them, there he'll be with a stupid grin on his face, and he'll say, "Boo," or some other cheesy bullshit, and then we'll sit here and he'll tell me what all has been going on all these years and he'll tell me I'm safe, that he'll protect me and I'll never have to be afraid again.

Voldemort, bitches, this ain't Hungry Hippos; this a Blood Sport, bitches.

Pathetic, I know. But I'd believe him. Hell, after what's happened in the past day, I'm likely to believe any ol' shit someone tells me.

I close my eyes. Open them again to the empty sky, the tombstones and trees. Beyond the trees, cars flash past along the glimpse of highway. I didn't know Ma Sinclair or Uncle Terence that well—they're just moments to me, a hand on my head, a squeeze, the smell of coffee percolating and mothballs. But I'd still be happy to see 'em. And they could explain some of this to me, and they could have my back too—that's what ancestors do, right?

Please step to me; by all means bring ya thunda
So I can watch the wack tide of ya rhymes drag ya unda

A flicker of movement pulls my eye off to the right. Nothing's there. I sit up, squint across the graves. Nothing.

I'd seen some shades already: tall, flowing shadows that drifted along like puffs of smoke. One of 'em had long shadow legs and strolled long strides. But they all kept their distance, didn't even turn and acknowledge me.

I'm thinking I mighta imagined that flash of movement when a shape slinks out from behind a crypt and lopes toward me.

Fuck with me now, but don't fuck with my style
Oblivious-ass bitches will get wrecked and compiled

I sit up straight, my heart blasting away in my ears over King Impervious's steady flow. Can't make out a face or anything. It's just tall and glowy with long arms.

Carlos told me to run if something comes at me. But Carlos doesn't know about Gio, doesn't know I've asked for help in my own silent prayers.

I probably shouldn't even be here. The dagger is nestled in my shoulder bag. I don't move though.

I wait.

The shadow crosses the walking path and looms over our

family plot. Carlos would kill me for not running. And he'd probably be right to.

Still.

"Hello?" I say. Only an asshole would say some dumb shit like that when a ghost walks up to them in a graveyard, but that's all I got right now. It slinks closer. Its long arms reach out and plant in the ground, and then it drags its sludgy torso along. I hear it panting as it slithers a shimmering hand on my grandma's stone and brings its face right up to mine.

Two wide, hollow eyes gaze from the shimmering shadow.

Time and again you cape up and defend / all these fuckboys and dickbags that come for my friends

I'm shivering.

One day you gonna learn that a bitch will get burnt / when she tries to deny that the tables been turnt

The shadow makes little sniffing noises, probes the air around me. Something jiggles against my thigh, and I almost jump up and just run. The shadow looks down—it's startled too, I guess—and I finally recognize my own ringtone bleating out under Impervious's voice. I pull off my headphones, carefully reach down and dig my phone out my pocket, and raise it to my face. The shadow tracks my hand from my ear to my leg and back to my ear.

"Hello?"

"Kia, you okay?" It's Carlos.

"Yep."

That pause'll be Carlos deciding if it's a lie worth investigating. The shadow, much too close, just stares at me with those hollow eyes.

"Where are you, Kia?"

"Nowhere. Doesn't matter. What's up? You find another pay phone? I'm proud of you, man. Good shit."

"I borrowed a friend's phone. Look, I—"

"Wait—you have friends?" A single bead of sweat slides down my forehead. The shadow watches it, panting.

"Kia."

"Alright, go 'head. What you need?"

"Can you meet me on Franklin Ave.? I gotta do some research, and there's someone I want you to meet."

I let a moment pass.

"I dunno, C. I'm kinda busy today."

"Kia . . ."

"Alright! Jeez. Be outside the train stop on Eastern Parkway in forty."

Carlos grunts and hangs up.

I look into the ghost's empty face. "You ain't my family, huh?"

It lets out a single, heartbreaking bleat. I stand. Nod at it. Touch Ma Sinclair's headstone one time and then walk out the cemetery.

"Nobody lives here?"

"Not exactly." Carlos closes the old wooden door and leads me into an empty room. The jangly din of Franklin Avenue becomes a muted whirr. Here, it's all silence and stillness; dust motes slow-mo cyclone through the sunlight.

"Creepy," I say.

"This is where I came back to life," Carlos says. The last time I saw him this serious-looking was when his girlfriend pinned him to the couch with his own sword.

"You die here too?"

He shakes his head. "Grand Army Plaza."

I cock my head at him.

"Long story." He shrugs. "And I don't know it. Yet. C'mon."

He leads me upstairs, then up some more stairs and into a huge room with tall ceilings and wide windows. Stacks of books cluster together in precarious mountain ranges.

They're all ancient-looking—those leather-bound ornate-type situations that wizards open in dumb kids' movies. "What is this place?"

"Mama Esther's library, child," a voice says from above us. "Carlos, you brought a friend." A face appears in the air, huge and smiling so wide it makes her eyes squint. "What's your name?"

"Kia," I say. "Kia Summers."

"This is Mama Esther," Carlos says. The old ghost takes up most of the upper part of the room; her rotund body disappears in a haze around the stacks of books. "She's saved my life more times than I can count."

Mama Esther scowls. "*Psh.* You were there when I needed you most, Carlos. That's what matters."

"Kia works at Baba Eddie's place. She got the Vision last night when someone's demon ghostling got its hands on her throat."

"Oh no, dear." She swoops down through the stacks, and suddenly I'm immersed in a warm, languid cloud. It smells like rose petals and mildew and it somehow feels like home. I close my eyes and submerge into a lava-lamp ocean, buffeted by a gentle amber tide. Somehow, I'm sure I'm floating inside myself, utterly at peace.

And then Mama Esther lets out a sigh and I blink back to this strange Franklin Ave. apartment.

Mama Esther smiles down at me. "Feel better?"

"I do, but I don't even know how." It's released some pocket of anguish I'd been walking around with. "What'd you do?"

"Don't worry about that. Carlos, who's training ghostlings to do their dirty work?"

"Funny you should ask. We have no idea. But you ever hear of a ghost named Garrick Tartus?"

Mama Esther squints at the ceiling for a few seconds. "Not that I can think of, no. That who did this?"

"I don't know," Carlos says. "I don't think so. There was

a spirit stationed outside the house where the ghostling led us back to. All he'd say was 'Garrick Tartus.'"

"Odd name," Mama Esther muses. She's eyeing one of the stacks of books, running a thick translucent finger along the spines.

"That's what I'm saying," Carlos says.

Adults are so cute sometimes. I already have 1,600,983 references to Garrick Tartus pulled up on my phone, but I let them hem and haw a little before I pipe up. "Do you mean the Garrick Tartus of 173 Devonshire Road that blogs about peregrine falcons or the Garrick Tartus of Tartus Realty & Construction Co. in Morningside Heights?"

Carlos shoots me a wild glare. "What the—"

"Or the Garrick Tartus that was a minor character in the late nineties sci-fi show *Blastagion*?"

"I think that'd be option number two," Mama Esther says. Carlos is still making how-the-fuck faces at me. I pull up the Tartus Realty site and turn my phone to face him.

"That the dude?"

"Shit," Carlos says.

I smile. "Things will go much easier for you when you realize that I know everything."

Mama Esther gets a kick out of that. Her whole hefty ghost body rears back, and for a second I think she's catching a seizure. Then she releases a belly laugh that I'm sure regular ol' non-the-Vision-having mothafuckas gotta hear too and then she finally calms down and sighs deeply.

"You done?" Carlos asks.

"Almost," Mama Esther pants. "She's right though. The child is of above-average intelligence."

I nudge Carlos. "Told ya. Says here the business has been closed since their founder's untimely death last year."

Carlos growls. I'm not sure if it's at me or at the information.

"The fuck kinda name is Tartus anyway?" I ask. No one seems to know. I scan farther down the site. "Says the dude showed up on the scene a few decades ago like some kind of architect child prodigy. Started his own firm at eighteen, ignoring offers from all the major companies."

"Yeah, you may need to talk with Dr. Tennessee 'bout this one," Mama Esther says.

Carlos cocks an eyebrow. "Dr. Tennessee?"

"Research librarian at Harlem Public. She doesn't have the Vision, but she understands shit. And her collection and research skills are unparalleled. I usually send folks to her when the topic's more modern like this or some real-world shit. Plus if the guy had offices up that way, she'll be able to dig up the records."

"You never told me about her before," Carlos says.

"You never asked."

While they banter, I scroll through a few more articles, including an obituary from some neighborhood Queens paper. "Says he drowned in one of his own tunnels," I announce.

Carlos perks up. "He made tunnels? That's our guy. Mama Esther, thanks for everything!"

"Of course, love." She grins down at me. "Come by anytime, Kia. And keep Carlos outta trouble for me."

I thank her. Carlos is already running down the stairs.

Carlos doesn't say much during the train ride to Harlem. He's thinking through something, plotting out three moves ahead and then scratching the whole thing and starting over. He told me once he could see what's going on with people, like little satellites of information dance around their heads. I squint, trying to will some dancing vision into existence, but all I see is the smiling model behind him.

Whatever he's working on, it's got him shook. That song he's always humming slips from his lips, a sad soundtrack to his every move these days.

I put my headphones back on and turn up King Impervious.

—————

"You gonna tell me what's going on?" It comes out louder than I meant it to, my demand echoing up and down the basement research section of the Harlem Public Library.

"Not just yet," Carlos says. He's leaning up against the information desk like it's a bar, scowling at the tidy shelves. "Still thinking it through."

"If you told me, I could help you think it through."

Carlos looks thoughtfully at me.

"Can I help you?" a gravelly voice asks. A short, dark-skinned woman stands behind the counter, eyeing us. Her gray hair is close-cropped, her silk dress shirt open a few buttons. She looks like she gets her way.

Carlos manages a forced smile. "We're trying to find some information 'bout an architect or real estate agent named Garrick Tartus. Any chance you'd have some info on him in the reading room?"

"The reading room for suckas," Dr. Tennessee says. "The back stacks where all the good shit hiding. If you workin' on anything deeper than a middle school book report . . ." She peers over her bifocals at him.

Carlos nods.

"Well, then, you gonna need to go into the back stacks. You smoke?"

"Cigars."

The doctor flashes a grin. "Gimme one." Then she ambles off down a corridor and around a corner.

I roll my eyes. "What kinda librarian smokes in the resea—"

"Well, c'mon, then, mister. Ain't you gonna join me?"

"Go on, C." I give him a little push. "I think she likes you."

The corridor lets out into a narrow open-air walkway that must lead between two wings of the library. Air conditioners and ventilation fans hum around us, and the sky is just a gray sliver behind crisscrossed pipes and a mesh of cables.

"What kind is it?" Dr. Tennessee asks, inspecting the cigar.

"Malagueña."

She perks up. "Ooh, like the song?"

Carlos shrugs. "I guess?"

The little librarian hums a melody as she flicks her lighter and inhales. "Ahh! This right here: absolutely. With this, I get you whatever information you need. You having one too, right?"

"You're not worried about, you know . . . ?" Carlos sweeps his hand at the vast library around us.

"My good sir, we are outside and standing on concrete. A cigarette would have to literally defy every rule of physics to set something on fire, and anyway, I dispose of my butts in this nifty little tin." She holds up a small lidded box. "And if you think for a second that I would let anything happen to these books, you've lost your mind. Now, sit. I can't smoke alone."

Carlos eyes her for a second, and I can tell he's wondering if perhaps we stumbled into some mad book-keeper's secret lair. In a way, we did, I guess. Finally, he relents and lights up the one he's been working on all day.

Dr. Tennessee looks at me. "You, young lady, are too young to smoke."

"Oh, I know. Trust me."

"The thing is," Carlos says, "this is a matter of some urgency."

"What's your name?" Dr. Tennessee asks.

"Carlos."

"Where do you work?"

"I . . ."

"Who your best friend?"

"Listen . . ."

"No? Okay. You can't come to my workplace demanding all kinds of answers and you ain't even really know me, just like you wouldn't like it if I did that to you. Dig? Now, have a seat and enjoy a smoke, Speedy Gonzales."

For a second, I think Carlos might cut her. I'm busy trying not to bust out laughing, but he looks like his blade hand's getting twitchy. Then he does whatever it is Carloses do to calm down, probably silently hums that damn song of his, and leans against the wall. He closes his eyes, takes a long drag, and smiles.

"That's better." Dr. Tennessee chuckles.

"You kick ass," I tell her. "I been trying to get him to chill for a year."

She smiles. "I'm alright. Now, whatchyall wanna know 'bout this Garrick Tartus guy?"

Carlos opens his eyes. "I thought . . ."

I punch him. "He had a realty and construction company up in Morningside."

"So?"

"He builds tunnels," Carlos says. "We need to know about the tunnels. There has to be some ordinances, some exceptions made, something. You can't just build tunnels under houses in New York City, right? We need to know where he did his work, who his clients were, everything."

Dr. Tennessee looks up at the sliver of sky. She closes her eyes and releases a stream of smoke. I watch it rise, very like a ghost, and then disperse. "Yeah, I can help you," she finally says.

Carlos smiles for the first time in a while. "Excellent."

Then King Impervious's voice blasts out of my hip: *Make me who I am what I do, I'ma be with you; mothafucka do what I say to mothafuckin' do, bi*—It's a number I don't know, so I answer with a curt "Hello."

A smoke-stained voice asks for Carlos. I scowl, hold the phone out to him. When he goes for it, I pull it back, cover the mic, and say, "Don't be giving all ya bitches my number, C."

He narrows his eyes and takes the phone out of my hand.

Then he stands up real quick, and that already grayish pallor goes a shade paler. "Just now? Shit."

Dr. Tennessee and I trade scrunched-up faces.

"Yeah. But it'll take me a minute to . . . At the Harlem Public Li . . . Oh, okay." He hands me the phone. "I have to run. Kia, you gotta handle this." He nods at Dr. Tennessee. "Thanks for your help, Doc." And then he makes for the door back to the main library.

"C," I yell. "I don't even know what I'm—"

"Tunnels!" Carlos yells over his shoulder. "Find out about the tunnels."

And then, like a dick, he's gone.

CHAPTER FIFTEEN

❧❧❧

Carlos

I hop into the Crown Vic idling outside the library and it screeches off before I can close the door.

"Well, alright then," I grumble when I've finally got myself situated. There's no seat belts, so I end up clinging to the doorframe for dear life as we blast over the 59th Street Bridge toward Queens.

The driver is huge, all shoulders and massive arms bulging out of a tiny Hawaiian shirt; he's got a boisterous goatee and no other hair at all. He grins at me in the rearview. "You Carlos, right, man?"

"Shit, I better be. We already halfway to wherever we going."

He busts out laughing and then suddenly scowls. "No, of course not!"

"Excuse me?"

He rolls his eyes in the rearview and gestures to the little blinking device in his right ear.

"Annie, how am I gonna be talkin' to you and ask if you name Carlos? Don't make no sense, Annie. C'mon, girl . . . No . . . no . . . yes." He does a little shimmy in his seat and then swerves sharply into oncoming traffic and dips back into his lane, avoiding massive disaster by milliseconds.

"Annie, baby, I need you to put that PhD to work and not say stupid shit, 'kay? I'm driving and stupid shit makes me accident prone . . . Oh, word, it's like that? Fa'real? Okay! Okay! Okay!" He claps at each "okay" and bleats the horn in between. "Yeah, bye! No . . . bye! Good-bye, Annie! Yes! Okay, baby girl. I see you tonight . . . yeah . . . mm-hm."

I'm not thinking about Sasha. I mean, yes, I am, but only just now. My thoughts don't dart back to her every ten minutes. It's because shit is happening, moving fast, in fact, so who has time to dwell? Plus, I made a new friend today, and she reminds me of me.

"White girls." The driver snickers. "They will destroy me one day, but I will die happy."

I'm not really sure what to say to that, so I just nod and look out the window.

"I'm Rohan, by the way. You can call me Fantastic."

"Do I have to?"

"That's what they call me, man, not my fault. Actually, they call me Mista Fantastic at the club, but you know, I don't wanna sound arrogant."

"I mean . . ."

"You mad gray, son—you know that?"

"I do."

"Aight. Just lettin' you know. Might wanna get that checked out is all I'm sayin'."

"Thank you, Mista Fantastic."

Industrial Queens whirrs by, and then we zip over the little Pulaski Bridge and into Brooklyn.

Reza stands in the center of a cramped Bushwick apartment. An older Mexican guy in a leather jacket fiddles with a laptop on the floor while a woman in a sharp business suit sorts papers at the kitchen table. There's a heavy by the far window—tall, muscled, and silent as a statue. In the corner, a white woman in her midtwenties sobs into a handkerchief that matches Reza's immaculate suit.

All of that is background noise though. My eyes pass over it all quickly and then land on the dead girl on the couch. She was maybe twenty-five, twenty-six. Caribbean with South Asian roots. Permed black hair frames her bloated face, tongue bulging, makeup smeared, eyes glassy, empty. One arm hangs over the edge of the couch, knuckles just grazing the ground. She's in Snoopy pajama pants and a Yankees tank top. There's an upside-down bowl of cereal by her side and a small island of milk seeping into the carpet.

"Diana, the roommate, found her an hour ago," Reza says, nodding at the crying woman. "She's . . . she was one of ours."

Rohan crosses to the far end of the room and folds his arms over his chest. In seconds, the chuckling chauffeur has become an unfuckwithable foot soldier.

I approach the body. "Do we know anything?"

"We were together last night," Diana says, sniffling back tears and snot. She has an oversized John Jay sweatshirt on and librarian glasses. "Had dinner at the Rosebud, and we were talking about how we were gonna make ends meet now that Charo's shutting things down. We both got tuition, and even when Shelly gets her MSW, what kind of salary does a social worker make? Ugh! I guess it doesn't . . . matter now . . ." She teeters on the edge of falling apart again, but doesn't. "I had a client last night, saying good-bye more than anything, tying up loose ends, and I stayed over. Shelly said she was just gonna go home and read; you know she loves those romance novels. Then I had class today and errands and . . . and . . . and then I came home and . . ." She shakes her head, face contorting into an ugly cry, but no sound comes out.

"You called nine-one-one?"

"She called us," Reza says. "Fortunately. Can you get anything from the body?"

"I can try." I kneel beside the couch.

"Memo," Reza says to the heavy at the window, "take Diana to the base. She doesn't need to see this."

He nods and helps the roommate gather herself. When they leave, Reza says: "This is Shelly, Carlos. The one from . . ."

I nod. I'd figured as much. "She's been strangled."

Reza nods. "But look at the marks."

I tip her chin up. Two tiny handprints discolor either side of her throat. "Shit," I whisper.

Reza considers me for a moment and then looks at the older guy on the computer. "Rolando, do you have what you need?"

"Oh yeah, got plenty here to work with."

"Alright, head back in with Memo and the girl." Rolando packs up quick and leaves. "Bri?"

The woman at the table grimaces at the handwritten pages of a small book. "Nothing going on in the journal so far," she reports.

"Keep looking," Reza says. "Carlos?"

"I'm on it." I close my eyes. Clearing the sobbing girl out of here opened up the space to me. All that shock and sorrow was getting in the way. What's left is Reza's cool efficiency, the jumbled diary entries Bri's browsing, Rohan's brooding stillness.

I place one hand on Shelly's cool forehead. Her last gasping moment blasts through me: something is off in the apartment; it's darker than it should be. No one else is home, but it doesn't feel that way. There's a presence. She sits, picks up the bowl of cereal she'd poured herself, takes a spoonful. Drops the spoon. Drops the bowl. Throat throbs with dull pain, breath gone. Holy terror courses through me, Shelly.

As she collapses in slow motion against the pillows, a face flickers in front of hers: a child, mouth twisted, eyes sunken back and wild. It's just a flash, and then everything goes black.

"Wait a minute," Bri says from the table. I grunt as I pull sharply back to reality.

"You okay, Carlos?" Reza asks.

I blink to clear the little spots dancing across my vision. "Fine."

"What you got, Bri?"

"Bugs." She holds up the journal. Crude drawings of cockroaches sprawl across the pages.

"Date?" Reza asks.

"It's from two months ago."

Reza crosses the room in a single long step and grabs the diary. "Fuck." She flips a few pages ahead and holds it up to me. More roaches.

"Fuck," I say.

"If it was before everything that went down," Bri says. "How . . . ?"

"She'd seen them before," Reza says. "Carlos?"

"I can try. No promises."

"Rohan," Reza says. "Poke around the boxes in her closet. See if there are any journals from earlier on."

I turn back to the corpse, shake my head. It's hard enough pulling last memories out of bodies. Two-month-old memories? This'll take some digging.

The most recent horror is a blur of gunshots in the darkness, screams, and the sense of a thousand creatures swarming from the deep. A dingy filter coats a cloudy street; Shelly's more remote memories look like they were filmed with an old movie camera through a dirty window. It's night. A white man in a suit walks beside her; his grasp on her forearm is too tight, his gait fast. He wants what he paid for. A light drizzle begins, and they duck into an alleyway and Shelly drops to her knees, fumbles with his fly.

Daylight blasts through the blinds; head pounding, Shelly stumbles into the kitchen, fusses with the dishes. Shelly in a wide-open garage, arguing with a stocky, tense-looking cat. He's not arguing back though, just shaking his head. Shelly at the movies, some rom-com where pretty white people fall in love, fall out of love, make speeches, fall in love again. Shelly on the toilet, studying. Shelly on the bus. Shelly bored out of her mind in class, trying to stay awake. Shelly riding another businessman, then another. Shelly with two men at once; neither of them can get it up and they both sulk and rage around the room at her. Shelly crying in the bathroom mirror. Shelly meditating. Shelly laughing with two other women at the Rosebud at daybreak. Shelly calling someone whose voice sounds very old and far away, talking about how well school is going. Shelly watching TV texting falling asleep to the sound of rain walking beneath the tracks lighting a clove ciga—

"Carlos!"

"Guh." The coffee table cracks against my back as I surge away from the body. I get up quick. Too quick—the world goes fuzzy for a few seconds, and I'm about to eat floor again when Reza puts a firm hand on my arm and eases me into a recliner.

She glares her question at me.

"I'm alright. And no . . . I went back months and nothing. No roaches. Something like that would've leapt out at me, unmissable."

"So it happened before. Why didn't she tell us?"

At the table, Rohan and Bri comb through a stack of cutesy inspirational journals.

"There's roach drawings in all of 'em so far," Bri reports. "Like, every couple months, all the sudden, it'll just be roaches." She holds up one, and you can tell from the swirly handwriting it must be from when she was a schoolkid.

Reza grunts and pulls a phone out of her jacket pocket.

"Yes?" She smirks and holds the phone out to me. "It's the twelve-year-old that doesn't want you to give her number out to us bitches."

I hold the phone away from my ear until Kia finishes her deluge of curses. "You done?"

"Not nearly, but I'll finish later."

"Thanks."

"I got an address for you."

"Oh?"

"1254 Sunnyside Lane, Queens."

I fumble for a scrap of paper and scribble it down. "What is it?"

"Where Tartus first started his tunnel work. And the payer address for all the other projects."

"Well, shit." I stand up.

"Weird thing is," Kia says, "that's, like, right around the area I lived for a couple years when I was a kid."

"That is weird. Real suburban, right?"

"Yeah." Kia takes a breath like she's about to say something, then doesn't.

"What?"

"Nothing."

"Kia, what?"

"I'll tell you later. It's too much to get into now."

"You okay?"

"Chillin'. Dr. Tennessee talking my ear off about John Coltrane or some shit, but I'll be alright."

In the background I hear the old librarian cough a laugh.

"Be careful, Kia."

"I'm fine, C. I gotta head off to capoeira anyway. Don't worry about me."

She hangs up, and I look at Reza. "Feel like a drive to Queens?"

"Always," Reza says with a disarming grin. "But I have a meeting to hit up first."

"Ooh, I love meetings. Can I come?"

"You could, but we'd literally have to kill you."

"I actually hate meetings anyway. I was kidding."

"I know. I wasn't. There's a taco spot around the corner from the garage though. You can hang out there till we're done."

CHAPTER SIXTEEN

Reza

A few years ago, Rohan rolled up into the garage in one of those massive Access-A-Ride vans the city uses to cart around folks too old for the regular buses. "City marshal auction," he replied to our collective what-the-fuck faces. "Someone had been smuggling drugs with it and they impounded the sucka, and now it's mine—uh, ours!"

Charo, always the tactical genius, let loose a rare smile. "Well done," he said. A week later, it was painted black and the tall windows and windshield were tinted and bullet-proofed. Charo presented it to us with a bottle of champagne. "Behold, the Partymobile."

"It's like an unstoppable death tank," Bri gaped. "But fun!"

Tonight the Partymobile is represented by a black circle that Charo has scribbled on a set of building plans tacked to the wall. "And that," he says, leaning over the table at us, "as they say, is that."

A heavy pause follows; then Bri says, "Damn."

A tangle of arrows and stars covers the plans behind Charo, and for a second he looks like some demonic saint, haloed by his own tangled plots of destruction. "Any questions?"

Rohan, who had been reclining on the back two legs of

his chair, leans in with his chin on one hand. "I mean, I have one: what the fuck, man?"

I cringe a little inside. Rohan's just about the only dude that can get away with talking to Charo that way, and that's only because Charo knows that's simply how Rohan talks. Still . . . I cringe.

Instead of blowing Rohan's head off, Charo smiles slightly and crosses his arms over his chest. "Problem?"

"No." Rohan shakes his head, eyebrows raised and lips pushed out. "That's just a helluva fuckin' shootout you got us in."

Memo snorts. "You can't handle it, man? That's alright. We'll go withou—"

"That's not what I said," Rohan snarls.

"Enough." Charo's smile is gone. "It's true, this is the most ambitious assault we've launched. And as you may have noticed, we've taken a turn as an organization. I've effectively shut down the prostitution ring, recalled our dealers. We're no longer going to be sitting passively waiting for whichever random conjunto of thugs decides to try to get cute on our territory next. We're taking the war to them."

"Fuck yeah," Bri says quietly.

"So coming up, you can expect more operations along these lines." Charo nods at the board. "If anyone has a problem with that, speak now and you can walk after this attack. No dishonor, no disrespect. You have my word we won't kill you so long as the words spoken here remain here and only here. Is that clear?"

Grunts and nods.

"Anyone want out?"

"Hell no," Rohan says. "We've all been waiting for this type shit for years."

"I'm in," Bri says.

Memo slaps the table unnecessarily. "You already know 'bout me, jefe."

Charo and I exchange a glance, the slightest of nods.

"Good," Charo says. "Any other questions?"

"Who are these cats we 'bouta kill?" Bri asks.

Charo closes his eyes, frowns. "Doesn't matter."

"Matters to us," Rohan says.

Charo shrugs. "It's a meeting. Two of them work for a conglomerate of multinationals that's building a free-trade zone in Central America. The other side is a guy repping the Solos, a paramilitary group down there that's been cleansing out whole villages for a few decades now in the name of—I don't know, whatever -ismo is popular that year. Seems the two parties realized their interests intersect and they decided to formalize things. But of course, e-mails aren't secure, and they're not gonna talk on the phone. They have to face-to-face it. The Barracudas brokered the sit-down and are doing security."

"Wait." Bri raises her hand. "The Barracudas brought us in, so there's a trail, no? What happens when . . . ?"

Charo shakes his head. "There's no trail."

"How . . . ?"

"Both the conglomerate and the warlords need this to be on lockdown for obvious reasons. No records, no communications, no nothin'. Barracudas are providing the space—their safe house out on the Island, security, and . . ."

"Entertainment," I finish.

"Right."

"The 'cudas got their own girls," Bri says. "Why they outsourcin' to us if . . . ?"

"Because," Charo says with a scowl, "they probably figure the girls will get wiped out when it's all over. And they probably figured right. Wouldn't be surprised if the conglomerate plans to wipe them out too, actually, but maybe the 'cudas think they're ready for 'em. I dunno. Doesn't matter really, cuz we're gonna wipe 'em all out."

———————

Later, when the room has cleared, Charo and I sit in silence for a few minutes, staring at the map of the Barracudas' compound.

"There's something else going on," I say. "Why are we starting with this group?"

Charo sighs. "Same people that took out my village."

A few more moments of silence slip past, and I think about all the chaos and hell we'll unleash in a few hours. "You don't wanna . . . take part yourself? Sometimes it helps."

He smiles, a warm and loving smile, looking suddenly very old. "The actual ones involved? I handled that. These guys weren't there that day. They're part of the same paramilitary group. And the people that funded them."

"So why even bother . . . ?"

"They're part of the same paramilitary group." He says it curtly, all warmth gone. "And the people that funded them."

CHAPTER SEVENTEEN

Kia

Man, fuck Carlos.

I put my phone away. "Dr. Tennessee, can I ask you something?"

"You wanna know how I'm sixty with the ass of a twenty-year-old?"

She's right though: that ass a ten. "I mean, one day, I would like to get that info out you, yes . . ." Dr. Tennessee looks a little crestfallen. We sit across from each other at a foldout table amid the forest of archival stacks. Garrick Tartus's paper trail lies splayed out between us. "Do you believe the dead watch over us and protect us?"

She squints and moves her mouth around like she's chewing something sour. "I guess they might. I mean, that's what the stories say, right? But the stories also talk about haints and other undesirable-type dead fools that come around and fuck with the living, right?"

"I guess."

"So really, I think if the dead do come back, and they pretty much act like the living in the sense that they do what they damn well please, then there ain't no one thing they do or don't do." She pauses, glaring up at the dim overheads like the answer waits in their buzzing glow. "Just like with everything," she finishes.

I sigh. Pack up the papers.

"Not much help, I know."

"Nah, it's alright. I just . . . I guess I got a lot going on right now."

"I see." The librarian nods at my black eye.

"Oh, this? Ha—this the least of my worries, trust." I think about Rigo for a second, that wily smile and the way he towers over me. That bulge. If I leave now, I can make it to capoeira more or less on time. "No, I mean . . . I mean, do you pray?"

Dr. Tennessee smiles, stands. "In a sense." We head through the stacks, a slow meander. "When I see a fine, fine woman, I close my eyes and say thank you. That's a kind of prayer, right? I do the same when I see a fine-ass man too, but that's so rare these days. Men ain't shit really, 'cept one or two, and aintshitness will make a fine man foul."

"Word up."

"When you get to be my age, you can smell it on 'em. And when I'm working my ass off in here for hours and finally look up and I'm surrounded by all these papers and stories and information and history, I say thank you. Then I come out here." We step into the dimming open-air corridor. "And light one up."

"A cigarette or a phatty?"

Dr. Tennessee shrugs. "Depends what kinda day I've had. But either way, when the smoke rises up to that little glint of sky, I say thank you. I consider that smoke a prayer. Even though it'll kill me one day, it's still sacred."

"Damn."

"The Yoruba have a saying: Once there was a man who didn't pray; then he was dead."

"Well, shit."

She shrugs. "So I pray."

We cross to the door of the main library, and Dr. Tennessee lights one up. It's a cigarette, so I guess it hasn't been too rough a day. "But I don't know who that prayer goes to. I never caught a name; ain't no face. Doesn't matter really, right? I just say thank you."

I smile at the librarian. "I think I understand."

She pats me on the shoulder. "Good luck out there."

There's a ghost on the A train.

All the other commuters must sense it too, because even though it's rush hour, this car is empty except for me and an old sleeping guy. And the ghost. It pulsates in the air above the old guy; I can make out great hulking shoulders, a mountainous back. It just hangs there, heaving with silent sobs. I stand very slowly and walk to the far end of the train.

At the next stop, I switch cars.

"Girl!" Karina squeals when I walk in. Everyone's partnered up and whacking at each other with sticks.

I'm mad late—it's a solid forty-five minutes into an hour-long class—but Rigo still looks up and flashes that come-sit-on-my-face grin when he sees me. Or maybe that's just his regular grin. Either way, I'm inclined to go sit on his face. I wave across the gym at him and apologize.

"It's okay!" Rigo yells. Everyone looks up and snickers. Fuck 'em.

"You aight?" Karina asks. Devon takes a swing at her with the sticks when she's not looking, but she blocks it anyway.

"What the hell!" Devon whines.

"Predictable ass."

"I'm cool," I say. "Just . . . it's been a long day."

"I see. I was worried about you after you ran off at the park last night. And then that creepy-ass dude went after you and fell out and then you weren't answering ya phone . . . What the hell's going on, girl?"

I shake my head. "Don't even know where to begin."

Rigo claps twice and everyone gathers in a circle around him. I gotta say, for this only being day two, he's made this impossible crowd pretty obedient. It's probably 'cause they all either angling to fuck him or taking notes on the suave, but whatever works, right?

"You have done good work today, yes?"

"Yep," Mikey B. says.

Kelly punches his shoulder. "It was rhetorical, arrogant ass."

"Hello?" Rigo says.

"Sorry," they both mumble.

"As I was saying, you are improved, yes? Yes. But . . ." He raises his eyebrows like even he is surprised by what he's about to say. "There is a long way ahead before you become true capoeira warriors."

Jerome curses under his breath. Guess he thought he was already there.

"Kia," Rigo says from across the room.

I freeze. Karina narrows her eyes at me.

"Can I espeak with you for a second, please?"

Everyone goes, "oooooooh," because I guess we're all really ten years old after all. I try to fight back the blush that I'm sure is blossoming across my face.

"Ay, girl," Karina says.

"I'm sure he just wants to discuss my tardiness, is all."

"Roight."

I scrunch up my face at her and cross the room to Rigo. My ears apparently catch fire on the way, so that's annoying.

He looks down at me, smiles warmly. "Are you okay, Kia? I still feel so bad that I kicked you in the face yesterday."

"I'm fine." I try not to squirm. "Thanks for asking. It's nothing really. And now we're twinsies!"

Rigo looks concerned. "What?"

Why do I open my mouth and say words though? Why?

"Twinsies." I point to the black-and-blue still shining on his perfect cheek. "Like, the same. We match." If I cringe any deeper, I'll crawl up inside myself.

"Ah, yes! Ha-ha! Yes. But this is, this is just a silly. Don't worry about this, yes?"

"Yes." I would like to die now.

"Anyway, the reason I asked you here is that . . ."

"I'm really sorry I was late today, Rigo. I was in Harlem and—"

"No, it's okay, Kia. It's fine. That's not what I was asking you."

"Oh?"

"I want to make sure you have understanding of the moves, yes? I want you to be a capoeira warrior, Kia."

I want to be a capoeira warrior too, shit. Sign my ass up. I nod.

"It's, how do you say . . . conhecimentos indispensáveis."

"Indispensable knowledge," I say. I picked up Spanish pretty quickly, so I started doing my homework in Portuguese a year or two ago. It's pretty straightforward, once you have one romance language down, to pick up another.

Rigo raises his eyebrows. "Wow! I did not expect that! Ah, listen, I hope this is not inappropriate, but I would like to teach you more in depth. Okay? Here."

He hands me a business card. There's an address written on the back. My words gridlock in my throat and none make it out.

"You come?"

Hopefully not this second. "Okay," I mumble.

"Tonight?"

"Sure," I say. "Tonight."

That winning smile. Efferfuckingvescent, Carlos would probably say. "See you then, Kia."

And he's gone, and I'm standing in a cloud of his too-much cologne, panting.

CHAPTER EIGHTEEN

Carlos

As soon as the door opens, I understand what Reza meant earlier about me not being able to lie. When I do my cop impersonation, I just throw a little extra snarl into my already dour demeanor. For all I know, people are more intimidated than convinced. It's functional grumpiness, that's it. The absolute personality makeover that Reza evinces when Mrs. Fern greets us on her doorstep: art.

"Good evening and sorry to bother you, Mrs. Fern," says the chipper person next to me that used to be Reza. "I'm Detective Jimenez"—she uses the Anglo *J* so Mrs. Fern can deduce she's one of the assimilated ones—"and this is my partner, Detective Morris." She flashes her fake badge and I flash mine; then she grabs Mrs. Fern's hand and shakes it vigorously. "Don't mind him. He's not very touchy-feely—you know how men are!" Reza giggles, and I almost drop my cover to boggle at her. Then Mrs. Fern giggles too.

I'm impressed.

"We are so sorry to trouble you on this lovely evening," Reza goes on.

"Oh, not at all, dear," Mrs. Fern says. She's in her mid-sixties, and wearing lovely pearls over a pink-and-yellow sweater. A perfectly coiffed halo of recently dyed hair surrounds her sagging face. "Richard and I just got back from dinner with some friends. I do hope everything is alright?"

"Golden Temple?" Reza says.

"Sorry?"

"The Chinese spot on Sunnyside. The one with the koi fish tanks in the windows. Their vegetarian wonton soup is unparalleled. There is no comparison."

"Oh!" Mrs. Fern giggles again. "I'll have to try that! I usually get their pad thai. You know, sometimes the Chinese out-Thai the Thai, so to speak."

Reza chuckles. I nod and smile.

"No, we went for sushi around the corner on 156. Phenomenal. An absolute delight."

"That's outstanding," Reza says, and then she sighs. "So, won't take up any more of your time; Detective Morris and I are on the Community Affairs Task Force, and we're organizing a committee of neighborhood volunteers to consult with developing a security affairs group."

"Oh dear," Mrs. Fern says. "Has something gone wrong?" She glances at the quiet street behind us.

"Ah, well, you know how this generation has become. Hip-hop music and saggy pants leads to petty offenses and marijuana-smoking, of course, and that's what we call gateway delinquency, as I'm sure you know."

"Of course. Oh dear."

"So, we don't want to alarm you. There's nothing to actually be alarmed about, just a recent uptick in marijuana-related arrests and some possible connections to more nefarious influences, including one international drug cartel, unfortunately."

Mrs. Fern pales. "Goodness!"

"Our thoughts exactly. So, a few other community members mentioned you and Richard as folks who would possibly be helpful in this measure."

"Of course. We'd be delighted to. I'm sure you spoke to the Blacks—oh!" She giggles. "The family I mean, of course, not the actual blacks."

Reza grins knowingly. "Of course, and of course we did. The Blacks have been very helpful. Anyway, it's late; we don't want to take up any more of your time, but . . ."

"No, please," Mrs. Fern says. "Come in!"

Sadness dampens the air in the Ferns' house. It's basically your standard suburban American home—a carpeted hallway leading off to the kitchen, photos grinning off the wall, a slightly worn couch and easy chair in the living room, a stairway up to the second floor. But it's sadder. That heaviness just hangs there, an entity unto itself.

Richard Fern strolls out of the kitchen with a cup of tea. "Who is it, Evelyn? Oh, hi!" He has a comb-over, light brown slacks, loafers, and an expensive watch.

"It's the police, dear. They say there've been some druggers in the neighborhood."

"Well, dang," Richard says. "I mean, you know how kids are, of course." He gives me a firm handshake, and I'm glad Reza convinced me to wear these leather gloves. "Good to meet you."

"Likewise," I say. "I'm Detective Morris. This is my partner—"

"Detective Jimenez," Reza cuts in with that grating pronunciation. She gives Richard's hand a hearty shake. "Great to meet ya and so sorry for the trouble."

"None at all," Richard says. "Anything we can do to help. Matter of fact, why don't you all step upstairs into my home office. We can talk there."

"Outstanding," Reza says. "You guys go ahead. I wonder if I could trouble you for the use of your little girls' room, Mrs. Fern."

"Please, Detective, call me Evelyn," Mrs. Fern clucks. "And of course, dear, just to the left at the end of the hall there."

Reza smiles and disappears down the hallway. Richard and Evelyn Fern lead me upstairs.

"Of course, ever since Jeremy disappeared," Evelyn says, shaking her head, "we've been as involved as we can be in the community." They sit side by side, their hands interlaced. Richard's office is cluttered with degrees, paperwork, a few file cabinets, and a gorgeous mahogany desk. A stunning photograph of some waterfall in Brazil takes up most of one wall. "The therapists all said, when you've lost a child, you can either disappear from the world or you can take part." She smiles at her husband, eyes glassy. "We decided to take part."

I have no idea how we got to this episode of *Carlos, Fix My Life,* but here we are. I barely said anything, just asked some bullshit perfunctory questions to give Reza time to do whatever she's doing down there. At least they're talking.

"It hasn't been easy," Richard says. "And of course it was especially hard on Caitlin."

"Caitlin?"

"Oh, that's our daughter," Evelyn says. "Jeremy's twin."

"Ah. Must've been very difficult for her, I'm sure." Is that what people say to those who've lost loved ones? The words seem stunningly pathetic, considering what we're talking about.

Evelyn sighs. "Just awful. She struggled, but she's really made a turnaround since those years after Jeremy died. First in her class at Yale. Now she's the executive vice-president at Adopt the World."

"That's a . . . ?"

"Adopt the World provides adoption services to the most

war-torn, impoverished countries," Richard says. Guess he memorized the flyers. "Real terrible stuff." Head shaking, brow creased, eyes faraway. "I mean, just . . . awful. But you know, they say if you want to heal yourself, you have to start by healing the world."

"Isn't it the other way around?"

Richard frowns, and then Reza walks in with the Ferns' cordless phone in one hand and a file full of papers and a framed family photograph in the other. "Call him," Reza says. She's back, the Reza I know and really like, and she's not fucking around.

"Excuse me?" Richard says.

"And where did you get that file?" Evelyn demands. "Have you been—"

Reza gets up in Richard's face and shoves the phone into his hand. "Call. Him."

Richard glares at us. "Who are you people? What the hell do you . . . ?"

"Stop speaking," Reza says. She says it quietly, but Richard gleans the threat in it and actually shuts the fuck up, to my surprise. Reza looks at me. "Give me your cane, please."

I hand it over, and she immediately unsheathes the blade. Richard and Evelyn Fern gasp. She puts the business end a few centimeters from Richard's nose and then says: "Call your son."

Evelyn sobs, her face shriveled into itself like a scrunched-up paper bag that's wearing too much makeup. Reza hands me the file and the photo. It's from a while back: Richard and Evelyn grinning widely and the twins in front of them: Caitlin is all teeth and dimples, baby fat carried over into early adolescence, and Jeremy—tall and lanky, arms crossed over his chest, head slightly tilted.

"Our son is dead," Richard says, raising his hand. "And you have no right . . ." Reza flicks her wrist, and the blade slices open a bright red line across Richard's forearm.

Richard gasps. "Jesus!" Evelyn yells. She jumps up, finds herself face-to-face with the blade, and sits back down. "How . . . ? What kind of! Richard!"

Richard stares at his arm, mouth open. He looks at Reza.

"Make the call," Reza says. "Put it on speaker. Tell him there's an emergency and you need him to come over. Fuck it up, cry for help, call nine-one-one instead: Evelyn eats sword. Clear?"

Richard's eyes look like they might pop out of his head at any moment. He nods, mouth still hanging open, while Evelyn quietly sobs.

Me? I just sit there and look surly. Ain't shit I can do but play along at this point, although Reza's turned into more of a wild card than I could've imagined.

Richard pushes a button and the speed dial blips out a number in quick succession. Slick-ass. After two rings, someone picks up, but there's only silence on the other end. Then a ragged breath.

"J-Jeremy?" Richard says.

Another breath, long and tortured.

"Jeremy, your mother and I need you to come over to the house. Tonight. Something's come up, I'm afraid. It's important. I know we haven't . . ." Tears pour down his face, and he has to pause to compose himself. "Sorry. I know we haven't seen you in a few years, but this is important. Okay? We need to see you, son." He closes his eyes. "I'm sorry."

One more shuddering breath fills the room and then the call ends. Richard drops the phone and stands. "Now, we did what you . . ." Then he opens his mouth to scream because Reza's raised my blade over her shoulder like she's waiting for the pitch. She swings, slicing clean across his neck. Richard's voice cuts off midsqueal. His throat gapes open, his light blue shirt suddenly bright crimson. He's dead before he hits the floor.

I jump to my feet. Evelyn Fern stands, opens her mouth

to scream, and then Reza slices across her neck too and she drops.

"What the fuck?" I say when my voice finally returns to me. "Wh-why?"

Reza's already on the ground, doing something to the bodies. She mutters a few words over each, eyes closed, and then says, "Because people tend to notice gunshots in these parts."

"I mean . . . why though?"

"Open the file."

Photos, printed out from a computer. They're all taken from across the street or through a crowd, stalker-style. It's all folks I don't know until . . . "Kia!" There's Kia in Von King Park, talking to a tall, overweight kid. There she's crossing Marcy Ave., backpack on, probably heading to school or the rec center. There she is laughing with her friend Karina.

"And the next one," Reza says. I flip ahead and find Shelly lighting a cigarette outside her apartment. Shelly running to catch the B37. Shelly talking on a cell phone in front of a bodega.

"Shit," I say. There are more pictures. Many more.

Reza wipes the blade on Richard's sweater and hands it back to me, handle first. "And that family photo. The boy."

I close the file with a shudder, look at the framed picture. "Jeremy Fern?"

"That's the long-armed motherfucker in the tunnel I told you about," Reza says.

I squint as the pieces come together. "Jeremy disappeared seven years ago and really became the ringleader of some maniac insect cult? And his parents knew the whole time?"

"Not just knew, clearly . . . Caitlin too, I'm sure."

"And now he's coming here? So we can . . . ?"

"End this shit."

"I mean, I get that, but did we have to . . . ? Have you no code?"

Reza stops what she's doing and looks up at me. "Angie," she says. "That's my code. Now, give me a hand."

We work in silence, rolling the bodies into rugs from the bedroom. We're lugging the second heavy bundle down the front stairwell when Reza says, "Carlos, when I said my code was Angie, that was . . ." She shakes her head. "That's true, but that's only part of it. I do have a code, a real one. And rule number one is cut shit off at the roots. I know to you it looks like what I did was wrong because we weren't under attack, but this is what I've learned from my years on the street—this is what I've learned from war: if you're going to kill a thing, kill it dead. If you half step, you'll be the dead one. That's it."

I nod. It's all still spiraling around my brain too fast to make heads or tails of. We round the corner at the landing. Beads of sweat slide down my brow, my back.

"And you also knew," Reza says between pants, "if you think hard enough about it, that they had to go from the moment we dropped cover."

"*You* dropped cover," I point out. Then I feel sort of childish. It's true though.

"Right. Point is, you think they weren't going to call the NYPD the second we walked out the door? They would've. And then we would've had explaining to do, if they caught us. And out here, cops come quick when they're called. So they mighta. And I don't know about you, but I got a trunk full of guns that I don't need the five-o asking questions about. Not to mention the charge for impersonating a police officer is no small thing. And you—you got ID, Carlos?"

I grunt a "no" as we reach the first floor. "And you know I don't. I still . . ."

"Do you know what they did to Angie, Carlos? They opened her up. Dr. Tijou told me there were eggs in her lungs, her stomach, all through her trachea and esophagus. Roach eggs, Carlos. She'd been tortured." Reza pauses for a moment as we angle the body right to get through the basement door. "She was still alive when they put those things inside her, C. I wish she'd had someone end her as quickly as I ended the Ferns. And all of that shit happened to her because these people let it happen. They've been covering for this monster all along. And clearly someone in this house is plotting on Kia and had Shelly killed. You see the look on Mr. Fern's face when he knew the shtick was up?" We clomp down the concrete stairwell. "Mrs. Fern too. They both know, they been knowing. They carry it with them. I'm sure the sister knows too. I get that you see innocent suburban America when you look at the Fern family, Carlos, but I need you to work past that delusion and see it for what it is."

The Ferns' basement is pristine. What kind of maniac has a pristine basement? Empty boxes are stacked neatly against one wall. A washer and dryer, immaculate, glisten in the far corner. There's a pool table in the center and a few lawn chairs set up under the one small window. At the other end, they've put up a little office area: a desk with some paperwork and a desktop computer on it. We lay Evelyn's carpet-wrapped body beside her husband's and then lean against the pool table to catch our breath.

"I understand," I say. "But you came outta nowhere with it. I had no idea 'bout all that."

"I know. I haven't worked with you before and I couldn't be sure you'd play along right." She pauses, shuffles her feet. "Sorry 'bout that."

I dig out a Malagueña, put it in my mouth but don't light it. "I just . . . The last time I took a life, a living one, I mean . . . I mean, mostly living—it never left me, is all. I'm still living the fallout of that kill, Reza."

"I understand," she says, her eyes looking suddenly weary. "Believe me. And believe me when I tell you this had to happen." Reza goes into a black duffel bag beside the bodies—she must've run out to the car for it when she was snooping around. She takes a Glock from the bag and holds it out to me, handle first.

"I don't really . . ." I say.

"What?"

"Not my style."

"Take it anyway. Try for headshots; seems to drop them quicker."

I nod, take the gun. It's too heavy and awkward in my hands. I tuck it into my pants and already feel it jacking up my rhythm.

"And I'm sorry I used your blade. If we'da done it down here, I would've used my guns. This place is soundproofed."

"How can you—"

"Extra-thick glass on the windows, that slanted angle they at, the sealing around 'em. The door is big enough to shut in a meat locker. They designed this room for *activities*."

"So now we . . . ?

Reza's already halfway up the stairs. "Now," she says, slamming the giant door at the top. "We wait." She clicks off the light. "And then young Jeremy will show up and work his way through the house, come down here, and we handle him."

It's darker than I'm comfortable with, but those windows near the ceiling would announce a lit-up basement in a dark house and ruin the whole thing. In my mind, the bodies at my feet loom large, take over the whole floor, stand up and walk around. Reza's beside me, rustling through her bag again.

"Rule number two is always be prepared. Now, take this." She hands me a little flashlight attached to a headband. "And this." A ski mask and some goggles. I put them on. "Now, hold still." She shakes a can of something and then sprays it directly into my face and all over my head and body. "It's extra-strength. DDT-out this bitch."

"Yay cancer."

She sprays herself down.

"And there's a corollary to that one." She stands, and now that my eyes have adjusted to the half-light, I can see she has a double-barreled sawed-off shotgun in her hands. "Never be outgunned. Anyway," Reza says, her own flashlight lighting up narrow pockets of the floor as she crosses toward the office end of the basement, "this gives me time to look over whatever they've been working on down here."

I light the Malagueña and lean against the pool table, trying to ignore the creeping, endless darkness around me.

I can't decide whether something is actually crawling around on the ceiling or if my troubled mind is just making shit up. Then a pale quarter-sized shape skitters across the patch of light thrown by the computer screen and disappears into the shadows. "Fuck," I mutter. "Reza."

There goes another. And another. I turn on the flashlight strapped to my head, and five of them scatter from the sudden glow on the ceiling.

I draw my blade. "Reza!"

"Hang on, Carlos. I'm onto something over here. They got more photos on this computer. I think it's Caitlin's and—"

"We got roaches, Rez. Lotta them."

"Well, kill them. I'll be right there."

I follow the line of skittering monsters back to the stack of boxes.

"Looks like they plotting on some of your people, Carlos."

"What?"

"This dude looks half dead like you."

I'm across the room in seconds, and there on the screen in front of Reza is Gregorio Franco, the gray-skinned man with the beard and fedora I'd seen Sasha meet with when I was trailing her. "Shit."

Reza moves out the way. "Let me go see 'bout this roach situation."

There's a few more shots of Gregorio, crossing a street, talking on a pay phone. And then I click on the next one and my breath catches.

Sasha.

She's carrying a baby in one arm, *our* baby. And she's pushing a stroller. There's a baby in the stroller. *Our* baby.

"Carlos," Reza says. "We have a problem."

There are two babies. We have two babies. Twins. They are tiny and round and brown and perfect. And they're ours. I . . . We have twins. Baby twins. Twin babies. Sasha's hair is pulled back into a bun. She's glancing sideways, looking fierce and beautiful as always. She wears a long jacket and a red blouse, jeans, and boots. Looks like she's in Brooklyn, but I can't place where.

"Carlos," Reza says again. "There's . . . Fuck. There's a door back here."

I have babies. Two of them. And they're being watched. Fuck.

Behind me, Reza yells, "Fuck!" and I swing around to see boxes fly away from the wall as she raises her shotgun. A wooden door swings open, and a man steps forward from the shadows. The blast rips out and devours this tiny dark world: everything echoes with it. The man flies backward and a thousand small shapes flutter out of the doorway. Another figure appears, and I hear the *chuk-chuk*ing reload of Reza's weapon.

These monsters want to destroy my family, my friends. My babies. Reza blasts again as I'm crossing the room. Two more of the roach men already clamber forward over the shattered remnants of their brethren, but they don't get far. My upswing catches the first one, cleaving a dark red gash across his midsection. He drops as my blade comes down on the second; it opens up his shoulder, and my next cut leaves his head dangling from a torn thread of cartilage.

The air fills with pale flying monstrosities. I swat through

them as a fifth and sixth roach man appear. One vanishes
into the shadows at the far end of the room before either of
us can get at him. Reza slow-steps into the darkness after
him, shotgun poised. I close on the doorway, where the other
stands watching.

He hurls toward me, arms swinging, and I catch him
midstride with a cross-body slice. The man spins and collapses, roaches exploding to either side, and I throw myself
out of the way.

"Reza?" I yell. They've moved into the far end of the
basement, and I can't make out shit for all these flying fuckers and the encroaching shadows.

"Hang on." She grunts, and I hear a dull crunch and then
the sound of a body dropping.

"Reza!"

"I'm alright. Just too close to blast him without getting
got too." I hear another thwack and then another and the air
gets even thicker with roaches. A few land on me and I brush
them off and then spin a wild circle, patting at my clothes,
and whirl directly into another tall pale man as he emerges
from the tunnel.

"Fuck!" is the only word that I get out before he smacks
my blade to the ground, and then his cool hands find my
throat and roaches surge along my neck and up my face,
under the mask. If I open my mouth to scream, I'll be inun-
dated. The world quickly becomes gray and cloudy.

Another figure steps out behind the one choking me, and
I hear Reza yell. The face staring into mine is emotionless,
pale, dead. I try to smash it, miss. A diamond-shaped chunk
of flesh detaches and adjusts its evil little body before settling back in.

Darkness begins to close in.

And then I remember Reza's gun, which I'd tucked into
my waistband. My hands scramble around it, retrieve it, and
put it under the man's chin. I don't close my eyes when I pull

the trigger; I want to see it. The blast throws his head back, shattering bits of flesh and skull as roaches burst outward. I drop to the ground, shaking. Brace myself against the pool table and stumble to my feet. Swat roaches or my own frantic imagination. Everything is alive and crawling.

Reza.

I look up just in time to see her bring the butt of her sawed-off across another roach man's face, spin the gun around, and then blast his head off. The image of Sasha and our babies flashes through my mind. The whole world goes dark red, and it's their blood that I won't stop spilling now that I've started; it's a red that's the promise I'll destroy every single one of these living parasites until there's none left to hurt the people I love.

I'm on my feet; my blade crashes down on another one as he launches out the door toward me. I free it from his flesh and stab directly into his chest, then kick him back into the tunnel. There's another waiting in the shadows and another behind that one. I flush forward, slicing, catching bits of flesh as roaches flutter and dance in the darkness around me.

"Carlos!" Reza's yelling, her voice hoarse. "We gotta . . . We gotta get the fuck outta here."

I don't want to leave.

I want to kill.

I slash again, take off an arm. A gathering crowd of roach men whistle and chirp as they rush forward, then stumble back from my blade. Reza's arm wraps around my shoulder from behind. "We can't, Carlos. We can't do this alone. You can't do this alone. We gotta get out of here, man."

She reaches past me, Glock in hand, and fires four times, crumbling a roach man with each shot. In the shadows beyond them, more skitter toward us.

She's right.

"Carlos, come on. I got something for 'em anyway."

I pull back, step over the fallen roach men and the rug-rolled

Ferns. "Get ready to run," Reza says. Halfway up the stairs she tosses something into the basement below. Three, now four of the roach men burst out of the tunnel and lurch toward us. The object Reza threw lands with a clink and then explodes with a sharp bang. Thick gray smoke fills the basement as the roach men scatter to either direction.

"Tear gas?" I ask, covering my nose.

Reza shakes her head. "Insecticide. Made 'em myself." She pulls out a silver lighter when we reach the ground floor. "Also, highly flammable." She lights it and tosses it down the stairs, slamming the door after it.

"Rule number three," Reza says as we run the fuck outta there. "Burn the whole shit down."

We don't walk away slowly while the Ferns' house bursts into flames behind us. We fucking beeline the fuck outta there and then fly forward when the blast sends burning chunks of wood and metal out over our heads.

I'm standing, the blast still ringing in my ears, as a figure emerges from the smoldering ruins and runs toward us.

Reza hasn't moved. I draw my blade. Flames dance off the man's charred skin. I sidestep as he closes, send a long, deep cut bristling across his gut and then another down his chest. He crumples.

Reza's up. Behind us, the fire rages. We run up the tree-covered hill behind the Ferns' house, crash through a neighbor's yard, and don't stop till we reach Reza's Crown Vic and, breathless, speed off into the night.

CHAPTER NINETEEN

Kia

"Rigo seem like the kinda dude wanna whisper sweet nothings to ya pussy before he dive on into it."

"Karina."

"*Bonjour,* beautiful kitten of the night; *mon Dieu,* what lovely leeps you have, *mon pussevou.*"

"Why he got a French accent all the sudden though?"

"Dudes automatically become French before they eat the box. That's the rule."

"I'm hanging up the phone."

"Kia!"

"What?"

"Be careful, okay?"

I'm standing outside the address Rigo gave me, a quiet block on Underhill Avenue in gentrified-ass Prospect Heights. At the end of the street, the Brooklyn Public Library emits a gentle glow like some magical palace. The second-floor apartment has its lights on and plants in the windows. How could I possibly be in danger if the man puts plants in his windows?

I know if I overthink this shit, I'll walk away. And look, I'm not stupid—I know Rigo ain't no love-of-my-life-type dude, but this, even if it's ridiculous and impossible and probably stupid too, this isn't some shit you just walk away from.

So instead of plotting out all the maybes and maybe nots, I just press the buzzer.

"Yes?"

"It's Kia."

"Ah, good!"

The door lets out a mechanical burp and then clicks, and I pull it open, take a deep breath, and walk in.

There's this boy Tall Adam that I let come over last summer and eat me out. I mean, he was my friend since we were little and whenever I was near him I thought about what it would be like. Could see from the way he looked at me he was hungry for it, but he was too shy to ever say anything. It was an energy thing—his eyes'd dance over my body real quick whenever they got the chance and a tiny earthquake'd erupt inside me and rumble straight up from my pussy into my brain and I wouldn't be able to concentrate on shit for like five minutes.

It was weird to have that power over someone—like, I knew I could have him, take him home, do what I pleased with him—I knew it without either of us saying a single word, so when I called him one hot-ass Thursday afternoon and said, "Come over," he knew better than to ask any questions. I don't think he was that bright, so it's better that we didn't talk much first. As Karina says, one dumbass comment turn that pussy from the Niagara Falls to the Kalahari. When it was over I think he thought I was gonna reciprocate, so I just rolled over and pretended I was asleep until I really did pass out, and when I woke up he was gone and we never talked about it and barely stayed friends after that, just a "hey, you" in the hallways every now and then.

And I mean—it was something else. That orgasm ripped through me like nothing I'd ever felt when it was just me and my hand. I think I went blind for a few seconds and I didn't even care, and I wanted all of him inside me so badly at that moment it scared me. He was ready too. His eyes flashed with it; his whole body tensed to pounce and devour me whole again and again. But I closed up shop. I didn't wanna lose my mind, and I was already spinning dangerously close to the edge.

Now I stand before Rigo's door and I know this is another thing entirely. And I wonder if I'm ready. If he'll answer the door in just a towel and then sweep me off my feet. If that bulge will tear me in half and if I'll die smiling. I wonder all these things, and then the door opens before I can knock and it's not Rigo standing there at all. It's someone else.

And then all my breath leaves my body and I fall forward. Arms wrap around me, real flesh arms, not translucent ones, and he still smells like he used to somehow, but that old scent is mixed in with some cologne and, beneath that, something tangy and citrusy. And I can't speak 'cause I'm crying so hard. His arms squeeze me closer, and the only word I can get out comes from somewhere deep, deep in the pit of my gut.

"Gio."

CHAPTER TWENTY

❧

Reza

"Smoke?" Rohan says.

And why the fuck not? We're flying along the Long Island Expressway in the Partymobile. It's almost midnight. I roll down the window and turn up the radio, some soca station Rohan insisted on, where the DJ keeps interrupting the music to shout out all his cousins. Rohan puts two unfiltered Conejos in his mouth, lights them both, and hands me one.

"Nervous?" he says.

"No, man. Why?" I can't remember the last time I felt nervous before a hit. Yes, this one's different in a way—the beginning of Charo's new war on a few strategically selected targets he's deemed worthy of utter destruction—but if anything, a new lightness has taken over me since we made it out of that suburban Queens hell house a few hours ago. Carlos didn't look so good when we parted, worry for his family etched across his face. But me? I felt that old ease begin to seep back into my bones.

Angie is still all over me. Her smile still haunts every few thoughts, but I feel lighter now. We take revenge in the name of those that have fallen, but really, I think it's just for us. Angie's gone. I'm the one left carrying the charge of her memories.

Rohan lets out a smoke ring. "You're smiling. And you reek of smoke and insecticide."

"It's been a weird night," I say. I showered twice, dressed and spritzed on plenty of my favorite cologne before running out the door, and I was only seven minutes late to meet the others and looking sharp. But some smells don't scrub off easy.

A tap comes from the other side of the partition. "Ay, we close?"

I push the button, and the thick glass doorway slides open behind us. "'Bout fifteen minutes," I say.

Bri pokes her head up. "Can we stop for coffee?" She's all made-up, pretty brown flesh spilling out of a tight blouse. A cloud of flowery girl fragrance fills the front seat.

Rohan looks at me. I shake my head. "We cuttin' it close as is."

Bri makes her pouty face in the rearview at me. "Memo's back here putting me to sleep with his frickin' life story."

"Hey!" Memo yells from the darkness.

"That's weird," Rohan says. "Memo never says shit to me."

Bri rolls her eyes. "You ain't cute like me."

I take my half-full coffee cup from the holder and pass it back to Bri. "Finish mine. I don't want it."

"Word? Thanks, Rez. You the best!"

"It's black though. No sugar."

"Ugh! Whatever." Bri sips at it, scrunches up her face, and then retreats into the back.

"It's always something," I mutter.

Rohan shakes his head. "Sure you're not nervous?"

The swell of the ocean grows louder as we roll down a series of dark streets.

Rohan taps the partition door. "Getting close."

It slides open, and Memo's big head appears. "You want Bri up front?"

"Yeah," Rohan says. "I'm coming back."

It takes some wrangling, but Rohan manages to squeeze his bulky frame through the small doorway. Bri ducks into the front a few seconds later and slumps into the passenger seat with a groan.

"Coffee didn't work?" I ask.

She rubs her eyes. "There's no stopping that guy. I just nodded off at some point around the third grade. Nobody even asked for his damn life story. I just said 'How ya been?'"

"Damn."

"Never. Again."

We drive a few more minutes in silence, and then a massive concrete wall looms out of the darkness. "This is it," I say.

As usual, Charo's description is spot-on: *There'll be a guard booth beside the gate. The booth is lit with a dark red light. That glass? Bulletproof. The gate? Reinforced steel. Cannot be broken through. Try to ram it, your crumpled corpse will be returned to me riddled with bullet holes and your dead ass will owe me twenty G's for the trash heap you turned the Partymobile into.*

I hit play on the CD player and an ecstatic techno beat blasts out, punctuated by shrill inebriated giggles. I have no idea where he got this track, but it really does sound like I'm driving a van full of wasted party girls. I roll up to the guard station.

If you fuck up and have to waste the front guard, don't bother going through with it. They got cameras all over him, and by the time you figure out how to get the gate open, you'll be dead.

A stern face emerges from the red-tinged darkness.

I smile. "Brought the entertainment." Beside me, Bri adjusts, ready to let loose her cleavage and giggles, but the guard just nods and then the gate groans and swings grudgingly open.

If you fuck up when you're inside, you're all gonna die. Once that gate closes behind you, you gotta make it to the

building at the far end of the lot without alerting the front
guard that you're making a move. He's got monitors in his
booth and he's watching everything that happens in the lot.

I swing the Partymobile in a wide circle and back toward
the doorway of the building. My backup lights throw lumi-
nous splashes across the open lot, then the plain cement
wall, then a single tall figure in a black suit. His hand is
raised. He's . . . helping me park.

"Should I waste him?" Memo asks from the back.

"You heard Charo," I say. "They got eyes on us. You
waste him, it's over."

"So what's the move?"

"Hang on." I swing the wheel hard, bringing the van in
at a sharp angle, and the guy waves his hands in agitated
circles. "Left!" he yells. "Cut left!" Then he runs to the other
side of the van so I can see him in the rearview mirror. "Pull
up and let's try it again," he says from the doorway. Right
where I want him. I throw it into drive, swing forward hard
and then lurch backward so fast he has to scramble into the
entranceway.

"Jesus, lady! Where'd you learn how to drive?"

A sliver of red light opens in front of me, back at the gate.
"You good, Silo?" the front guard yells across the darkness.

I wait a beat, holding my breath. Bri smacks her bubble
gum beside me.

"Yeah, just another bitch that doesn't know how to drive."

"Alright." The light disappears and our back doors fly
open. I hear the curt whisper of Memo's silencer and then
a shuffle of motion.

Don't take out the guard at the front door either, not
right away. You need him to get you in the elevator.

Memo, I'm sure, put a bullet in the guy's gun arm, and
Rohan followed it up with a solid crack across the face.
When those two get in the zone, they're like a pair of impen-
etrable brick walls with one deadly mind. I kill the engine.

The darkness in front of us remains unbroken. Bri and I trade a look and then pop open our doors.

Inside, the guard is slumped against the wall, glaring defiantly at the pistol Rohan has pointed at his temple. He clutches a bloody spot on his right arm, but the mess isn't bad, just a few drops, which means Memo took care to miss the artery.

"Take us up," I say. The guard growls and then straightens himself and leads us down a narrow, dimly lit corridor. At the far end, an elevator waits beside two doorways. One leads to the front stairs, and the other goes into a lounge area with a back stairwell at the far end.

The cameras in the elevator gotta go. It's only a minute and a half ride, so by the time they figure out something is wrong you'll be in their midst. If you don't take out the cameras, they'll see it's you and not the girls and when the door opens you'll face a roomful of guns.

Rohan and Bri disappear into the doorway without a word. Memo reaches up into the elevator and crushes the camera with one hand, then shoves the guard in. I follow. Push the 2 button.

This is the moment when everything could go wrong. We're separated. We're relying on someone else's inadequacy and the promise that this elevator won't deliver us to certain death. None of this is to my liking, but there's always a moment when you have to give up control—those dizzy silent seconds before the storm. I adjust my collar, unholster my handgun, and tap the knife strapped to my ankle, the gas mask on my thigh.

Everything is in place.

"You good?" Memo says under his breath.

"Perfect," I say.

With a calm electronic *ding*, the elevator door slides open to reveal four tall men, their guns pointed directly at us.

The first shot is mine. It tears through Silo's head and then shatters the chin of the guy directly across from me. The world explodes as Memo and I fall back against opposite walls of the elevator and Silo's body is decimated by gunfire before he drops. There were six counting Silo; now there are four. Memo is hit—a hole in his suit trickles blood down his shoulder, but it doesn't look bad. Memo either hasn't noticed or doesn't care.

If they were stupid they'd come one by one and we'd pick them off. It's easy to get cocky when you have your enemy cornered into a twelve-foot death box. They're not stupid though. I hear them shuffling backward, overturning tables as they retreat to defensive positions. The automatic doors close on what's left of Silo, make a squishing noise, open again. I steal a glance and then duck back as a hail of bullets ricochet off the steel elevator walls.

Memo already has his chemical grenade out. I give him the nod as I'm pulling my mask out. Memo doesn't wear masks in these situations—some high-intensity military training he did that makes him feel that much cooler than the rest of us. Dude can wade into a cloud of biological hellfire and come right back out with barely a sniffle. His aim sucks though, which is why his big imprecise ass gets to play with the big imprecise-type weapons. He chucks the grenade into the room as another barrage of gunfire bursts out.

Usually, this is when folks panic. *Oh shit, a grenade!* And various other unhelpful responses. This one's already spilling out its foul milky haze, and in less than a minute it'll fill the room. These guys are good though. They really are. They haven't yelled once since we arrived, no boastful threats, nothing. And now the silence lets me know they're not fucking around. When I peek, one of them is bum-rushing the grenade. He's not gonna jump on it and take one for the team like they do in movies. He's gonna drop-kick that thing directly back into the elevator, where it'll fuck our vision to pieces. Gas mask or not, paramilitary training or not, an elevator full of smoke will make us an easy target. It'll be game over.

Very, very over.

I'm raising my gun when a chunk of the guy's head explodes upward. He slides to the ground, lands twitching. Bri stands in the doorway behind him, gun out, and then ducks back as bullets splatter the wall around her. It's too late though: the smoke has done its thing. The room becomes an impenetrable, empty fog.

We don't have much time.

The gunfight will have sent the primary targets into a scatter. They're in a room down the hall from here, presumably with three other armed guards. One will probably bust through the far door in another couple seconds. He'll be heavily armed, one of the paras, and probably more than a little panicked to find the place thick with chemical smoke. The other two bodyguards will escort the conglomerate rep and the warlord down a back stairwell and then make a break for their armored cars.

No one gets out alive, Charo told us. *No one.*

I holster the Glock and crouch low, loosening the dagger from its ankle sheath. Close combat and near blindness is no time to be shooting. I duck out of the elevator, cut a hard left, and then stride through the smoke in the direction of the closest 'cuda gunman, staying low. He'd been crouching behind a toppled wooden table. He appears suddenly out of the fog, turning toward me as he wipes at his watering eyes with one hand and waves his gun with the other. I catch his gun wrist lest he try anything cute while he's dying and then jam my blade up through the soft meat of his jaw and into his brain. He drops as I hear the far door swing open across the room—that'll be the bodyguard. I crouch and inch forward. Someone yells, "¿Qúe carajo?" and I hit the deck. Another 'cuda guy comes flailing out of the smoke just as machine-gun fire explodes through the room, eviscerating him. The 'cuda's top half flails forward over his tattered midsection, spraying me with innards; then he drops to his knees and crumples on top of me.

Presuming they're not hit, Rohan and Bri will be converging on the gunman now. Memo's probably somewhere down low, making sure no one has a pulse. I crawl forward, reach the edge of the room just in time to see Bri emerge from the smoke, gas mask on, gun pointed at the bodyguard's temple. He swings around a second too late—her bullet cuts through skin, skull, and brain and explodes out the far side of his head in a splatter of red and pink. He drops.

I stand, nod at Bri, and turn back into the fog. "Memo?"

His voice comes from the floor a few feet to my right. "Aquí." Then he rises out of the fog, still maskless, like some hulking angel of death.

"Rohan went back down the stairwell to head them off," Bri reports.

"Good. Memo, make sure everything's clean up here. Bri, come."

We're halfway down the stairs when my phone vibrates. Charo usually doesn't call during hits, but I tap my earpiece one time to answer in case there's a change of plans. "Go."

"Uh . . . hello?" It's a girl's voice. Vaguely familiar. I pull off my gas mask. Last time I answer during a job without checking the number. "Is this Reza?"

Ah, yes. "Listen, Carlos's little friend, right?"

"This a bad time?"

Ha. But there's something in her voice that catches me. She's terrified. There's no imaginable way she'd be so polite if this wasn't serious. "Very. What's wrong?"

Bri shoots me a concerned look as we reach the first floor. She puts her ear against the door leading out to the front corridor.

"It's Carlos," Kia says. "Something's wrong with him."

"We did a thing . . . earlier tonight. He might've taken it a little hard. Tell him to get some sleep and I'll give him a ca—"

"No. Listen. He's like . . . unconscious. Or no, his eyes are open, but he's not responding. He's just saying shit."

"Saying what?"

"Like . . . words. Lots of them. I don't know what to do. If I call nine-one-one, he'll never forgive me, and that EMT guy Victor isn't picking up his phone. And I don't know how to reach of any Carlos's . . . other . . . people."

Spirits. I mean shit, neither do I.

Bri cracks the door, slides through gun first. I follow. The corridor's empty.

"Kia, I gotta go. I'm in the middle of something . . ."

"But . . ."

Gunfire erupts a few rooms away.

"Reza?" Kia says in my ear. "Are you okay?"

"Listen, I promise I'll swing through as soon as I can, okay? Text me Carlos's address. I'll be there . . . tonight."

"Come soon," she says, sounding very much like a small child.

The door to the lounge flies open and Rohan barrels through it backward, guns blazing. Bri and I flatten against the walls on either side. Rohan rolls off to the side as automatic fire bursts out of the lounge. He leaves a splatter of blood on the white linoleum floor. I make a mental note to make sure that gets cleaned before we make our final exit. Rohan crouches in front of the elevator, panting. He shows me two fingers and nods. That means he took out the two main targets. Which means only the paramilitary bodyguards are left, not counting the front gate guard—and he's probably about to make an unscheduled appearance.

I motion to Bri, and she soft-steps along the corridor wall and disappears around the corner. A rustle of clothing and scattered footsteps from within the lounge means at least one of the bodyguards is making his move. Rohan ducks behind a metal wastebin. A thick guy runs through the door, AK-47 pointed ahead of him, and pauses. I blow his brains out the front of his head. The big guy collapses, and the stairway door opens a crack. All our guns train on it. Memo steps out, gun first. "Hey, guys!" He flashes a winning grin. "The para dude came running up the back stairs. I broke his neck. That everyone?"

Bri strolls around the corner. She's breathing heavily, and her usually immaculate makeup is smeared. She cleans blood off an arm-length knife with a dark blue uniform shirt. "That's everyone," she says.

"It's done," I tell Charo an hour later as we slide through scattered late-night traffic on the LIE. The blood has been cleaned, security footage destroyed, bodies stripped of IDs and laid side by side on their backs. One of the 'cudas will find them tomorrow and they'll be incinerated. They will have their suspicions, sure, but Charo's right—the thing about taking out secretive people is they do your work for you: their concealing conceals us too. The conglomerate exec will be a missing person, "a tragic disappearance," "a terrible loss," and then an unsolved mystery, gathering dust in some detective's archive.

"How'd it go?"

"Mostly smooth. Rohan got grazed on the arm, Memo took one to the shoulder, in and out."

"I'm fine!" Memo yells from the back.

"Neither serious," I add.

"Good," Charo grunts. "Tijou is here and ready. Anything loud happen outside?"

"No, Bri handled that." Beside me, Bri extends a fist and I dap it.

"Well done," Charo says.

"You don't sound happy, Charo."

"When, in the years we've known each other, Reza, have I ever *sounded* happy?"

"You sound concerned."

"I don't know. Doesn't feel like enough."

"You want to kill all the evil men in the world, Charo? It'll take some time."

"Lo sé. But that's not it."

"What, then?" I exit onto the Jackie Robinson. Cypress Hills Cemetery flows past on either side of us.

"I don't know, Reza."

"Have a coffee, man. Get some sleep. You can't be having these existential crises every time we . . . well, every time."

"Alright, Reza. How far out are you?"

"We're close," I say. "But I'm dropping off the crew and then dipping."

"Oh?"

"Gotta see about a friend."

CYCLE THREE

❦

INTO THE UNDERGROUND

Cuentan los que vieron
que los guapos culebrearon con sus cuerpos
y buscaron afanosos el descuido del contrario
y en un claro de la guardia
hundió el mozo de Palermo
hasta el mango su facón.

Those who saw it told the tale:
two fine young men, writhing like snakes,
each searching for a lapse of vigilance in the other;
until the young man of Palermo found his moment,
and buried his dagger into the cop,
all the way to the hilt.

"La puñalada"
milonga, 1951
Celedonio Flores

CHAPTER TWENTY-ONE

Carlos

    Fence plate a butter knife a pillow a rail a pigeon a stick of bubble gum a plastic flower a menu a prosthetic leg a pound cake a bag of chips a car radio an old man on a respirator his wife waiting quietly beside him a slice of pizza a rusted-out boat in an abandoned lot of trash overgrown weeds two carved figurines a bicycle a chair a lawn mower a change machine a toy robot a bow and arrow a balloon stuck in a tree branch and mostly deflated a pile of leaves a hand, open, light brown with one ring swinging toward me

"Carlos!"

the turnstile at a metro stop a pit bull a radiator a pair of scissors an envelope a hand, open, light brown skin with one ring swinging toward me.

"Car!"

Again.

"Fucking!"

Again.

"Los!"

Reza releases the collar of my shirt and stands over me, panting. "The fuck happened?" I say.

Kia pokes her head out from behind Reza. Her eyes are puffy like she spent all of last night bawling, and I want to know why but words aren't making sense in my mouth yet. "Is that all it took?" Kia says. "I coulda done that."

"The fuck . . ." I'm in my apartment. On my bed. My face is burning like someone threw hot water in it. Reza. Kia. ". . . happened?"

Sasha.

I thrash around uselessly for a second.

The twins. Our twins.

I'm up, breaking for the door. Reza stops me with a hand on my chest. Only takes a slight shove to hurl me back on the bed. This is the second rude awakening in as many days, and I'm surly about it, but more importantly: Sasha.

The twins.

Reza just shakes her head. Kia steps in front of her, crosses her arms over her chest. "You were *out*, man. Just lyin' there mumbling all kindsa . . ."

"I gotta . . . I gotta . . ."

"Gotta what, man? We don't know where they are. You don't know where they are. What you gonna do?"

"I was searching."

"Is that what you call it?"

This is also the second time I've cast my spiritual net too far and blown out my circuits trying to reach Sasha. I stand, and a million tiny lights erupt across my vision. Reza and Kia are on either side of me, and then another set of hands wraps around me and lifts me; they're firm but not unkind. The hands let me down into the easy chair next to my bed. A tall, well-built young man looks down at me, his brow creased with concern. His hair is shaved close to his head, and he's wearing track pants and a T-shirt. Got that same defiant chin Kia has, face inclining sharply from the cheeks, the same sharp eyebrows making him look somewhat put out, probably even when he smiles.

"Carlos," Kia says, appearing even tinier than usual beside the guy. "This is my long-dead cousin, Giovanni."

I rub my eyes. Too much happening. "Nice to meet you, Gio." He takes my hand and shakes it with both of his, almost crushing it.

"The pleasure is mine," Gio says.

"You're not dead though," I say. "So that's nice."

"I'm gonna make coffee," Reza says. "We have to talk."

"I love you," I mumble. Reza snorts as she leaves, but I mean it.

They make a big deal out of setting up everything all nice for me on the kitchen counter. Reza puts my coffee on a saucer and Kia places my Malagueñas next to me with an ashtray like I'm at some fancy cigar lounge. Giovanni sits across from me and opens a pack of cookies. He's maybe in his midtwenties, body long and lanky but well toned: a gymnast or a dancer. Each movement is crisp and precise like Reza's, but he flows better; it would seem like a performance if it wasn't so smooth and genuine. His muscles ripple beneath his tight gray T-shirt as he removes a cookie with two fingers, appreciates it momentarily, and then takes one bite, chewing with consideration.

"Carlos," Reza says. "We've put some pieces together while you were . . . napping."

"Oh?"

"There were some elements in the equation we weren't aware of." Reza looks pointedly at Kia.

"More specifically," Kia says, "we found a link." She places a laptop on the counter, opens it, and turns the screen to face me. "Which may turn out to be a pattern. The Blattodeons, that's what they're called apparently"—she looks at Gio for confirmation and he nods—"are trying to make a clean sweep."

A chart of names and interconnected lines spreads across Kia's laptop screen. "How do you mean?" I ask.

"They're going after anyone that knows they exist," Reza

says. "There was Shelly, right? She'd seen them before. Her own diary said so. They targeted her. The call that came in the night I found Angie requested Shelly directly. When she got away, they went after her again, and they got her in the same way Kia was attacked."

"Right," I say. "But . . ." My stomach turns a small somersault. "You?"

Kia nods.

"We both saw them," Giovanni says. "Seven years ago, in Queens. This boy I liked back then kept talking about strange men outside his house, and one night I took Kia with me to check up on him and they came. They . . . they took him."

I look at Kia.

"Close your mouth," Kia says. "It's all true."

"The boy they took that night was Jeremy Fern," Reza says. "The house was the one we . . . visited earlier."

I take a long sip of coffee, my eyes wide.

"And I was all the way fucked up," Giovanni says. "I fought off one of them and went into his house after the others. When I got to the second floor, they had already started to swarm him." His eyes betray nothing; he tells it like he's remembering something merely odd or unusual. "They were all over his body, his face, coming out of his mouth." Giovanni shakes his head. "I should've run, done something, but . . . I just stared, transfixed. It was just a few seconds, really. I snapped out of it and charged them, but he held up his hand. *He* did. Jeremy. The three of them just looked at me. The cockroach guys had already sent most of their roaches on to Jeremy, so they were just raggedy skin on bone. Corpses. Jeremy stared out from behind that swarm and then just shook his head. Then they left, the men escorting him on either side, sort of like kidnappers but sort of like bodyguards."

The room is very, very quiet. Then Giovanni puts a cookie in his mouth and chews it loudly. I release two Malagueñas from the pack and give one to Reza. "And then?"

"I found him," Kia says, nodding at Gio. "A few minutes later. And we went home. And he was never the same again." A swirl of anger laces Kia's words. These two have some more talking to do.

"I . . ." Giovanni falters for the first time. "I lost my mind after that. I couldn't get rid of that image: Jeremy looking at me through that haze of pink roaches, and somehow, even though I knew I did everything I could, somehow it was my fault. Like, I felt guilty. Even though Jeremy himself held me back, I just, I replayed over and over how I could've stopped it anyway. I could've overpowered them both *and* Jeremy and saved him and then he would've come to his senses. I made up a hundred different endings to that day, and every time I did it, I sank deeper into my own pit: guilt, depression." He's talking to Kia more than me now, looking down at his own hands.

Kia stands with her back against the wall, arms wrapped around her stomach, frown severe.

"I wanted to die," Giovanni says. "First just a little, like, it was the answer to every guilt-drenched thought I had. Every movie of the scenario I would play in my head ended with me dying. Giving myself instead of Jeremy, or just taking my own life in some ridiculous way, in the middle of the school cafeteria or walking into the ocean and never coming back. I don't know. I couldn't find anything to hold on to."

Tiny streams slide down Kia's face. Giovanni just looks at the counter and shakes his head. "And then I just slipped away. The only way to not die at that moment was to disappear, so I did. And for a long time, I still clung to death like it was some kind of escape hatch. A lot happened . . ." He laughs and widens his eyes at his own memories. "A lot. But then I started clawing my way back out of that hole. And I started investigating. And training. A lot of martial-arts shit. Weapons. I traveled."

I realize there's an unlit Malagueña in my mouth. I'd been too caught up to bother with it. "Investigating what?" I ask, and then I light up and pass the lighter to Reza.

"The roach men. Blattodeons, they're called. Jeremy is, like . . . their chosen one. There's a long lineage of these guys, I guess, going back to the first European settlers. Each new roach master is found through a complicated ritual based on some prophecy. Jeremy fit the bill, and when they started showing up, somehow he knew, he understood on some level, even though he was terrified. And when his time came . . . he went. And I saw it."

"Shit," Kia whispers.

"They prey on folks, implant themselves in flesh to create these human hives, basically. The corpse becomes a nesting ground and their collective consciousness animates it. And it all goes back to the High Priest, in this case, Jeremy, who commands the whole situation and figures out how to get new bodies for them. They go for people they think won't be looked for, of course: prostitutes, the homeless."

"And the parents?" I throw a sideways glance at Reza.

"They funded his whole operation. Left money in a bank account that he could withdraw from with an alias. They never saw him after he became the High Priest, but I think they got updates through Caitlin."

"The sister," Reza says.

"I don't have much on her. I mean, she has to know, right? She's gotta be the connection Jeremy maintains to his old life. Kia and Reza are right about the link with Shelly."

"The tunnel entrance in the Ferns' basement," I say.

Reza nods. "The sister's involved. Gotta be."

"I just haven't figured out how," Giovanni says. His eyes are still off somewhere in the saga of his last seven years. Kia sniffles a few times and wipes her nose.

"The computer," I say, "was Caitlin's. She's probably in charge of something, cleaning up her twin brother's messes, I'd guess. She's the one . . ." Targeting my family. The family I barely know. "She's gotta die."

"Easy, C," Kia says. "We're getting to that."

I tense. Stifle the yell rising in me. I'm not used to this teamwork thing. Usually it's just me and Riley and whatever group of soulcatchers we got backing us up, and they do what we say.

"We wanna find out whatall's going on," Reza says, "before we go offing any more random white ladies and bringing the full force of the NYPD and daily tabloids on our heads."

She's right. They're both right. And I'm usually the one cautioning against the quick kill. In fact, I was last night, right up until I saw that picture.

"You're probably wondering what Sasha and your kids have to do with all this," Reza says.

I'd been trying not to ask. Considering I already had one meltdown while tracking her, I'm sure I already look like a maniac to them. And I knew they'd get there eventually.

"We're pretty sure the Survivors made a move on the Blattodeons at some point," Reza says. "Gio's crossed paths with them a few times over the years, and he says the roaches have gotten at least two of them."

I close my eyes, but all I see are winged monsters closing in on Sasha and the babies. "It makes sense," I say. "The Survivors are off the grid. They fit the profile of folks who won't be looked for."

Giovanni looks at Kia. "A lot of folks do, when you start thinking about it."

Reza and Kia are staring at me. I raise my eyebrows at them. "You guys have a play in mind?"

"As a matter fact," Kia starts. The Council transmission blares through my brain without warning, first a shock of white noise, then: *"Council of the Dead to Agent Delacruz."* I straighten and hold up my hand to stop Kia. *"Your presence is required immediately at Council Headquarters for a special-asset protection detail."*

Special what? I don't even—

"Please report posthaste and without delay."

I shake my head. "Repetitive-ass dickholes."

"What's wrong?" Giovanni asks.

"Oh," Kia says. "Remember I told you C's into some dead-people telepathy-type shit? That's the face he makes when it happens. He probably has to go."

"I do," I say. "But tell me the plan first."

"Not a plan," Reza says. "But we're gonna reach out to the Survivors."

"Great," I say. "When do we do it? You have a lead? I can . . ."

"Carlos," Kia says. Then she shakes her head.

I look back and forth between Kia's and Reza's unsmiling faces. "You want to do it . . . without me?"

"Initially," Reza says. "To feel them out."

"My . . . family . . ." I say, and a heaviness squirms to life in my chest.

"The thing is," Kia says, "we have no idea how Sasha's gonna react to you or how you're—"

"My fucking kids!" My hands slam down on the counter before I realize they're closed into fists. Everything is fire.

Kia stares at me. ". . . gonna react," she finishes.

My words hang in the air. The fire abates. I want to swallow up the last ten seconds of life. I want a do-over. That heaviness swells, rustles; it is gigantic.

"I'm gonna go call Rigo," Giovanni announces. He lets himself out.

"What just happened," Reza says, "is why you won't be going with us when we make contact with the Survivors." She doesn't say it cruelly; it's just a fact. When I meet her eyes, they're gentle.

"She . . ." But the words catch in my throat, and then instead of making a sentence, I let out a low moan. The heaviness dislodges, rises. I put my head down in my arms and burst into tears.

"More?" Kia says, rubbing my back.

My body heaves a few more times. Turns out crying is like vomiting—you do everything you can to hold it off, and then it happens and you feel eighty pounds lighter and more clear-headed and wonder why you didn't just do it in the first place. I lift my head from my arms and wipe tears and snot off my face. Reza pours a fresh cup of coffee and hands it to me over the counter. Kia passes me some more tissues.

"I just . . . I mean . . ." I stutter. "I can't . . . and then . . ."

Reza nods. "Of course, man. It's your kids. And their mama." She pours herself a coffee and looks at Kia with eyebrows raised.

Kia shakes her head, rubs my back a few more times. "The way I see it, you're like thirty or whatever yeah, but in a way you're like a tall five-year-old. Emotionally speaking. I mean, you lost all your memories, right? So you don't have, like, the emotional ABCs that a normal fully alive adult does. You haven't been through the ringer in the same way, right?"

I sniffle. "I hadn't thought of it that way." Not sure whether to be offended or relieved. Either way, she has a point.

Reza shrugs. "Most grown-ass men I know ain't got shit for emotional vocabulary either. Far as I'm concerned, C's ahead of the game. But I feel you, Kia. It's a good point."

Kia pats my back. "You good, man?"

I nod. Blow my nose. Shake my head. "I . . ." It comes out clogged by another sob. I clear my throat and try again. I got this. "I will do whatever . . ." Now a hoarse whisper, much better. ". . . the fuck I have to do to make sure they're okay."

Reza nods. "We know, man. And right now what you have to do is get your life together."

"So that when shit starts getting even realer," Kia says, "we can count on you to be the regular ol' fuck-shit-up Carlos we know and sometimes love."

I laugh through sniffles. Blow my nose again. "How the fuck did y'all get so close that you're finishing each other's sentences? How long was I out for?"

"Gio and I were here for a few hours, trying different shit to wake you up. Then Reza came and gave it a shot. Then we figured we'd let you work it out some more, and we started talking and comparing notes 'n' shit, and I mean . . . time kinda slipped away some, I guess."

"You forgot about me?"

"I mean, we didn't forget," Reza says. "We just had other things we were dealing with besides you."

"And anyway, you were good," Kia insists. "We wanted to make sure you got your search in, you know, fully."

I raise an eyebrow at her.

Reza puts down the coffee. "Well, I don't know 'bout y'all, but I've had a helluva night and now I want a big-ass breakfast."

Kia hops off her stool. "I'm in. C?"

"I gotta go see what my fucking bosses want."

"Aw, man!" Kia says.

"I know. Isn't it a school day, young lady?"

Kia just stares at me, and I relent. "Anyway, it's probably better you guys get breakfast without me. You can . . . talk about how you're gonna . . . find the Survivors." There it is again, that trembling heaviness rising inside me. I know it now though. I can see it coming. I fight it back, stand.

"You good?" Reza asks.

I nod.

"We'll check in later," Kia says, dapping my shoulder. "Be easy, bruh."

We head outside into the gray light of a brand-new morning. Giovanni sits on my stoop, whispering sweet nothings into his cell phone in accented Portuguese. He laughs a good-bye and pockets the phone when he sees us, then hugs me surprisingly hard and pounds my back. Reza offers to drop me off at the Council even though it's on the other side of town, but I shake my head, thank her, and head off into the morning.

I need, as they say, a moment.

I swing down Marcy Ave., past the projects, Hasidic supermarkets, and hipster cupcakeries. All the graffiti-decorated metal gates are down still. The day is only beginning to break across Brooklyn.

I am alone.

And I move once again with ease, like there had been rusty chains cluttering up my joints and suddenly they're gone. I damn near float past Von King Park, where wilted flowers and rained-in liquor bottles still mark the near-dozen kill spots of the ghostling's slow-motion massacre.

I have a family.

We are separated, yes, and they are in danger, but that's right now. And I'm not some random schmo with no recourse. I have skills, a mind that untangles these kinds of messes on the daily, a blade . . . And Sasha is not to be fucked with. I've seen her use a sword—two in fact—and she outshines me on her worst day. And I have a team: Kia's brilliant ass, Reza, the human angel of death, and Riley and Squad 9. The full force of the Council could probably be wrangled into my corner if need be. Riley and I would figure it out.

I pick up my pace, cut east and south, pass Fulton Street with its twenty-four-hour fruit stands and then Atlantic, just beginning to bustle with the morning commute.

By the time I reach Prospect Park I have become an unstoppable force. The city urges me forward; those early-morning winds rustle the trees and the occasional plastic bag and me. A chorus of morning birds erupts nearby as I move through the park, invincible, unbreakable, a well-dressed warrior.

Balance: it's mine.

If some obstacle were to rear up in my path, my hand would release this blade from its cane sheath without thought or hesitation, a single smooth movement, one with my stride; a slice through air and foul flesh and I'd sail past my fallen foe without breaking the rhythm of this speedy saunter.

The morning air swishes through me, brightens me with its freshness. Life. The world teems with it, each dew-covered blade of grass, the morning birds' song. I had a full one once. I was complete. I may have had a family, been in love. And then it was torn from me and I became this . . . semi-wraith. Kia's words about being an overgrown five-year-old echo through me as I cross the fields of Prospect Park and wind through a path in the woods. What if I'd lived, fully lived? Who robbed me of a full life?

I can't get caught up in that mental circle jerk now though. I don't have time. It's just . . . life, my life, it matters more and more every time I think about Sasha and the babies. It looms— a great, impenetrable shadow over my morning, my life. My half-life. I stop in a still-dark coven of drooping trees. When all this is over, when Sasha and the babies are safe and these Blattodeon roach fuckers dealt with, I will find out who the fuck I was and who the fuck killed me. And I'll kill their ass.

Or asses.

The sun cuts through the trees, turns the gray morning suddenly resplendent. Kia, Reza, Riley, Sasha . . . Giovanni now, and Sylvia Bell. Squad 9. My team, however disparate and weird. That's the present. My babies are the present. Sasha. I keep walking, heading south through the park and then across Park Slope as the rising sun throws my lopsided shadow across the block ahead.

The Council's misty embrace surrounds me as soon as I walk through the rusted door. The murmur of souls rises through the chilly air, a never-ending susurration, and I climb the metal stairwell up to the second floor, stroll down the dilapidated corridor, and enter the conference room, where Bartholomew Arsten sits at a long rotting wooden table beside Chairman Botus. Botus is massive, takes up half the table, and the first thing I think is that it's rare he'd make a showing for something as menial as a job assignment.

"Ah, Carlos." Botus smiles with all his ghostly teeth. "Wonderful of you to show up."

Something is off.

Botus stands, and I realize someone had been sitting behind him all this time.

Someone alive.

And then I realize who she is.

"You're on a special protective detail until further notice," Botus says. "Carlos, this is Caitlin Fern. She's very special to the Council. And she needs our help."

CHAPTER TWENTY-TWO

Kia

Reza takes us to some greasy-spoon diner out in Bushwick that hasn't been cleaned in eight centuries and doesn't give a fuck. The eggs are bangin', though, and the bacon's just right. Reza and Gio both get something called the Lumberjack Smack, which turns out to be two of damn near everything on the menu.

"People always ask me," Reza says as she forks some more bacon in her, "how the fuck I eat so much and stay tiny." She rolls her eyes.

"I hate that question," Gio says. He puts a fried egg on his whole-wheat toast and takes a huge bite. The yolk rains thick yellow drops over his plate. "People really want to act like everyone's body works the same." He shakes his head.

"Exactly," Reza says.

"Well, if these aren't two people I never thought I'd see in the same place at the same time," an excited voice calls in a thick Creole accent from across the diner. Dr. Tijou makes her way past the other booths. She's short, with one gray streak breaking her otherwise jet-black hair. "Gimme the Lumberjack Smack, Cathy," she says to the old lady waiting tables. "Kia, right?" She grins down at me. I nod. Her smile goes all the way across her face. "My friend Dr. Voudou's little helper. How is he?"

"Baba Eddie's alright," I say.

"And Carlos?"

I tilt my head and shrug. "He'll be alright. This is my cousin, Giovanni. Gio, this is Dr. Tijou, the best surgeon in the world."

"Stop," Dr. Tijou says, extending her hand to Gio. He kisses it, charming bastard that he is, and then Reza says, "Sit." They exchange kisses on the cheek, and then we get down to business.

"Well, the Survivors are willing to talk," Dr. Tijou says. "But they want to meet in the middle of Highland Park."

Reza raises an eyebrow. "I don't like it."

"Like, the middle-middle," Dr. Tijou says. "Not some field. They're talking about way in that woodsy area."

"I really don't like it."

Dr. Tijou shrugs. "The Survivors are some of the most skittish folks I know. The only reason they trust me is because I helped Sasha deliver the twins. And everyone trusts me."

"Why don't you like it, Reza?" I ask.

"It's an ambush waiting to happen. We go in as is, yeah? But they pick the spot. They probably know it well, so for all we know the woods'll be crawling with 'em. I mean, I've done some business out there, but it's been a minute. We're surrounded before we begin with no way out, no good sense of where the fuck we are, probably no cell reception. It's a death trap."

"I am sure," Dr. Tijou says, "that's part of their logic. Not because they want to kill you but because they run a tight ship. They don't trust you yet."

"I'd do the same thing," Gio says.

"Me too," Reza says. "That's what worries me."

In the back of Reza's Crown Vic, I put my head on Gio's shoulder and close my eyes. And it all comes back with his smell: that Gio smell—it's just a hint of funk beneath whatever light cologne he's wearing. The funk paints a picture: Gio, age fifteen, smile so wide his whole face is creased with it. He's sitting in my living room, playing with Aunt DiDi's Chihuahua. His T-shirt's way too big for him and his hair is tucked beneath a baseball cap.

That Gio is gone.

I let him go.

I mourned. I held on for so long and then I finally let him go and mourned. And I'd been mourning all along; mourning had become my friend, even if I tried to hold it at a distance. Because even if he wasn't dead—and he wasn't, he wasn't, I told myself night after night until I didn't anymore—he was still *gone*. So very gone. And the loss was a hole in me, and so I mourned, and eventually I released even the possibility of him showing up. And then he did show up, and I cried until I couldn't breathe, from sorrow and from joy.

And now his shoulder holds up my head. It's real: flesh and blood, not some spook; it rises and falls with his breath. And he's humming along with some salsa song Reza has on and looking out the window like it's just another day, but it's not.

Gio is alive.

And part of me wants to kill him for ever making believe he was dead.

"What's wrong?" Gio asks, and for a second I think he's been reading my mind. It would be just like Gio to be a goddamn telepath on top of everything else. But no, my breathing's gotten fast and labored and I hadn't even noticed.

I shake my head at him, tears worrying the edges of my eyes, because I don't have the words to explain how happy and furious I am that he's back.

Reza finds a spot on a suburban street near the park. She steps out of the Crown Vic and makes a call, mumbling with a fierce whisper into her earpiece. Then she pops the trunk and pulls out a duffel bag, which she slings around her shoulder.

Gio looks at me, opens his mouth and closes it again when I shake my head. "I'm coming," I say. "That's the end of it."

"I'm not," Dr. Tijou says happily. "But give a shout if someone gets shot or something. I got my stuff with me. Not that I can do much, eh? But hey—better than nothing." She clicks on the radio and reclines her seat.

Gio and I get out and follow Reza down a grassy slope into the park. A middle-aged white guy walking a Dalmatian nods at us as he strolls past and says, "Morning!" A group of old ladies genuflect in slow-motion Tai Chi as a chilly breeze sweeps across the meadow. The day is gray and overcast, the sky a murky white.

When we walk into the shadowy wooded area, Reza sets down her duffel bag and unzips it. "You can shoot, I'm guessing?" she asks Gio.

"I can, but I prefer knives." He pats his pockets.

"Alright, well, take this just in case." She hands him a small revolver and then takes an automatic rifle out the bag. It looks like something I'd see on the news in a war-torn country. "And you." She aims a sharp glare at me. "Stay the fuck outta sight if shit pops off. Understood?"

I nod, my heart galumphing through my ears. We walk deeper into the woods. Reza freezes, one hand up. A young white couple jogs out of the underbrush. They're wearing the brightest shades of green and pink I've ever seen and matching headbands. They stop in their tracks when they see us, their eyes glued to Reza's automatic. The woman whispers, "Oh my God!" and then we just stand there for a few seconds.

"Call the police," Reza says very slowly, "and I'll find you and burn down your house. Then I'll kill your parents. Nod if you understand me."

I believe her. They both nod, eyes wide.

"Now, go."

They do, first at a jog, then an all-out scramble.

"That's why I hate shit like this," Reza says, falling back into her stride. "They'll prolly call the damn police any-damnway."

I look at Gio and he shrugs. A light drizzle speckles the woods around us. Nearby, two headless chickens lie beneath a tree, one of Baba Eddie's friends leaving an offering, no doubt. Farther off, an open building foundation has become a sullen pool of dark water, reflecting the swaying trees back up at themselves.

Deeper in the forest, the pale sky blotted out above us, Reza stops again, one hand raised. All those years of killing must've gotten to her. I'm sure every twig snap is a gunman moving into position. I mean, really . . . who brings a damn automatic rifle into Highland Park?

Then I freeze, because up ahead a tall bearded man in a Stetson hat and an overcoat stands aiming a shotgun at Reza. His skin is a dull brownish gray like Carlos's, and his black beard is tinged with red. He's smiling—a wide, unnerving kind of grin that shows way too many teeth. Other folks stand in the woods behind him. They're gray like he is and armed, and that's all I can tell before Gio shoves me roughly behind him, pulls a knife out of each pocket, and flicks them open.

"I would say we come in peace," the man's voice booms through the forest, "but that would be a lie." Then he chuckles in a way that sounds forced.

Peeking around Gio, I see Reza shift the rifle to one hand and unsheathe a Glock from her shoulder holster with the other. She points the Glock at the bearded man's head and waves the AK in a slow circle around the forest. "Before you do anything else," she says, "understand that since I have no fear of death, my only concern is taking as many of you with me as I can. Don't doubt that if I go down, Gregorio here falls too."

Gregorio chuckles again.

"This AK can take out at least four of you in a single spray; count on that. Gio there will probably finish you off. There are what, eight of you? Your organization will be decimated when we're through."

There's an uncomfortable shifting among the Survivors.

"And finally, know that my people are converging on the outskirts of this forest as we speak. If I don't come out smiling, they will hunt down each of you, one by one."

"Reza," Gregorio says, and it's clear she's wiped the smile from his face. "No need to be dramatic. You called this meeting, after all. We are your guests. And you know as well as anyone that precautions must be taken. These are precautions. That is all."

"Fuck your precautions," Reza says. "I don't talk to people pointing guns at me. I kill them."

"That's a shame," Gregorio says, and I brace myself. In the seconds of silence, I hear the forest breathe, the gentle cricks and cracks of life; somewhere above us a mourning dove coos and another replies.

"Wait!" I yell, stepping out from behind Gio.

"Kia, no!" Reza snarls, but I brush past her and plant myself in the epicenter of all that firepower.

"This is bullshit," I say. My hands are shaking, so I clasp

them behind my back. "We're here to talk about working together, not to blow each other up."

"Kia?" a woman's voice says. I turn, and Sasha steps out of a shadowy grove of trees. She holsters a serious-looking handgun and, before I can do anything about it, wraps her arms around me. "My God, what are you . . . ? What's going on, Kia?"

Last year, when all the shit happened with Carlos, Sasha got herself possessed by some ancient evil dude that shredded up people's insides. Plus she was pregnant, and on top of all that she helped Carlos destroy the evil dude even while she was basically dying. Again. So she ended up comatose on Carlos's couch for a few days, as people tend to do, and when she woke I was the first person she saw. I made her tea and told her, best I could, what I knew, and called Carlos and Baba Eddie and Dr. Tijou back, but everyone was away doing stuff, so for a few hours, it was just me and Sasha. She spent most of the time crying, sipping tea, crying some more.

At first I just looked at her. What was I gonna say? It's okay? It wasn't, for all I knew. She could've lost the baby. She could still be dying. I didn't know shit. So I sat there. And then I moved from the easy chair to the couch beside her. When she kept crying, I put my hand on her back, same way I did for Carlos earlier today, and just made circles while she heaved up and down. She wrapped her arms around me and put her face in my shoulder and just sobbed and I made little *shh* sounds the way my mama usedta do, and eventually she got it all out and I gave her the tea I'd made, now cold, and then we talked quietly until the others came.

When she left, I felt like I'd just made a friend and lost her in the space of twenty-four hours. I had pictured us hanging out, telling each other secrets even, if nothing else because we'd just been through this moment, huge and tiny, and even though we barely knew each other, there was something easy and true about her that I was drawn to, that I wanted to be like. Plus, I heard she was badass with that blade.

Now it's Sasha rubbing my back and I don't even know why. Somehow, she feels the whirlpool of sorrow and rage that's been swirling up inside me since Gio showed up. I almost shatter, right there in her arms, because her touch is just right, but I resist. There's too much firepower around us to go all emo.

When I look up from Sasha's hug, I see the guns have lowered. The crew of Survivors around us are staring with awed expressions. I take it they don't have many non-half-dead friends, these guys.

Reza holsters her Glock and points the AK at the ground. "First of all, we wanted to let you know that the Blattodeons have you in their targets," she says. "We got access to their computers last night, and they have Sasha, Gregorio, and probably a few other of your gray asses marked to kill."

"They've come for us before," Gregorio says. "We tried to wipe them out last year, after they kidnapped and murdered some of our people. We did some damage and they returned the favor. They are a formidable threat in those tunnels, where they have numbers and the cramped darkness on their side—their natural habitat. But they are clumsy, and those decomposed bodies don't hold up well under a solid thrashing."

"It won't be the roach zombie guys," I say. "They're sending ghosts now. Child ghosts."

The Survivors murmur in surprise.

"How do you know this?" Gregorio demands.

"That's how they came for me," I say. "It was a ghostling, but trained to kill a specific target. That's what Carlos said, anyway."

His name sends another ripple of conversation through the Survivors. "You are working with Carlos? With the Council?" Gregorio says, his voice almost a roar. "Then we are finished here. The Council is our sworn enemy."

"Wait," Sasha says. "Carlos saved my life. He—"

"Yes, we all know what Carlos did for you," Gregorio snaps.

"Don't you da . . ." Sasha says, but she stops when a short white woman steps forward, one hand raised.

"That's enough, Gregorio." She's older, maybe in her sixties, but who can tell with these half-dead folks? She says it calmly enough, but Gregorio looks like he's been slapped. "We will hear what these people have to say." She turns to Reza. "What is it you are proposing?"

"The Blattodeons are a plague on both our houses," Reza says. "We join forces to annihilate them once and for all. Their leader, Jeremy Fern, and his sister, Caitlin, whatever her involvement is. And all their roach zombies. The elder Ferns were involved in funding their son's activities. They've already been handled."

"You killed the Ferns?" one of the Survivors asks.

"They've already been handled," Reza says again. "Which means the roaches are probably in disarray right now, trying to figure out what the next move is. Carlos is speaking with the Council at this moment, to see what their involvement will or won't be. Either way, we have a fair amount of fire-power from my end—I'm sure you know Charo isn't one to be trifled with. And Giovanni here has been studying their movements for several years now."

"I don't like it," Gregorio says.

"Neither do I," a tall guy in wraparound sunglasses says. He's still clenching his pistol like he wants to splatter us all across the forest.

Gregorio shoots him a look. "Easy, Blaine. Easy." He makes eye contact with the older woman and then exhales sharply. "Marie is right. We came here to hear you out, and it's not my call to make. We will take it back to the others and send word through Dr. Tijou of our decision."

Reza nods. The Survivors are already fading back into the shadowy woods, one by one. Soon, only Sasha remains. "Can we talk?" she asks in a voice so quiet I want to just wrap around her again right then and there.

"Of course," I say. I signal to Gio and Reza and they walk ahead, casting a few dubious glances back at us.

The rain slows to a gentle sprinkle and the sun peeks through the swaying branches above us. Sasha and I stroll along at an easy pace; she could be my older sister or one of those concerned teachers that takes a liking to a student and goes the extra mile.

"I need to," Sasha says. And then she stops. Looks up at the sky. Searching for words, I guess. We walk another couple of steps in silence. "I need to talk to Carlos," she finally spits out.

I laugh. "No shit. He spent all night trying to track you down after they figured out the roach guys were gonna send their baby-ghost assassins after you."

"I know." She shakes her head. "There was too much going on. The Survivors are in turmoil, as I'm sure you just saw. Gregorio and Marie have been going at it more and more. And with the babies, it's just . . . I don't know . . ." She stops walking, so I stop too. She takes a deep breath that's almost a sob. "I don't know how to talk to him."

"Then you'll be on equal footing," I say. "Cuz I promise he doesn't know how to talk to you."

She allows a slight smile. "Some days I'm terrified. Of it, what I've done, what's happened. What he must feel. How angry he must be."

"I don't think he's—"

"How angry I still am."

I nod. He killed her brother, even if he didn't know it at the time. "What are their names?"

She smiles again, wider this time, but still unendingly sad. "The girl's Xiomara. The boy's Jackson."

"Beautiful," I say. "Glad you didn't go the corny petty route and name 'em Trevita and Carl or something. I can tell him?"

We start walking again. The rolling fields of Highland Park appear in spots of bright green through the trees. "Yes," Sasha says. "Please do. And tell him I need to speak to him. It's urgent."

"Any details? You know he's worried sick about you. And them."

She shakes her head, eyes narrowed. "I'll be taking care of myself. He should know by now I'm perfectly capable of that." Her hand rests on the hilt of a short blade strapped to her belt. "But no, it's about the past. There's . . . information. A way to get information. About what happened to us. How we died. Ol' Ginny, the fortune-teller in Flatbush, as it turns out."

"Oh yeah, he'll be excited about that. So you want me to . . ."

Another deep breath, this one strong, unbroken. "Tell him I'm ready to talk. Tell him the southwest entrance to Prospect Park, tonight at nine."

For a half second, I wonder if this whole thing is some setup. Carlos would be easy to take out if he thought he was going to meet Sasha. Wide-open to attack. But it's not for me to figure these things out. All I can do is pass the message along and pray he's pulled it together enough to not get got. Anyway, I trust Sasha. I don't know why, but I do. There's nothing put-on about what she's said.

"Alright," I say as we step out of the woods. Up ahead, the wide-open field stretches up a small hill. There, three tall men in gray suits stand looking down at us. Reza is beside them, the duffel bag still slung over one shoulder. They cut an imposing tableau.

Sasha stops walking. "Damn. Reza wasn't bluffing, huh?"

"Nope," I say. "Reza don't bluff."

CHAPTER TWENTY-THREE

Carlos

Caitlin Fern looks older in person. Of course, it could be the sudden death of her parents or the wear and tear of being a homicidal necromancer etching those worry lines across her sallow face. Her dirty-blond hair is pulled back in a loose ponytail; some stray strands frame her wide forehead in a chaotic halo. Her eyebrows sit high above her eyes, giving her the look of someone perpetually surprised. She steps outside of the chilly warehouse and stands beside me as a flock of pigeons rush past us down the deserted street.

"Let's take a walk," Caitlin says. It's still chilly, and she wraps her arms over her chest, shivering a little even in the heavy cardigan she wears.

I nod.

Inside, her voice had trembled as she described being called out of an important late-night meeting at the adoption charity. She'd paused, gulped back a sob, and then shook her head, eyes closed. "I'm sure he . . . I'm sure he wants to kill me too," she'd said as Arsten cooed sympathetically and Botus looked on.

Now that frightened woman begging for the Council's

protection is gone. The new, unimpressed Caitlin walks ahead
of me to a fence blocking off the industrial harbor area.
Beyond it, the gray ocean swirls beneath the gray sky. "C'mon,
let's go by the water," Caitlin says. She lifts a detached section
of the fence and ducks through.

Listen: not only am I half dead with nary a legit docu-
ment to my name, but I'm Latino. Beneath this gray, I'm
still brown; the cops remind me with their suspicious sneers
every chance they get. Since I died and came back, all I've
known is a life under the radar, blending in, avoiding arrest,
questions, prisons, hospitals, institutions of every kind. So
when I trespass, it's because I have to. That's it.

But Caitlin stares back at me, her high eyebrows arched
in challenge, a slight sneer across her face. I won't kill her.
I promised Reza and Kia, and anyway, they're right; we need
to know more about what the fuck she's up to. Still . . . I'm
on a mission, I remind myself. This is work. And anyway,
she's clearly hiding something from the Council that she's
not afraid to show me. I glance up and down deserted-ass
First Avenue and then duck through the fence after her.

"I know about you, Carlos."

Again, I resist the urge to draw this blade. We stroll past
massive freighter crates along a narrow strip of concrete
beside the choppy waters of New York Bay. Way out over the
waves, the Statue of Liberty is barely visible in the mist. If
things get messy, there aren't many options for escape. If
Caitlin works for the Council, that means she is the one that's
been necromancing all those baby ghosts. I haven't seen any
of the little guys floating around, but who knows? On top of
that, I'm pretty sure some security schmo will pop out any
second and arrest us both.

"What do you mean?" One clean slice. That'd be that.

I'd reach across myself, grip that handle, and the cut would catch her neck from below, lopping her head clean off. The head would bounce once and then roll into the waves; the body would tumble and with, a little kick, follow suit.

"I've heard about you, who you are, what you've done."

"All good things, I'm sure." I force a smile that I'm quite sure looks forced.

"I heard about Sarco and how you tricked that other halfie from the Survivors into helping you."

So *that's* the story about me and Sasha the Council's going with these days. Figures. I shake my head. "Complicated times."

"Indeed. So I'm not going to pussyfoot with you. I need your help. I need someone I can trust, a soldier. I believe that's you."

"What makes you so sure?"

Find the part of the lie that's true, Reza had said, *and tell everything else to fuck off.*

"First of all, you strike me as the kind of man that can't lie for shit."

I laugh a little too eagerly. "Well, that's true."

"And second of all, I believe you'll do what has to be done. You're not overly burdened by conscience or identity like the Survivors. But you're not trapped by protocol and bureaucracy like most of the Council drones."

I shrug. Everything else can fuck off. And the less I say the better. We wind along, past a pier and into a corridor between more brightly painted shipping crates. "My brother, I don't know what the Council told you about him, but he is . . . special."

I try not to laugh, and it comes out a grunt instead. Caitlin ignores me.

"He was always on some deeper stuff, you know?" She squints, remembering the Jeremy that Giovanni once fell so hard for. "Other kids had their after-school activities or little Magic card games, whatever. Jeremy was reading all the apocryphal books of the Bible by the sixth grade. He loved to dance. That was his one indulgence, I think, but besides that he approached even his childhood like he was training for something."

Back out in the open now, we stroll along some abandoned train tracks. A seagull caws at us from its perch on a tire heap. "When they took him, when he disappeared, I think I was the only one who felt it coming. I had my own gifts—not unlike yours, although I didn't have to die to get them—and even though I didn't know how to use them yet, the whispering universe had given me some clouded sense that Jeremy had more to him than just a quiet, overachieving life in suburban Queens.

"So while my parents mourned, I prepared. That's a whole other story, but I began learning how to use my talents and honed them. Why? Because I knew Jeremy'd come back to us, and when he did, he'd need my help."

"And he did."

When she nods, her frown deepens like she's holding back a sob, and I wonder if she's putting on that same Oscar-worthy show she gave the Council earlier. "About a year later. You have to understand, Jeremy has tapped into a kind of power that's deeper than anything humanity has fathomed yet. I mean . . . I know that sounds ludicrous, but it's true. We humans are so wrapped up in this idea that the magic of the universe revolves around us, our needs and desires, and it's so much deeper. You think Christianity is old? Buddhism? Just babies. The shit Jeremy's wrapped up in—the magic flowing through him—that shit predates humans, predates monkeys, predates the supremacy of these ridiculous hairy bipeds. It's deeper."

She stops walking, closes her eyes, and takes a deep

breath. It looks like a trick she might've learned in therapy. When she opens her eyes again, they're sharp, unapologetic. "What do you think power means, Carlos?"

I shake my head. "How 'bout you just tell me what you have to tell me. I don't like riddles."

"Power is survival. Against all odds. Power is the ability to maintain, through any circumstances, whatever may come: nuclear holocaust, arctic freeze, flood, and fire. We think we're powerful because we can bring that storm, but power isn't in destruction. It's not even in creation. That's kid's stuff. Tonka Toys. I'm talking about power that outlasts all that."

Roaches. I hate everything.

"Those powers, they function in a kind of collective consciousness that's way deeper than anything we could understand, right? And through those millions of minds functioning as one, they chose Jeremy. Jeremy is the one destined to bring about the dawn of this new power, this global power."

She's proud of him. Proud of her one and only psychopath roach master brother. Family is an amazing thing.

We stand at the edge of the docks. The fog has swept in fully, wrapping Manhattan in a cloak of gray. A light drizzle begins.

Caitlin turns to me, looks me dead in the eye. "You want to get a drink?"

"Absolutely."

"Man!" Caitlin yells. "It's good to be able to talk about this shit without having to explain everything and coddle a man!" She slaps the bar. "And take his little hand and walk his stupid little ass through each!"—slap—"and every!"—slap—"step! Jesus!"

She's four martinis deep and Quiñones the bartender is shooting death rays out of his one eye at her.

"This the spot you Council goons frequent, right?"

I nod and swish my rum and Coke around. It's the same one I've been nursing for the past hour, staying meticulously sober while Caitlin rambles on about everything except what exactly the fuck is going the fuck on. I haven't been drinking that much this year, not since everything went down with Sasha, but hearing the nonspooky half of Caitlin's autobiography has made me want to empty this place into my liver. Still, I gotta stay on point, especially if Caitlin plans on drinking herself into an oversharing stupor.

"Where are all the ghosts, then?"

"Must be a busy day," I mutter. Truth is, they all ducked out pretty soon after we walked in. Caitlin seems to have a reputation among the dead.

"Anyway, yeah, I dated this guy Rex for a few months. I mean . . . his name was fucking Rex, right? How much should I really have expected? Ugh. He worked at a different nonprofit, did fieldwork actually, which was you know, sexy? I guess. In theory more than practice, but yeah . . . at some point, you know, it got more serious, and he met my . . ." Her voice trails off.

I wait.

"And the truth is, and I know you know this as well as I do, Carlos. Can I call you Carlos? I mean, I have been, but . . . I mean, it's your name!" She spits a laugh out and I catch some in my eye. "Ha! Anyway, as we both know, at some point, no matter how fucked up your"—she shoves a finger into my chest, then hers—"or my nighttime activities may be, at some point, you gotta let people into your life. You can't keep living in your . . . in your parents' you know . . . *basement!* Forever. Right?"

She might cry. The sob hovers in wait. Then she bursts out laughing. "Shit! I tried to explain to Rex about stuff. About you know, *ghosts* . . . and *Jeremy.* Shit. I walked him through it *slowly,* Carlos. I was really . . . I was careful.

Didn't spring it on him. And I'd been dropping little hints along the way, right? I can be subtle when I want to be. Caitlin can be subtle."

Caitlin has reached the speak-about-yourself-in-the-third-person stage of wrecked.

"So what does he do? Loses. His. Shit. Carlos. Carlos! How did he lose his shit?"

I just stare at her, because I think it's a rhetorical question. She stares back.

"How did he lose his shit?" she says again, quietly this time.

"I . . . I don't know?"

She gets real close to my face and whispers: "Like a little bitch."

We both lean back and stare at each other for a few seconds. I have lost all patience. I'd been operating on a What Would Reza Do principle for the past hour—not asking her too many questions so I don't seem overly eager, letting her say what she has to say so she can ramble around to giving me whatever information I need. I've been patient, balanced. But I'm fucking done. I down the rest of my rum and Coke and order another. Quiñones grunts.

"Caitlin."

"Eh?"

"What happened with your brother? Why do you think he's trying to—?"

"I've been cleaning up that little motherfucker's messes for a long time, Carlos. You know about cleaning up messes. You're a cleanup man. You are to the Council what I am to Jeremy. Understand? When he gets sloppy, when one of his . . . when someone gets out. Or there's a witness, or whatever . . . I'm the one that tidies up. Why? Because he's family, and that's what family does. We do our part. And Mom and Dad, they've been doi—they did their part, for years. *Years,* Carlos. They never even saw him, all those years, but they knew. They knew everything, because *I* told them. I held their fragile little hands while they cried and shook and carried on and then calmed down, because eventually, Carlos, everyone calms down. The shock is a performance. We're *supposed* to be horrified by the weird shit our family does. It's expected. So they went through their motions, and I waited by their side, and when they calmed down and were ready to help their son step into his destiny and become what he was meant to be, well, I was there to transfer the funds and keep everything on the level. Do you understand?"

Very slowly, I nod.

"So they gave. And gave and gave and gave. And me, I did what I do, closed all the open doors, so to speak." Open doors like Shelly and Angie. Kia . . . Sasha. I suppress a shudder. "And fulfilled my contracts with the Council on the side. *And* worked at the agency, which is no easy work either. But he always wanted more. It was never enough. They . . . the thousands and thousands of them, all thinking as one, all manifesting through Jeremy and the weird underground universe he created around him . . . *They* want and want and need and it was never enough.

"They were always, always arguing. The back-and-forth was incessant and it happened through me, always. Why? Because they could never see him, never see what he'd become. He was ashamed, even through all his heightened sense of self, all his big talk about channeling these primordial energies, and he is, he is, but still . . . it's made him a monster and he knows it. Somewhere deep down, he still feels shame, and he loved and hated our parents for that shame, because he knew if he looked at them face-to-face he'd see the horror reflected back at him, of everything he once was and everything he had become."

Quiñones drops off my rum and Coke and then Caitlin and I sit side by side in silence for a few seconds.

"So yes, I'm sure. The police found no bodies in the ruins

of my house, Carlos. None. They found the tunnel, of course, but the tunnel just goes into the sewer system. It's weird, but nothing they could do much with. Jeremy finally got fed up with the back-and-forth and he killed them and took their bodies out and burned down the place. He's threatened to do it before." She looks up at me, her eyes wide and wild. "Sick fuck," she whispers.

"You don't want my help keeping you safe, do you?" I say.

Caitlin shakes her head. "I want you to help me find my brother and fucking kill that piece of shit, Carlos."

Very slowly, I nod. "I can do that."

"Great. Eleven p.m., here." She puts a scrap of paper on the bar. The Bushwick address we followed the ghostling to is scrawled on it in neat handwriting. "Bring your sword."

And she's gone.

Twenty minutes later I'm alone and on my third rum and Coke, putting all the pieces together, when I feel the prickly awareness of a small presence by my side. I turn and then stumble backward, groping for my blade. The . . . the thing . . . The killer child ghost sits on the barstool next to mine. He's staring at me, expression calm, if not a little lopsided.

"The fuck . . ." I stammer, reaching for my blade.

"Easy, Carlos." It's Riley, his shimmery ass chuckling as he long-steps across Burgundy Bar with his hands up. "It's cool, man."

I resheathe but don't sit back down. The ghostling just stares at me. "You . . . It's . . . What the fuck?"

"It's uh . . . reformed? Whatever, it's okay now." Riley sits on the other side of the ghostling, and I warily take my own seat and signal Quiñones to bring two drinks.

"How, man?"

Quiñones is used to creepy motherfuckers like myself

ordering more drinks than necessary and carrying on whole conversations with folks that ain't there. If anything, he was probably more surprised to see me walk in with an actual person earlier.

"Sylvia figured it out," Riley says. "Said she used to teach private school when she was alive and so reforming the homicidal deep programming of some wee errant soul was no big deal. I think she got some secret powers she's not telling me 'bout though, to be honest."

"If I told you, they wouldn't be secret." Sylvia Bell takes the stool beside Riley and nods at me. I signal Quiñones for another drink as he puts the first two down, and he growls. The Burgundy is filling back up. I recognize most of Sylvia's crew from Squad 9 taking up an entire corner. They're carrying on about some inside joke, glancing at us every now and then to make sure everything's alright.

The child ghost hasn't stopped staring at me. "Is he . . . Is he okay though?"

"We don't really know," Sylvia says. "Probably not, considering all he's been through. But he's not trying to murder everybody, so that's a step in the right direction."

"Word," I say, and clink my glass against Riley's and Sylvia's. We drink, the two ghosts leaning forward to sip so as not to freak out Quiñones any more than necessary.

"What's the play, C? I heard you were in here having an interesting conversation."

I shake my head. "To say the least. I mean, it was boring as fuck for ninety percent of the time, but yeah, I think I found out what I needed to."

"Listen," Sylvia says. "If Caitlin is the one behind this situation." She throws a curt nod at the child ghost. "She has to die. I'll do it. I don't give a fuck. But she has to die."

"She is," I say. "And believe me—there's already a long line for that job. Took all I had not to end her right quick just now, but not yet. She wants me to help her make a move on her brother—thinks he's the one that took out their parents the other night."

"He's not though, is he?" Riley asks.

I shake my head.

"Got it."

"Reza and Kia are trying to bring in the Survivors to help us too."

"The Survivors as in the group outlawed by the Council?" Sylvia says.

Riley and I both nod and then stare at her.

"I'm in," Sylvia says. "Council's out here trying to protect the complete failure of a human being that tortured these children into being murderers—they're dead to me."

"No pun," Riley says.

"Shut up, Riley," Sylvia says.

I like her.

"So I said to Botus, 'No, mothafucka, you're gonna pick up the dog.'" It's two hours later and I'm standing in the far corner of the Burgundy Bar, surrounded by the shimmering shrouds and laughing faces of Squad 9. We're all utterly wrecked.

"You ain't really call Botus a mothafucka, C," Riley says.

"I'm paraphrasing, mothafucka." More riotous laughter.

"I did actually call Bart Arsten a dickhole one time," Sylvia says. She's less outwardly sloppy than Riley or me, but her eyes are narrowed and teary.

"Get the fuck outta here," Gordon scoffs. He's the tallest Squad 9 'catcher, and the loudest.

Sylvia glares at him for a solid four seconds, just long enough to quiet the room. Then she blurts out a laugh. "I really did though." Everyone relaxes and chuckles. "It was right after I got out of the academy. He wanted to send me on some runaround to get back this ghost of a teacher I knew."

Angry, incredulous noises from the crowd. Sylvia shakes her head. "Like . . . I knew this man. I worked with him. Arthur, his name was. We were friends even, in that easy sort of not-too-deep way you have with coworkers. Taught eighth-grade earth science. He, you know, he made sense, in a way that most teachers at that ragged fuckhole of a school didn't. He was kind. Got hit by a car the night before his wedding."

The whole bar's quiet now. Quiñones wipes down the counter, muttering to himself. We all shake our heads, taking in Sylvia's story.

"Took him a day or two to actually die, so the shit wasn't sudden, didn't wipe out his memory. No offense, Riley." Riley shakes his head. "So *of course* the guy's gonna come back over. If nothing else to try and comfort his mourning fiancée or whatever. Shit. And Bartholomew McFuckshit wants me, still fairly recently dead myself—heart attack, by the way," she adds. "Anyway, this piece of shit wants me to go drag him back down to Hell? Two days after he was supposed to get married? Um, no."

"You didn't go?" Andrea asks. She's long and thin, and from what I hear, the fiercest of the new batch of fresh-out-the-academy 'catchers.

"Oh, I went," Sylvia says. "And I stood beside him the whole time while he did what he had to do, said his good-byes, handled his business. Then I let him know what was what with the Council, how to stay under the radar, whatever, and sent him on his way."

Squad 9 lets out a cheer for their commander. Riley slides into the seat next to Sylvia and throws an arm around her. "Proud of you, babe," he says, smiling drunkenly into her shoulder.

Babe? I'm too drunk to think too hard about it. All I know is, it's an overcast afternoon and I've just met with the woman that wants to kill most of my favorite people in the world and now I'm surrounded by outrageous, happy souls that I barely know but somehow love.

CHAPTER TWENTY-FOUR

Kia

At the botánica, NY1 blares news about the Ferns' house blowing up. A reporter with a young face and receding hairline explains that no bodies were found and the elder Ferns are still unaccounted for. He sounds genuinely upset about it, and then it's time for Traffic on the Ones. I mute the TV—you have to stand up and turn the remote at some hypotenuse-ass angle while pressing the button eighteen million times to get it to work—and then slump back into my swively stool and cross my arms over my chest.

I'm sick of this, all this. Sick of feeling the icy sensation that some dead eyes linger on the back of my neck, sick of flinching at every passing shadow, glancing at corners to see if some skittering, six-legged pale agent of death is there, sick of checking the skin on strangers' faces in case it tries to crawl away. Sick of ghosts and guns. Sick of death. Sick of myself. Sick of being sick of shit. After the standoff in the park, I headed to Carlos's, tacked a note on his door about meeting Sasha, and then came here, tired and irritable and over it all.

I put on my headphones, which I never do when I'm behind the counter, and at first, even King Impervious's words feel faraway and useless. It's one of her slow joints—slow by

Impervious standards anyway—and she got some dude that sounds like he's a day away from dying of throat cancer to sing the hook. Yes, *I am the riot son / the king of chaos come,* and in the back a chorus of sexy girls—you can tell they sexy; it's not a debate—chants, *I am the riot, the riot, the mothafuckin' riot,* and then the King comes in, spittin' machine-gun thunder: *Come chaos, come from the barrel of the gun / Fuck the path fuck the way fuck the method fuck the sun.* She just said "fuck the sun." I know it's coming; I still smile every time. *Find me in the fire line / Floatin' like a satellite / Fucking mothafuckas in the face with a Cadillac.* Like . . . How does one go about fucking a mothafucka in the face with a Cadillac? I don't care. She doesn't care. We don't care together. Anyone who cares can fuck off.

I'm just letting a smile cross my face when the door chimes erupt through my music, through my skull, and a group of white boys rumble into the store. I pause the King, take off my headphones. They pass without a glance in my direction.

"No, Kenny, no, it's over here!"

"Shut up, Bill!"

"And so I told her, 'No, girl, it's not even like that!' She just shook her head. I'm so fucking tired of her shit, man."

"Yeah, man. Yeah."

"It's over here! Kenny, come here."

"I'm coming, man, relax."

"Bill, you gotta shut up, man."

I can't keep track of who's Bill or Kenny or getting curved by whose girlfriend, and really, I don't care. I just want them out. The air fills with them—their banter and boy smell and whiteness, their exaggerated ease with one another and the world.

"Ahahahaha, these are potions though! Like, for real, this soap is supposed to scare away ghosts."

"Oh shit, man."

"Kenny, what's this mean, a love potion?"

"Yeah, that's supposed to bring the ladies right to you, man."

"Let's get it for Bill. Maybe Christine will stop friend zoning his ass."

Wild laughter. Because really, what's funnier than other people's cultures and sexual coercion?

"No, no, this one, this one: brings in the money!"

"Woo-woo!"

"We can pay rent this month! Get three!"

More laughter. My right hand has found its way to the short blade Carlos gifted me; my fingers wrap tight around the handle. I wonder briefly if my body has figured out something my mind doesn't know yet. But no floating translucent weirdoes clutter the air, and no child demons emerge from the shadows. It's not fear, this need to hold something lethal. It's rage.

The boys drop eight packets of Baba Eddie's soaps and herbal remedies on the counter. One of them, Bill, I guess, says: "We'll take 'em all." And for the first time, in their world, I exist. A transaction is needed; my presence matters now.

"No," I say.

I'm not sure what it is. White people have been coming in more and more these days. Sometimes they're respectful, sometimes not, but I've never felt like this. When I say *no,* really it means *fuck you,* and I relish the sizzling denial lingering in the silence that follows.

"Uh . . ." Bill says. Then they all laugh, but it's forced. Surely I must be joking.

Really, the dried herbs and soaps, on their own, are a quick fix. Baba always tells people that himself. It's like getting some generic over-the-counter shit when you could go get diagnosed and prescribed a true, tailor-made remedy just for you. But they're also cheap, and folks are struggling.

Anyway, the product's not the point: I'm fed up.

"What do you mean, no?" Bill says into my icy glare.

"I mean, you can't buy them."

The chuckles stop.

"Why not?"

"Because"—I dig up a smile—"I said so."

Suddenly, I can taste violence in the air. It must be their sweaty fight-or-flight glands going into collective overdrive. An unexpected ripple has been torn in their meticulously cultivated ghetto paradise, and I'm the mothafuckin' pebble. I feel like King Impervious would be proud.

I smile wider.

"Wha—?" another stutters. "We want to see your manager."

"Kenny," Bill says, lip curled into a sneer. "Forget it. She's just a stupid kid."

"No, that's not the point, man! Where's your manager?"

"You're looking at her." I'm not just a pebble. I'm a stone. A rock. Their whirlwinding frustration curls and crashes around me. "How may I help you?"

"Fuck this," a third says. "Where's this Baba Eddie guy, then? We want to file a complaint. Because this is some bullshit, seriously."

I take a piece of paper from the printer and poise a pen above it. "I'll take your complaint. What seems to be the trouble today, sir?"

They erupt into a fury of protest. The air thickens. Their wiry bodies tense; that flailing gets erratic. If a hand crosses the counter at me, I'll take it off.

"This is *so* unacceptable!"

"Yeah, Christine?" one of them says into a super-expensive-looking cell phone. "You won't believe this shit!

We're at the store around the corner where they sell the voo-doo stuff and . . . What's that? Oh wow, that's cool, yeah."

I probably wouldn't really chop a hand off. I don't need to go to jail right now. Baba Eddie would have to handle the fallout, and it'd be a whole thing: *Satanic Black Girl Lashes Out.* Whatever. But now this game is getting old and I want to go back to King Impervious. And I have no idea how to get these assholes to leave. What if they decide to occupy the place, and then I'll have to explain everything to Baba Eddie?

The door chimes jangle again, and Baba Eddie walks in with his boyfriend, Russell. Russell's Native, Ojibwa, I think, but folks always confuse him for regular ol' white. He's wearing a slick business suit as always and looking vexed as fuck, as always. For a few seconds, nobody says anything. One of Baba Eddie's eyebrows goes up. Russell furrows his brow, then says, "These boys bothering you, Kia?"

"Wait a minute!" one of them yells.

"She was the one . . ." another starts. But then they all get quiet, cuz Russell raises his hand. He's wide. Not fat. It's just a long way from one side of his shoulders to the other. You could fit three of these scrawny hipsters across Russell's large frame. "I didn't ask you a question, son," he says real quiet-like. "Now, Kia. Are these . . . boys . . . both-ering you?" He squeezes each word out like it hurts.

"Yeah," I say. "They're being assholes."

Russell turns to them, frown deepening. The boys look at each other and then scatter. They have to go past Russell and Baba Eddie to get to the door, so there's a lot of sim-pering "Pardon Me"s and "Sorry"ing and then they're gone and the jangly door slams shut, and Baba Eddie and Russell lean against the counter and glare at me.

"They *were* being assholes," I say.

"You didn't provoke them at all?" Baba Eddie asks. "Not that I think you would, but . . ."

"They were making fun of your herb packets." I sound like a petulant little kid, and I don't care. The fire still rages through my insides. "And being disrespectful. And loud."

Baba Eddie sighs. "Then I'm glad you held it down."

"She's still mad," Russell says. I'm annoyed that he's talking about me like I'm not there and even more annoyed that he's right.

"What's wrong, Kia?" Baba Eddie asks, coming around to where I'm sitting. He's pretty small, looks even tinier next to his wide-shouldered boyfriend, and he has to pull up one of the stools to really be comfortable at the counter. "Tell Baba Eddie all about it."

I shake my head and stupid tears start to form in my stupid eyes like I'm a stupid . . . well, teenager. I just faced down a throng of unruly hipsters without flinching. There's no reason I should suddenly become a whimpering douche bag.

Alas, here I am.

Russell passes me a silk handkerchief, and I wipe my eyes with it and then shake my head again and then just put my head down on Baba Eddie's shoulder and sob silently for a few minutes while he rubs my back.

"I'm fucking angry," I finally say.

"At who or what?" Baba Eddie asks.

"I can't"—*sniffle*—"talk about it."

"This have anything to do with whatever fuckshit Carlos been on? Because you sound an awful lot like him right now."

I manage a choky little laugh. "Only kinda. I don't even really know what I'm mad about. I mean . . . I got everything I wanted. You ever . . . you ever get exactly what you wanted and then realize that you're still mad for not having had it all that time and it just doesn't seem fair at all?"

Both Baba Eddie and Russell nod, faces glum.

"That's me. I just . . . Why didn't he ever tell me? Why didn't he reach out? Anything? I just want to be happy, but

I'm so, so mad. All this time. I feel like a terrible person. I am a terrible person."

"Ah, Kia." Baba Eddie shakes his head. "You're all right. I don't know what you did or didn't do, but your feelings don't make you terrible."

Russell snorts. "That's not what you said last night when I—"

"Quiet, old man," Baba snaps. "We're going out to dinner— Russell made partner today, and we have some celebrating to do."

I blink away tears. "Congrats, man!"

Russell shrugs. "Thanks. I plan to rain even more havoc upon the motherfuckers."

"Excellent," I say, and hock some boogers into his handkerchief. "I would come, but I gotta meet someone. That situation I was just talking about, as a matter of fact."

"I'm sure," Baba Eddie says, "that if you tell the person why you're mad, they'll understand, even if it feels like it doesn't make sense."

I punch his shoulder. "When did you get so touchy-feely, man? I can't deal with this shit."

"Pay him no mind," Russell says, walking to the back. "He'll be back to his old fuckery soon as you dry your tears. I'm gonna go take a piss."

"You alright?" Baba asks.

"I will be. I'll say what I have to say. And then we'll do what has to be done."

"That sounds ominous. I'm not sure how I feel about you and Carlos teaming up. I love Carlos like the weird half-dead son I never particularly wanted, but he runs in a dangerous world, Kia."

"I've noticed." I want to tell Baba the whole story, from the night Jeremy disappeared on, but he has dinner to go to and I'm not gonna sully Russell's big night. "I'll be careful," I say. "I promise."

———————

Last time I came to the walkway along the Brooklyn waterfront, it was a pretty but haphazard boardwalk, starting and
stopping, the fresh ocean air blending with the exhaust and
clutter of the Brooklyn-Queens Expressway. There were
lovers and rats and parts where you probably shouldn't go
at night and parts that looked like postcards. I was with my
dad. We had slipped off from some summer-fun program
where the facilitators spoke in all caps with too many excla-
mation points until my dad finally shook his head and muttered, "Let's get out of here, kid," and we did. Wandered all
through downtown Brooklyn, my little hand in his and white
men in business suits and old brown men selling children's
books and teenagers popping gum. We stood on the boardwalk, the bay sparkling beneath the midday sun, and a few
feet away, a white woman with bags under her eyes got high.
Across the bay, Manhattan's steel towers glared back at us,
reflected the perfect sky.

Now the waterfront is brand-new. Every plank and screw
has been plotted, planned, oh so carefully placed. Nothing
is left to chance; nothing deteriorates or scuffs. There's a
carousel and playing fields and the walkway stretches all
along the edge of the water, rising and falling around little
wooded areas. Gio and Rigo walk hand in hand beside me,
a picture, essentially, of perfection. Rigo wears a long leather
jacket over a light hoodie and a silver button-down shirt—
tacky as hell, but . . . he's Rigo. He can literally do whatever
the fuck he wants and still look like a god. The top bunch
of buttons are open, and he's practically got cleavage, those
pecs are so flawlessly defined. I think he has more cleavage
than me, dammit.

And Gio's just Gio. Still struts with that unceasing flow,
even after all the . . . whatever it is he's been through. He's

in cargo pants, a T-shirt, and that green European-looking overcoat he wears, probably where he keeps all his cool weapons.

That first night—the night I thought I was going to have sex with Rigo and instead found my long-lost cousin—I finished sobbing into his shirt and then we all sat down to eat. Some incredible seafood stew served in a stone gourd that Rigo called mocqueca. It was red and still bubbling, and little shrimps and mussels lounged around half submerged in the thick broth. And we chatted. Just chatted. The three of us. Like, small talk. Like Gio hadn't been gone for seven years and I hadn't finally accepted he was dead and . . . and . . . and . . .

I played along.

Because what else could I do? I wasn't going to overturn the table. Vanquish the instant ease we'd all found with each other. Rigo cracked jokes and talked about his adventures getting lost on the subway. Gio smiled and looked on. I let myself laugh, because it really was funny, but also to stifle that simmering, seething rage trying to claw its way up from inside me.

How dare he?

It became a chant, one I was barely aware of. It just cycled on and on like the chorus of hot chicks singing *the mothafuckin' riot* behind King Impervious. *How dare he not tell me? How dare he just show the fuck up one day out the blue and pretend everything is alright? How dare he disappear in the first place and leave me all alone trapped in a fuckass school system that didn't understand me? How dare . . . ?* The entries piled on and on and I felt more and more selfish each time.

It wasn't about me.

It wasn't about me.

It wasn't—

"What's wrong, Kia?" Gio asks.

"How dare you?" I blurt out.

The sun has set, the sky finishes off the last touches of night around us. The streetlights blinked on a few minutes ago. Freighters glide silently along the inky water, cutting the shimmering reflections of Manhattan's skyscrapers.

Gio and Rigo stop walking. Gio frowns at me, squinting, and lets go of Rigo's hand. Disappointed? Enraged? I am an asshole for being mad; I want to stop being mad, but I can't. I want to swallow the words back up, take them inside of me and let them keep wreaking silent havoc, but I can't. I almost apologize, as if that could scrub away my question, but I don't do that either. That would be a lie. And anyway, there's no unsaying what's been said. You can't uncast a spell, Baba Eddie always tells me with a chuckle.

Gio rubs his eyes, mutters something.

"What?"

He looks me dead in the face. "I'm sorry."

"You are?" I waver somewhere between laughing and crying. "For . . . what?" That probably came out sounding like a challenge, but I really want to know.

"You're right."

"About what, man? All I said was 'How dare you?' It's a question, not a statement."

"About everything. What your question implies. I had no right to disappear, no right not to tell you where I went or why. I had no right to pretend that it wouldn't hurt you, but I did pretend that because that was the only way I knew how to keep going."

"But why didn't you just . . . ?"

"I couldn't. I couldn't. First I was too depressed and I thought I was gonna kill myself, and reaching out to you would have only made it harder. And I was terrified that the roach guys would go after anyone I talked to, anyone I touched. So for a long time I just didn't touch anyone. I kept it moving, literally and figuratively. Never stayed in the same town two nights in a row, did horrible, stupid things to stay alive and . . . and I was ashamed. I was ashamed that the only way I knew how to keep going was to be a ghost, cut off from you and everyone I else I knew and loved."

"It's not just me," I say, feeling brave and feeling awful about feeling brave. Feeling like I'm driving the knife even deeper. "My dad. He . . . he raised you, Giovanni. He thinks you're dead."

Gio nods. Shakes his head. "I didn't know how. I didn't. And then, at some point, I started training. I had a goal, a focus. And I . . ."

"You have to make it right," I say. I don't want to hear about his training and globe-trotting anymore. Not right now. "You have to tell Dad."

"I will," he says, a little too fast. "I will. Once we . . ."

"No. You can't let him go another night thinking you're dead. Not after all he's been through for you."

"Kia, I don't know if you understand the danger we're in right now."

"Don't understand it?" I stomp my foot. "Did you forget the part about me getting choked out by a floating toddler? Did you miss the whole thing where I was standing right next to you in the woods with a dozen half-dead guys pointing guns at us? Was that someone else? Get the fuck outta here."

I turn around and I'm stomping off, literally stomping the fuck off, when a man comes running down the boardwalk. I hear Gio yell, "Kia!" and then the man bucks forward, sliding into a crouch. For a fraction of a second, he looks suddenly much slighter, just decayed flesh on bones, and then all I see is a swarming cloud of pinkish hell blasting toward me.

And then I see Gio, his spinning form blotting out the swarm. He swooshes forward, lands in a squat facing me, his hood up. Then he grunts as the mass of pale roaches crashes against him and splays out to either side. He throws one leg back, plants the other foot, and then flies up into the scattering swarm and cracks the guy across his face. The roach man drops, all flaked-off skin and shiny bone. Gio lifts one foot. I can't look away. I don't want to see, but I can't look away. Gio's foot smashes down, demolishing the guy's skull with a mushy crack.

Rigo's already behind him, swatting off a few stray roaches from his coat. They both turn to me.

"You okay?" Gio asks.

I nod but then shake my head, because three more of them round the corner and sprint toward us.

Gio and Rigo follow my gaze, then look at me. "Run," Gio says. And I do.

Furman Street runs a long, dusty stretch in the shadow of the Brooklyn-Queens Expressway along the waterside park. We come out somewhere in the middle, not close enough to either end to matter. Gio has retrieved daggers from his jacket and holds one pressed against the inside of each wrist, his eyes behind us as Rigo charges forward, checking the bushes and fenced-in areas beneath the overpass

Up ahead, a Mustang idles halfway on the curb. As we approach, the driver's-side door swings open. Rigo stops and tenses into a fighting stance. I know the man that emerges—he was there in the park this morning: one of the Survivors. Blaine, they called him. He's tall with a shaved head and wraparound sunglasses. And of course, he's gray-ish. He smiles when he sees us, a little too wide, but I'm relieved, because surely he's come to whisk us off, away from these fucking monsters, which also means the Survivors have come to their decision and will help us take out

Jeremy Fern. And then Blaine raises a pistol at us and smiles even wider, showing his large teeth, his gums.

"The fuck?" Gio says.

The three Blattodeons walk out of the park behind us and just stand there, panting.

"That's a good question," Blaine says. I want to knock his teeth out. "I'll make it simple. Get in the car."

I'm pretty sure Gio could take him out if he had a chance, but we're outnumbered and outgunned and I don't think Gio would risk losing either of us in the fight. Then again . . . we may not have another chance.

"If we don't?" Gio says.

He's buying time. I want to burst into tears, but I don't. I twist up my face into a fuck-you scowl and leave it there.

"I think we both know what'll happen if you don't," Blaine says. His smile's fading a little. He doesn't want trouble. Behind him, headlights approach, and he lowers the gun to his side.

"You might get one of us," Gio says, "but you won't live long after that."

Blaine laughs as the car whooshes past and then holds the gun up again. "Funny thing about that. You care about these two, whether they live or die. I don't give a fuck about these cockroach pieces of shit. They're just business associates. In fact, I hate them."

Gio shakes his head. "Then why . . . ?"

"Because we're partners now, me and these roach motherfuckers, and that's that," Blaine says. "So while us killing you all would be a terrible tragedy for you, you killing a few of these freaks but still getting caught in the end is fine with me. Do you understand? You're not just outnumbered and outflanked: you lose because I don't give a frosty fuck and you do. Clear? Now get"—he cocks his gun and levels it directly at my face—"the fuck"—I don't flinch; I just stare him down—"in the car."

First we hear tires screech, then an old diesel engine revving and the low thrum of some bass and drums beat. It comes from just around the bend. We all turn to look. The three roach guys mutter and click and shift their weight around. Blaine lowers his gun—last thing any of us needs is some asshole calling the cops.

One of those Access-A-Ride vans comes flying into view, brights blaring into all our retinas. It's painted black, and techno music blasts out, getting louder as it approaches. At first it looks like it'll just zoom past. Then it swerves onto the sidewalk as it's passing the Blattodeons. It catches the first one full-on, before he has a chance to run. I see his body somersault through the air as the roaches explode into flight around him. One of his arms detaches, lands with a clutter a few seconds before his shattered body crashes down in a heap. The van doesn't slow, just screeches slightly to the right so it ends up clipping the other two roach men at the same time. Both collapse under its tires and are pulverized instantly in a flash of tangled limbs and pale fluttering wings.

I've been gaping. Everything seemed to freeze the second the Access-A-Ride deathmobile veered off the road. Rigo's strong, perfect arms wrap around me from behind; he's screaming in my ear, but I can't make it out. He pulls me backward. Blaine raises his gun, mouth wide-open. He gets off two shots—both ricochet off the windshield—and then yells as three tons of metal slam into him at thirty miles an hour, throwing him against the back window of the Mustang. The huge black van keeps coming, smashing full force into Blaine and his car, and turning them both into a shattered pile of blood, flesh, broken windows, and twisted metal.

I'm getting to my feet when the Access-A-Ride reverses out of the wreckage. I didn't even realize I'd been on the ground. The van is barely dented. The crumpled bodies of the roach guys lie perfectly still. Across the road, Gio emerges from the bushes he'd jumped into. Rigo stands beside me, his body tensed for a fight.

The driver's-side window lowers, and a bald brown guy with a goatee grins out at us. The *double-thump clack* of a house beat pulses out of the van, punctuated by the coy giggling of party girls.

"We're with Reza," he says. "Come with us."

CHAPTER TWENTY-FIVE

❦

Carlos

One night, when I was still in the early throes of Sasha being gone as suddenly as she'd appeared, I was at the Burgundy, guzzling rum and Cokes like water, and I made the mistake of confiding in an old ghost. In living years, he'd probably passed at sixty or so, but he'd been a Council soul-catcher for a few decades and he let every year show.

"I mean," I said for the eight hundredth time that night, "I don't even know."

"Carlos, what the hell are you talking about, man?" His name was Barry, but everyone called him Barometer—no idea why. Some inside joke I never cared enough about to know.

Sasha and the Survivors were and will always be public enemies in the eyes of the Council, so I wasn't telling folks about what happened at that point; still don't. Instead I'd been repeating "I don't even know" like a self-destructive mantra, each time the slur enhanced.

"I don't . . . know," I said, grasping for some woozy truth amid all the shit I felt but couldn't say or could say but couldn't feel. Or something. ". . . I don't know . . . whether I feel guilty or angry."

Barometer shrugged. "Why not both?"

And that's probably where I went wrong. The guy made

one little ounce of sense, so like a jackass I opened the flood doors. "And so she walked out," I muttered twenty minutes later. I'd managed to omit her name and the fact that she was half dead like me, but otherwise, the story spilled out unedited.

Barometer leaned over to sip his gin and tonic throughout, nodding and shaking his head at all the right parts. When I was done, he sighed and said, "Oh, you're good."

I raised my eyebrows. "I am?"

"Yeah. It wasn't love."

I signaled Quiñones to bring another round. "It wasn't?"

"Nah, man. You said you only knew her for, like, a few months, right?"

"I mean . . ."

"Right. You can't love someone in that amount of time. I mean you literally were in her presence for what—eight, nine hours? C'mon, man."

"I hadn't thought of it like that."

"I mean . . . technically."

"So how many . . . ?"

"Minimum, and we're talking bare minimum here, Carlos: eighteen months. Up till that moment, it's really not love."

"What is it?"

"It can *feel* like love, whatever that means—am I right?"

"I don't . . . know."

"It can *taste* like love, if you know what I mean."

"I really don't."

"But it ain't *love* love."

"What is it?"

"It's prelove."

"The fuck is—"

"And prelove ain't love. Nope."

"How the fuck—?"

"In fact, even prelove is often not prelove; it's just mistaken for prelove."

"So what's—"

"It's really that you just love the pussy."

"Wait . . ."

"And that's all well and good. I support good sexing and whatever, but just cuz you love the pussy doesn't mean you love the woman."

"Can you prelove the pussy?"

"Carlos, I feel like you're not taking me seriously at this point."

"No, I'm really just confu—"

"You can prelove the pussy *one* time; that's it. After that, you just know and it's love love."

I really didn't have anything to say to that, so we just sat in silence for a few minutes, sipping our drinks and letting that last bit of wisdom resonate. A few hours later, I turned over and over in bed, wrestling with a hundred more questions, wanting to throw on my coat and run across Brooklyn, bust into the Burgundy, and yell, "No, Barometer, this is love. This ache I feel, this need, this fire that stirs every time she crosses my mind, that is love, and more than that, what we felt between us when we walked through the park, when our eyes met, the way we both knew without saying the truth that lay dormant but undeniable on the tips of our tongues, *that* is love, Barometer, not some x on a calendar or setting on a stopwatch."

Instead, I rolled over again, cursed the echoes of each unsaid word, and passed out.

Now I'm standing at the southern gate of Prospect Park, my back against a carved stone pillar, and I still want to yell at Barometer, yell at the sky, yell at myself, yell at Sasha. She'll be here any minute, and somehow I feel like for all the time I've had to process and prepare, it's not enough; it's never enough.

The night sky laughs at me. The kids skating past laugh at me. Old drunks laugh at me, swig and then pass the bottle to other old drunks, and they laugh at me too. And why shouldn't they? For all the grace and ferocity I've summoned within myself in the thick of crises, facing down hellfire and tragedy, my stomach still knots at the thought of Sasha strolling through the dim park toward me.

And then Sasha strolls through the dim park toward me.

Our eyes meet and we both smile at the same time. Hers is wide and unafraid; I think even she's startled by it, and mine matches. She walks right to me, pauses. We size each other up for a half tick—that post-pregnancy weight looks amazing on her—and then fall into a deep embrace. Her smell surrounds me, that Sasha smell, some coconut shampoo she uses and the gentle hint of whatever essence of her seeps through. There's something long and hard strapped to her back, beneath that jacket—a sword, I'm guessing—but I just ignore it for now. Her face is in my neck, and I feel her lips smiling against my skin, my chilly skin and her chilly skin, and our hands find each other, and the moment when normal hugs cease to be comes and goes and still she smiles into my neck and still my arms wrap around her and still . . .

Now the sky smiles at me, winks even, and the kids skating past snicker and the old drunks shake their heads and remember. Something true has happened, cut through all the fear and overthinking and trying endlessly to decide what is and isn't, what should and shouldn't be, and what's left is just this: the two of us, holding perfectly still, bodies pressed together.

"Did you . . . ?" she says, but her voice trails off and she shakes her head.

We let a few more moments pass.

"Did I what?" I ask.

"Never mind. I don't even really know what I was going

to ask. I was just breaching the silence, but then I changed my mind."

I nod. She wiggles in my embrace and then takes something out of her pocket. A picture. Two smiling babies.

My babies. Our babies.

They're fat and brown and almost identical.

They're ours.

I don't cry. I think I'm all dried out from earlier anyway, but I do gulp and gasp a few times. I step back from her, just to take them both in, and there they are. Little chubby cheeks and three chins each and those weensy-ass little fingers. Jesus. I hand her the picture back, and she shakes her head.

"Keep it. I wanted to bring them, but what with everything going on . . ."

"I understand. It's better." I stare at the picture some more and then slide it into the inside pocket of my jacket. Then I look back up at Sasha. "I don't know what to say."

"You and me both. Look . . ."

"I'm sorry," I blurt out. "I know I said it before, but that was . . . before. In the midst of everything." The trees shush and tremble around us—it's a chilly night, and that breeze doesn't help. It's a night that we should be under covers, fogging up windows. "And of course I was sorry then, but it might've sounded like I was just saying it to . . . to keep you, and yes, I wanted you to stay, with all of me, I did, but . . . and, I know these words can't change what I did or bring him back, but the truth is that doing what I did . . ." I pause because I know I have to say it, but I don't want to. I can't. I won't. "Killing Trevor has haunted me since I did it, not just because of what it did to you but because of what it did to me and . . ."

She silences me with a finger to her lips. "I know."

"You do?"

"I assumed. And . . . even though I had every cause in the world to walk out on you, I'm still sorry I did. I'm sorry I hurt you. I know that I hurt you. I wish I could've stayed."

The wind in the trees is a song. It's the theme song to my heart waking back up. The world it wakes to is cold, cruel even, but it is awake, my heart. And somehow, smiling.

"But I also know that if I'd stayed then, I would have resented you. And maybe never . . . forgiven you." She shakes her head. "Not that I have, necessarily, forgiven you. Or ever will. But I knew if I was to ever see you again, I needed to first get away."

I nod. It all makes sense. It did then too, in a horrible way, but it makes much more sense now. "The babies are . . . ?"

"They're fully alive and healthy."

I exhale.

The wind in the trees is a song. All those leaves shuddering and shushing against each other on this cool night; one falls and slow dances through the breeze, touching gently down on the pavement. The song is about my life and the lives that came from me. I am a father. We have made life, these two half wraiths, these impossible children of death, have come together, and from two halves came not one whole but two.

I want to run. I'm sure I could lap the park in seconds if I took off right now, laughing the whole way, but instead I smile.

"Come," Sasha says. "We need to see about something."

We head out of the park, past her looming prewar apartment building on Ocean Avenue, and deeper into Flatbush. "Kia's note said one of the Survivors found a way to tap into our lives?"

She nods. "Who woulda thought, of all the things Ol' Ginny can't do for shit, hypnosis is one she rules at."

"Say what?"

I hadn't even realized where we'd walked to. Large purple letters announce GINNY'S FORTUNE-TELLINGS AND SPIRITUAL READINGS in some *Wizard of Oz* font across a storefront. I haven't talked to Ol' Ginny in months; in fact, the last time I saw her was the night Sasha and I finished off Sarco on the roof of the Grand Army Plaza.

"Well, if it isn't the dude that's always about to die!" Ginny cackles when we walk in. She tells me I'm going to die every time I see her. She sucks at fortune-telling, but I guess she picked up on the fact that I already did die. I'm somehow overjoyed to see her; chalk it up to the fact that I have two beautiful babies and they're okay and this beautiful woman is beside me.

"How are you, Ginny? It's been a minute."

"Minute and a half!" she crows. "And how are you Miss Brass?"

"Good, Ginny. I hear you met my friend Francine the other day."

Ginny's face grows long and sullen. "Ay."

"She said you had quite a conversation."

Ginny nods.

"We . . . well, I want to go under. I want to know what's back there . . . before."

Ginny nods again. She's a whole other person now, her eyebrows furrowed and tight. "Once you know, you can't unknow."

"I know," Sasha says, eyes narrowed.

Ginny looks up at me. "And you?"

Sasha and I exchange a glance. Of course I want to know. The only moments of my past I have are from my murder: I'm fighting, then looking up at masked faces. I know I've lost, that it's over. The certainty of my impending death sweeps over me. Then there's nothing. I managed to ignore the questions for the first three years of my new life. They nagged—who was I? What led me to that final desperate struggle at Grand Army Plaza?—but I shrugged them off and they stayed at bay. Then I met Sarco, who had somehow orchestrated the whole event, and Sasha, who had died beside me along with her brother, Trevor, who I'd then killed a second time. And the questions returned, and this time they lingered. Was I married? In love? Did I have parents, children?

I needed to know. I'd been a living question mark for too long.

"Yes," I say to Ginny. "I'll go after Sasha."

Sasha smiles, kisses me on the cheek, and then disappears behind the curtain into Ginny's reading room.

I plant my ass on the love seat and lose myself in fantasies about what might have been.

Sasha steps out from behind the curtain. She looks grayer than usual. Her eyes wander the room, unresting.

"Sasha," I say. She looks at me, face stricken. I half stand, realize I'm rock-hard—the remnants of a dream—sit back down. "What's wrong?"

She shakes her head. Tires screech outside, and then the door flies open and Reza steps in, gun leveled at Sasha.

"The fuck is going on, Reza?" I'm up, erection obliterated, confused as fuck.

"You tell me," she says to Sasha.

Sasha shakes her head. "I have no idea."

"She didn't try to kill you?" Reza says, catching me in the corner of her eye.

"What are you talking about? Sasha?"

"Carlos, I . . ." Her voice trails off.

"Alright," Reza says. "I don't know what's going on here, but the Survivors just made a move on Kia and Gio."

"What?" Sasha and I yell at the same time.

"And they had roach guys with 'em." Reza stares at Sasha.

"They what?" Sasha gasps. "I don't understand . . ." Her eyes narrow. "Gregorio. He . . . he . . ."

Reza eyes her for another half second, the Glock steady.

Then, ever so slightly, her jaw unclenches; her brow lightens. Whatever silent signal Sasha's giving up that she has no idea what's happening, it's been received on Reza's end.

"We have to go, now." Reza takes a step outside, holding the door open. "I'm sure they . . ."

"My God," Sasha says. "The twins!" She runs out.

"Where are they?" I start after her.

Ginny pokes her head through the curtain. "Carlos."

"I can't now, Ginny. I . . . I'll be back."

Out on the street, a family strolls past: a mama with a baby carriage, three giggling little ones and a teenager fully immersed in her phone. The bodegas are beginning to close down for the evening. "I left them with Marie," Sasha says. "But if Gregorio allied the Survivors with the Blattodeons, it means he went against Marie, which means . . ."

She's cut off by the teenage girl's scream. We whirl around, hands reaching for weapons. A man comes barreling past the family; one of the kids is sitting on his ass, looking stunned. Sasha moves first, stepping directly into his path and swinging up with a short sword I hadn't even seen her unsheathe. Her slice nearly rips the man in half—now the whole family is screaming and collecting each other as they hurry down the block. The man stumbles once, then drops to his knees. He flails forward, dark ichor seeping from Sasha's slash, and then buckles. Those pale nightmares stream off him in a sudden, relentless throng, and in seconds, Sasha is covered.

"No," I gasp as Reza and I launch toward her.

My jacket is off, swatting the monsters from Sasha's arms and chest as Reza wipes them off her face. A few land on me, and I swat them away, ignoring the tiny pinprick of their pincers.

Two more roach guys round the corner as we're finishing up. "Let's move," Reza says. She jumps in her Crown Vic and revs the engine.

"I'm okay," Sasha whispers, seeing the fear in my eyes. "Come on."

We both jump in the backseat and slam the door just as the first guy smashes up against it. Pale roaches splatter across the window, and then Reza peels off into oncoming traffic and a cacophony of horn blasts and tire screeches.

CHAPTER TWENTY-SIX

Reza

Assaulting a house isn't like delivering a pizza. You can't just double-park out front, roll up in there, *pop, pop,* and zip off. Not unless you have a fully locked and loaded team and body armor. And even then . . . Nah. I pull up on the corner of the quiet residential block in Kensington that Sasha directed me to. Oak trees swoosh in the chill, early spring breeze over parked hoop-dees and SUVs.

I almost have to physically restrain Sasha from jumping out of the car the second we stop. "Wait," I say. "We can do this the right way or the wrong way, but if you fuck it up and go in hot, there's a lot less chance of your babies making it out alive."

She freezes, already halfway out the door. Nods. Carlos, who had been about to open the other door, stops too.

"Someone needs to stay with the car."

They look at each other, both restraining the urge to tell the other to stay.

I nod at Carlos. "You stay."

"I don't know how to drive."

"I'm not worried about a goddamn parking ticket, C," I say, getting out. "I need to be sure no one runs off with it while we're inside. Can you do that?"

"My ba—"

"I know." My voice leaves no room for argument. "And I will get them back. I promise."

He slumps into the seat, and Sasha and I brisk-walk down the block past plain two-story houses and plain front lawns. "There a back entrance?"

She nods, every part of her tensed with the effort of not bursting forward in a fury of mama-love and destroying the whole world.

"You can handle the locks?"

She smiles dimly. "I still have a key."

"Good. I'll take the front; you take the back. I don't need to tell you not to take any prisoners."

She shakes her head one time and then slips into the shadows of the front yard and disappears behind the house. I see how this woman could own Carlos's heart. She moves with effortless grace, even this rattled. Also: she's a killer. It's all over her. There's no hesitation in her lethal flow, and I'm positive it's not just because of what's going on.

I soft-walk up the porch stairs and then my Glock is out, lowered casually by my hip and concealed from any chance passersby. I'm about to take the lock when I realize the door's slightly open.

Which is probably a bad thing.

Yes, a very bad thing indeed: the first splatter of blood I see is a handprint on the foyer wall. Beyond that, the living room is in shambles: overturned chairs, shattered glass. And bodies: three in this room. One's the older woman from the park, Marie. There are no bullet holes, I notice. Everyone involved wanted to stay discreet, and a single shot in this neighborhood would've brought a hundred cops. As it is, it's incredible the place isn't a crime scene, considering the battle that must've happened here. Sasha stands perfectly still in the middle of all the carnage. Our eyes meet, and for a terrible second, we just stare at each other.

Then she brushes past me and up the stairs, but I already

know, can feel it in the awful stillness of this house: the
twins are gone.

In this dark inlet somewhere deep in Prospect Park, the Partymobile idles next to my Crown Vic. Carlos storms back
and forth in the glare of their headlights, muttering to himself: "Something . . . We're missing . . . something . . . Fuck!"

Bri, Memo, and Rohan are spread out along the perimeter
of the little clearing in the woods. Since everyone else is too
busy freaking out, trying to make sense of shit, it's on me
to make sure we're all safe in the meantime.

Kia sits in the Partymobile with Rigo. The door's open,
and they both peer out as Sasha, Gio, and I huddle in the
darkness, cobbling together a plan.

Or trying to.

"So what happened at the Survivors' safe house?" Gio
asks.

"Marie was dead," Sasha says. She looks like she's barely
holding it together. Every couple seconds she gulps in a
mouthful of air and wraps her arms tighter around herself.
"One of our leaders. You saw her in the woods."

Gio nods. "I remember."

"Also six other Survivors." She exhales, looks away. "And
the twins were gone. My children."

"I'm so sorry," Gio says.

"Fuck!" Carlos yells. "Something . . ."

"And no roaches?" Rigo asks.

I shake my head. "But they came at us in Flatbush just
now. And you by the river. If I hadn't put Rohan and Memo
on Kia-detail, this would be an even grimmer situation.
Sasha, how many Survivors are there total?"

"We were eighteen," Sasha says. "Now eleven."

Gio shakes his head. "Ten. Blaine got got."

"Always hated that prick," Sasha mutters.

"And the remaining ten are probably gonna be siding with Gregorio?" I ask.

Sasha scowls. "I'm not so sure. The lines haven't been clear for a while, just a lotta infighting and politicking and bullshit, to be honest. And only about seven of those ten are really much use in a fight. A few don't even really come around much, so I doubt he'd bother tracking them down for his coup. Especially if it was off-the-cuff like this. I don't think he's been planning this long—probably the Blatts reached out to him sometime after the meeting this morning. Most likely he grabbed up Blaine and one or two others and ran."

Best to prepare for the worst. "We'll put them at seven, then. The question is where."

"Listen though," Gio says. "Carlos is right. They're acting different. It's part of why we came back . . ." His voice trails off, and he casts a pained glanced at Kia. She looks away. "Finally. We got word from a contact here that there was a lot of Blattodeon activity—more than their usual now-and-then kidnapping. Something's different."

"It's true." Rigo climbs out of the Partymobile and stands next to Gio. "And this thing where they throw their whole roach hive off their skin? They almost never do that. The Blattodeons are not very skilled fighters. They rely on luring enemies down to where they can gang up in great numbers to destroy them, yes?"

"Right!" Gio's getting excited now. "They've almost never attacked in public the whole time we've been after them. They'll show up now and then, always cleaning up their dead quickly when it's a public melee, but they never launched a full-scale lash out like the one by the river today."

"I mean," I say, "we did take out Mom and Pop Fern. That's gotta . . ."

"That's the thing," Gio says. "That's not how they function. Jeremy doesn't come first; the hive comes first. Always. His needs don't dictate their movements; theirs do his. Look, we

captured one once, Rigo and this guy Ishmael we were working with. We did everything we could to get that corpselike
motherfucker to talk."

"And?" I say.

Rigo shakes his head. "The Blattodeon Trinity. That's
all we got out of him. The Blattodeon Trinity, the Master
Hive. He croaked and whistled and hummed for hours, but
the only actual words he said were those."

"It's like they're hardwired to protect it," Gio says. "But
that's all we got. The Blattodeon Trinity, the Master Hive.
Everything for them revolves around that. So if they're
breaching their normal protocol now, it's for that. That's been
put into play somehow. And they're protecting it is my guess."

I growl. The weight of incomplete information hangs
over all of us.

"But it's still not adding up," Gio says. "Why would they
grab up the kids? What do they have to offer Gregorio that
would get him to take out four Survivors?"

Kia hops out of the Partymobile and walks around to
where Carlos paces.

"Not this second, Kia. I gotta . . ." He doesn't even look
at her. "There's something missing . . ."

"Carlos, man, stop for a sec. We all tryna figure this out
together; you over here wildin'."

He stops. Closes his eyes and then opens them again.
"You," he says.

"Huh?"

"After I left the library, you stayed and talked to Dr.
Tennessee more, right?"

"Yeah. We got high. She's the shit. Why?"

"You kept looking up info on the architect though, right?"

"Of course. You asked me to, didn't you?"

"And?"

"He worked on the Ferns' house, the one in Bushwick that

you found him at and another behind it, a few others around Queens and one way out in Long Island."

"Tunnels?"

"The houses in Bushwick and Queens had tunnels linking up with the sewer systems. That's how they move back and forth between 'em, I guess. The Long Island one's a tower or something. Got a network of tunnels underneath, but it's like way out there. They don't connect to anything that I could tell."

"That's where they are. That's it." He starts pacing again. "Carlos?"

"There's something else. We're missing something."

Sasha's by his side in seconds. "Carlos, why do you think they're out there?"

"I—I'm sorry," Carlos says. "I know I'm being weird. I'm . . . thinking . . ."

"We don't have time," Sasha says quietly.

"Time!" Carlos yells. "What time is it?"

"Ten twenty," I say, walking up next to Sasha. "Why?"

Carlos stops pacing again. The headlights throw a tall Carlos shadow back toward the woods. "I forgot to tell you about Caitlin."

I scowl. "Caitlin Fern?"

"The Council asked me to protect her. That's what they were calling me in for this morning. Apparently she's done work for them."

"Figures," Sasha scoffs. If the Council dis reaches Carlos, he doesn't react.

"And she asked me to help her take out her brother."

Gio comes around to where we're standing. "That makes no sense."

"Said Jeremy always blamed their parents for not giving enough to support him, and he'd threatened to kill them before, so she figured he'd finally done it when the house burned down and there were no bodies."

Carlos and I trade the slightest of glances.

"Anyway, I'm supposed to meet her at eleven in Bushwick. And I presume we'll go handle Jeremy."

Gio crosses his arms. "And you don't think it's a trap?"

"I do think it's a trap," Carlos says. "I mean, I think it might be. But I don't know how yet. And the twins might be down there with Jeremy, if the Blattodeons are leagued up with Gregorio."

"I'm guessing they're at the Long Island safe house," I say. "Or headed there. But we don't know the address."

"We can call Dr. Tennessee," Carlos says. "See if she'll rustle up the maps for us."

Sasha steps forward, puts a hand on Carlos's shoulder. She looks like she's pulled herself together in the past few minutes. Her eyes have narrowed from terrified to determined. She's ready to make moves. "Carlos. You might be walking right into an ambush. You don't know a damn thing about these roach men."

"Hell, I barely know a damn thing about them," Gio says. "And I been trailing them for years."

"I know," Carlos says. He looks Sasha right in the eyes, and for a second I see it all: everything between them, how gigantic it's become and how little time they've even gotten to spend together. They look like they're alone in a whirlpool, like the rest of us are just spinning smudges. "I don't like it either, but . . . the Blattodeon Trinity, Gio said . . . Maybe . . ." He snaps his head at Kia. "Mama Esther . . . She'll know . . . maybe."

I roll my eyes. "We need full sentences, man."

Carlos squints a half smile. "I have a plan."

CHAPTER TWENTY-SEVEN

Kia

A lright, listen," Carlos says, twisting his body so he can see us from the passenger seat of the Partymobile. "Kia, whatever Mama Esther's got, you get it. There's something, *something*, and if anyone knows it, she will. Reza's dropping me off a few blocks from my meet-up point with Caitlin. When you get what you need, you tell Gio, and they'll put him at the entrance to the tunnels. Riley and Squad 9'll be there and they'll go in after me with Gio and Rigo and one of Reza's guys. Got it?"

"Who is this Esquad 9?" Rigo asks.

"They can't see ghosts, C." I try not to roll my eyes—Carlos is going through a hard time. "I gotta go wi—"

"No," Carlos almost shouts. He breathes deep, tries again. "No. You can't put yourself in any more danger. Tell Gio and get somewhere safe. Understand?"

I nod my head yes, but there is absolutely no way in hell that's how it's gonna go down. But okay, Carlos. Whatever makes you happy.

"Reza and Sasha, y'all gonna head to the Long Island safe house after you drop me off. Dr. Tennessee is opening up the research library right now. She's gonna call Reza's phone once she has the location sorted out."

"And then?" I ask.

"And then we . . . take it from there."

I hate this shit, but there really isn't much else we can do. I know one thing: Gio's not going into those tunnels without me. It's not happening. Roaches and baby assassin ghosts be damned. I'm not losing him again. I put a hand on Carlos's shoulder that I hope is reassuring, nod at Reza and Sasha, and then hop out the Partymobile. Gio and Rigo follow. Another Crown Vic pulls up behind us. The hazard lights blink on, and three of Reza's people get out—Memo, the insanely tall and muscled bald dude; the sly-looking woman they called Bri; and Rohan, who I may have fallen in love with. But maybe that's just cuz he saved all our lives. That and those thick-ass arms, Jesus. Bri and Memo glance up and down Franklin Avenue, looking like those security guards that stand there mean-mugging when an armored truck rolls up for a delivery. They exchange looks with Rohan and then climb into the Partymobile. Reza peels off doing about Mach ten as soon as the doors slam.

Rohan looks at us, and my heart somersaults one time. "Ready to do some research, kids?"

Rohan, Gio, and Rigo stay downstairs. They say it's to guard the front door in case the roach men or Survivors show up, but I think they're just uncomfortable with all this spooky ghost shit. I don't blame 'em. I'm not that happy about it either, to be honest. But Mama Esther is the coolest ghost I've met in the short time I've been able to see them, and if she has whatever key Carlos thinks she does to helping destroy the roach men, I'll fuck with her.

The old empty brownstone seems to get warmer as I march up the rickety staircase toward the top-floor library. None of the lights are on—I'm sure the power got cut decades ago—but a gentle glow emanates from above. I wonder what it was like for Carlos in those early days of his new life. He must've learned to walk again on these dusty planks, must've felt that first surge of emptiness at having no memory, no past, in these same corridors.

"Kia!" Mama Esther grins down at me when I walk in. A soft saxophone melody wails from an old radio. Her smile fades. "What's wrong?"

Where to begin . . . "Carlos's kids are in trouble."

Mama Esther boggles. "Carlos's what now? Wait . . . Never mind. How can I help?"

"The Blattodeon Trinity. Need to know everything about them. But, like . . . quickly."

Mama Esther squints. "That could take more time than you have. Any additional questions to add along with your initial inquiry, young lady?"

"Yes, but I don't know how to say it."

"Try."

Carlos kept saying a piece is missing. Gio said they don't act this way. We need to know what's going on. "Why . . . now? They've changed their pattern. We want to know why."

Mama Esther nods, whirls around, and it's like a tiny hot tornado has entered the building. Books scatter, replace themselves, turn on their sides. About ten great tomes fly open simultaneously; pages whip past. I hear Mama Esther's voice muttering different languages all around me.

"*Cantari . . . eloquis . . . baronti . . . quan quan quan . . . eji . . . eji . . . oko . . . oko . . . cantari . . . septimus . . . l'vailche. . . . siguroy . . .*"

The hell kinda incantation . . . ? Downstairs, something thuds loudly against the outer wall. Mama Esther's face whirls back around toward me. "Shto etta?" she demands, in what I can only guess is some Russian-type language. She must still be immersed in whatever she was reading.

"My cousin and his boyfriend and this hit man are downstairs guarding the door." Words I never thought I'd say.

Strange days, these. "Those guys we're researching are after us, so I'm guessing they're here."

Mama Esther snorts and turns back to the books. The air heavies up, and her murmuring voice gets louder, drowns out the saxophone ballad and the occasional honks and growls of traffic passing along Franklin Ave. *"Cantari celosis meji bara meji qui pantosa quel'arte befoulo chi barra chi oji chi meji chi sotano bara mi bara si obasi . . ."*

Another thud and then yelling from downstairs. My heart screams in my ears. Gio. What if . . . ? Gio. "Can I help, Mama Esther?"

"Thank you, child." She halts her chant, and I hear more yelling downstairs, the shuttle train rumble past, the sorrowful sax. "This one," Mama Esther says after a few seconds, "is in English. Ignore that it's kitschy. There's something in there for us. Try page three seventy-eight."

A slender, faded orange book hovers through the air and lands on a stack in front of me. *"Cantari celosis,"* Mama Esther mutters. *"Bara si bara o bara questiquanticus palacio teneriscow pajoli."* I flip open the book, trying to ignore the fighting sounds getting louder below us.

Lore of Yesteryear, the book is called. It's from 1904, all frayed edges and tattered binding. On page 378, woodcut illustrations show an amorphous shadow whisking across the night sky over a moonlit meadow. Two figures gape up at it; one of them seems mangled somehow, his body bent over and twisted all wrong.

The threscle hain, the caption says. But the facing page is all about crop shortages and some kind of fungus. I flip to the back, holding the place with one hand. According to the index, *threscle hain* shows up eight times, including on 378. They're clustered around 250–255 so I flip there. *Which begins again, for mine uncle has seen this with his own Eyes, he reports to me. 'Tis dark and fluttering, almost not there but Unmissable in the Sky against a moonlit cloud. The*

*threscle hain can be seen only every seven years, 'tis said.
My uncle was never the same since that night; he took to the
Drink and could be found Babbling about the Shadow that
Flies. Luther was never seen again, but it wasn't only Luther.
It was after that night too that the children of Shallow Brook
began to Vanish, one by one, until the Town was full of
mourning, only the wailing of Mothers and drunken rants
of Fathers as Funeral after Funeral Procession took to the
sullied streets.*

Another thump shakes me from the words. The fighting's
louder now, just one floor down.

"The threscle hain," I say out loud. "A shadow that flies
through the night sky every seven years."

"¡Eso mismo!" Mama Esther yells, startling the shit outta
me. "Bring it here."

I walk down the corridors of stacked books. The air is
prickly and thick. Below, there is silence, and I can't decide
whether that's good or ominous. I place the old book on top
of three much older, much larger ones on a claw-foot wooden
table.

"What are we looking at?"

"Seven years," Mama Esther says. "This is from what is
now Belarus. Describes the smlechnya, a kind of rabid
locust swarm that destroys acres of crops every seven years."

"Ooh . . ."

"And here, in Venezuela, reports of a monastery on a hill
whose hooded acolytes would emerge to massacre the vil-
lagers below, also every seven years."

"I see the pattern," I say.

"And your threscle hain."

"Seven years."

"And now this." She reaches down from either side of me
and places another book open on the table. "The roach." A
careful ink sketch of one of those hideous pale water bugs
takes up the entire page. Half its body has been removed, and

its filthy innards are visible, complete with pointers explaining various parts. The facing page shows the monster viewed from above, just the shell-like wings and awful little antennaed head.

"This is a natural science book from Hungary, the 1790s. Says they're a rare, endangered breed of parasitic land arthropod."

"Hmph, not endangered enough." I scowl.

"Parasitic because they rely on a human host to survive. They lay eggs inside the stomach, lungs, and esophagus generally. The males leave and burrow in the actual flesh of the host human, become a second layer of skin, basically."

"Yep, seen that."

Another bang from downstairs. My heart flails and pitter-patters. Then a yell, but I can't make out whose voice it is.

"The females though," Mama Esther continues, "are removed while still in the pupa stage and deposited inside a singular host, a living host, creating what's basically a hive in the esophagus and abdomen. This is known as the Master Hive, and the whole operation functions with some kind of groupthink-type insectoid telekinesis, hormones, and whatnot. Yadda yadda. Let me see . . . Ah! Here we go: an unusual, spectral kind of cult has emerged around the creatures, the Blattodeons. The singular living host with the Master Hive inside is known as the High Priest. The Blattodeon acolytes, their skin made up of the male roaches, lie in wait, tending to their own foul affairs. That is, except for a bloody series of months, every seven years. Then the entire cult flurries into a kind of homicidal rampage."

Three illuminated figures appear in the dusty air above me. The one in the middle is hunched over with long, creepy arms and fingers.

"The cult revolves around three central roles: the Petari Vox, the Petari Gi." The two upright figures on either side light up. Mama Esther is providing audiovisual enhancement,

and I love her for it. They wear long robes and complicated
hats with lowered face guards. Miasmas of power swirl
around their raised arms. "The Petaris act as kind of con-
siglieri, or a support team, using necromancy and manipula-
tion to protect and preserve the High Priest, and ultimately,
the Master Hive."

The long-armed figure lights up. "Jeremy fucking Fern,"
I whisper.

"The High Priest cultivates the Master Hive within his or
her body for a period of seven years, at which point the entire
hive must transfer to a new High Priest, which can only
happen if the original High Priest expires."

"Ugh."

"They can only survive outside of a host for a few hours,
so in olden days, the transference of hosts became a sacred
sacrificial ritual. In modern times . . . Hold on . . . In modern
times, this would be accomplished by a complicated series
of conspiracies ending in the murder of both Petaris and the
High Priest and the abduction of whoever was deigned the
new host body for the Master Hive. The Petari Vox and Petari
Gi transfer their spirits into new human bodies in an act of
phantasmagoric mimicry that shadows the Master Hive's
transferal to a new host."

The figures vanish, and Mama Esther's furrowed face
appears above me. "Ah, this is important. The Blattodeons do
not believe in suicide. According to their cosmology, self-
destruction is a cardinal sin—part of the whole roaches-can-
survive-anything theme, I suppose. These three figures, the
Blattodeon Trinity, are like ancestral archetypes, still surviving in spirit form. That's why the septennial ritual becomes
such a bloodbath and must end with their murder."

"Caitlin Fern," I say. "That's why she . . . asked Carlos
to . . . She must be one of the Petaris. It's not an ambush. It's
worse . . . But who's the other? And who's the new host?"

"Says here two of the new hosts tend to be children—one

for the High Priest, one for the Petari Vox's spirit, and preferably related."

"Caitlin and Jeremy. They were both teenagers that night, seven years ago . . ."

"While for the Petari Gi, the Blattodeons seek out a mastermind of some kind that will be able to protect the other two while they develop into their roles."

"Someone else that they will try to have Carlos kill, so they can send the spirit into . . ." Clarity, partial clarity anyway, comes like a blinding ray of sunlight after a night of partying. "Jesus," I whisper. "Gregorio made a pact with the Blattodeons and kidnapped Carlos's twins . . . They must've promised him the role of Petari Gi and the . . ."

Mama Esther takes her eyes off the page and gazes down at me. "What?"

"The twins!"

The library door flies open and Gio tumbles through it. He's covered in roaches. Rigo bursts in and starts swatting him with his jacket. Rohan backs in behind them, gun pointed at the door.

"What is this?" Mama Esther booms. "There is no combat allowed in Mama Esther's house!"

A roach man appears in the doorway. Rohan's gun pops with two silenced shots, and the man falls backward even as two more crawl over him and run into the room. Rigo spins into the air with some kind of flying Mortal Kombat tornado kick and smashes one of them. Two more burst in.

"STOP THIS!" Mama Esther's voice is an earthquake between my ears, but of course, they can't hear her. She's suddenly directly over the fray, her wide face tensed, eyes half-moons of fury. She shudders, and the whole room shudders with her; I expect the foundations of the building just moved. Rigo, Gio, and Rohan collapse and roll out of the way. The Blattodeons must sense her presence above them. Who knows what the fuck those walking abominations can fathom? All four of them look up at the same time. They pause for a half second, then rear backward, I guess about to hurl their collected roach swarms at her.

I wonder, briefly, how that would go: ghost versus evil death roach. Then I find out: Mama Esther hollers. It's a terrifying, guttural thing. I'm pretty sure my liver and spleen are on the verge of rupture when it's over. Her wide-open mouth takes up the whole upper part of the library. Then her giant ghost hands come crashing down from either side of the room. The roach guys have enough time to be startled, and then they explode, utterly obliterated between Mama Esther's giant palms.

It sounds like four bodies hitting the pavement from ten stories up. Shards of bone clink against the glass windows along with the singular wet splatter of entrails and blood exploding across the room. Thousands of crinkled roach bodies lie motionless in the puddled gore.

"What . . . the fuck . . . was that?" Rigo gasps.

I'm the first one standing. I hadn't even realized that I fell, but—I feel alright. I don't seem to be bleeding from any orifices, so that's a plus. "That was Mama Esther."

"Can we bring her with us?" Rohan says.

"If only." I stumble toward Rigo and Gio. They're both sitting up, dazed. "You okay, cuz?"

Gio nods, but he looks more shaken than I've seen him since his return. Rigo stands, and we both help Gio up. "We have to go," I say. They start getting themselves together, sidestepping the giant splatter in the middle of the floor. "Mama Esther?"

She appears above me. "Did I scare you, child? I hate fighting."

"I'm okay. And you saved our lives! I'm sorry we can't stay to help you . . . clean up."

"Don't worry 'bout that, dear. Did you find everything you need?"

"Yes," I say. "But it's worse than we thought."

———————

Five minutes later we're barreling up Bedford in the Crown Vic. Rohan is still picking roach guy innards out of his goatee.

"Drive faster," I say as I wrestle my hair into some semblance of a bun and then secure the whole situation with pins and a du rag. It'll have to do; I'm pretty sure we're all about to get wet.

"I am," Rohan grunts. "But we also need to not get pulled over and whatnot. Makes things more difficult, if you know what I mean."

"Don't you have PD bought off, or whatever it is you guys do to get away with shit?"

He shoots me a look that lets me know I've crossed a line, so I settle back and watch Bed-Stuy fly past.

"What are we telling Carlos?" Gio asks.

"He was right," I say. Rohan screeches around a corner onto Myrtle Ave. and zooms toward Bushwick. "The Caitlin thing is a setup. But not the kind he thinks. They're not trying to kill him. They need him to kill Jeremy and Caitlin and someone else I haven't figured out yet."

"That's my kind of setup," Rohan says. "Anything that involves those two getting got, I'm with."

I shake my head. "You don't get it. It's not about them. It's about the roaches. Jeremy and Caitlin are just the conduits. They're . . . they're allowing themselves to be used. And that includes being sacrificed so that the roaches can live on. In another body."

"Whose?" Rigo asks.

"I'm pretty sure it's gonna be Gregorio," I say. "And . . . Carlos and Sasha's twins."

Rohan drives faster.

CHAPTER TWENTY-EIGHT

❧

Carlos

"Garrick! Tartus!"

I'm sitting on the steps of the Ferns' creepy safe house in Bushwick, smoking. Pretending that a thousand pinpricks of fear aren't doing the wave inside my gut. Pretending to be the indomitable badass I'm supposed to be. Those two perfect pudgy, brown faces surface in my mind and I shake them off. I can't get caught up. Sasha's worried eyes—what did Ol' Ginny show her that frightened her so damn much?

I hate not knowing shit.

I shake my head and pull my unimpressed mask back on. The ruse is both for my own sake and Caitlin's. I can't look all freaked-out when she shows up.

If she shows up.

If I'm not just sitting here waiting to die. Seems unlikely. Why drag me all the way out here to murk me when she could send her baby demons to murk me any ol' place?

Or try.

"Garrick! Tartus!"

The old ghost hangs in the air beside me like he's suspended from a clothesline. His sad bulging eyes gaze out into the night. His bottom lip quivers. Tears still stream steadily down his cheeks. I shake my head, pull long and

deep on the Malagueña, and sigh a smoky mountain toward
the sky.

"Garrick!"

"I get it, man!"

"Tartus!"

"Garrick Tartus. I know. I'm happy for you."

If she doesn't show soon, I'll have to figure out a plan B.
Go in myself and try to find Jeremy and off him? Seems
iffy. Iffier even. Riley and Squad 9 should be lurking around
the premises, hopefully well the fuck out of sight.

I stand, stretch, exhale more smoke.

"Garrick! Tartus!"

I shake my head. "Garrick fucking Tartus."

"Oh, just ignore him," Caitlin says. She strolls up the
block looking cool as can be, a bodega coffee in one hand.
I wonder if her chill is a ruse like mine. If so, it's overplayed,
considering the circumstances.

"You seem pretty calm for someone about to have her
brother killed."

She shakes her head. "That's my defense mechanism.
Been doing it since I was sixteen. I'm terrified."

I study her tired face, frayed hair. Try to picture her
radiating with joyful light instead of worn-out and prema-
turely sullen. Doesn't take.

She sips her coffee. "You ready?"

"No. I don't know a damn thing about what's going on. I
don't know where we're going or how we're supposed to do
this. I don't know anything about you. I am not ready."

"Garrick! Tartus!"

Caitlin narrows her eyes at me. "That's fair. We don't have
much time though—Jeremy is down there now doing one of
his rituals, but he won't be for long. They're supposed to go
out tonight on some mission. I stopped keeping track. I just
know this has to end, Carlos. This has to end. It's gone on too
long. Let's walk as we talk."

I imagine her saying this to some coworker in the adoption industry: "Let's walk as we talk," and then fast-strutting along a well-lit corridor in their Manhattan offices, files and photographs stuffed under their armpits and coffee thermoses in their hands, a whole world of data, names, geopolitical connections, and intrigue cluttering the air between them. I wonder if the agency has any hint about the monster that lurks in their midst.

"Alright," I say. I can see any more delaying will shatter whatever delicate trust she holds in me. Hopefully Caitlin's lateness has given Kia time to find out what the fuck is going on. I try to imagine them barreling toward us in Rohan's Vic.

The street is deserted, another quiet residential block in Bushwick. I turn and follow Caitlin inside. Behind us, Garrick Tartus's ragged ghost hangs in the air and announces his name to a world that can't hear him.

"I need you to understand something," Caitlin says as she leads me through a typical drab front hallway and into the kitchen, clicking on lights as she goes. "I know you know a thing or two about the dead."

"You could say that."

"I mean, working for the Council, of course. We deal with their dumb shit all the time, right?"

I don't like thinking about Caitlin and me as coworkers, but there it is. "Indeed."

"So, you need to understand that the ghosts you're about to meet were all considered BRH status by the Council."

"Barely Really Human?"

"Ha . . . That would make sense, knowing how the Council can be. But no: Beyond Rehab."

"But . . ."

She stops in front of the fridge and holds up a hand. "I know. Don't think too hard about it. It's the Council. They were spirits that the Council, for whatever reason, didn't feel would um . . . shall we say, play well, with the other ghost kids. I know I seem blasé about it, but remember this is my life's work."

I raise an eyebrow.

"Come," she says. "Help me move this." We edge the fridge to the side. A small wooden door waits behind it. Down a flight of stairs in the darkness, and then Caitlin flicks on a light.

Around me, a dozen or so small snarling child ghosts gnash their teeth; their sunken-in eyes dart back and forth. The room is long and immaculate. Children's toys lie scattered around, which somehow makes me feel sick to my stomach. I had figured on stumbling into a place more or less like this tonight, but still—I feel like a slab of steak in the lion's den, and all the lions are small, translucent, and rabid. Sorrow and fear flood me in equal parts. If things turn ugly— uglier rather—surviving will mean chopping down slews of already dead children.

Even if I win I lose.

"I know it looks bad," Caitlin says. "But these ghosts wouldn't exist at all if it weren't for the work I've done with them. Council would've sent them to the Deeper Death a long time ago. Hell." She chuckles. "They might've sent you to deal with 'em. So in a way, I'm saving you work."

I don't even bother pretending this shit is in any way cool or funny. I can't. I'm not that good a liar. "How did you . . . train them?" I don't really want to know, to be honest. But I do.

She shakes her head, smiles. I think she's . . . proud? "Wasn't easy! Right, little guys?" I swallow a little bit of vomit. "They gave me plenty of trouble. Well worth it, though. Well worth it. You guys ready?"

A wretched smile arises from the throng. I take a step back, my hand gripping my cane-blade.

"Relax, Carlos. They do what I tell them." Her smile stretches wide across her face; little crow's-feet appear beside her eyes. "So, look—there's no way Jeremy will fall to ghost hands. First of all, they know him well, and I'm not sure how they'd take to attacking him, reliable though they are. Second of all, he knows how to fight ghosts." A chilling thought, but I just nod. "And anyway, we need them to handle the Blattodeons. Basically"—she opens a hatch in the floor and starts climbing down—"they'll run interference while we go in. The Blatts aren't particularly coordinated, but when they gang up on you, it's over. And," she says right before disappearing into the darkness, "it's a horrible way to go, trust me."

I shake my head. Panting and muttering, the ghostlings stream around me and vanish down the ladder.

"Carlos!" Caitlin whisper-shouts from below. "You joining us?"

Darkness and dripping water.

For a few breathless seconds, that's the whole world down here. That and the occasional pant or grunt from the host of killer ghost kids. My eyes adjust. Up ahead, a dim light shimmers over dark water. Caitlin nods at my cane-blade. "You might wanna have that ready," she says quietly.

"It's always ready. Nothing for you?"

She sneers. "I hate weapons. And anyway, these guys are like the best bodyguards a woman could ask for. And loyal to a tee. Let's go." I edge forward through the tunnel, stop when my feet reach the murky water. "Stay close to the right wall," Caitlin says behind me. "The rest is deep and . . . occupied."

I place one foot in the mire. It laps up against the top of my boot but no farther. That's quite enough. I step across, hear Caitlin follow. She slides past me and walks to the opening at the end of the tunnel. There's movement up ahead—a rustling noise and shadows pass in front of the light.

"Caitlin," a shrill voice whispers. "I've been looking for you."

Caitlin raises her arms. The ghosts break into a frenzied run, streaming past her into a wide-open chamber.

"Caitlin . . ." the voice sighs. "Why?"

Then I hear screaming. A tall figure shoves Caitlin out of the way, hurdles into the darkness toward me. My blade comes out. In the dim corridor, I can just make out the man's silhouette as he lurches forward and a hundred writhing shapes fling off him. Roaches. I'm about to spin and cover like Gio taught us, when the remaining ghostlings vault into the air, forming a shimmering spectral wall between myself and the Blattodeon. The insects slam into the translucent child barricade and suddenly slow, like they've been trapped in molasses. Then, one by one, they burst; tiny splatters of roach guts cascade in slow motion through the interlinking ghosts.

The roach man roars. He's skinnier now that his protective layer has flown off. The light glints off a stretch of exposed muscle framed by tattered, rotting flesh. He charges, tearing through the ghost wall, and catches my blade in a solid upswing across his chest. Up close, his face is worn down almost to the grinning skull. Just shredded rags of skin dangle here and there like evil laundry hung out to dry. His yellowed, feverish eyes glare out from mostly skeletal sockets.

For a second or two, he just stands there as thick, dark blood seeps from the gash I tore from his navel to his shoulder. When he drops to his knees, I lop his head off just to be sure. The last of the ghosts flush through the opening, and I hear Caitlin yell, "Jeremy, no!" and that high-pitched screaming again.

The tunnel opens up into a cavernous room. In the center, a raised platform looms over knee-deep dark water. Chains hang from the ceiling; at the far end, other tunnels lead off

into darkness. A few flickering industrial lights throw dancing shadows across the walls. About ten Blattodeons move
toward me through the water, but the ghostlings are all over
them, clawing away at their faces, sinking sharpened, shining ghost teeth into roach-covered, decaying flesh.

One Blattodeon tears a ghostling from his face, shreds it
with three quick swipes, and then breaks into a run. Three
other ghosts are on him in seconds. He slashes two out of the
air as they pounce; the third latches on to his torso and seems
to be burrowing into him. The roaches scatter into a swirl,
and for a second he's just rotting skin on bones. Then they
return, all of them landing on the ghostling. A howl rings out,
and in a few seconds the tiny phantom is just a sprinkle of
glimmering flesh, then nothing at all.

Caitlin is nowhere to be seen. Neither is Jeremy. I start to
work my way around the edge of the cavern. Another Blattodeon breaks free from the ghostlings and stumbles three
steps before two tiny writhing hands wrap around his neck
from behind. He flings his arms outward and falls back, disappearing beneath the black water. A few seconds later, hundreds of shiny pink backs surface and swarm circles where
he fell.

I keep it moving. Caitlin and Jeremy must be around the
other side of that platform. Something long-armed and pale
swings down from the ceiling at me. At first I think it's a
fucking albino orangutan. But it's not; it's fucking Jeremy
fucking Fern.

I don't know what the hell being the High Priest of Roach-
ville has done to warp his body this way, but he barely looks
human. I don't care to know, actually. I just want this over
with. I leap out of the way, and Jeremy lands in a crouch.

That smiling boy from the photograph is just a faded
shadow in this creature. Jeremy's mouth is a crusty, dribbling
slash across his long face. His tongue hangs languidly out.
His once-bright eyes have narrowed to slits over furrowed

dark patches. He lunges forward, spinning those spaghetti arms in a wild circle. When a ghostling charges out of the mire toward him, Jeremy destroys it with one slice of his long, gnarled fingernails.

These guys must've powered up with whatever magic allows my own blade to destroy spirit matter. I've never seen a living being do that to a ghost. He lunges at me, those long fingernails splayed, and I backstep just out of reach. Caitlin's nowhere to be seen, and I'm not sure if I should . . . One of the roach guys is on the platform behind me. I catch him out the corner of my eye, rearing back to hurl his swarm. I don't have time to sit here and pick roaches off my face. I decapitate him with a single cut. When I turn back, Jeremy's right up on me.

There's no room to wind up for a good swing. I thrust, catch him in the right side of his bare yellowish chest. We just stare at each other for a half second. Then Jeremy's gaze lifts to something behind me, and his long mouth creases into a smile. With both hands, I pull my blade upward, tearing through flesh, lung, and brittle, decayed bones, cutting Jeremy almost in half. He peels open, and a swarm of roaches bursts out.

They're bigger than the others, like small chitinous pigeons. They don't attack me though. They just flutter in a slow, awful mass toward the tunnel we came through.

And then they're gone.

And I hear laughter. Around me, the whole cavern has become still. No more fighting. The surviving ghostlings and Blattodeons stare at me. I turn, follow the sight line of Jeremy's final, grinning stare.

"You did well, Carlos," Caitlin says. She's standing over the beheaded roach man. One of the roaches crawls along the side of her face and disappears into her mouth. "You did well."

I shake my head. "It was a . . . setup . . ." Pieces fall into place and then back out. All this? A ruse? All those Blattodeons and ghostlings sacrificed . . . for what?

"Now that you have freed the Master Swarm from its mortal cage," Caitlin says. Her smile makes little dimples form along her cheeks. "It will need a new one. Fortunately, we've arranged for that . . ."

"My . . . the twi—" I can't finish the word, because before I do, Caitlin nods, and all I see is red.

I lunge.

CHAPTER TWENTY-NINE

Kia

That dead guy Riley was waiting for us when we rolled up. Had a whole team of floating, glowy badasses with him too, including Sylvia Bell, the stern white-lady ghost who was there the day I almost got choked out.

"C went in a couple minutes ago," Riley said as I ran up to the front steps. Gio, Rigo, and Rohan were behind me, getting heavy with weapons and body armor and shit. "We're about to go down."

"We gotta tell him not to kill Jeremy!" I blurt out.

"What?" Sylvia said.

"Can't explain. No time. You ready?"

"Garrick! Tartus!" one of the ghosts yelled.

"The fuck?" I said.

It was an older tattered-up phantom I hadn't even noticed before. The architect ghost Carlos mentioned.

"Oh yeah, pay him no mind," Riley said. "We ready."

"Garrick! Tartus!" Garrick Tartus yelled even louder.

"That's weird," Sylvia said. "It had only been every couple minutes up till just now . . ."

"Garrick! Tartus! Garrick! Tartus!"

I look at Riley. "Uh . . ."

"Garrick Tartus Garrick Tartus Garrick Tartus!"

Riley shrugged, and then Garrick Tartus flung himself into the street. "It's time!" he howled.

"Goddammit!" Riley sighed as the old ghost began floating away. "Let him go. We need all hands for this shit."

"Kia." It was Gio. He looked worn-out. "You sta—"

"No."

"Kia . . ."

"No, I said. I'm not losing you again. I'm not watching you disappear into some hellhole and never come out. I'm not—"

"Kia, I promise I'll—"

"I said no!" I stomped my foot. "That's it."

We stared at each other for a few seconds as the ghosts started filing into the house. Rigo and Rohan hurried past. The door slammed. I narrowed my eyes. The face that meant I'm not giving in. Gio remembered it, I know he did. He sighed. I smiled, but only slightly: victory meant a horrible death probably, but it was better than waiting, waiting, wondering, waiting . . . no.

This path, I chose.

We ran up the steps together and inside.

"This way," Gio said, walking unknowingly through a crowd of geared-up, ready-to-throw-down ghosts into the kitchen. We followed him in. He opened a little wooden door behind the fridge, which had been shoved aside, and ran down the stairs.

Rigo ducked in after Gio, then Rohan, then me. The ghosts streamed around us, rustling and furious as they readied for battle. Next came a wide, well-lit playroom of some kind. Creepy as fuck, to be honest, but we didn't stay long. Gio clearly had the whole place mapped out in his mind: he had already thrown open a trapdoor in the floor when we got down and was climbing into the darkness below.

The fear sits in my stomach, a squiggly lump, just wrastling and tumbling around. Still: I'm calmer than I ever would've thought myself capable of, considering everything. In the tunnel, the dark walls keep squirming to life, but it's just my feverish daydreams making hell where it isn't.

Yet.

We're trodding through their den, after all. They sure to show up. I think about Reza's girl Angie, what she must've felt like living her last however many hours or days or whatever in this dank pit, being tortured, used as a human nesting ground. Then I think about Carlos's babies. We're rushing forward through the tunnel, but it's not fast enough. It's probably already too late.

"You scared, little lady?" It's Rohan. He's beside me, even bulkier with that bulletproof vest on, and cradling his shotgun.

"Nah," I lie.

"Good." He flashes a gigantic smile. I want to ride his face.

I know. I know: *right now, Kia?* I can almost hear Karina say it. But yes, because those arms are lined with muscles, and together they could just lift me up and place me back down, spread, and yes, because goatee, and yes, Jesus, that smile, and most especially because just the thought of it pushes that ball of fear out of my tummy and I realize I'm smiling too.

And then Gio yells, "Incoming!" and flattens against the wall of the tunnel.

"Squad 9," Sylvia hollers as the dim light ahead of us flickers. "Brace for roach impact."

Then I realize: the light's not flickering. It's being covered up. It's a swarm. They've entered the tunnel and are barreling toward us. Rohan, Rigo, and I throw our backs to the wall. Squad 9 assembles in front of me, those dim shadows shoulder to shoulder, three wide and about eight deep, hel-meted heads leaning in. The swarm crashes into them and slows in midair, like they're flying through Jell-O. They're huge. Bigger than any roaches I've seen.

The Master Hive. They've taken wing.

Which means Jeremy is dead, and maybe Caitlin is too.

My heart beats in my mouth, my ears; my whole face pulses with it.

After a couple seconds of struggle-flight, the Queen Hive bursts through Squad 9's barricade and whooshes through the tunnel past us with a buzz and flutter. The ghosts of Squad 9 stumble to either side, coughing and collecting themselves. Musta been one of the more awful feelings of their weird ghost lives, having a whole swarm of evil queen roaches penetrate through their translucent flesh.

But there's no time to dwell or check on our dead friends. I break into a run. Ignore Rohan grabbing for me, ignore the weird chill that slivers along my skin as I brush through Squad 9, past Sylvia and Riley and Gio and then slide knee-deep into a pool of black water.

Something's rubbing against my legs, but I don't care. It's dead, whatever it is. Or was. I keep going, wading through the mire, and come out into a wide-open cavern with a plat-form in the middle. Six or seven Blattodeons stand in the water, staring. A few of those evil baby ghosts are there too, hovering, staring. I follow their eyes to where Carlos is lung-ing at a scrawny white girl, blade-first.

Caitlin.

She's still alive.

I yell with everything I got: "CARLOS, NO!"

Carlos freezes, eyes wild, blade inches from Caitlin's neck. The ghostlings and roach men turn to me as one.

Caitlin whimpers: "No . . ."

Then the ghostlings flood toward me and the roach men begin to wade through the mire. I pull the blade out, hold it over my head like Ishigu in the Valley of the Damned. Magically, I don't shit my pants. There isn't time: the first pediatric fuckspawn of Satan rears up, sharp teeth, mouth wide, pupilless eyes, and long fingernails. And then it flies backward before I can slice it in half. For a second, all I see is Sylvia's big translucent soccer-mom ass as she dives past me, her arms raining Holy Ghost hell on that little fucker. Squad 9 bursts into the room; they tackle the ghostlings and plaster themselves like Saran wrap over roach guys, sending explosions of six-legged mothafuckas into the dank air. Gio and Rigo vault into the action after them, splashing through the murky water. Rohan follows, swinging a huge machete as he lumbers toward a charging roach guy. Gio drops his foe with a single, skull-shattering spin kick. Rigo ducks a swarm and then lifts back up a second too soon, catching a few in the face. Gio yells and runs toward him as Rohan swings his machete into the head of the roach man he's fighting, chopping him in half. The Blattodeon lingers for a few seconds, twitching, until Rohan spartan kicks him into the water.

I edge along the perimeter walkway toward Carlos. Caitlin whirls at me, enraged. "Carlos," I say. He peers at me around Caitlin.

"Quiet, brat," Caitlin snaps.

"She wants you to kill her; that's the whole thing. Some kinda resurrection-spirit transference plot. Just like she wanted you to kill Jeremy." Carlos glances down at an arm and a hideously mangled torso half submerged in the icky water.

Jeremy.

Carlos looks back at me.

"Either way," Caitlin says, "you can't stop the Master Hive. They are well on their way to their new host."

Something flashes in Carlos's eyes, and for a second I think he's gonna kill her on general principle. I know I want to.

I hear Gio grunt and turn to see another Blattodeon

collapse beneath his flurry of kicks. Rohan helps Rigo wipe the roaches off his face.

"We have to go find the twins," Carlos says. I can hear the sorrow and rage fighting inside him. "Now." His voice is a hoarse whisper.

"How we lookin'?" Riley yells from across the room.

"We have to go," Carlos says again. "Now." He's about to explode. "Rohan!"

"What it do, gray guy?" Rohan pulls a final roach off Rigo and strides through the muck toward us.

"You guys have any way faster than driving to get us to Long Island?"

Rohan belly laughs. "Faster than—?" A ghostling flashes up into the air in front of him, then splatters across his face. Little arms scratch at his throat. Rohan gurgles, stumbles backward.

I'm in the water, and it doesn't matter. I clear the ten feet between us in seconds, reach up without even thinking about it and pull that nasty little monster off Rohan's face. Gio and Rigo are on either side of him, holding him up.

"The . . . the fuck . . ." Rohan gasps. Dark splotches mark either side of his neck.

The ghostling squirms in my hand, growling and hissing, but his little arms can't reach me. "I'll take that," Sylvia Bell says, hovering up beside me. She snatches the little guy and shoves him in her bulging sack with the rest of the ghostlings.

Behind us, something splashes into the water.

Caitlin.

She's gone.

"Riley!" Carlos yells. "You gotta handle this. I gotta . . . I gotta go."

"Go, man!" Riley says. "We'll find her."

"Kia, I need your phone." He breaks into a run along the walkway. "Rohan, you okay, man? I gotta . . . I need to . . ."

"I'm alright," Rohan says. "But there's . . . there's . . ."
Carlos has already disappeared into the tunnel.

"Who are those glowing people?" Rohan says.

Oh boy.

"I'll explain later," I say. "Right now we gotta make moves."

Outside, Carlos borrows my phone. He pushes some buttons
and then just stutters into it, so I take it away from him.
"Who this?"

"Victor, Carlos's friend. Who this?"

Ah. I get it. "The EMT?"

"I'm a paramedic."

"Whatever, man, nobody gives a fuck. We need your help."

"What's wrong? I'm working. I—"

"Perfect. I'll explain when you get here."

"Get . . . Listen, I can't just—"

I step away so Carlos can't hear me. "Listen, mothafucka,
the twin babies Carlos didn't even know he had are about
to get turnt into a festering hive of evil prehistoric-ass cockroaches of death. We need to get to Long Island to stop them,
and you're gonna help us get there, because I know for a fact
that Carlos has helped you out or saved your pernil-eating
ass at least once, and if he hasn't, then I'm quite sure he one
day will, so I don't give a full-fathomed fuck if you're working. I need you to pull whatever bureaucratic shenanigans
you need to do to make this happen and still have a job. And
then be here. Fast."

"Fuck," Victor says. "Where are you?"

Fifteen minutes later we're flying down the Jackie Robinson.
Cemeteries stretch out to either side. Flickering shrouds rise
out of the darkness like glow bugs, but they're not bugs at all:
it's the dead. I wonder if my family's out there in the night.

"Yes, this is five-seven X-ray," Victor says from the cabin behind me. His voice sounds shaky. "Calling for a transportation decision out of the regulated parameters. Yes, I'll hold."

In the driver's seat, this huge West Indian dude named Del shakes his head. "This is ridiculous," he says in a thick Russian accent. I don't ask.

"Yes, can you connect me to the telemetry doctor?" Victor says. "I understand that the protocol is to talk to the phone medic first, and I'm saying, connect me to the . . . Hello? Yes? No."

"Fuck," Del snarls. "Give me phone."

"I have a patient that needs to be transported to . . ."

"Victor! Give me phone!"

Victor grumbles something under his breath and hands the phone up. We swerve hard around a corner, and my stomach almost flies out my mouth while Del shoves the cell into his shoulder. "Yes? Hello? Telemetry medic? Listen: we have a sixty-five-year-old male with history of endocarditis, hypertension, and pulmonary edema complaining of right-sided chest pain times four hours; patient states he was released from Long Island Jewish two days ago following open-heart surgery and would like to be transported back to this hospital as they are aware of the particulars of his medical condition." We swerve around another corner, then hit a snarl of traffic. "Patient is morbidly obese and refuses transport to any other hospital in the area and has been appraised of risks involved with bypassing other hospitals."

In the back, I hear Carlos whispering curses.

"Vital signs," Del finishes triumphantly, "are stable."

There's a pause. Then he nods and says, "Spasibo." He tosses the phone over his shoulder. "Permission requested: granted. Let me just turn off GPS . . ."

"Just got a text from Reza," Rohan says from the back. "The Long Island Expressway's backed up."

"No problem," Del grunts. He flicks a switch on the dash panel, and the night around us explodes with a pulsing red splatter of lights. The siren bleats out a frantic, ear-shattering staccato, and the gridlocked cars haul ass to either side in front of us.

"Put on seat belts," Del says. "Now, we fly."

CHAPTER THIRTY

Reza

I was off the night Angie went missing. I had learned to tame my mind, mastered the once-incessant barrage of *what's she doing?* and *who's she with?* I'd made dinner and was settling in to eat when Charo called.

We tore through the house she'd been sent to, Charo and I. Didn't turn up a goddamn thing and had to pull out when one of the neighbors came by and threatened to call the cops. We burned up and down the block, sent Rohan and Memo and Bri out in a frantic scurry through the whole neighborhood.

Nothing.

Went back to the house later in the night, and I felt the exhaustion of hopelessness grind down on me. My hands shook. It never happens, not in these decades of facing down my own death. But Angie . . . Angie. Someone had her, and the sheer wall of impossibility between me and getting her back cast its shadow over my every move. The house was abandoned, emptied out completely, and I put my back to one wall and slid to the floor while Charo raged silently through it one more time.

I held my hands in front of my face, willed them to still.

They trembled on.

Closed my eyes.

I knew she was gone, even that first night. Everything in me knew, everything held tight anyway. Hope was gone, the whole search a lie. But it was all I knew how to do. Which meant I had to create some sliver of possibility and anchor myself on it.

I stilled my hands, slowed my heart, unclenched my guts, all on the strength of a lie called hope.

Stood.

Followed Charo through the house, eyes scanning endlessly like searchlights, eyes empty as searchlights. Lost. But I had stilled myself, braced by the lie.

And now we're in traffic. On the fucking Long Island Expressfuckingway.

Fuck.

"How long ago did you lose her?" Sasha says. Her eyes are closed. She's been deep breathing since we dropped off Carlos. Trying to calm the urge to destroy everything, I'm sure. I see a little bit of me in her, the me from that night, willing the stillness into my hands. I hope she doesn't have to anchor it on a lie.

"What?"

"I'm sorry," she says. "I know it's invasive. I didn't mean to . . . I just . . . I need to take my mind off this."

Right. Carlos had mentioned his weirdo supernatural abilities, the way folks' memories and thoughts swirl around us like little satellites to him, whole histories unraveling from a simple touch. Makes sense that his weirdo girlfriend would have the same skills.

"It's fine," I say. "I don't mind. Four months ago. The roach guys got her."

"I'm sorry," Sasha says. Her eyes are open now; she watches the side of my face.

I shake my head. "Not as sorry as they're about to be." But it sounds weak, considering we're stuck in fucking traffic on the fucking LIE instead of storming the fortress or whatever this place is.

I'm just thinking how I don't even know where the fuck we're going when my phone buzzes. I click the earpiece.

"Reza?" a gravelly voice says. "Dr. Tennessee again. How you guys moving?"

"Not well. What you got?"

"I'm at the library, looking through the file now. Seems Garrick Tartus's third structure is located on the marshlands at Caumsett Park. It's a little outlet on the north coast of the Island, connected by an isthmus."

"An isthmus, huh? Fancy vocabulary for a librarian."

Dr. Tennessee lets out an amiable chuckle. "That's why they pay me the big bucks."

"This by Oyster Bay?"

"Yeah. Remote as fuck, marshy, nasty, godforsaken. Home to some obnoxious wildlife and a bunch of scenic outlooks and abandoned little roads."

"Sounds like my kinda dive."

"If you're looking to bury a body, yeah."

"I just might be."

She sips something, and then I hear a lighter flicker.

"Having yourself a nightcap?" I ask.

She chuckles again. It's a warm, raspy sound. "Rum and a blunt. I'd offer you some, but technology's just not there yet, alas."

"Alas." I'm smiling. It feels strange. We're going to find this maniac half-dead dude and save kidnapped twin babies from the wrath of an evil swarm of cockroaches. I shouldn't be smiling. I am though. Soon, Sasha will notice, and I'll feel like shit. She's back to her trance though—eyes closed, hands in prayer position against her face.

"I'm gonna get off this highway and take the local streets," I say.

"Okay," Sasha says quietly.

"Great," Dr. Tennessee rasps. "Lemme pull up the map app on my tablet and see if I can guide you along."

"I'm by Jericho."

"Oh, I don't even need the app." She takes a sip and then a drag. "Take Route 25 past Crest Hollow and then head north on West Oakwood."

"Old stomping ground?"

"I used to fuck this divorced supermodel in Huntington."

"Ah, of course."

"She was a volunteer firefighter in her spare time. Some of the best head I've ever had in my life, Reza."

"You know what they say about divorced volunteer firefighter model chicks . . ."

We both laugh as I pull off the expressway. Sasha opens one eye at me, and I tell Dr. Tennessee I'll call her back when we get closer.

The darkness closes in around us.

"Listen," Sasha says as I maneuver us through the endless Long Island nightways, "I know you all have your ways of doing things."

I already know what she's going to say and I don't like it, but she's right. Memo says, "Whatsup?" from the back.

"And I hate when people tell me how to do my shit," Sasha continues. "But my babies . . . will be there somewhere. And . . ."

"No guns," I say. "Until the twins are secured."

Sasha exhales.

"But, Reza . . ." Bri says. In the rearview, I see Memo put a hand on her arm. She shrugs it off. "We don't even know . . ."

"No guns." My voice doesn't leave room for debate. "There's machetes in the back. There's a chain in there too. And some other shit you can kill with. And I got some insecticide grenades. I know we usually roll with more going for us, but I'm not opening up a shooting gallery with two babies in the mix. Fin de cuento."

Bri sighs and retreats to the darkness of the back.

"Thank you," Sasha says.

My phone buzzes once. These roads are narrow, and the dense marshland forest rises up on either side. Somewhere not too far away, the ocean roars. I'm doubling the speed limit and praying not to pass any cops, so I only glance at the text. It's a rambling mess from Rohan—Jeremy's dead and that turns out to be a bad thing; something called the "Master Hive" is swarming our way and apparently going to infest one of the twins. That seems to be the gist of the plan anyway. And something about shining people and the spirit world and Kia, but really, I can't be bothered.

I text him Dr. Tennessee's cell number so he can find out where we're going and then pocket my phone.

The Blattodeons are up to some sick reincarnation game. Makes sense, what with Caitlin fake recruiting Carlos to do her dirty work. I can't tease out the whole scenario while I'm driving, but I'm sure Jeremy approached the Survivors with a deal, or one of them anyway. Gregorio must've weighed out the options and put his money on the Blattodeons. Charo tends to let other organizations underestimate us, and that comes in handy during surprise attacks, but in this case . . . well, here we are.

The phone buzzes again, and I click my earpiece.

"Still on the Island?" Dr. Tennessee asks.

"And ain't it fine."

"You hit West Neck Road yet?"

"Yeah, we on it now."

"You're fast."

"That's what they tell me."

"You'll cross the isthmus soon then."

The sky opens up to either side of us, dark, dark water spreading out into the night. To the right, trees darken the horizon in the distance. "As we speak, in fact."

"Great. Hook a right down the first dark unmarked road after you're over. It'll be muddy—you're in swamplands now—and you'll go through a wooded area. Past that, there's an open, marshy field and a lighthouse at the far end. That's Garrick's."

"A lighthouse?"

"Not on the shore, I know. He was clearly a freak though, so I'm not that surprised. The door'll be on the far side from where you're approaching. Other than that, best I can tell, it's your average random ol' lighthouse in the middle of nowhere. And seems there're some tunnels underneath; don't see them lead anywhere though. All the guy did his whole career basically was build tunnels. Tunnels, tunnels, tunnels. The human fricken mole. And this one tower."

The turnoff comes quicker than I thought it would, and I have to screech the brakes to pull onto it. In the back, Memo curses.

"Gear up," I say.

"Who, me?" Dr. Tennessee asks.

I chuckle. "Sounds like you're already set for the night."

"Yeah, I'm just gonna pull an all-nighter here at the library since y'all got me up at crazy hours and at work anyway."

"Yeah, sorry 'bout that."

"Nah, I'm a night owl. Plus I wanna . . . you know . . . make sure you come out alright."

A few seconds of silence pass.

"Thank you," I say.

"Call me when it's all over, whatever the hell it is. And who-ever the hell you are."

"Thank you," I say again, this time allowing some warmth into my voice.

"And be careful, Reza. If you get through alive, maybe we'll grab a drink somewhere."

"I'd like that." It comes out before I think too hard about it. Which is probably for the best.

"Unless you smell bad. I don't date smelly women— sorry."

"I don't," I say through a smile. "Promise."

"Yeah, you don't talk like you smell bad. Bet you smell like fresh Egyptian cotton sheets and rainy mornings."

I stifle a chuckle. "And the occasional Conejo."

"I prefer Malagueñas now that Carlos introduced them to me, but I can get with that."

I cut the headlights, plow forward carefully. The forest becomes the whole world: shadowy branches blot out the moon, the light from the street behind us, everything. Dr. Tennessee says something, but her voice keeps cutting in and out. An unexpected emptiness settles in me when the call blips off.

"That librarian an old friend of yours?" Sasha asks.

I squint to see the dark road ahead. "Apparently so."

"Think they know we're here?" Bri asks.

We're gearing up: long hooded jackets and flak vests, firepower holstered; a belt with various death-bringing goodies strapped to it, including three of my custom-made insecticide grenades; Memo with his ax and chain; Sasha has a monstrous-curved scimitar and a short blade; Bri and I have machetes in each hand. I don't like how little we know and like even less that we're relying on this hand-to-hand bullshit, but there's no other way.

"We have to assume so," I say. "But realistically, they're short-staffed when it comes to nonroach dudes. By my count, Gregorio only had a small handful of Survivors at his disposal after he betrayed Marie. Minus Sasha, minus Blaine. And I don't think the roach guys can function as lookouts."

"Let's go," Sasha says. She's already at the edge of the forest, peering out into the moonlit field. For a woman with her babies in enemy hands, she's holding up impressively. Sasha's a warrior though; I see it all over her. She knows where to store up that anguish and fear so it doesn't get in the way of what needs to be done. I just hope she knows how to let it out when it's all over.

We move in silence across the field. The marshy soil squishes beneath our feet. Up ahead, the lighthouse forms a towering shadow against the dark sky, one dimly lit room at the top. We keep a wide berth between us: Memo and Sasha on either side, Bri and me in the middle. Feels too easy, but it always feels like that right up until all hell releases and you hate yourself for ever thinking it was easy. It's only when we're about twenty feet from the lighthouse that I remember the tunnels.

Tunnels mean entrances. Which means—

"Watch the grou—" I start to say. The crack of a rifle cuts me off. Bri's head flies back—in the dark I see a chunk of it hurl upward as she falls. Sasha and I drop into the tall grass. The field comes to life around Bri's fallen body. First it's just move-ment, squirming shadows. I brace myself for another swarm. Instead, a man lifts himself out of the earth, then another.

Then another.

Five, now six roach men rise, converge on Bri. Memo yells, "No!" and another shot rings out—this one I hear thump into the dirt a few feet from us.

Memo is a damned fool.

Bri is dead.

He swings the chain in a wide circle, clobbering two roach guys, then lops off the head of a third. Two lurch forward at the same time, splattering him with their swarms.

Ahead of me, the tall grass rustles and a shadow begins to

squirm free from the tunnel below. I roll toward it, kneel. Both my machetes come down at the same time. Behind me, Sasha grunts and then Memo starts screaming. It's not a sound I've ever heard him make before, and he's been shot how many times now? Then his scream becomes a muffled choke, and I know it's because they've entered him. I bring the machetes down again and again, until the thing beneath me is just a muddled pool of flesh stopping up the tunnel entrance.

The third shot rings out as I'm dropping back into the grass. One of the Blattodeons working on Memo falls backward hissing.

Then I see Sasha. She appears behind the horde of them; that scimitar flashes in the moonlight, and she starts cutting. As they turn, she slides backward into the night, seeming to disappear, and then shows up on the other side with a sharp upswing, decapitating another. She destroys three, four, five of them before another shot sends them all scattering.

"No pulse," Sasha whisper-yells from where Memo fell. Bless her for caring enough to check. And damn it damn it damn it.

Memo is dead.

Bri is dead.

Later, we will mourn. Now we have to survive. And kill these roach motherfuckers.

We rise at the same time and sprint the remaining fifteen feet to the lighthouse in a wide, ever-changing arc, arriving breathless against the wall. Behind us, the Blattodeons close back in on Memo's body.

The lighthouse stretches above us, its peeling plaster facade illuminated in soft moonlight. I unholster my Glock, block out the feeling that a hundred roaches are swarming toward me. If I were the shooter, I'd be peeking over now, seeing if there was an easy shot to take. I can't make out anything against that night sky though. Any second now, Sasha will see that my gun is out and—

"Reza!" Sasha hisses.

Above us, a shadow adjusts; the barrel of a rifle glints in the moonlight.

It's all I need.

My first shot catches the gun itself, my second the shooter. Both land in quick succession a few feet from Sasha. She jumps out of the way, then closes the deal with a swift scimitar chop. "Fuck," she gasps, pulling her blade out of the woman's skull. "That was Francine. Fuck. She was a . . . friend."

Some of the roach guys have left the fray over Memo and turned toward us.

"Come on," I say. "Dr. T said the entrance is on the other side."

The woods we came from pulse with the strobe of an approaching ambulance. Above us, a baby cries.

CYCLE FOUR

❧ ∽⧸∾ ❧

THE MAD ARCHITECT'S LIGHTHOUSE

La noche era oscura como boca'e lobo;
testigo, solito, la luz de un candil.
Total, casi nada: un beso en la sombra . . .
Dos cuerpos cayeron, y una maldición;
y allí, comisario, si usted no se asombra,
yo encontré dos vainas para mi facón.

The night was dark like the mouth of a wolf;
a candle's flame the single witness.
And so, nothing; a kiss in the shadows . . .
Two bodies dropped, and just one curse;
and there, Commissioner, if you can believe it,
I found two scabbards in which to plunge my blade.

"A la luz del candil"
tango, 1927
Julio Navarrine

CHAPTER THIRTY-ONE

Carlos

They're shooting.

The rifle shots echo in the cool Long Island night.

They're shooting, and my babies are there. Sasha's there. As long as I've known I have twins, they've been in mortal danger. I haven't even seen them yet and some disgusting madman is shooting near them. Sasha's just come back into my life and now this . . .

I don't care if the bastards see us coming. I'll erase them from existence. As soon as the ambulance stops beside the Partymobile, I fly out and break for the clearing. I only stop because Kia jumps out after me and grabs my shoulder.

"C, hold up!"

"No." My voice is cold. Death is all over me: mine. Theirs. I will bring the world down on them.

"Carlos, listen to me. We gotta do this right, man. You can't just go all kill kill kill."

"I can." She always reads me. "I will."

"No, mothafucka, you won't. You'll run twenty feet out into that field and get clipped, and then you'll be dead and we'll be short one useful-ass pair of hands. And then those roaches will do what they've been trying to do and we will fucking lose. Do you hear me?"

She's on her tiptoes, all up in my face. And she's right. Kia's always fucking right. Damn telepathic teenager. I exhale a breath I didn't know I was holding.

"It's true, Carlos." Rohan walks up behind Kia. His gigantic smile is a long-lost memory. Those two bluish handprints on either side of his neck are gonna be there for a while. "We need to do this right." Rohan will never be the same.

"Together," Gio says, walking up with Rigo.

I nod at them. "Kia, you—"

"We've been through this already, C, and we don't have time to go through it again. If you leave me behind, I'll do something stupid like follow you all by myself and get killed and then you'll feel guilty. Let's save ourselves an argument we both already know I'm gonna win."

I rub my eyes and nod. "Fine, but . . . stay . . . careful." No words can make sense of a time like this. "And no shooting. Not till we know where . . ."

"I know, man," Rohan says. He drops the gym bag he'd grabbed from his taxi on our way out here. "I brought machetes."

A grim smile creases my face. "Let's do this, then."

"I'm staying here," Victor adds, unnecessarily.

Another rifle shot breaks the night. "Alright," I say. My breath slows. The red veil has lifted. I have to remember to thank Kia when this is all over.

Out in the field, shadows move back and forth.

Blattodeons. I can see from their off-kilter stagger.

"How you wanna play it?" Gio asks as we step out into the moonlight.

"There's no way to approach undercover," I say. "The edge of the forest is too far away in either direction."

"Bum-rush," Rohan says. "Like we usedta do in the Bad Years."

"Roll up on them fast and vicious?" Rigo says. "I am with this plan."

"What about the shooter?" Kia asks.

Rohan snorts. "I'm guessing Reza and them 'bouta handle that."

"Either way, it'll be a tight fray," I put in. "There won't be much of a shot to take."

"Except they won't care about taking out a few of their own," Gio says.

We're halfway across the field. Most of the figures are clustered around one spot, moving rhythmically. A few more sprint toward the abandoned lighthouse.

Rohan squints as he walks, his fingers opening one by one. "Eight . . . ten . . . a dozen. I count fourteen. Carlos, soon as we carve a good chunk outta them, break for the lighthouse and see what's what. We'll handle the rest, yes?"

"Keep Kia safe," I say.

I can almost hear Kia roll her eyes. "Keep yourself safe."

"We got Kia," Gio says. "You get yours."

"Ain't nothin' to it but to do it," Rohan says.

We run.

CHAPTER THIRTY-TWO

〜⟡〜

Kia

There's this King Impervious line: *A bitch'll bite this breaker / in the fight to die a faker / think ya love her, boy, I'll make her / bring ya bitch so I can take her.*

Whatever bite this breaker means, the King keeps winning, one way or another. If the words themselves don't tell you that, her delivery makes it abundantly clear. She spits it like she's actually on fire, like she's got a sword that's on fire and she's slashing through all the haters one by mothafuckin' one. Like, all the fools that told her how she would never be shit are just exploding in flames around her and she's laughing through the smoke rising off their smoldering corpses.

Something like that.

Anyway, that's what keeps rolling through my head as we charge through this field toward the Blattodeon horde. I'll be honest with you: after the past couple days of holy terror and emotional mindfucks, running feels amazing, even if it's into certain death. The momentum of these four badasses running beside me carries all the way up to the edge of the horde. Then they must hear us coming. They turn, and between their shuffling feet I see two bodies torn to pieces.

I've never seen a human being reduced to shredded hunks of meat like that. I slow my steps, then stop. Gio and Rigo fly past me, both spinning up and smashing blades first into the crowd like they've been waiting all their lives for this moment. I see their machetes flash in the moonlight as bodies fall all around them and swarms of roaches burst into the night air.

Rohan and Carlos spring ahead to the Blattodeons approaching the lighthouse. They come up quiet behind them—this group doesn't even have a chance to turn around before those blades begin cutting them down one by one. Within seconds, five have fallen and the rest scatter to either side, regrouping for a counterattack.

One of them ends up away from the rest. He spins a slow, uneven circle, arms flailing.

I realize suddenly I'm out of breath. "A bitch'll bite . . . this breaker," I say between pants. "In the fight to die a faker." The Blattodeon's gaze settles on me. My hands wrap around the handle of this machete. He snarls. The short sword Carlos gave me is hanging from my waist. "Think you love her . . . boy, I'll make her." He starts walking toward me. "Bring ya bitch so I can take her." I'm a machine of death. I'm Reza. I'm Carlos. Gio.

I can't breathe.

"A bitch'll bite this breaker." He's gonna stop like five feet away and spray those roaches. And I'll turn like Gio does. Wrap this jacket around me and the roaches'll scatter and then I'll smash him. But I don't even want to feel their fucking feet against my back, don't want those one or two errant ones to crawl through my clothes and poison me with their tiny horrible touch. No.

No!

I charge. He's in front of me before I thought he'd be, just there, suddenly, and I can make out the individual roaches squirming over his face as he leans back and I draw my blade across my shoulders with both hands. I swing it upward over his face without stopping, using the momentum of my own running body as leverage. Half his head flies into the air in a swarm of bugs. I keep running. His body thumps to the ground behind me.

It's done.

I still can't breathe, but it's done. I try not to think about how that thing was once a person, had a family. The sounds of grunting and tearing flesh fill the world.

And then another one lopes toward me. He's already leaning back. I don't have time to even swing, so I barrel into him full force and we both topple. They're on me—I can feel the horrible gentle brush of wing and antenna against my skin—but it doesn't matter. The whole world becomes the blur of thrashing arms and expressionless face in front of me. I catch a hand across the face but there isn't much force behind it, slap both his arms away with my left hand, and bring down the blade with my right. It's not the best hit ever. I'm off balance and distracted by the hundreds of tiny legs, but the weapon finds its mark in the center of his face and then I put my shoulders into it and drive the point home, through flesh and bone and into whatever dusty mush is left of his brain. I throw myself away from his body and roll over a few times in the grass to get the remaining roaches off me.

There isn't time to freak out, even though it's all my body wants to do. When I rise, Gio is a few feet away spinning up from the ground, a tornado of feet and blades, and a roach man, now just a shriveled core, falls, squirting dark blood, beneath his onslaught.

Out beyond the fighting, something flickers. It's farther off in the field: a silvery shroud plodding along through the darkness, tall but drooping over. I step toward it, squinting.

The figure takes long strides through the field. It's heading for the lighthouse. I walk past Gio as he brings his machete down again and again on the writhing form beneath him. The far tree line, the sky, the lighthouse, the sounds of battle: they all swirl into an irrelevant haze around this single, trudging spirit.

I run. The wind catches my fro, kisses my face. My hand finds the blade handle in my belt. A few steps from the figure, I slow my roll, catch my breath. And then I realize who it is.

"Garrick! Tartus!"

But what is Tartus doing all the way out here? I fall into step behind him, blade ready. The fighting rages on to my left, yells and steel slashing flesh as shadows converge and collapse. I pray my friends are okay.

"Garrick! Tartus!"

We're not lined up with the lighthouse after all. If we stay on this line, Tartus's trajectory will bring us a few feet wide of the tower. He can't be up to any good, can he? Considering how desperate and fucked up everything is, I should probably just cut him down right now and have it done with. He either doesn't notice me or doesn't care I'm here. It would be easy: one slice through the back, just like Carlos taught me. *You trying to really kill a ghost for good,* C said, *you stab or slice at the head or torso. One or two good cuts and that's it; the deal is done.*

"Garrick! Tartus!"

In theory.

But C also fucked up his whole entire half-life by cutting down Trevor too quick. *Never rush to the kill,* he also said, and I could see the memories flood through his eyes. *Find out what's going on. But stay ready. Shit gets hairy fast with the dead.*

So I keep my steady pace behind Tartus as he slouches along, past the lighthouse he built. He stops suddenly, not far from it. His beady ghost eyes dance admiringly along the tarnished structure. "Yes, ah yes, but no, not yet, but soon, yes, soon and yes, all is so, just so, yes."

Is he talking to me?

"Garrick! Tartus!"

I wait. Sweat slides down my back and chills me in the cool night air.

"Soon . . . soon . . . soooooon . . . but see the angles, rivets, slipstreams of divinity that collide upon this structure, eh? The best structures are collisions, of course, of course. The best structures are collisions. And here, oh child, we collide. We collide and continue, yes, but only because one such as I made a structure such as this, oh, one with foresight, eh, one who Garrick! Tartus! Saw what would be, was called mad for it, mad . . ."

A weepy hiccup interrupts his ramble. Tears stream down his shimmering face.

"But aren't we all? Mad or called such when the time is not ready for the gifts we have brought, yes. Yes and yes, and here we are alas, child, amid the collision. They said madman, but here we are and soon, soooon comes the time as the tide turns, the sea brings salt, the salt brings dust, makes decay the crumbling bay collapses with a sigh. It is a relief, to drown, until the wind takes up the tide again and we begin . . . again . . . and collide."

Mad architect *and* cheesy coffee shop slam poet. I'm intrigued.

"Garrick! Tartus!" he yells suddenly. "It's come! Incomplete by half but still . . . whole, always whole. The alignment shall still be true, if lessened. It's come!"

I follow Tartus's gaze to the sky, out above the trees. A dark splotch stains a moonlit cloud. It's moving toward us.

The Master Hive.

Tartus beelines for the lighthouse.

Blade out, I follow.

CHAPTER THIRTY-THREE

～⁕～

Reza

A spiral staircase leads up to an open-air platform that winds around the center of the lighthouse. A low cement wall and then thick glass encase the central area, bulletproof if I had to guess. A closed door on either side. No giant bulb glares out to the ocean, just a dim neon in the ceiling, and that's probably all there's ever been. Tartus built this place with his own twisted intentions in mind—the lighthouse motif is a ruse.

I stay low. Signal at Sasha not to move.

Gregorio will be standing in the center. He'll be in a frenzy—his gunner is dead, last line of defense probably, and he knows we're coming. Heavily armed, a gun and a blade at the very least. The babies will be at his feet, hopefully in a bassinet of some kind.

He's out of his territory, caught up in someone else's game now, and he knows the full wrath of Sasha and Carlos is headed his way.

He doesn't know about mine though.

I peek up just enough to see the top of Gregorio's head, his wild brown hair and sweaty brow. I dip back down. Sasha's been composing herself again. She fixes a steady glare on me, fighting, I know, the need to run up there and bring down death in a fury. Whatever deep-breathing shit she's doing to keep under control, I'm grateful. This is gonna be touch and go straight through.

"The far side," I whisper. "Stay low. There's a door over there. I'll come in from the end. You'll know when to move."

Above us, one of the twins gurgles and then cries. Sasha cringes, her eyes watery. She pushes it away. Nods.

I want to hug her. It's not a feeling I'm used to. I make a mental note to do that when this is over. Blot out the dangling "if" phrase that wants to tack itself on. We hold eye contact for a few seconds, finding, I hope, mutual stabilization. Then she slides past me and crawls onto the platform.

I let a few more seconds pass for Sasha to get in position, then rise from the stairwell, machete in one hand, Glock in the other.

Gregorio sees me and fires five quick pistol shots that pockmark an unruly constellation across the glass. Both babies are screaming now; I glimpse their tiny brown faces, mouths wide-open, eyes squeezed shut. They're huddled together in a little wicker basket on the floor. Gregorio yells, charges the door as I open it. My machete smashes the gun from his hand. He's already swinging the blade in a wide arc at me from the other side, and all I can do is throw myself backward, out of his reach. The blade clinks off the doorway, and then Gregorio looks past me, up at the sky in a frenzy, and yells, "They come!" He pulls back into the room, slamming the door with a scowl, and turns. The thick glass muffles his howled curses.

The twins are gone.

Gregorio lurches toward the far door—I imagine Sasha has huddled back out of sight with the babies. I'm about to enter and finish the job while he's distracted—but he doesn't make it; something catches his eye and he spins back, sweat flying around him, and stands in the center of the glass enclosure.

Finally, I look up. A trembling horde blots out the whole

sky: the Master Hive. They swarm toward the top of the light-house, whistling and clicking in the night wind. They're bigger than the other ones, their flight an ungainly flutter. Gregorio looks up as the Hive bursts downward out of an opening in the ceiling like a squirming reverse oil fissure from the sky.

They don't flutter; they dive-bomb, directly into Gregorio's open mouth.

It only takes a few seconds. By the time I get a grip on myself and lunge at the door, Glock out, the bugs are all gone and Gregorio is . . . changed. His arms extend past the jacket sleeves, end in too-long fingers. His mouth hangs open, a string of brown drool trailing out. His eyes have glazed over with a yellowy film.

I pull open the door and squeeze off four shots, clipping him twice. He's faster now, each movement sharp and guided by that precise, collective intent. He dips and darts in a wild circle, stopping suddenly, then jumping into the air. Thick blood seeps from his shoulder and one thigh, but the wounds don't seem to register.

I'm trying to track his erratic movements for another shot when he suddenly swings the far door open, grabs something off the ground, and rushes around the catwalk toward me with a snarl.

I have just enough time to holster the Glock and raise my machete with both hands to meet the scimitar strike. Steel glances off steel and my arms feel like Jell-O from the rever-berations. I'm still recovering, backstepping, but he keeps swinging, mouth open, eyes wide. I parry, parry, and then I'm behind the door and he shoves it forward with a kick, smashing it against me, and I'm on my ass and he's howling, clamoring down into the darkness of the lighthouse, gone.

CHAPTER THIRTY-FOUR

Carlos

I'm barreling up the spiral stairwell full throttle when Gregorio emerges. He swings out of the shadows and clatters onto the landing a few steps above me. Moonlight from a dusty window throws a trembling illumination over his contorted face. He moves with that same lopsided, impossible agility Jeremy did, lunges at me in quick, jerky shocks with a huge curved blade.

I parry his first swing, and the next rains down half a second later.

"Traitor," Gregorio gasps, his voice a raspy, buzzing whisper like Jeremy's was. "Traitor to the Survivors, traitor to yourself."

I have no time for poetry. I sweep away another slash and then advance, clipping Gregorio in the shoulder as he backwalks up the stairs.

He howls, lurches forward.

Someone is behind me.

I can't take my eyes off Gregorio's onslaught, but that ghostly presence slides like an icicle along my spine.

"Traitor," Gregorio yells over the clanging steel.

He's getting faster in his fury. I can barely keep up.

"Garrick!" a voice yells from down the stairwell. "Tartus!"

I almost roll my eyes. This babbling, self-centered fool . . . still in the game?

"Oh, findling I see, findling out the field has altered quite, I see, I see," Tartus mutters, his voice growing gradually louder as he approaches. I still can't look back, because Gregorio keeps swinging at my face, and his long-ass arms give him that extra-lethal reach. "The Master Hive has selected another, which means I too must select another, and then one day soon the Trinity will be complete, the Trinity Blatodeo will be complete! Ah, fortune smiles upon he who makes decisions in the mire, eh. It is simple really. What appears to be chaos is truly providence. The swarm knows, always, and their moves are true. I must select another, and lo, another lays himself before my path."

Enough playing. My babies are upstairs. Sasha is upstairs. I put some extra oomph into my next block, sweeping Gregorio's scimitar far to the side, and then slice into his chest before he can bring it back. He snarls, backsteps again, and I fake left and then stab for his heart. He parries just in time, but my blade still catches him in the gut. He looks up at me with obscenely wide eyes, mouth hanging open further.

I wind up for the kill shot while he's still stunned. Icy fingers wrap around my throat. A hand closes around my blade arm; I'm yanked backward.

"See," Tartus's voice whispers in my ear, his frigid breath against my neck. "You'll do nicely."

In front of me, Gregorio raises his scimitar and smiles.

CHAPTER THIRTY-FIVE

Kia

Oh, this mothafucka.

CHAPTER THIRTY-SIX

◦～◦◦～◦

Reza

I stumble down the stairwell, loosening the grenade on my shoulder sash as I go. I steady myself on the handrail and glance over. Kia hacks and slashes the air just behind Carlos's back, and for a second I think she's attacking him. But no, this is some ghost shit happening; I see her blade catch in the air and slow as it carves through the darkness. Something is on Carlos. Or it was. Whatever had been strangling him from the back is in tatters now; Kia unleashed a thorough murking on it. Carlos, suddenly freed, propels forward blade-first into Gregorio. Gregorio's raised scimitar flies out of his hand, clatters down the stairs.

"Carlos," I yell. "Up here." He puts his shoulder into it and charges up the stairs, pushing Gregorio on the blade ahead of him. I take three steps back until I'm on the walkway again, motion Sasha to stay down with the kids, and throw open the door to the center room.

Gregorio emerges seconds later, those long arms flailing, Carlos's blade sticking out of his back. "In here," I yell as Carlos passes. "And then get back." He pushes one last time, putting Gregorio right in the doorway, then pulls his blade free. I step in front of Gregorio, shove the grenade into his mouth, and pull the pin. A swift kick throws him backward into the room. Then I slam the door and throw myself to the ground.

He yells, a muffled howl cut short by the sharp crack of the stun grenade, then a splatter. Thick yellow smoke congeals in the room. Entrails encrusted with crumpled roach corpses slide down the inside of the glass.

Kia runs up the stairs and freezes. "What the entire fucking fuck though?"

CHAPTER THIRTY-SEVEN

Carlos

My babies.
They are tiny and wrinkly and their fingers are even tinier and their tiny faces have tiny creases. Their little squinty eyes squeeze shut; their little chins double up as they scream.

They are perfect.

And most of all, they are alive.

"You're bleeding," Sasha says. She's huddled against the wall, cradling one howling ball of perfection in each arm. A slab of intestine slides slowly down the other side of the glass above her head. Thick yellow smoke still clouds the inner room.

"Can I . . . ? Can I hold them?"

"Carlos, you're bleeding."

"I'm fine. Can I hold them?"

"Sit."

I do. Put my back to all that ichor and hell and slide down beside this woman I've missed and barely know and, somehow, still love. She looks over at me, eyes red from crying, and I see something else there. There's a sorrow beyond all of this.

"Are you okay?"

She shakes her head. "But this isn't the time for all that. Here." One, then the other. They're warm. Their tiny hearts beat through their tiny bodies, telegraph itty-bitty messages into my arms, my own heart. Life is so fucking fragile. Death lurks all around us. For as long as I've had a memory, life has been a tenuous, trembling thread that I'm only barely attached to. I had a whole life once. Memories, a childhood. Parents. Kids maybe. Maybe I was in love. Maybe heartbroken. Someone wiped that all away. I look down at the gurgling bundles. How could anyone hurt these tiny things?

"Carlos?"

I don't realize I'm crying till I look up at her and tears slip down my cheeks and off my chin. Sasha actually smiles. It's the saddest smile in the universe, but I'll take it.

"C?" It's Kia, sounding way more tentative than usual. "I hate to interrupt, you know . . . but there's ghosts out there."

I don't care.

It's the damnedest feeling, after all that caring. Since I saw that photo on Caitlin's computer the other night, I've done nothing but care. My entire being became a projectile hurtling toward whatever I could do to keep them safe. And now it's over, these two bundles nestle in my arms—their crying has turned to satisfied little lip smacks—and this woman sits beside me and—

"I think that's Riley and Sylvia. And there's the rest of Squad 9. The roach guys are all splattered. There's Gio and Rohan. There's Rigo; he's limping though. They're alive."

Alright, I care about that. Beyond that though? I just want this . . . I want this moment right here. One of the babies opens a single tiny eye and looks up at me.

I'm crying again.

"Carlos . . ."

"Kia, I need a . . ."

"There some other ghosts at the edge of the woods. They're tall as fuck. What's going on?"

CHAPTER THIRTY-EIGHT

Kia

Carlos shoots me the illest shut-the-fuck-up face, but I don't take it personal. He passes the babies back to Sasha, and I help him stand. That shoulder wound doesn't look too bad, but he should probably get it disinfected. Who knows what kinda fuckdemon cooties were on that scimitar? He looks out on the dark field. I follow his eyes to the moon-lit killing ground and then the towering shrouds out at the edge of the trees.

"Shit," Carlos says. He shares a look with Sasha and then runs downstairs.

"I'm not gonna bother asking if you're okay," I tell Sasha, "cuz that would be ridiculous. But do you need anything?"

She shakes her head and scowls a smile. "Thanks. I will be okay though. Go find out what's going on, Kia. Don't worry about us."

Reza's in the lighthouse room with a gas mask on. I walk in, my sleeve over my mouth and nose, as she brings her boot down on another crumpled roach. "Just tidying up," she says. "I'll be down in a minute."

"Alright," I say. I head down the winding stairwell, side-stepping blood splatter, and out into the field.

———————

"And then *they* showed up," Riley says as I walk up. Beside him, Sylvia Bell casts anxious looks back at the tall, glowing shadows.

"The fuck are they?" Carlos asks.

Riley scowls. "Throng haints."

"The fuck's a—"

"Many spirits bound together against their will into one angry, awful core," Sylvia says.

"I don't like them," Carlos declares. "Why are they here?"

"Last I heard," Riley says, "it was a rumor whispered along back channels at Council HQ. That was a few months ago. Didn't take it seriously. Some kinda pilot program out on an island somewhere in New York Harbor. Enforce the enforcers or some shit. They mentioned them at the academy once, but it was like a warning: look out for throng haints. Don't engage with 'em, just run. That's about it."

"Until now," Carlos says. "Enforce the enforcers as in some internal affairs type thing?"

Around us, Gio, Rigo, and Rohan pull corpses toward the underground tunnels. Two bodies, one gigantic, the other small, lie off to the side, covered by jackets.

Riley makes a face. "Something like that."

Sylvia turns to Riley. "We're out."

"What?"

"I'm not doing this. I'm not doing another investigation for the Council. Not putting Squad 9 through it. Nope. Too many unanswered questions, too much bullshit. They're gonna wanna know why we engaged in an unlawful assault, and all we wanna know is why they are protecting a monster like Caitlin Fern. I'm not doing it."

Riley raises his eyebrows and looks like he's about to retort, but instead he just sighs. "I get it."

"We have the ghostlings subdued and safe and we're

taking them with us." With a flash of her hand, Sylvia has the entirety of Squad 9 in a tight formation around her. "You're not coming." It's a statement, not a question.

Riley shakes his head, very slightly. "Not . . . yet." A choked whisper.

Sylvia nods. "I understand." She closes the space between them. "Soon though. Don't let them steal your soul, my friend."

She looks at me and Carlos, nods one time, and then she's gone, lost amid the rush of Squad 9 as they flash across the field, beyond the lighthouse, and disappear into the forest.

"All I am is soul," Riley says quietly. No one laughs. And then everyone shudders, because a bone-chilling shriek cuts the quiet night. Even Gio and Rigo look up with worried faces. It sounds like a hundred wolves, auto-tuned by Satan. The shriek gets louder and the throng haints sweep through us, all icy tendrils and towering shrouds covered in screaming mouths, and then they're gone, vanished into the woods, hot on the trail of the newly renegade Squad 9.

No one says anything for a few seconds, we just stand there stupefied. It felt like the passing frozen wind took shards of our souls along with it.

Footsteps approach from the lighthouse, but I don't even have it in me to turn and see who it is. "Come on, people," Reza barks as she stomps past. "We got dead to bury."

EPILOGUE

La vez que quise ser bueno en la cara se me rieron;
cuando grité una injusticia, la fuerza me hizo callar;
la esperanza fue mi amante; el desengaño mi amigo . . .
Toda carta tiene contra y toda contra se da!

When I tried to do right, they laughed in my face;
when I raised my voice against injustice, they shut me up;
hope was my lover; disillusionment my friend . . .
Every card has an opposite side, and that's the side we're
*   dealt.*

"Las Cuarenta"
tango, 1937

Francisco Gorrindo

Carlos

How'd he take it?" Reza asks. We're at the diner. A big meal is in my belly, and I'm sipping coffee and staring across the table at Kia like a concerned dad. Which, I guess I am, just not hers.

Kia shrugs. "Good as any dad would, I guess. Maybe better even. He still mad though."

"I would be too," Reza says. "But I get it. I dropped out of school in the sixth grade, never looked back."

"I'm not dropping out," Kia says. "I'm just taking a break. Doing something that's right for me for once in my life, instead of trying to please everyone else."

"Was he happy to see Gio?" I ask. All of this family stuff is a mystery to me, but I guess I better start figuring it out.

Kia's smile is more of a grimace. "Happy's a funny word for it. He broke down crying when they hugged. Then my dad held Gio at a distance and looked at him, and Gio just shook his head and kept apologizing and they both cried and then we all cried and then we ate a big lunch just like Gio and I had planned, and *then* we told him about how I'm leaving school and going to Brazil with Gio and Rigo."

"Smart move," Reza says. "Always feed people before you deliver crushing news."

"And *then* he lost his shit."

"Ain't mad at him," I say.

Kia shrugs. "It's been an emotional day."

"Week," I say.

"Year," Reza adds.

We all nod.

"Anyway . . ." Kia perks up. "I wanted to thank you both. You know, for saving my life and letting me help out and all that shit."

I smile. "I mean, you really saved my life."

"If your half-dead ass hadn'ta been in the way, that big ol' half-dead-ass cockroach monster dude woulda had nothing between me and him. So yeah, maybe I pulled the Tartus ghost off ya, but I'm gonna still give you credit for the save on that one."

I doff my cap in acceptance.

"And you." She looks at Reza. "I just . . . I want to be like you when I grow up."

Reza rolls her eyes. "Here I thought I could make it to sixty without anyone ever saying that to me. Please don't be. Seriously. Just be like you. Hell, I wanna be like you when I grow up."

"Whatever," Kia grumbles. "Thank you."

We clink mugs just as Cathy appears holding a cupcake with one of those white emergency-supply candles shoved in it. "Happy birthday, little darlin'," she rasps. Then she places the cupcake on the table and lights her cigarette off the candle flame.

"Oh my God!" Kia squeals. "You guys didn't have to—oh my God!" She leaps out of her seat and hugs Cathy, who looks slightly terrified, and then shoves into the bench with Reza and me, squeeing like a—well, like a teenager.

She almost never cracks that tough facade, I realize. I'm going to miss her when she's gone. "Of course we had to," I say. "It's your birthday, right?"

"I mean, shit, yeah, but . . . I dunno. Wow!"

She tells us about all the exciting things she plans to do in Bahia when she gets there, how Rigo lives a ten-minute bus ride from the ocean and she's going to go every day and how the orishas are *everywhere* down there, not just in botánicas. She goes on and on, face lit up by the birthday candle and all the future has in store.

When three o'clock hits, the last thing I want to do is leave, much less deal with the vapid, senseless explanations of the people upstairs.

But.

"Alright, y'all," I say. "I gotta go speak bureaucracese to the Council and see what's what."

Reza's smile becomes sly. "And I got some other business to attend to."

"Oh?" I shoot her a glance, eyebrows raised. She just grins.

Outside, the afternoon is wrapped in gray; rain teases the edges of the sky. I give Kia a huge hug, holding tight till she taps my shoulder to let me know she can't breathe. "Be careful out there," I say. Everything I could think up sounded pretty stupid, so I opted for the least stupid.

"Yeah, yeah." Kia rolls her eyes. "*You* be careful."

"You got the blade I gave you?"

She pats her shoulder bag. "Of course, C. Chill. I got this."

If this is even a microscopic slice of what parents feel like sending their babies off to college, I'm not sure I'm cut out for the job. But I guess I'll figure it out one way or another. Kia gets into Reza's Crown Vic, waves one more time, and then they take off down the dusty backstreets of Bushwick.

"Basically," Riley says, "Tartus was the third leg of the Blattodeon Trinity, but he bit it early—we think one of the Survivors got him when they were warring with the roaches—and so the Ferns had him frozen in ghost carbonite so to speak until the time was right. Then, when all didn't go according to their plan to resurrect the Master Hive and two Petaris, they started improvising. Didn't work out though."

Botus's frown reaches all the way down his shimmering face.

Usually, that lights a dancing candle of joy within my heart, but on this overcast afternoon, it's cause for alarm.

He leans his long, angular body all the way across his desk at Riley and me. "What I fail to understand, gentlemen, is how you ended up beneath the city fighting pests while the individual we asked you to protect slipped away. She could've been kidnapped by her brother's minions, for all we know!"

"Funny thing about that," I say, my voice cold as death. "Turns out Caitlin Fern was involved in the illegal torture and weaponization of ghostlings."

Botus narrows his eyes at me.

"Which I know is strictly forbidden by Council protocols."

"Of course," Botus says icily.

"So, I took it upon myself to unravel the Ferns' schemes. As I'm authorized to do. Which led me to the lighthouse, where we destroyed most of the Blattodeons and the head of the Survivors, along with one of his henchwomen. And since the Survivors have long been a public enemy of the Council, I was surprised that someone the Council asked me to protect was aligned with them."

Bartholomew Arsten emerges from the shadows behind Botus. "Are you implying, Agent Delacruz, that—"

"I'm implying that instead of this interrogation," I growl, "perhaps a simple *thank you* would do."

Botus waves his arm. "That's enough." Arsten fades back into the darkness. The Chairman swings back to us. "As to your concerns, Agent Delacruz, the Council was unaware of any of the indelicate activities you describe regarding Miss Fern, and of her connection to the Survivors."

"Imagine," Riley says. "And it was all happening right under your nose."

"Caitlin Fern was a private contractor with the Council," Botus continues. "Much like yourself, Agent Delacruz. She has a special talent for working with the dead, and she's done excellent work for us in the past. The allegations that she snatched children from the adoptive agency she worked for are, of course, troubling and completely out of line with Council policy."

Riley and I just stare at him so he knows we're not eating his bullshit. What's the point of arguing though?

"Anyway, our throng haints are seeking her out, and they'll surely turn her up soon. After all, she trained them. The throng haints know her ways better than anyone else at the Council."

I don't release the hundred curse-outs rising inside me. Of course the throng haints won't catch Caitlin; they're probably helping her escape right now. And Botus damn well knows it.

"When she's caught," Botus goes on, as if his words have

meaning, "she'll have to answer for her crimes, as well as those of her associates."

Charming.

"Speaking of associates." Botus whirls around, his eyes boring into Riley's. Riley doesn't blink, doesn't flinch. "We would love to have a word with Soulcatcher Bell and the recently defected Squad 9. Just a word, is all. If they reenlist and answer a few questions, all will be forgotten, of course. The Council takes care of its own."

Silence.

"Well, do let them know, if you should happen to . . . bump into any of them out in your travels."

I stand up, because if I'm here any longer I'll do something reckless. "We done?"

"Just one small matter," Arsten simpers.

I stare at him.

"Your next assignment, he-he." He looks around. No one's laughing with him. "Mount Prospect Park. It's the one squished between the museum and the public library, over on Eastern Parkway?"

"I know it." My voice: ice.

"A bum got squashed there last night. Like . . . flattened. Horrible stuff. Got a certain supernatural flare to it, it seems. See what you can find out."

Botus is smiling.

I shake my head and walk out the room.

"You *know* those mothafuckas knew exactly what Caitlin was doing the whole goddamn time!"

We're facing the water, past the fence that Caitlin recklessly led me through just yesterday. I nod. "She's in the wind now though."

"We tried to find her, man. Shit was chaos for a minute

after you took off. Sylvia's guys say they musta had an underwater tunnel in that pit somewhere. She was just *gone*, man."

"Nothing you coulda done." I pass him a Malagueña. Cup my hands into a shelter and light it for him. I don't even feel like smoking.

"Thing now is," Riley says. "What do we do?"

I just stare at the crashing gray water. "The Council protected Caitlin while she plotted the destruction of my family. They gave her resources, looked the other way while she enslaved and tortured baby ghosts. Baby ghosts she sent against Kia, was gonna send against my . . . children and Sasha. I just . . ."

Riley shakes his head. "Council gotta die, bruh."

"I know. Reza said if you're going to kill a thing, you gotta kill it dead. And I want to light them up, but . . . we can't yet."

Riley drags hard and releases a mountain of smoke. "Word. I been doing these filthy shitsuckers' dirty work for my whole afterlife. I'm through. But I'm not tryna go out in a blaze and just scratch the surface. We gotta move with strategy. I'm talking 'bout: we tumble the whole situation on its head."

"Start from scratch," I say as a grim smile creases my face.

"Not a lotta spirits would be very sad to see the Council fall," Riley says.

"But way fewer would lift a finger to make it happen."

"My man." He slaps his chilly translucent hand against my outstretched one. "We got work to do."

"Carlos." I don't have to look to know it's Sasha. But I do, and once again those eyes rob the breath from my body. She's in the peacoat she wore the second night we saw each other, collar popped. A winter hat holds her hair back, and her slender face would fit perfectly in my hands.

"And I'm out," Riley says. "Later, Sasha."

She smiles at him as he goes and then she stands beside me at the fence, staring out at the bay.

"Awfully close to the Council Headquarters for a public enemy," I say.

"Oh, they pardoned me." She puts little bunny ears around "pardoned" and rolls her eyes. "For helping take down Gregorio and the Survivors. Told them to go fuck themselves with their fuckass pardon, but it still applies, apparently."

"I'm glad." Something giant hangs there in the air between us, but I have no idea what. "Do you want to—"

"The fortune-teller," Sasha says. Her face when she walked out from the curtains. She saw something, something about her life.

Suddenly, Sasha looks like she's about to cry.

"Wha—" I start, but she holds up one hand, palm out, and I shut up.

"I'm sorry, Carlos." She puts the hand on my forehead, her cool skin on mine, and then I'm looking at myself, and it's pouring rain, and behind me the ornate archway of the Grand Army Plaza looms against the dark sky.

And I know what's about to happen.

I watch myself slash to one side, then the other with something, then look up in shock as a blade slices downward across my left leg. My bad leg. I see my own eyes grow wide, and then I whisper one word as the blade stabs into my chest: "Aisha."

My whole body goes cold as the rainy night vanishes and the world becomes gray again. "This is your memory," I gasp. "You . . . it was you. You killed me."

Sasha's crying, nodding. "If you need to . . ." she says.

I turn around, head south along the dusty speedway beneath the Brooklyn-Queens Expressway. I've spent the last year of my life yearning. First came the stretch to find her, a constant reach since that night in the park when I first saw her picture in the hands of her dying brother. Then we met, we loved and lost, and memories overtook me. I cross

Bensonhurst, move toward the shore. Memories overtook me, and regret and the slow burn of a justified rejection. And all the while, a deeper strain rumbled beneath: the growing, insatiable hunger to know what my life was before I died, what kind of man I was, and more than that, to know my own death past that singular, blurry snippet.

And now I do.

And now forgetting tugs at my whole being like the icy hands of a hundred decrepit ghosts as I cross the highway and stand at the foot of the towering bridge to Staten Island. Remembering tore open the scab again and again. The twins are a singular beacon of light in my mind. Everything around them is pain.

The waves snarl and spit at the concrete legs of the Verrazano.

Sasha. *Aisha*. The last word I spoke, her name.

I turn back toward Brooklyn, toward my next assignment, whatever murderous shroud awaits me in the park. My whole body sags with the urge to forget, to finally, fully, let go.

So I do.

Kia

"How were they?" I ask. "The services this morning." We're speeding through Bushwick toward the Stuy, and Reza's wiping cigarette ashes from her pin-striped suit and cursing while salsa blares on the radio.

"Sad," Reza says. "They were good people, both of 'em. It's always sad. But they died in battle; it's how they would've wanted to go."

I nod, because what do you say to that? Really, no one wants to die beneath a horde of evil roach-covered corpses, but I get it. And then another angry text comes in from my dad. The snarl escapes from me without asking permission.

"What's the matter?" Reza asks.

"You get along with ya daddy, Reza?"

"Ever since I shot him in the face when I was in the fourth grade . . . yeah. Before that? Not so much."

"Whoa."

"He stays at the old folks home on Lorimer now. I visit sometimes. We play checkers. The coffee's not so bad there, actually."

I have no idea what to do with Reza's random barrage of information. She knows how to paint a picture though, I'll give her that. I imagine Reza in a big dining area surrounded by little old Puerto Ricans gibbering away; she's in her nice brown suit and sipping coffee with a slight smile while she triple jumps a little red plastic coin across the board, and an old man with half a face curses across from her.

Seems about right.

"I swore if anyone ever hurt my mom, I'd shoot them in the face," Reza says after a pause. "And he did. So I did."

"I mean, you a woman of your word, Reza."

"He got me too though. Just clipped my elbow. Which, all things considered, was considerate of him. My dad knew how to shoot back then. And he wasn't the man to put a gun on. So he did what he had to do while causing the least amount of damage possible, in the twisted logic of his world. Our world."

"But?"

"He didn't do it fast enough."

I'm trying not to laugh, because what the fuck, but then I look over at Reza and she's smiling. "Apropos nothing," she says, "one of these days, someone's gonna have to buy Carlos a goddamn cell phone."

"Word!" We both get a good chuckle out of that. Then Reza pulls up in front of Karina's and shoots me a sharp look.

"What I do?"

"Nothin'." She shakes her head. "Just don't get hurt out there. We need you. You give us . . . you know . . ." Reza looks like she has to wrestle with her tongue to get the word out. "Hope. And there's not much of that around."

"Okay, Princess Leia." Then I feel like an asshole because that really was touching. I get serious. "Thank you."

"I'd take you to the airport, but I got somewhere to be."

"Don't worry 'bout it. I think Gio called a yellow cab." Karina squints into the tinted windows from the stoop where she sits. "Anyway," I say, "I gotta say bye to this heffa first."

"Wait. Hold up," Karina says. "You mean you *didn't* sit on Rigo's face?"

"Karina."

"Don't Karina me, bitch. Did you sit on his dick?"

We're on her stoop, watching Bed-Stuy pass, not talking about what's really on our minds. It's just easier this way.

"No, Karina."

"Did he sit on your—"

"Girl, shut the fuck up."

"I'm disappointed, is all. But I guess it's fine. Now he's open for me to make my—"

"Rigo's taken, boo. He don't want you."

She puts a stick of gum in her mouth and looks down the block at nothing in particular, chewing loudly. "Man, fuck this."

Drasco shuffles past and then his army of cats, single file as always. He nods at us without breaking his endless stream of mumblings. We nod back.

"You really leaving," Karina finally says.

I shrug. "Yeah. I'll be back though. I promise."

"The fuck am I sposta do in the meantime? Selfish ass." I scowl at her, roll my eyes.

"I'm kidding, Kia. I'm happy for you. Really. I know you

gotta see other things besides these streets and do what your spirit's calling you to do." She punches my shoulder and then we're hugging, and I really will miss her ass, I realize. The past few days of hell well up inside me for a second, and I just let Karina hold me until it dies down.

"Don't be a noncalling or e-mailing heffa though," she says when we finally break the embrace. "I'll replace ya ass with a quickness. Best friends a dime a dozen in this here county of Kings, bitch."

"I promise," I say through my laughter and maybe a tear or two.

"Well, shit," Karina says. I look up, and there's Rigo and Gio, both looking glorious and golden in the fading afternoon sunlight. Rigo's muscled arm wraps around Gio's waist and Gio's is over Rigo's shoulder.

"I think I just came," Karina whispers.

"Ready?" Gio says. "Flight's at seven. Got your stuff in the trunk." He nods at a taxi double-parked behind them.

"Hi, Karina!" Rigo smiles and waves. Karina gurgles something in response and then I hug her one last time and we crawl into the cab and I'm snuggled between these two men who I've been through so much with and still barely know, and the cab pulls off and the future stretches ahead, a wide-open road.

Reza

A slight tremble slivers through me as I walk up the steps of the Harlem Public Library.

It's just I really don't do shit like this.

Usually, I just go still, and be me, and whichever she-it-needs-to-be comes sliding up beside me, drawn in by the gravitational pull of my slight smile, these hands that know patience, this tongue that knows reach. I just allow myself to be read as the unstoppable force of nature that I am, and when I like what I see, I move.

But this business of pursuit? Not my style. The best hunters are patient ones.

Still . . . it's been a week of breaking rules, beginnings and ends, and if anything, the universe is whispering that it's time for new tactics.

I know how to read.

And anyway, she made no secret of her intentions.

And anyway, I'm curious. And it's good to be curious again, after so long of just being cold.

And anyway.

The little white lady at the front desk tells me the research library is down the flight of stairs to my left, and yes, the librarian is in right now. She flashes a gigantic smile, and I retreat quickly before she tries to make small talk.

Down the flight of stairs, I straighten my collar, check my hemline—immaculate—and walk through the double doors into the research library.

"How may I help you?"

Dr. Tennessee is short. She has thick glasses that advertise her profession. An impressive array of jeweled rings decorate her hands, and a necklace of big mahogany-colored seeds hangs down her chest. Her hair is gray and pulled back beneath a silver headband with an owl on it. I can tell from across the room that her ass is phenomenal. Her black turtleneck hangs just at the top of a gray skirt and my God . . . my God.

"I'm looking for a saucy librarian that likes to break into her workplace late at night and drink rum and Coke while talking to strange women driving through the Long Island backcountry," I say. Came out almost as smooth as when I rehearsed it. "Perhaps you could be of assistance."

Just the edge of Dr. Tennessee's mouth curls slightly upward. "We have a special section on that topic, actually."

I raise my eyebrows. "Really? Could you direct me to it?"

"I could in twenty minutes when I get off. Are you available?"

I don't have to go looking for the smile that stretches wide across my face; it shows up on its own. "Yes. I'm completely free."

ACKNOWLEDGMENTS

Many thanks to my terrific editor, Rebecca Brewer, for helping bring this book to life and believing in the Bone Street Rumba series from the beginning. Thanks to publicist Alexis Nixon and the whole team at Ace/Roc Books, particularly the cover art department for working overtime to get this one just right—it's a terrific work of art. I'm forever grateful to Eddie Schneider and everyone at JABberwocky Literary for all their hard work and excellent advice. Thanks to Carl Engle-Laird and Liz Gorinsky at Tor.com for publishing the stories that would later become part of *Midnight Taxi Tango*. Thank you, beta readers: Sorahya Moore, Maya Davis, Maria Jackson, Isake Khadiya Smith. Shout out to all the good folks on Twitter that kept me laughing along the way and particularly to Kevin Glethean for advice on guns and Teri Brock for ballet info. And many, many thanks to Sorahya, Ashley Ford, Mikki Kendall, Patrice Fenton, Emani Ramos-Byam, Nastassian, and Shaadi Devereaux for consulting on the cover and general Black Girl Excellence.

A great big thank-you to Anika Noni Rose for optioning the Bone Street Rumba series and giving it a whole new life beyond the page.

To the elegant, mysterious gray-haired woman in leather

fingerless gloves and a dapper vest who lit a cigarette in her idling Crown Vic while I stood outside my ambulance watching—thank you.

Huge thanks to the legendary Afrofuturist John Jennings for the taxi medallion at the front of the book and Cortney Skinner for the amazing Bone Street Rumba map. Thanks to Johnny Blackchurch for help securing the copyrights for the songs.

Thanks always to my wonderful family. I love you. To Iya Lisa and Iya Ramona and all of Ilé Omi Toki and my good friends in Ilé Ashe. Thanks to Jud and Tina and Sam for always being there and to Le Paris Dakar on Nostrand for always having delicious crepes, big smiles, and strong coffee.

The tango translations are my own, but I couldn't have done it without the help of my mom, Dora, who is always ready with a huge copy of *La Real Academia Española*; the brilliant Daniel Bellm, who was my translation professor at the Antioch MFA program; and the indispensible site TodoTango.com, which contains lyric sheets, recordings, and best of all, a Lunfardo dictionary. All translation errors are my own, and tango purists will notice that I chose to go with Rolando Laserie's Cubanized version of "Las cuarenta," if nothing else because it was my introduction to the song, and hope seems like a better lover than experience.

I give thanks to all those who came before us and lit the way. I give thanks to all my ancestors; to Yemonja, Mother of Waters; gbogbo Orisa; and Olodumare.

And finally, thanks to Nastassian, who makes it all worthwhile.

ALSO AVAILABLE FROM

Daniel José Older

Half-Resurrection Blues
A Bone Street Rumba Novel

Carlos Delacruz is one of the New York Council of the Dead's most unusual agents—an inbetweener, partially resurrected from a death he barely recalls suffering, after a life that's missing from his memory. He thinks he is one of a kind—until he encounters other entities walking the fine line between life and death.

One inbetweener is a sorcerer. He's summoned a horde of implike ngks capable of eliminating spirits, and they're spreading through the city like a plague. They've already taken out some of NYCOD's finest, leaving Carlos desperate to stop their master before he opens up the entrada to the Underworld—which would destroy the balance between the living and the dead.

But in uncovering this man's identity, Carlos confronts the truth of his own life—and death....

R0215